JACOB'S APARTMENT

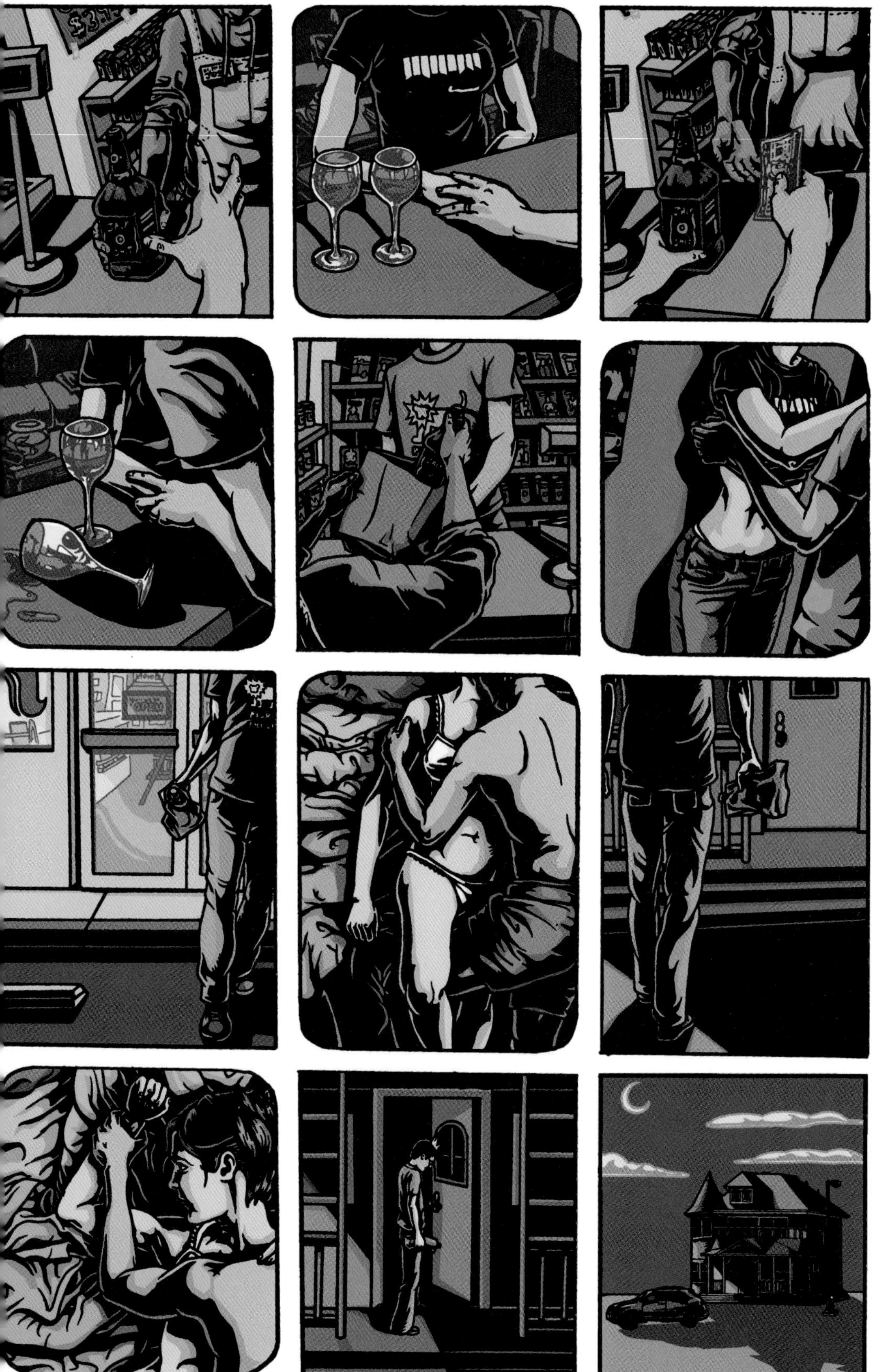

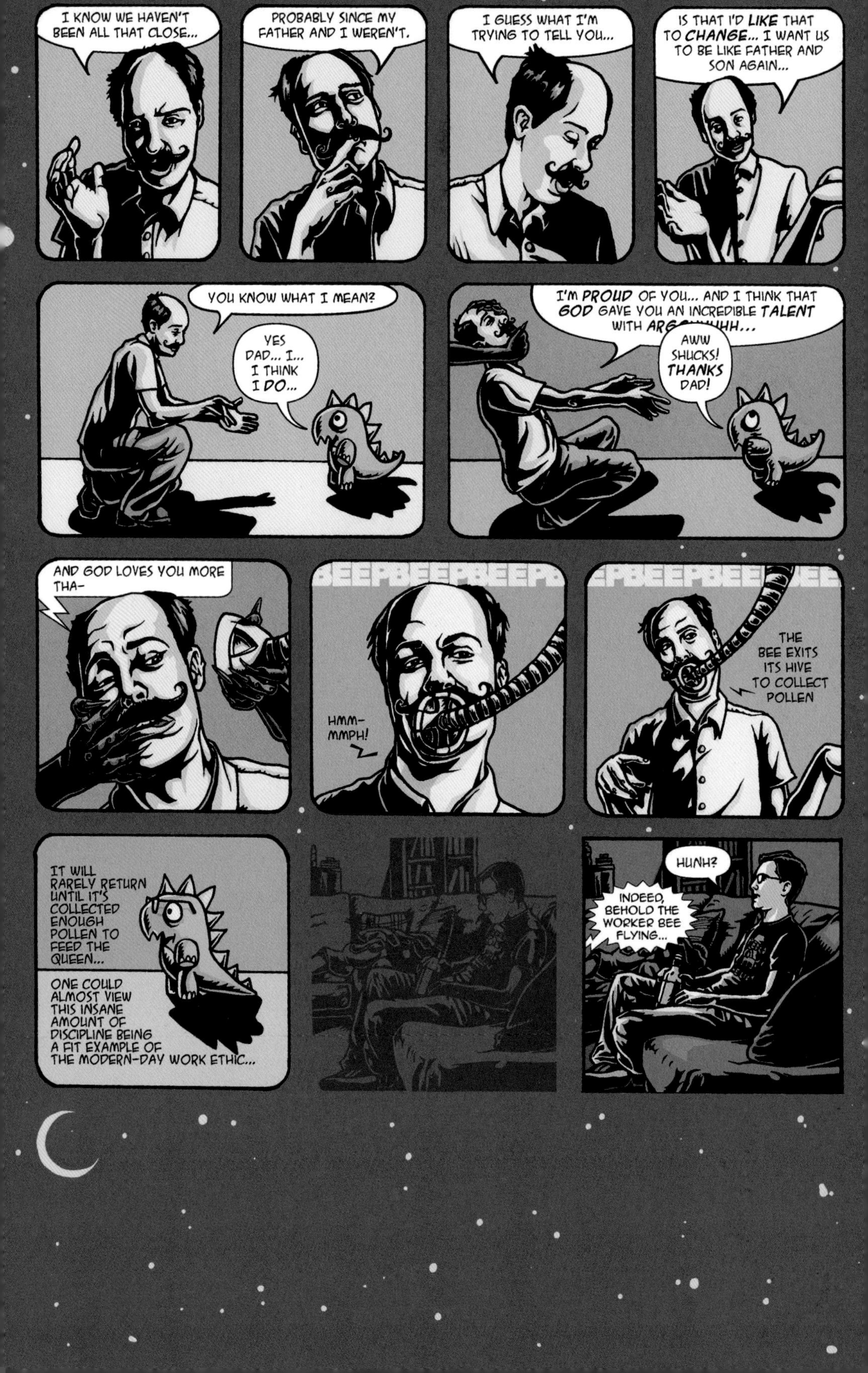
I KNOW WE HAVEN'T BEEN ALL THAT CLOSE...
PROBABLY SINCE MY FATHER AND I WEREN'T.
I GUESS WHAT I'M TRYING TO TELL YOU...
IS THAT I'D LIKE THAT TO CHANGE... I WANT US TO BE LIKE FATHER AND SON AGAIN...
YOU KNOW WHAT I MEAN?
YES DAD... I... I THINK I DO...
I'M PROUD OF YOU... AND I THINK THAT GOD GAVE YOU AN INCREDIBLE TALENT WITH ARG
AWW SHUCKS! THANKS DAD!
AND GOD LOVES YOU MORE THA-
BEEPBEEPBEEP
HMM-MMPH!
EPBEEPBEE
THE BEE EXITS ITS HIVE TO COLLECT POLLEN
IT WILL RARELY RETURN UNTIL IT'S COLLECTED ENOUGH POLLEN TO FEED THE QUEEN...
ONE COULD ALMOST VIEW THIS INSANE AMOUNT OF DISCIPLINE BEING A FIT EXAMPLE OF THE MODERN-DAY WORK ETHIC...
HUNH?
INDEED, BEHOLD THE WORKER BEE FLYING...

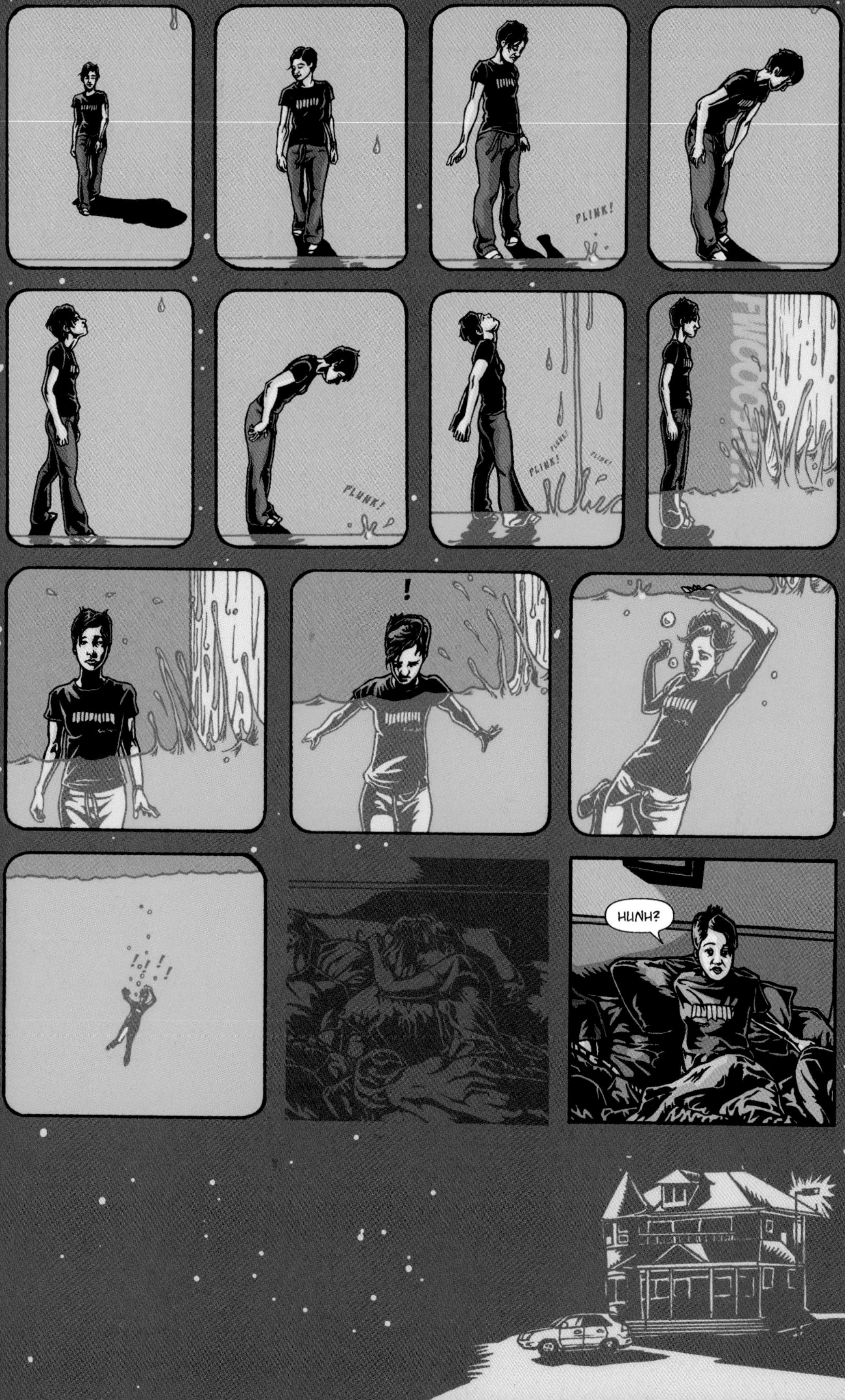
PLINK!
PLUNK!
PLINK!
PLINK!
PLINK!
!
HUNH?

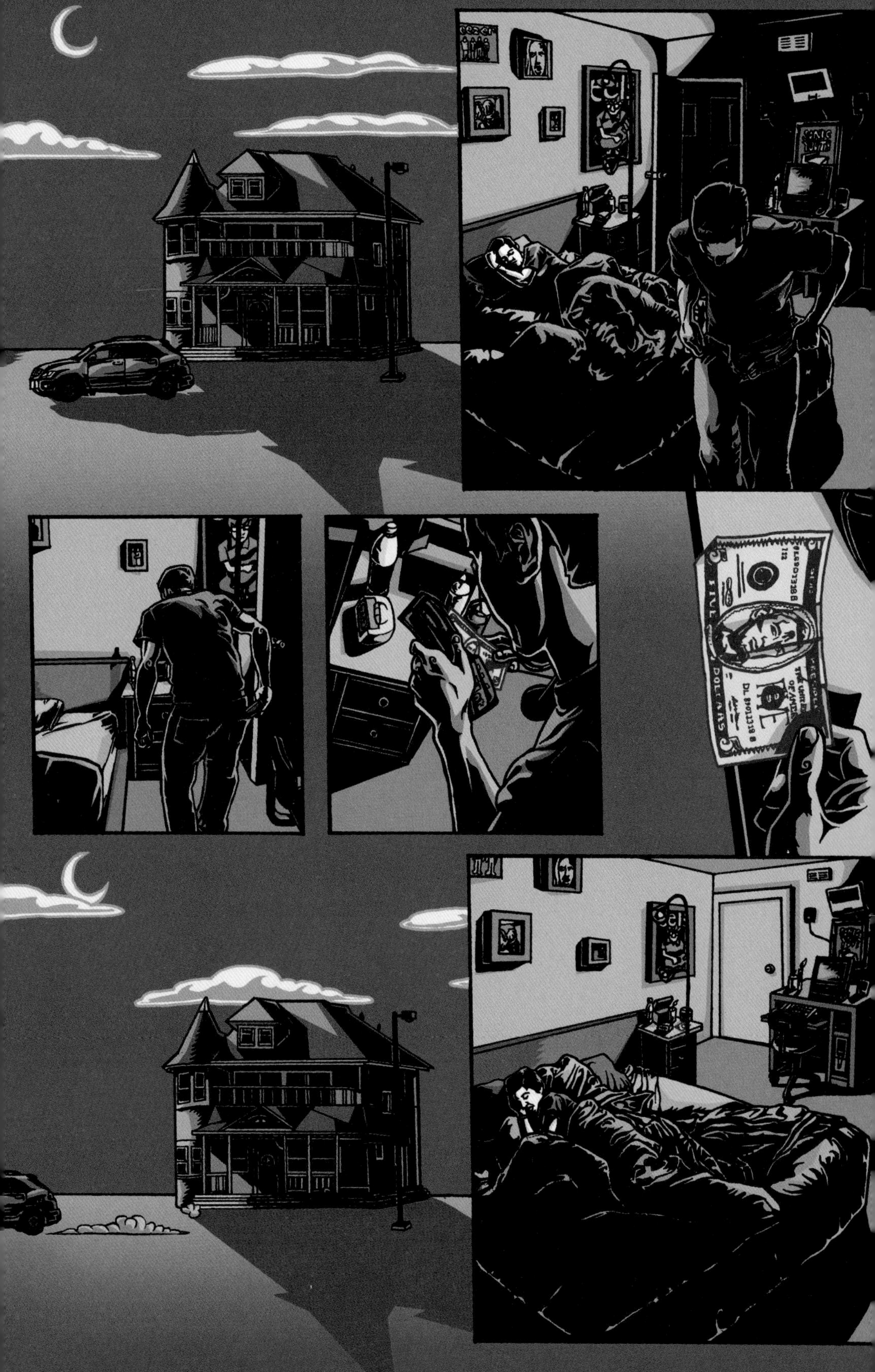

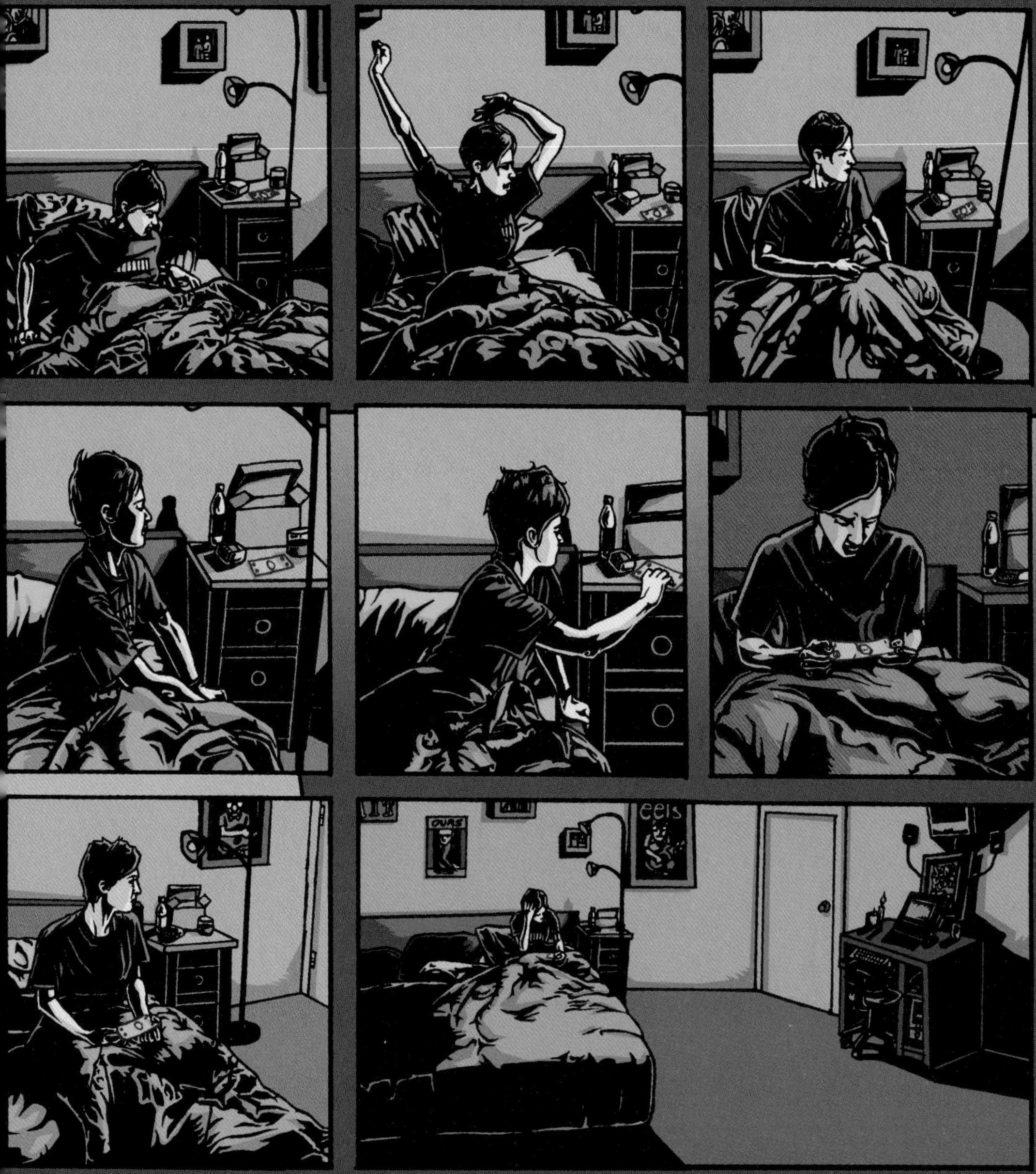
OURS
eels

JACOB'S APARTMENT

JOSHUA KEMBLE

GRAPHIC MUNDI

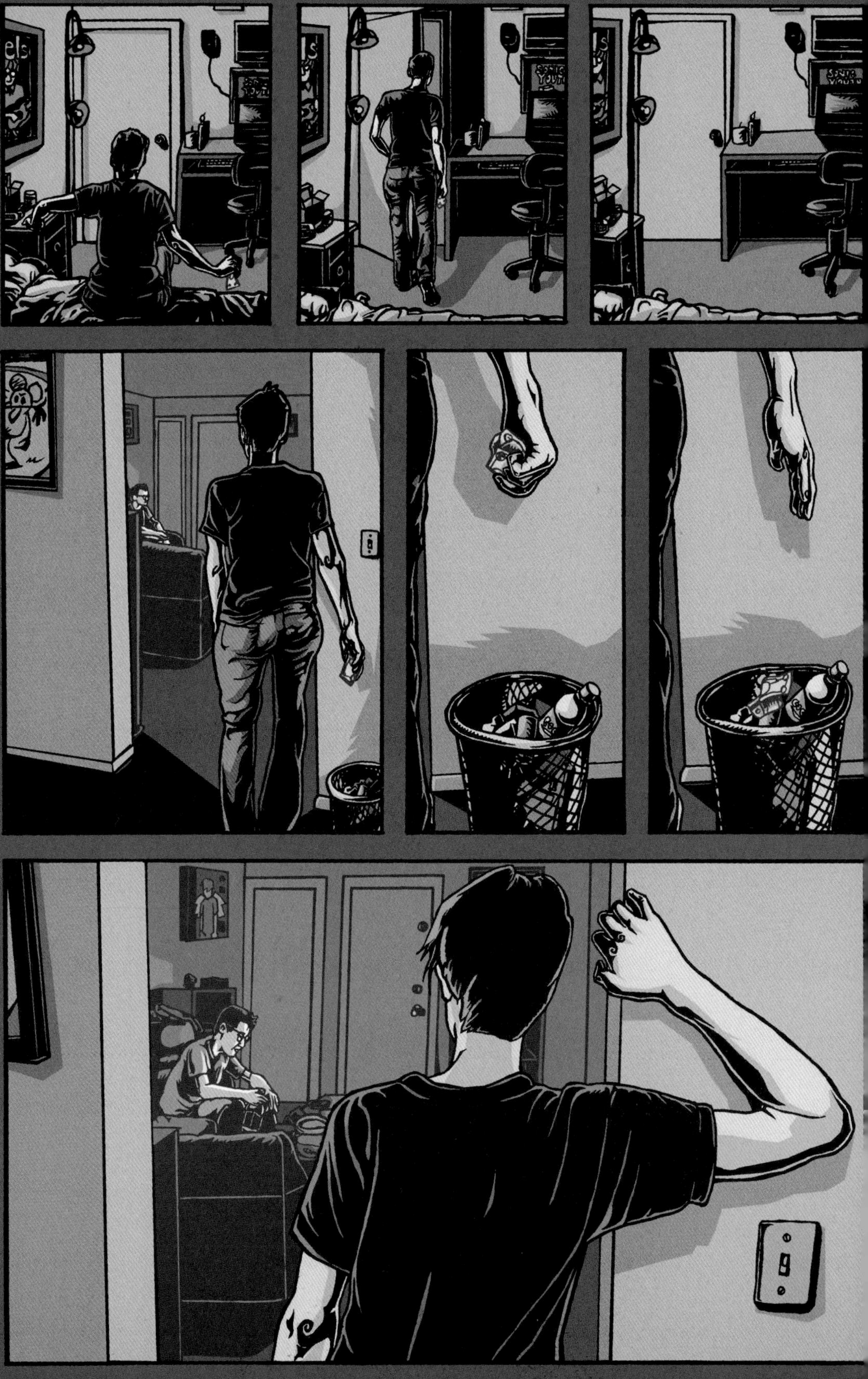

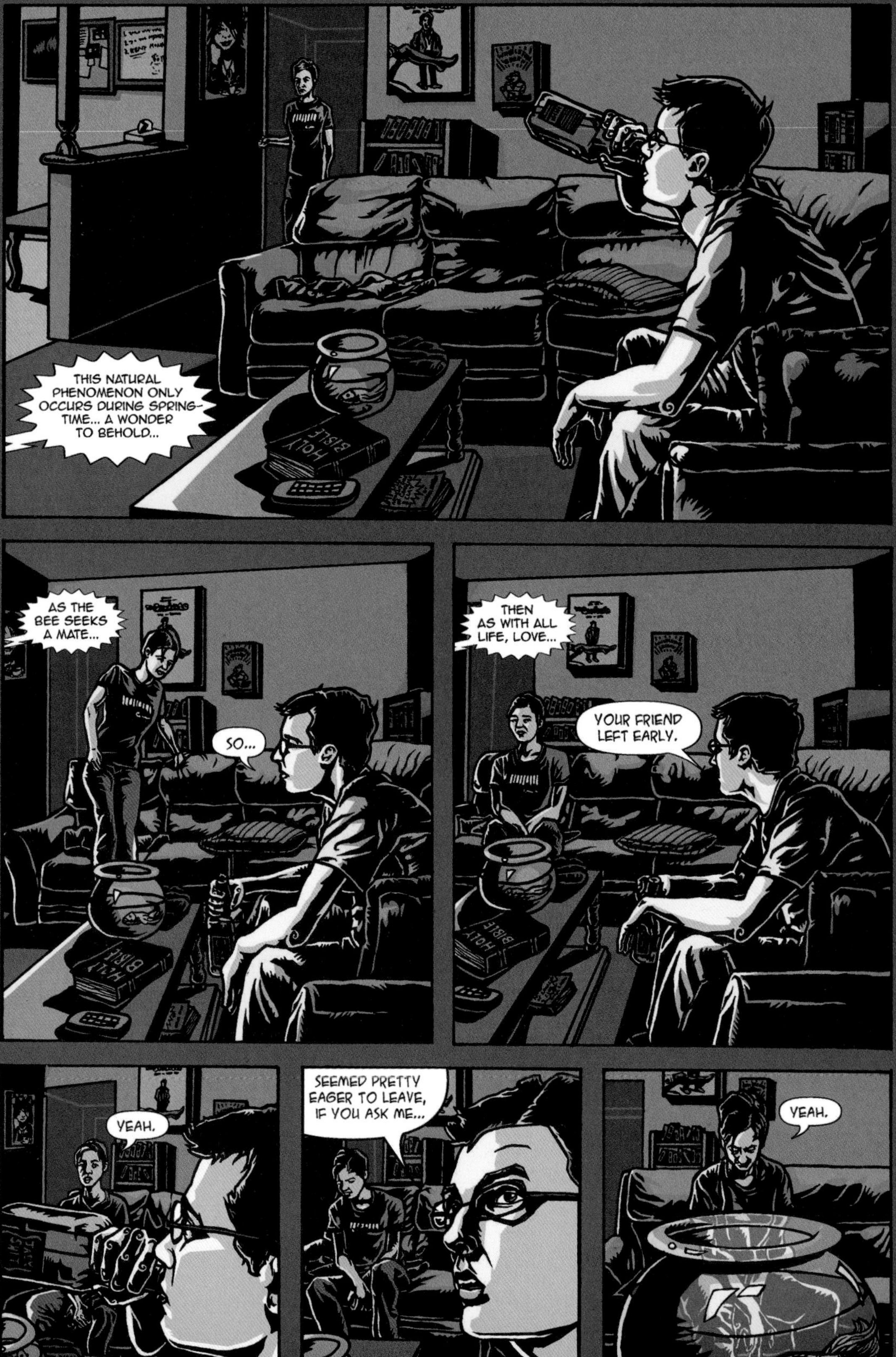
THIS NATURAL PHENOMENON ONLY OCCURS DURING SPRING-TIME... A WONDER TO BEHOLD...
HOLY BIBLE
AS THE BEE SEEKS A MATE...
SO...
THEN AS WITH ALL LIFE, LOVE...
YOUR FRIEND LEFT EARLY.
YEAH.
SEEMED PRETTY EAGER TO LEAVE, IF YOU ASK ME...
YEAH.

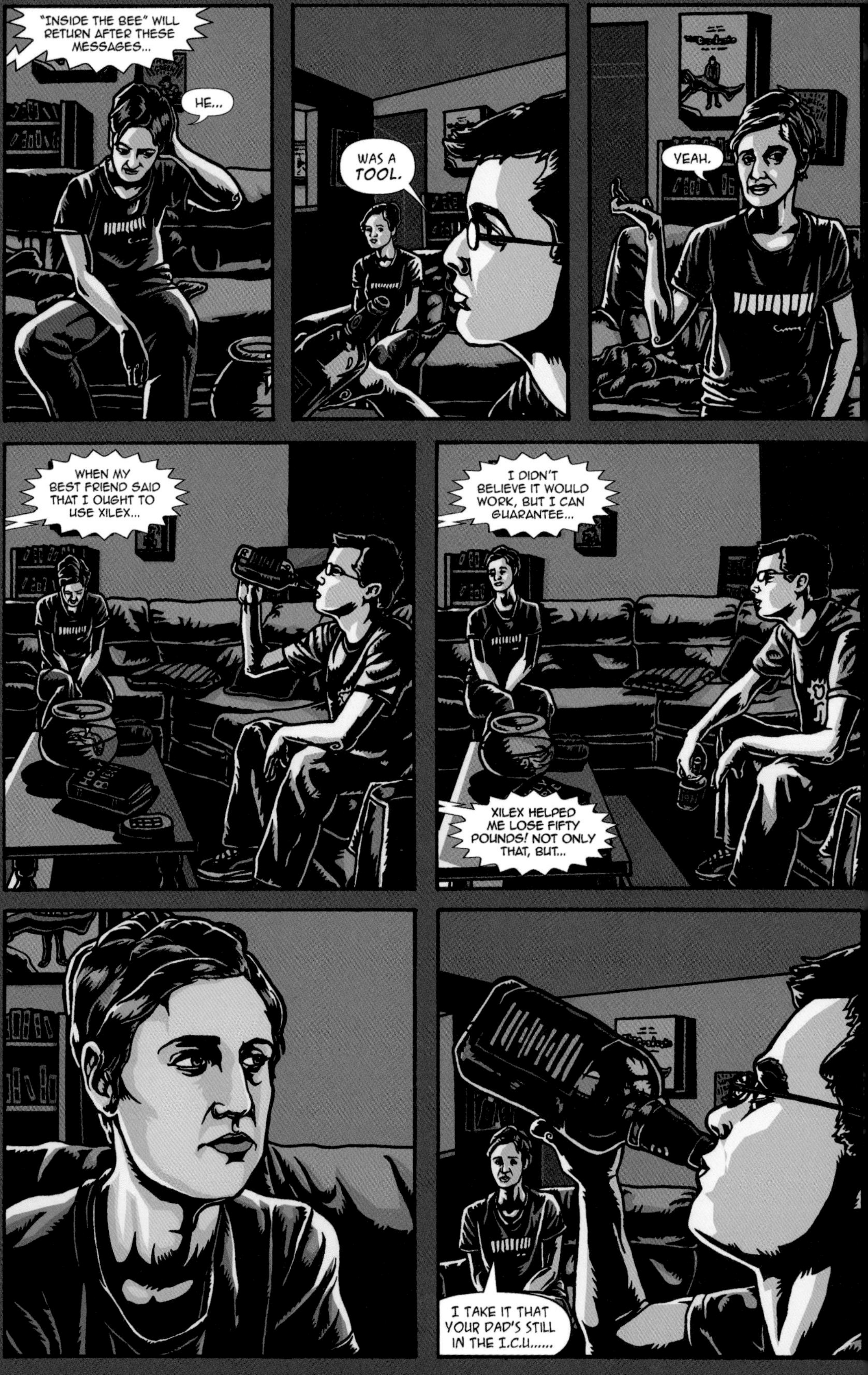
"INSIDE THE BEE" WILL RETURN AFTER THESE MESSAGES...
HE...
WAS A TOOL.
YEAH.
WHEN MY BEST FRIEND SAID THAT I OUGHT TO USE XILEX...
I DIDN'T BELIEVE IT WOULD WORK, BUT I CAN GUARANTEE...
XILEX HELPED ME LOSE FIFTY POUNDS! NOT ONLY THAT, BUT...
I TAKE IT THAT YOUR DAD'S STILL IN THE I.C.U......

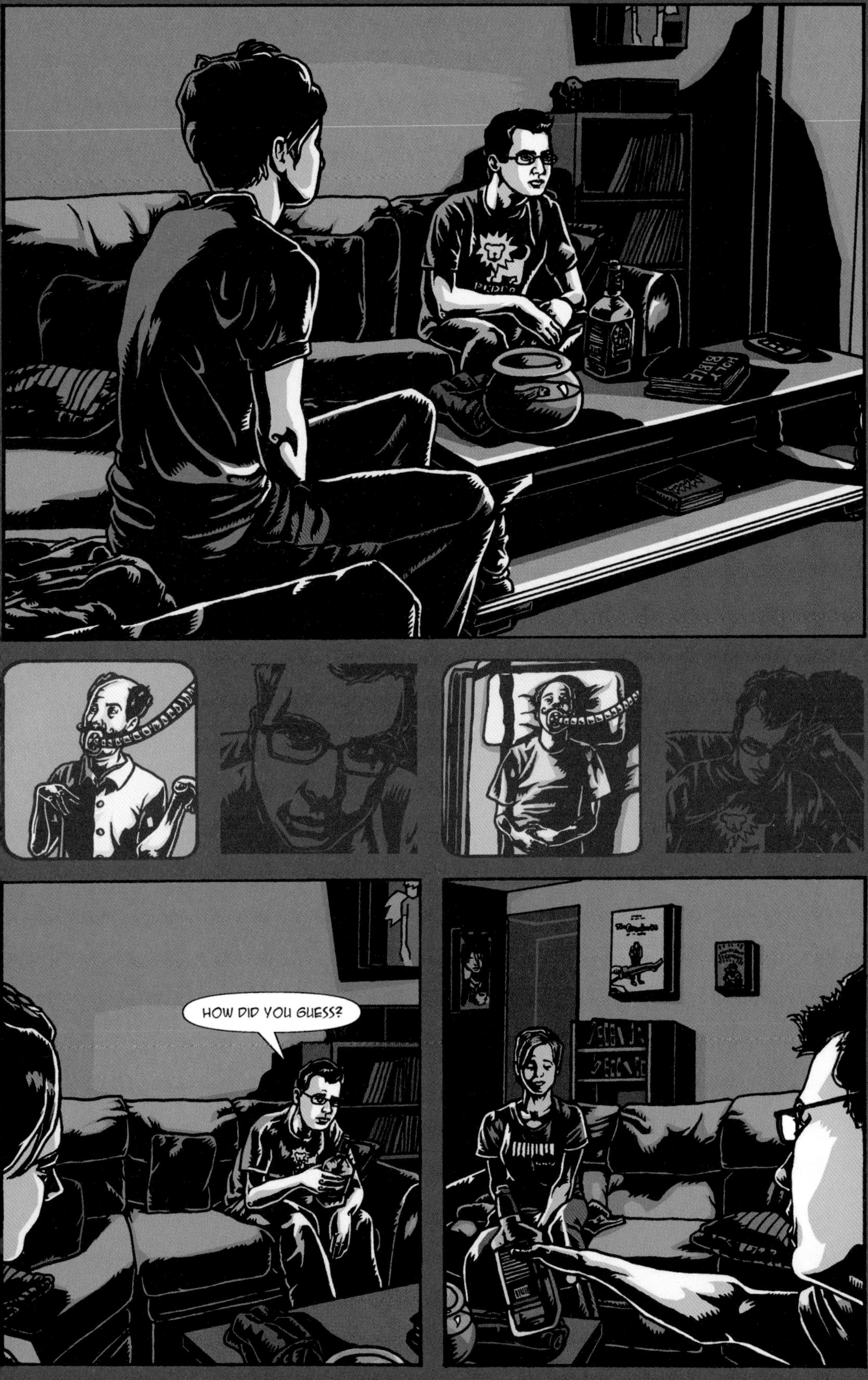
HOW DID YOU GUESS?

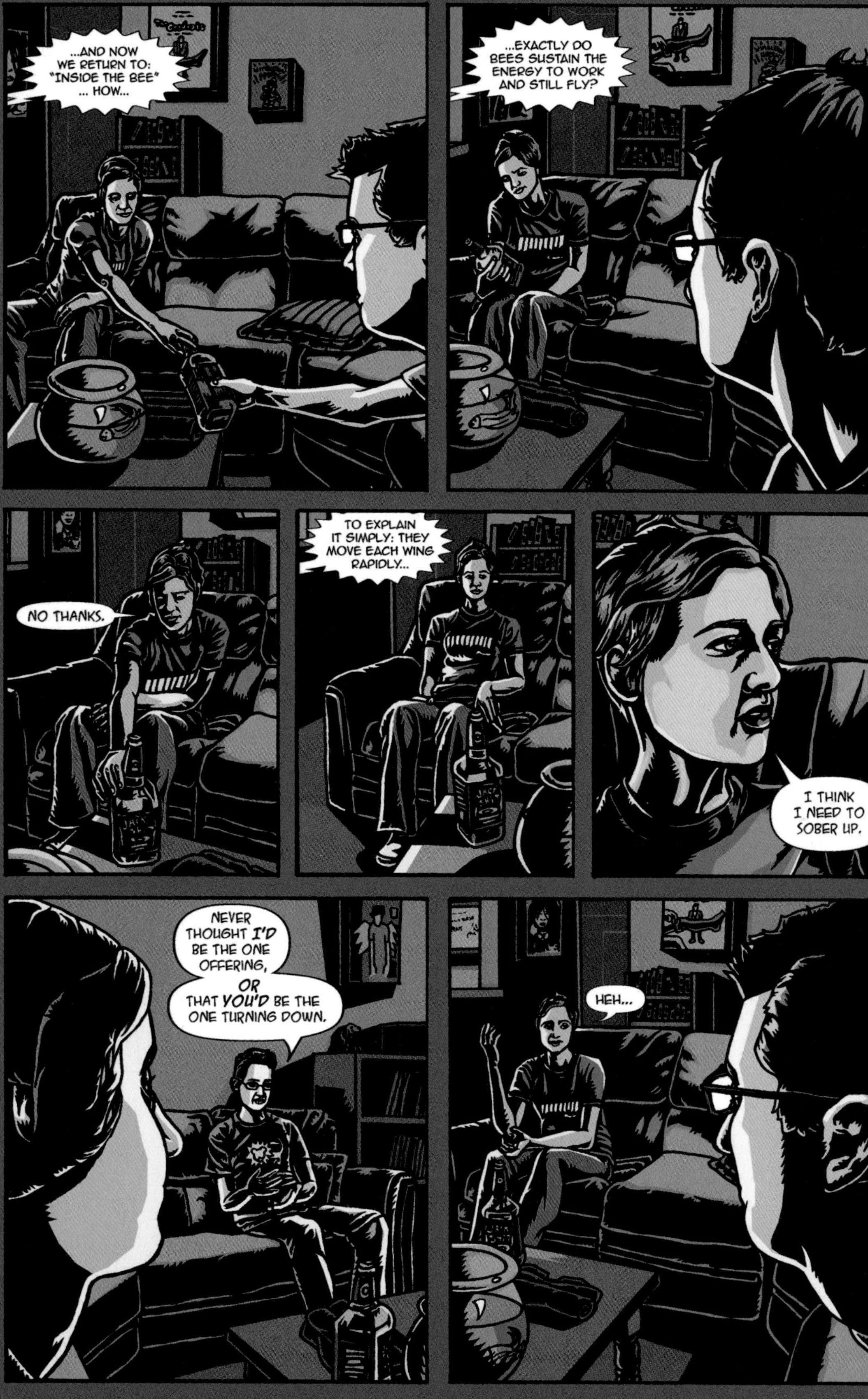
...AND NOW WE RETURN TO: "INSIDE THE BEE" ... HOW...
...EXACTLY DO BEES SUSTAIN THE ENERGY TO WORK AND STILL FLY?
NO THANKS.
TO EXPLAIN IT SIMPLY: THEY MOVE EACH WING RAPIDLY...
I THINK I NEED TO SOBER UP.
NEVER THOUGHT *I'D* BE THE ONE OFFERING,
OR THAT *YOU'D* BE THE ONE TURNING DOWN.
HEH...

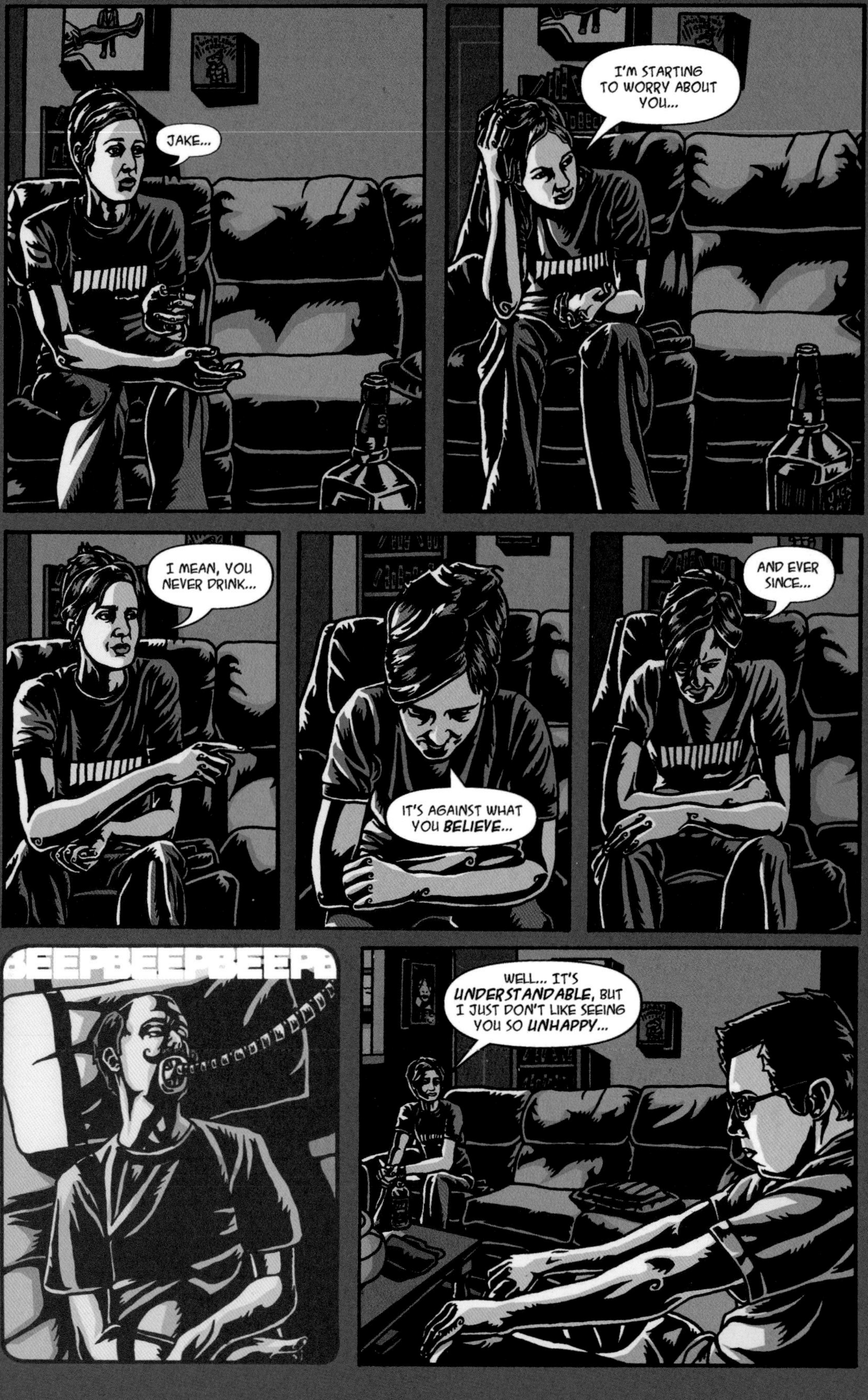
JAKE...
I'M STARTING TO WORRY ABOUT YOU...
I MEAN, YOU NEVER DRINK...
IT'S AGAINST WHAT YOU BELIEVE...
AND EVER SINCE...
BEEPBEEPBEEPB
WELL... IT'S UNDERSTANDABLE, BUT I JUST DON'T LIKE SEEING YOU SO UNHAPPY...

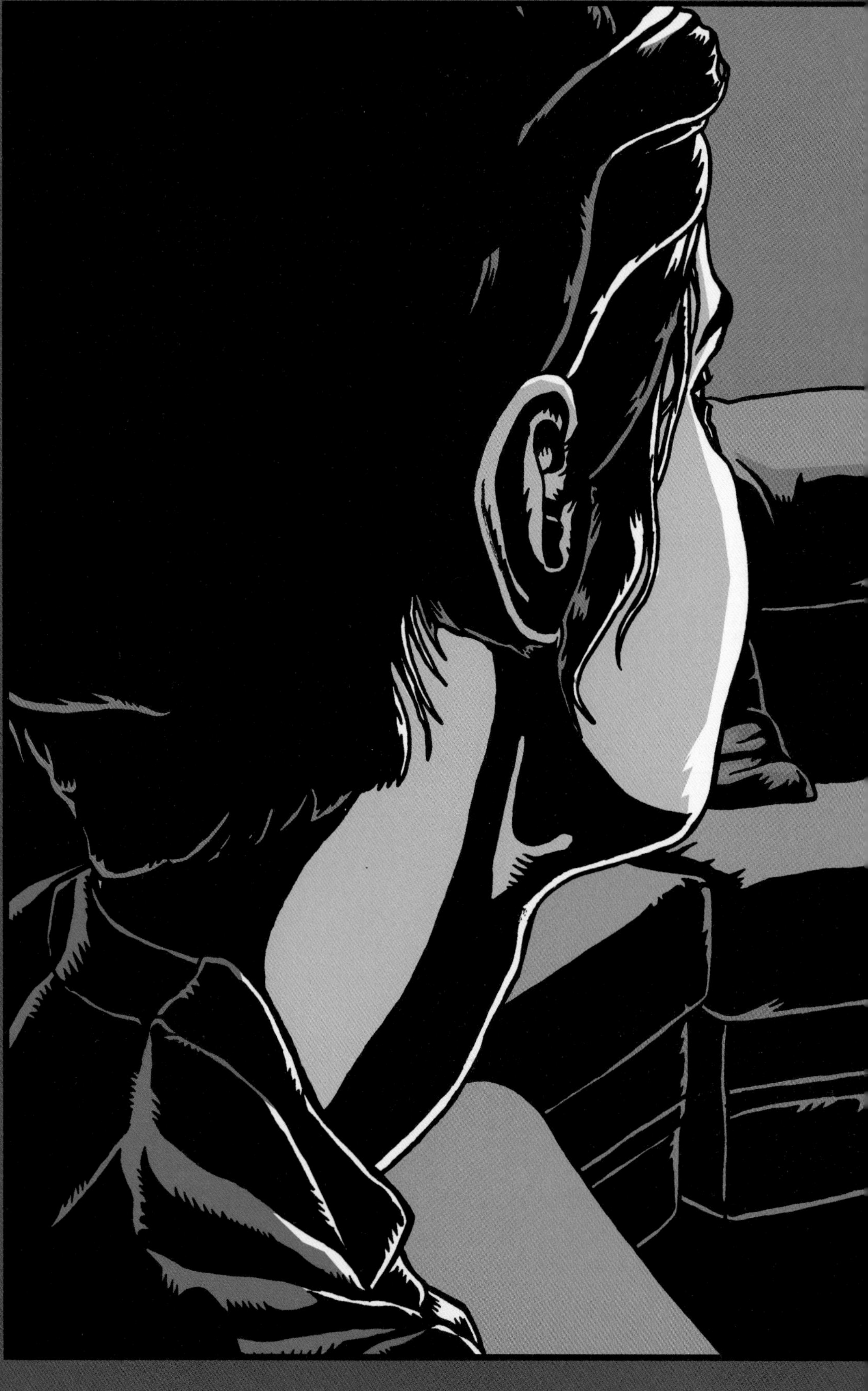

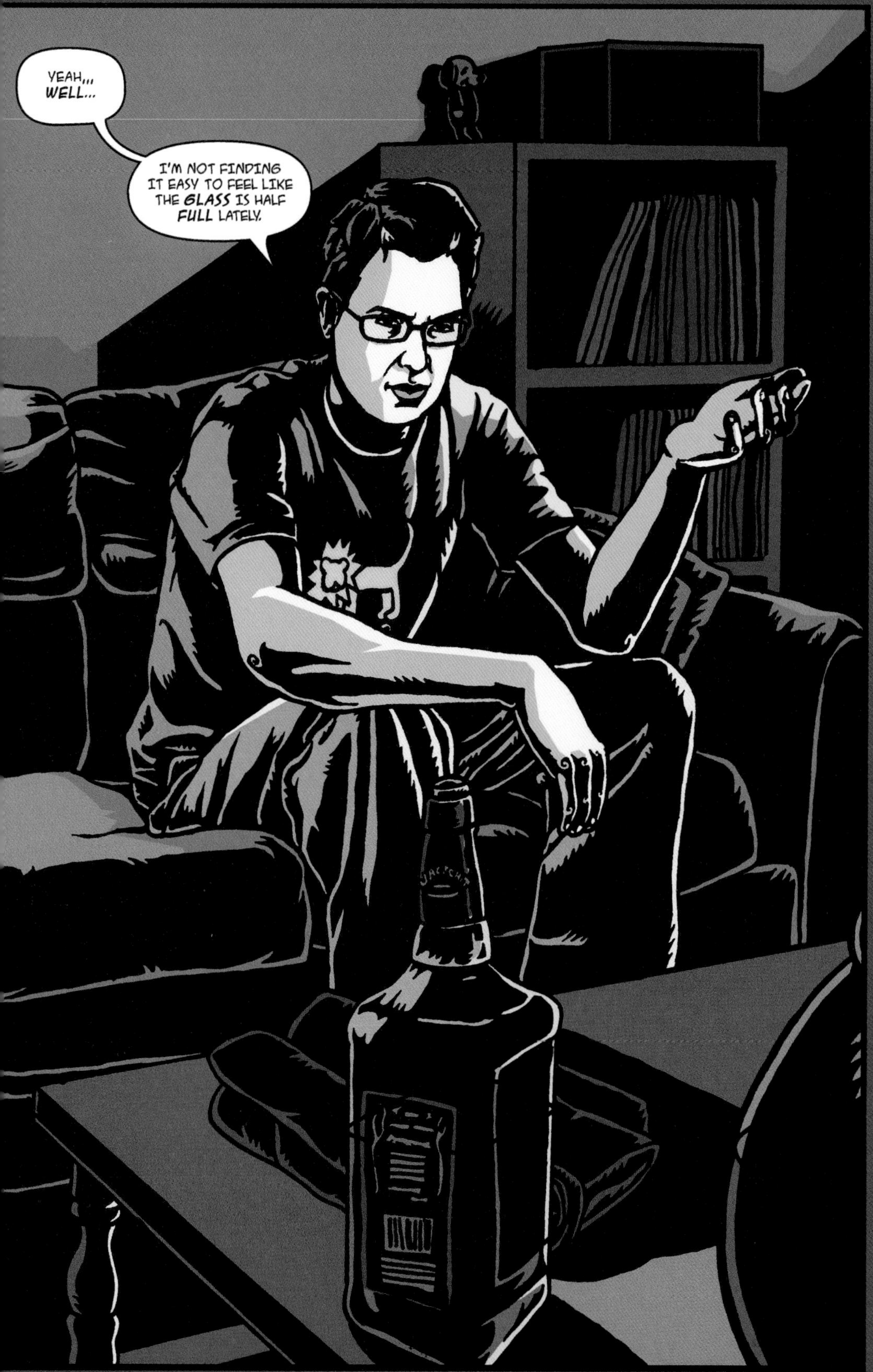
YEAH,,, WELL...
I'M NOT FINDING IT EASY TO FEEL LIKE THE GLASS IS HALF FULL LATELY.

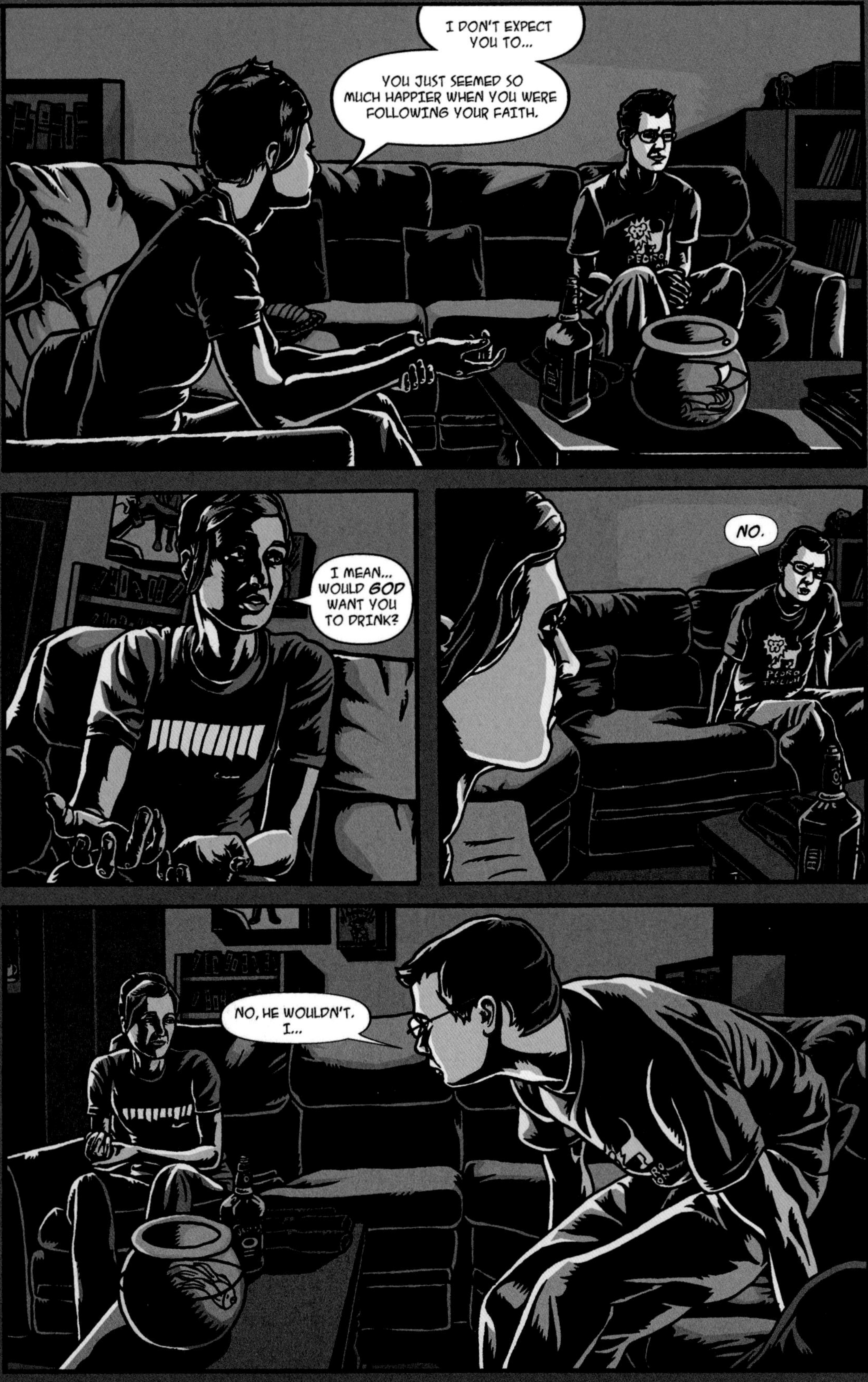
I DON'T EXPECT YOU TO...
YOU JUST SEEMED SO MUCH HAPPIER WHEN YOU WERE FOLLOWING YOUR FAITH.
I MEAN... WOULD GOD WANT YOU TO DRINK?
NO.
NO, HE WOULDN'T. I...

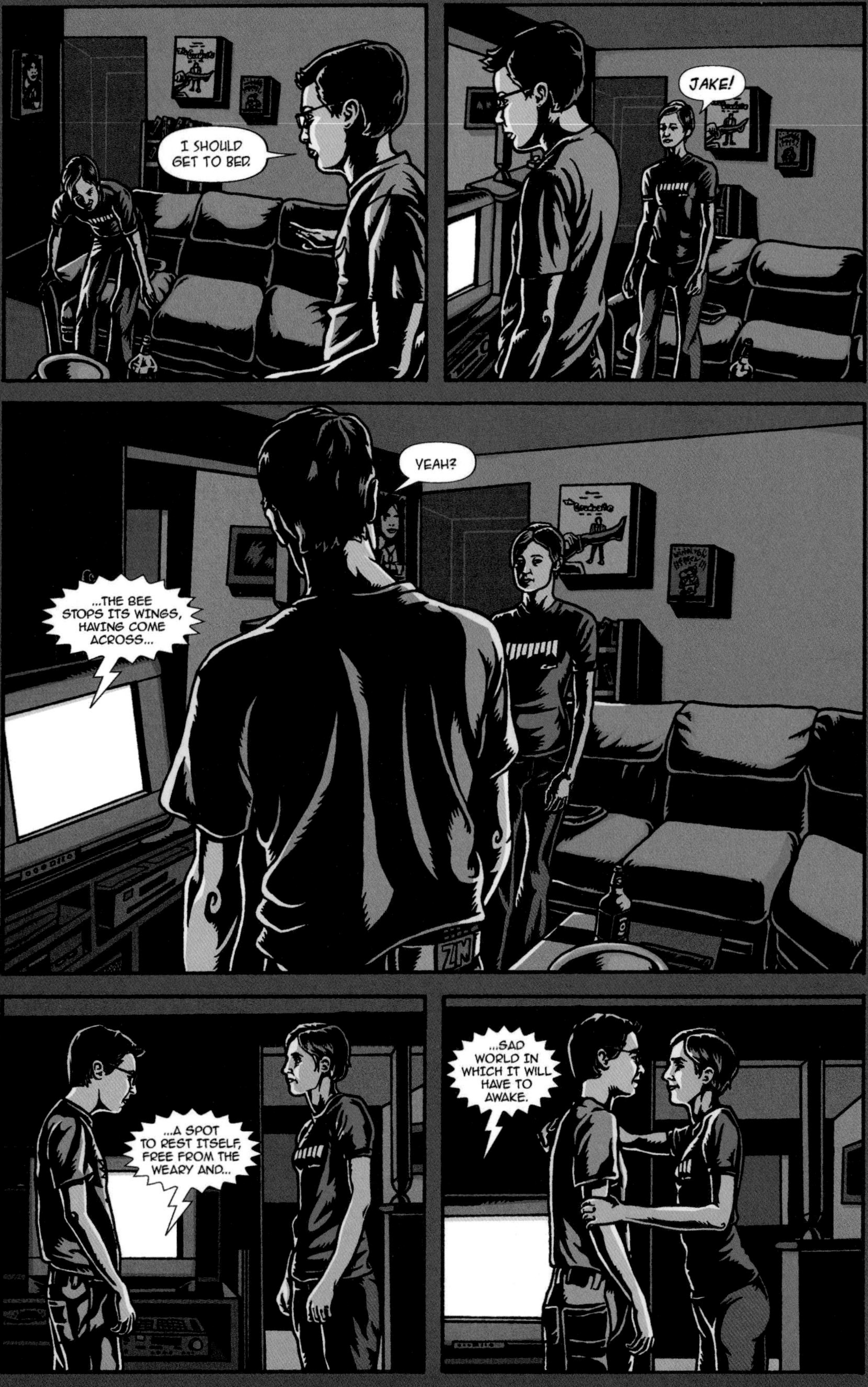
I SHOULD GET TO BED.
JAKE!
YEAH?
...THE BEE STOPS ITS WINGS, HAVING COME ACROSS...
...A SPOT TO REST ITSELF, FREE FROM THE WEARY AND...
...SAD WORLD IN WHICH IT WILL HAVE TO AWAKE.

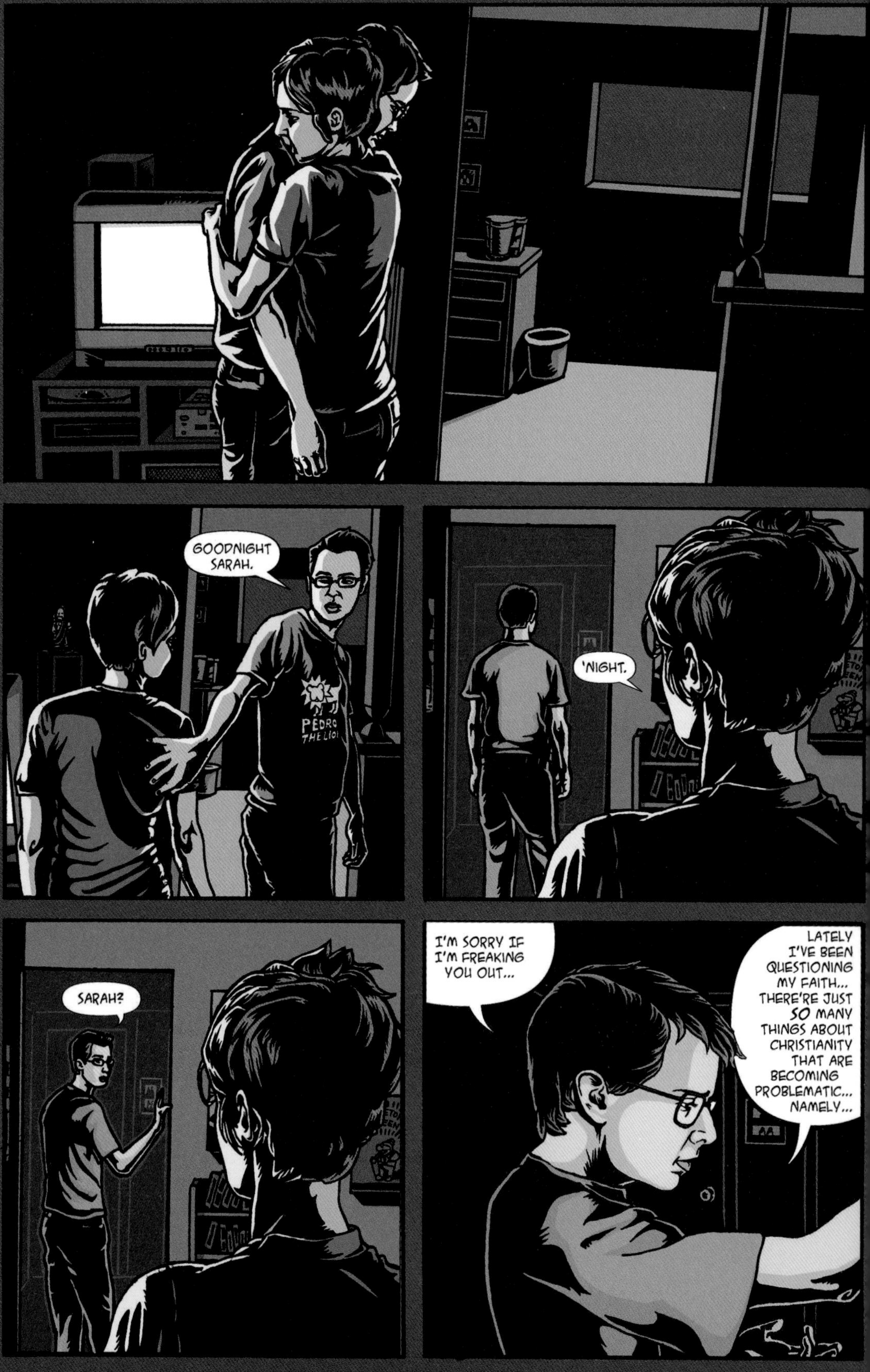
GOODNIGHT SARAH.
PEDRO THE LION
'NIGHT.
SARAH?
I'M SORRY IF I'M FREAKING YOU OUT...
LATELY I'VE BEEN QUESTIONING MY FAITH... THERE'RE JUST SO MANY THINGS ABOUT CHRISTIANITY THAT ARE BECOMING PROBLEMATIC... NAMELY...

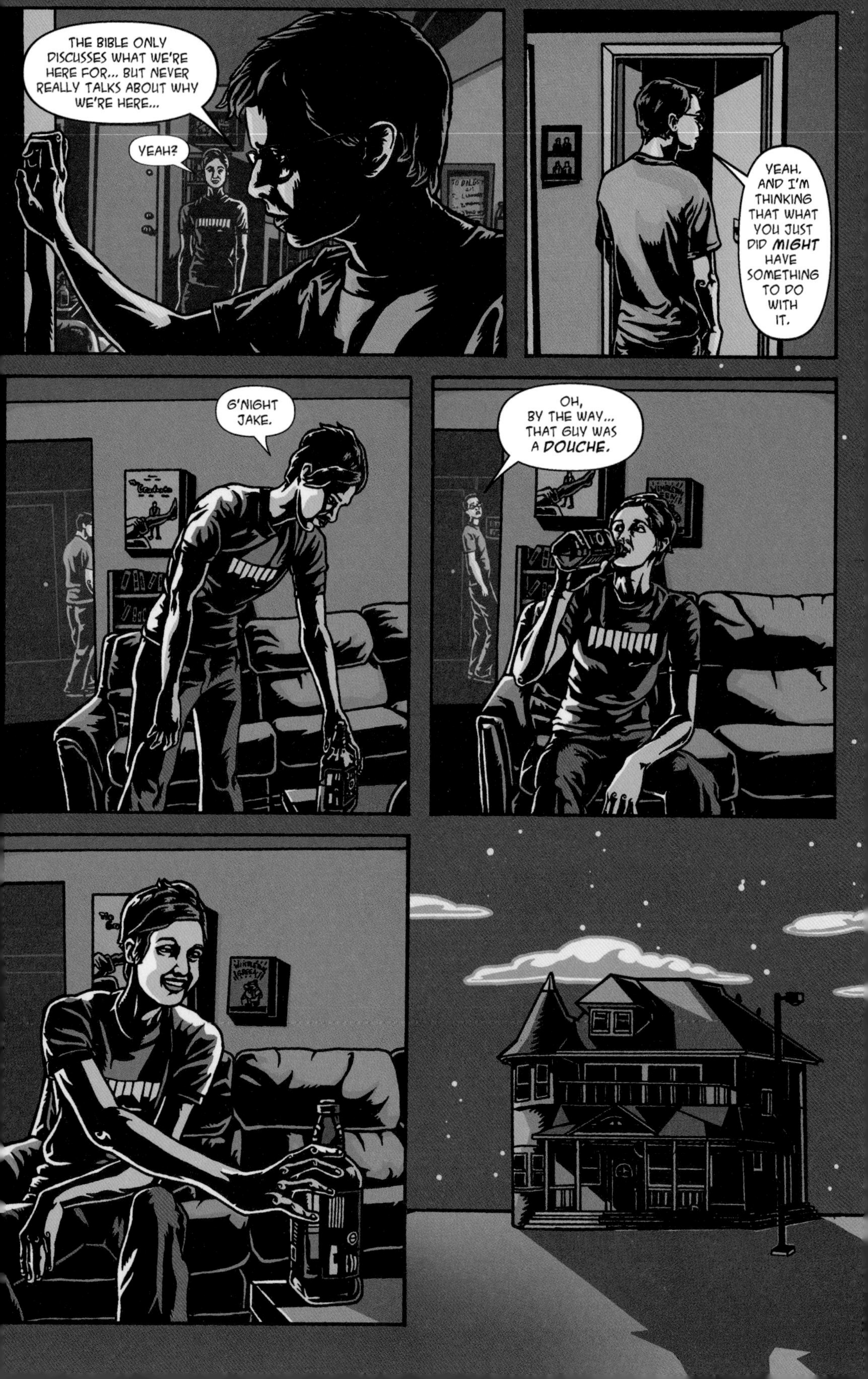
THE BIBLE ONLY DISCUSSES WHAT WE'RE HERE FOR... BUT NEVER REALLY TALKS ABOUT WHY WE'RE HERE...
YEAH?
YEAH. AND I'M THINKING THAT WHAT YOU JUST DID MIGHT HAVE SOMETHING TO DO WITH IT.
G'NIGHT JAKE.
OH, BY THE WAY... THAT GUY WAS A DOUCHE.

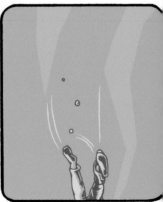

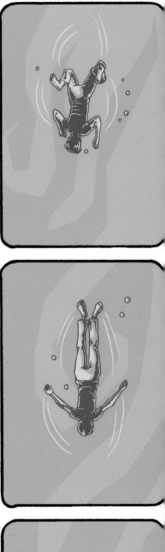

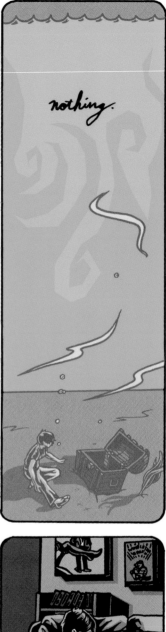

nothing.

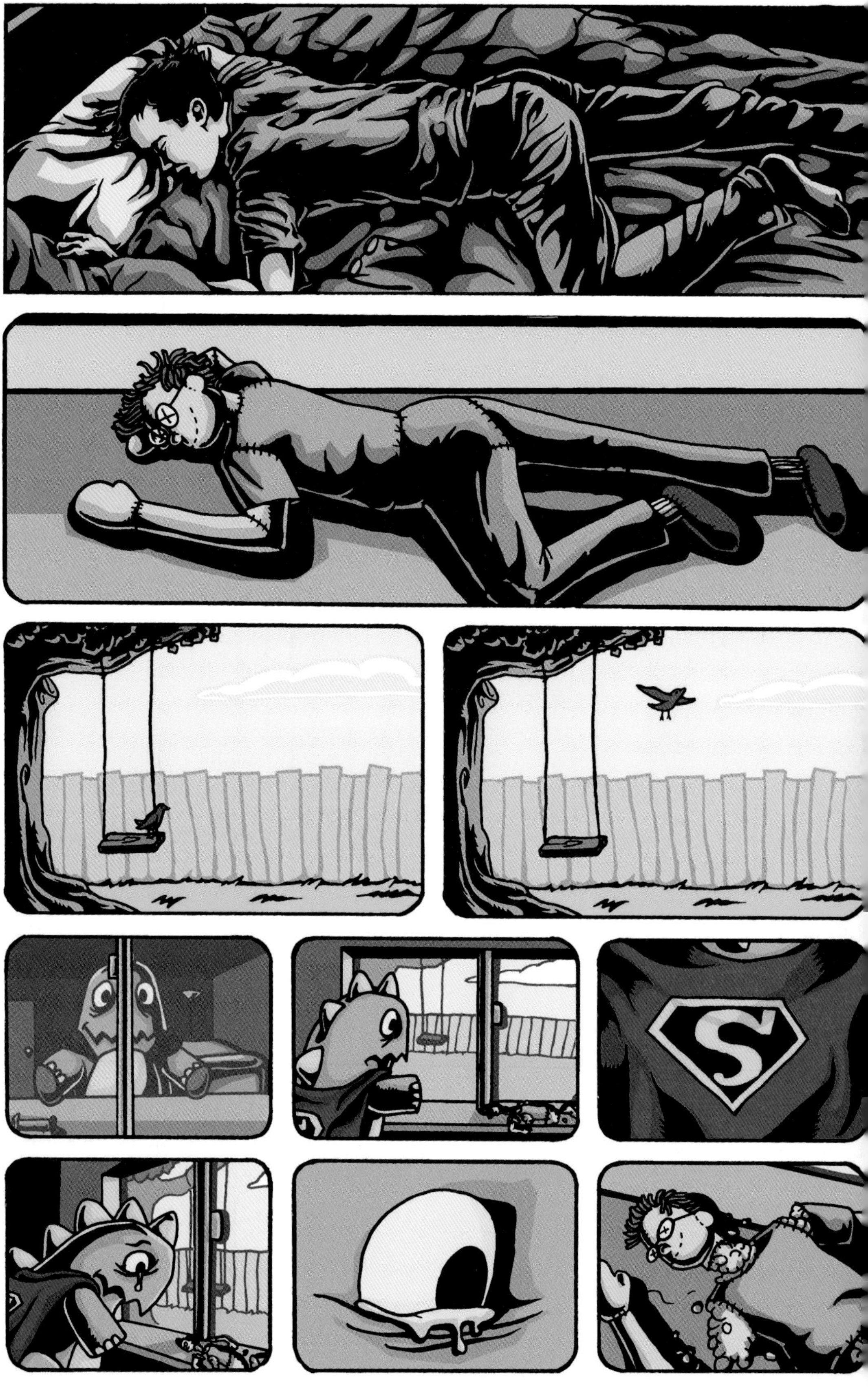

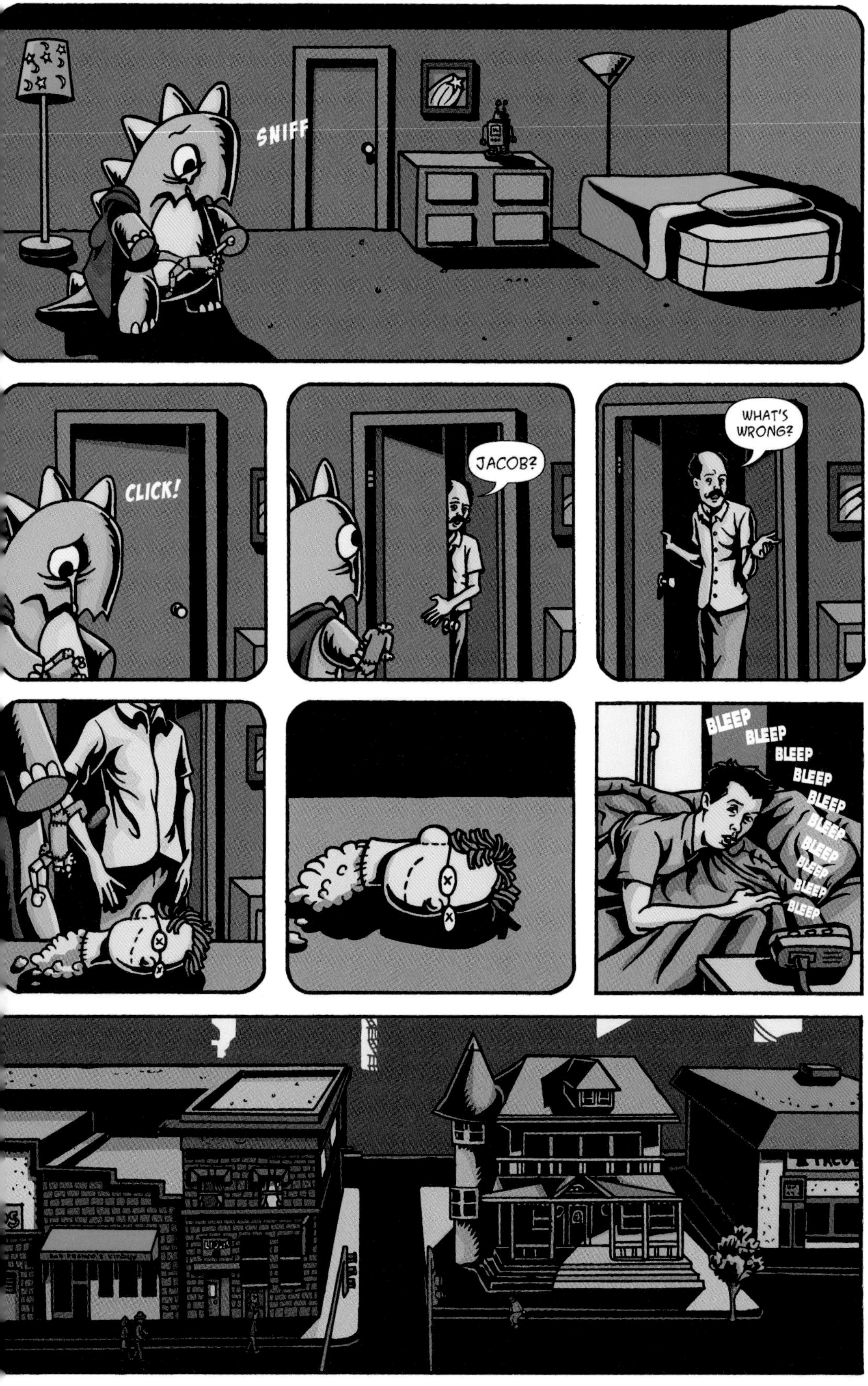
SNIFF
CLICK!
JACOB?
WHAT'S WRONG?
BLEEP
BLEEP
BLEEP
BLEEP
BLEEP
BLEEP
BLEEP
BLEEP
BLEEP
BLEEP

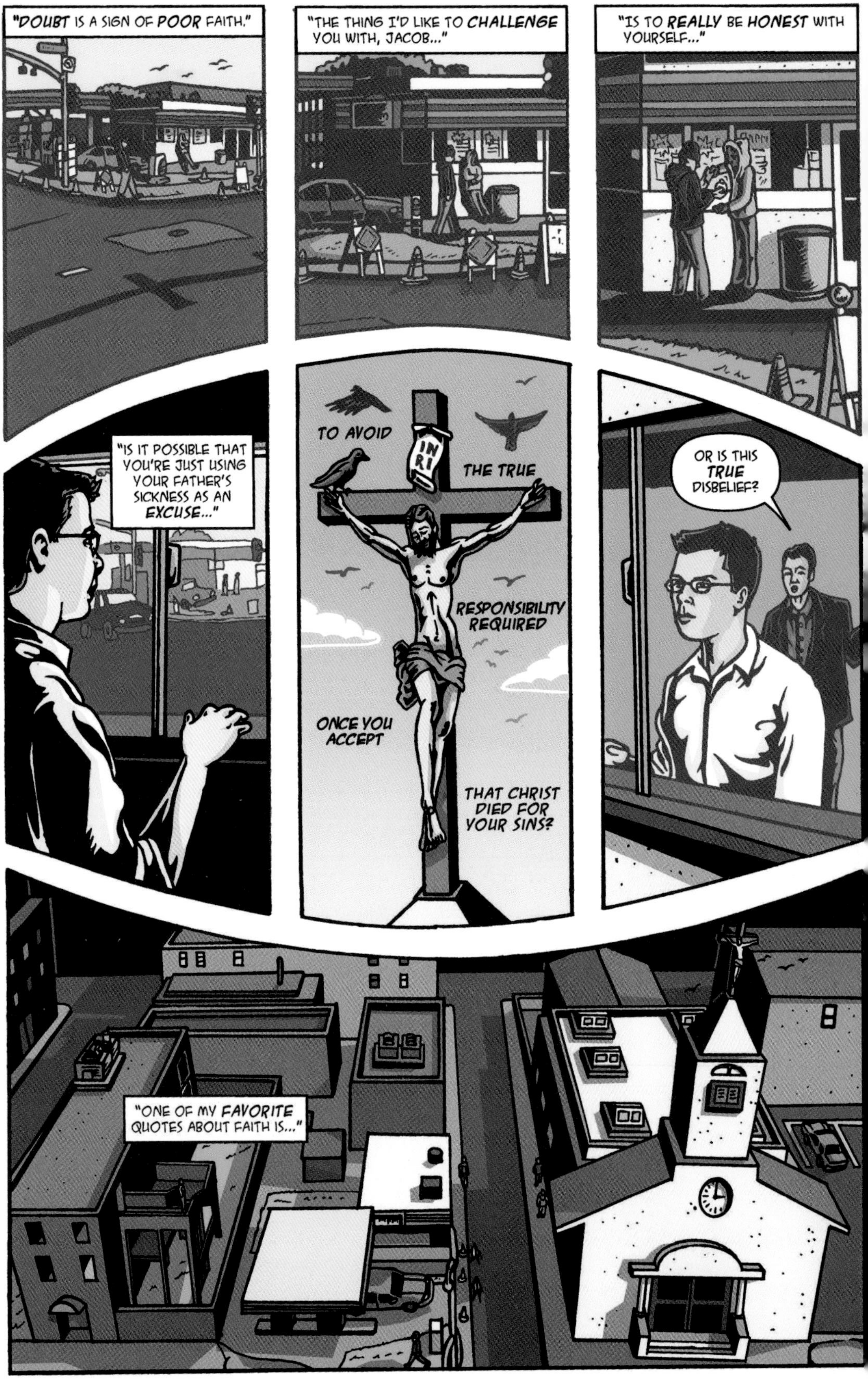
"DOUBT IS A SIGN OF POOR FAITH."
"THE THING I'D LIKE TO CHALLENGE YOU WITH, JACOB..."
"IS TO REALLY BE HONEST WITH YOURSELF..."
"IS IT POSSIBLE THAT YOU'RE JUST USING YOUR FATHER'S SICKNESS AS AN EXCUSE..."
TO AVOID
INRI
THE TRUE
RESPONSIBILITY REQUIRED
ONCE YOU ACCEPT
THAT CHRIST DIED FOR YOUR SINS?
OR IS THIS TRUE DISBELIEF?
"ONE OF MY FAVORITE QUOTES ABOUT FAITH IS..."

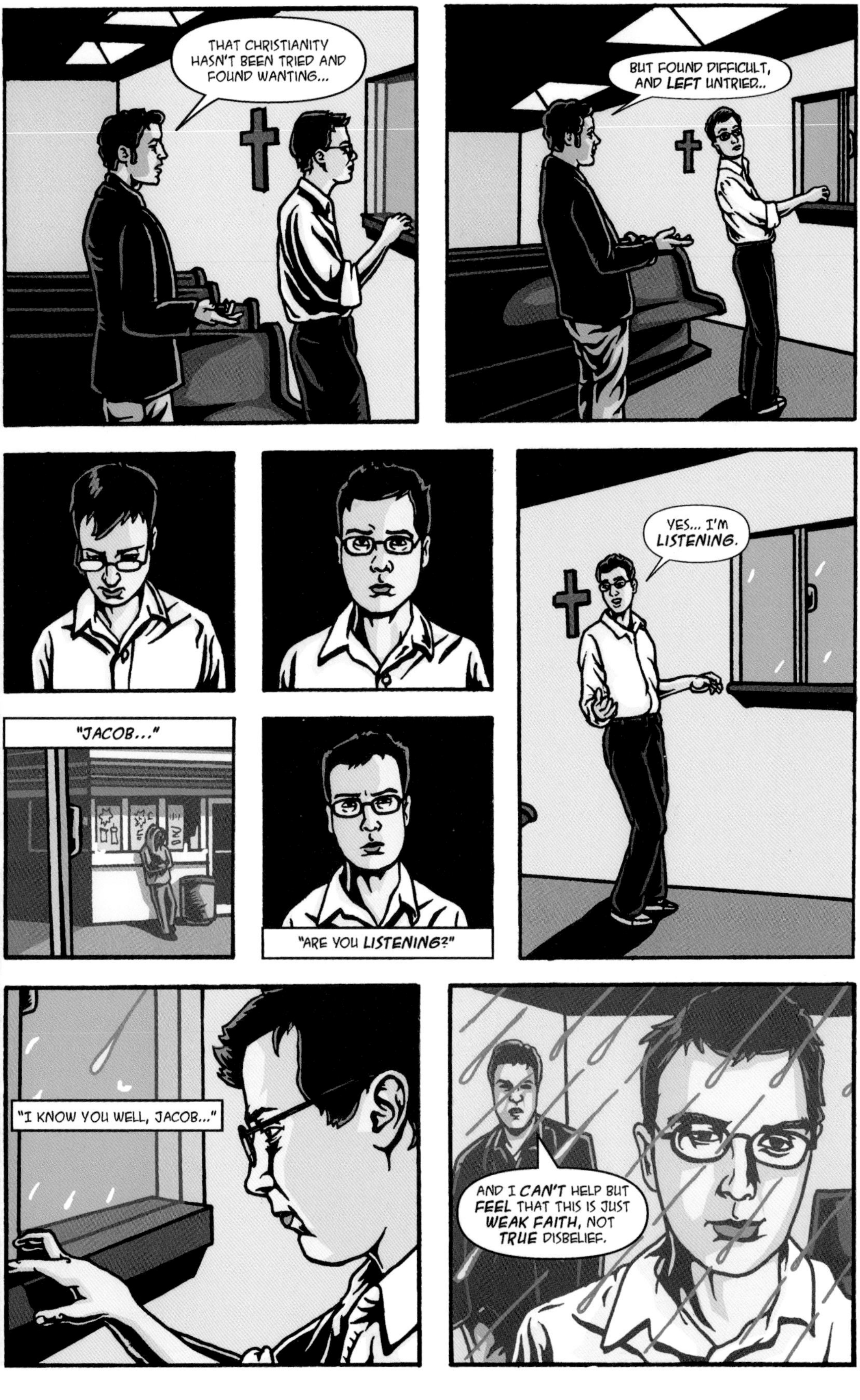
THAT CHRISTIANITY HASN'T BEEN TRIED AND FOUND WANTING...
BUT FOUND DIFFICULT, AND LEFT UNTRIED...
"JACOB..."
"ARE YOU LISTENING?"
YES... I'M LISTENING.
"I KNOW YOU WELL, JACOB..."
AND I CAN'T HELP BUT FEEL THAT THIS IS JUST WEAK FAITH, NOT TRUE DISBELIEF.

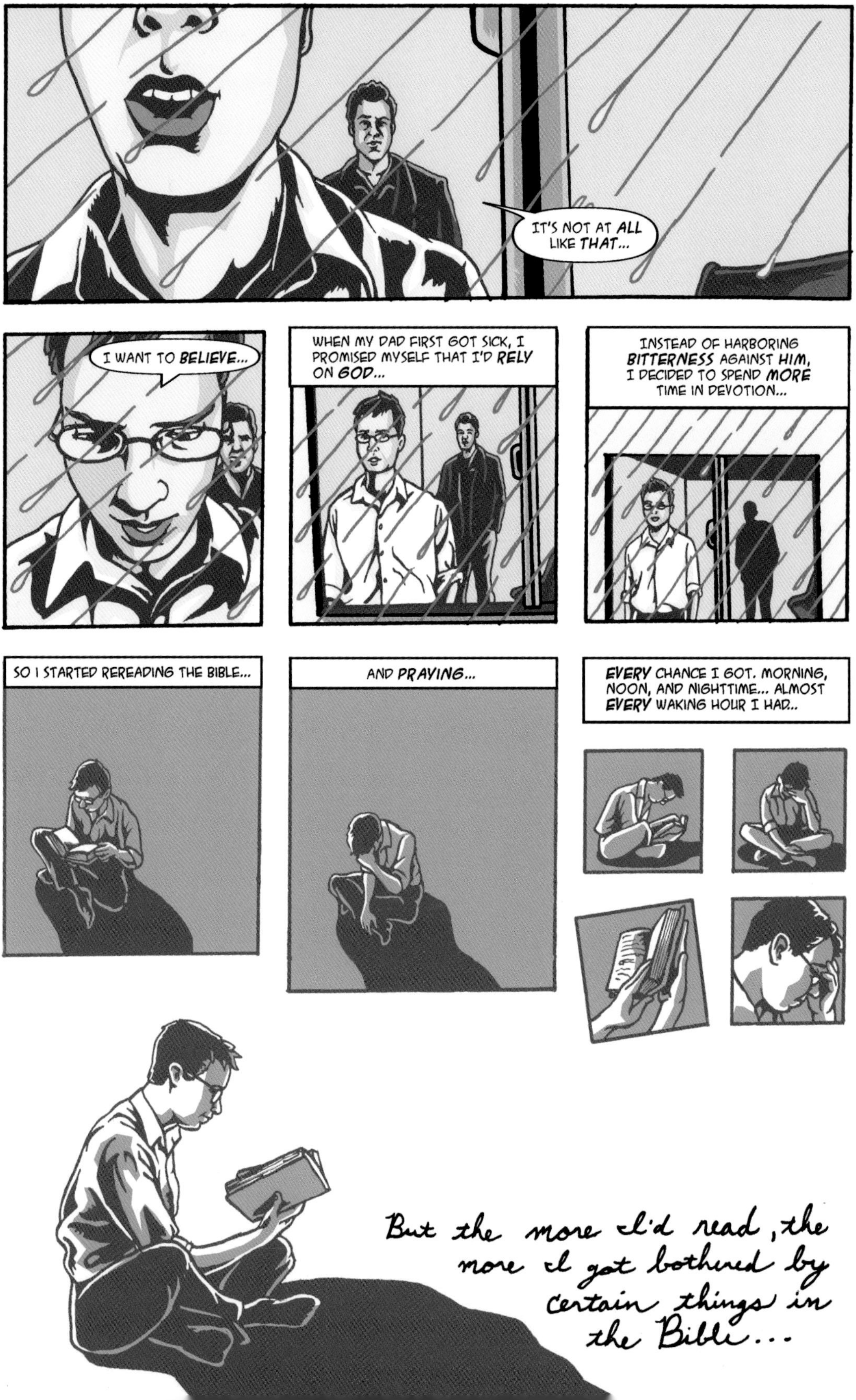

IT'S NOT AT ALL LIKE THAT...
I WANT TO BELIEVE...
WHEN MY DAD FIRST GOT SICK, I PROMISED MYSELF THAT I'D RELY ON GOD...
INSTEAD OF HARBORING BITTERNESS AGAINST HIM, I DECIDED TO SPEND MORE TIME IN DEVOTION...
SO I STARTED REREADING THE BIBLE...
AND PRAYING...
EVERY CHANCE I GOT. MORNING, NOON, AND NIGHTTIME... ALMOST EVERY WAKING HOUR I HAD..
But the more I'd read, the more I got bothered by certain things in the Bible...

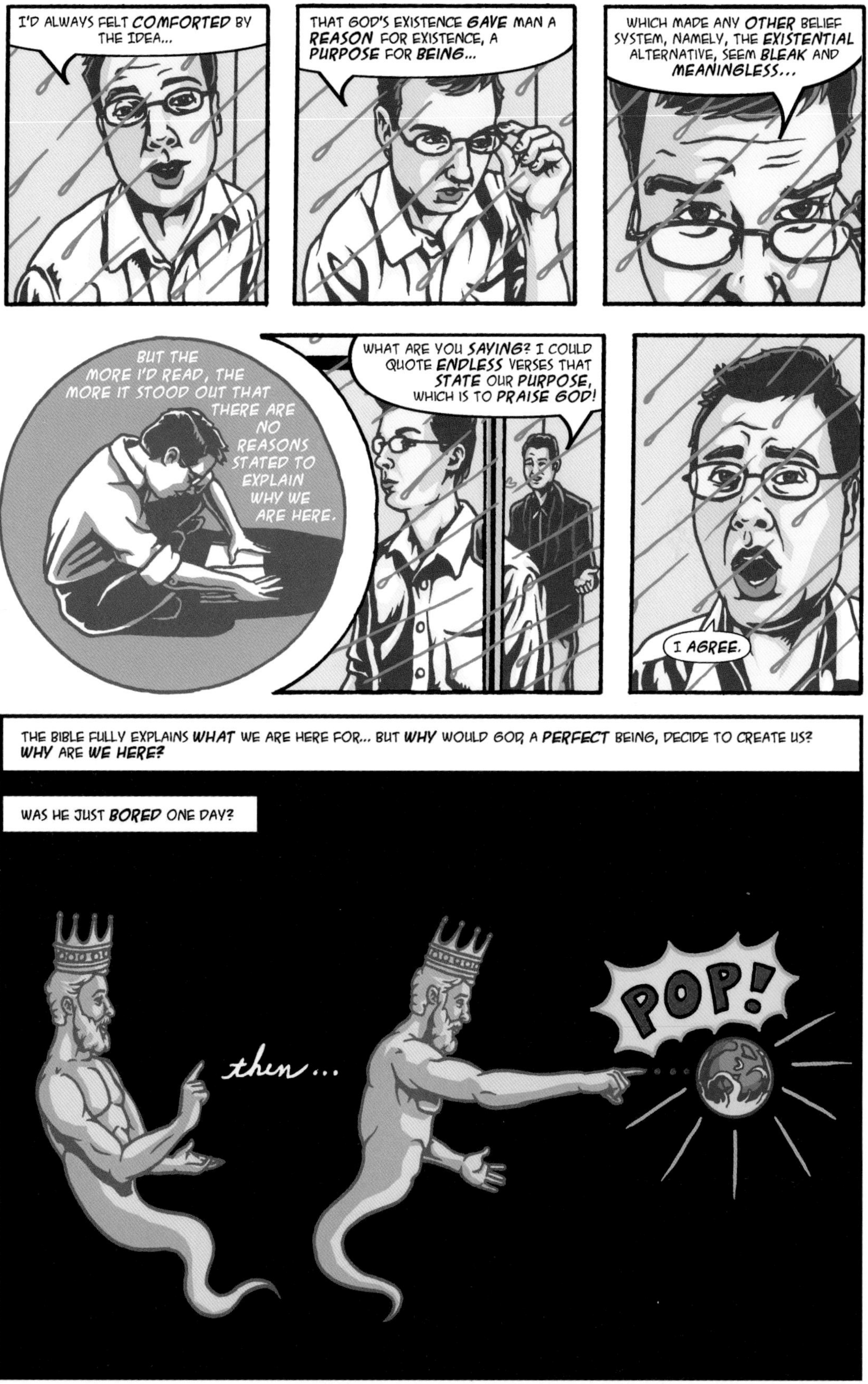

I'D ALWAYS FELT COMFORTED BY THE IDEA...
THAT GOD'S EXISTENCE GAVE MAN A REASON FOR EXISTENCE, A PURPOSE FOR BEING...
WHICH MADE ANY OTHER BELIEF SYSTEM, NAMELY, THE EXISTENTIAL ALTERNATIVE, SEEM BLEAK AND MEANINGLESS...
BUT THE MORE I'D READ, THE MORE IT STOOD OUT THAT THERE ARE NO REASONS STATED TO EXPLAIN WHY WE ARE HERE.
WHAT ARE YOU SAYING? I COULD QUOTE ENDLESS VERSES THAT STATE OUR PURPOSE, WHICH IS TO PRAISE GOD!
I AGREE.
THE BIBLE FULLY EXPLAINS WHAT WE ARE HERE FOR... BUT WHY WOULD GOD, A PERFECT BEING, DECIDE TO CREATE US? WHY ARE WE HERE?
WAS HE JUST BORED ONE DAY?
then...
POP!

Or is it that existentialists had it right, that God or no God, there is no purpose... that we're just spinning in an empty void?

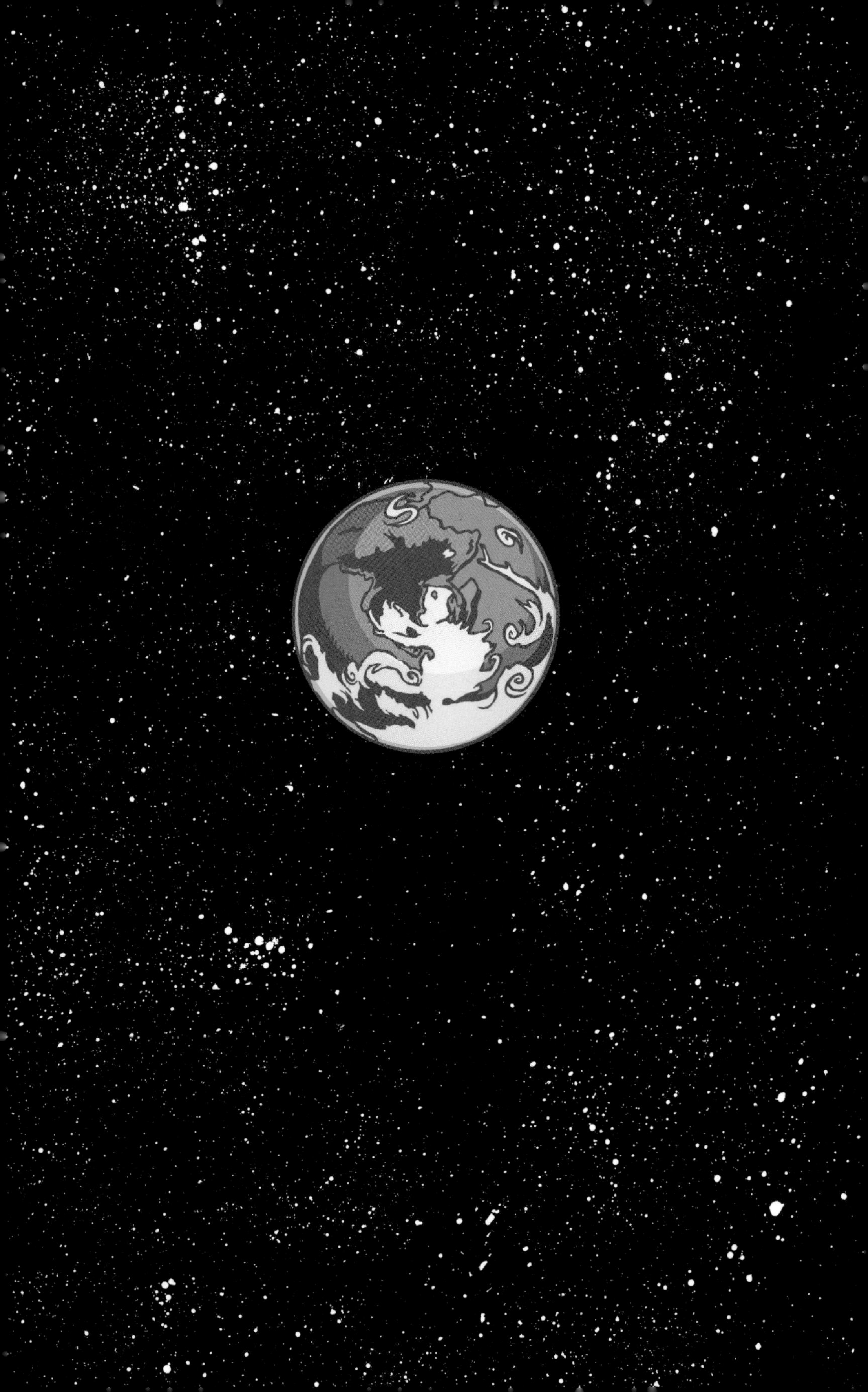

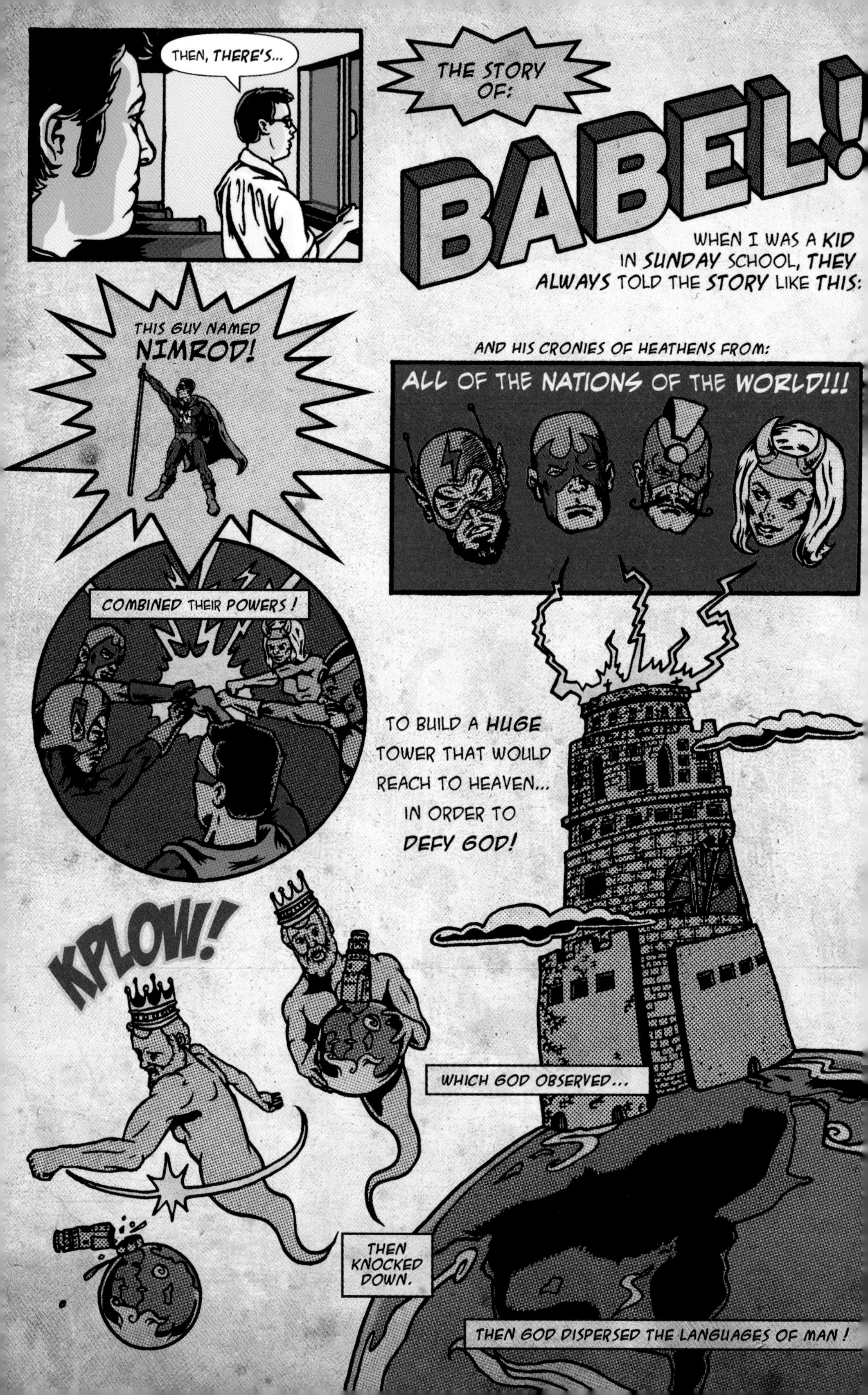
THEN, THERE'S...
THE STORY OF:
BABEL!
WHEN I WAS A KID IN SUNDAY SCHOOL, THEY ALWAYS TOLD THE STORY LIKE THIS:
THIS GUY NAMED NIMROD!
AND HIS CRONIES OF HEATHENS FROM:
ALL OF THE NATIONS OF THE WORLD!!!
COMBINED THEIR POWERS!
TO BUILD A HUGE TOWER THAT WOULD REACH TO HEAVEN... IN ORDER TO DEFY GOD!
KPLOW!
WHICH GOD OBSERVED...
THEN KNOCKED DOWN.
THEN GOD DISPERSED THE LANGUAGES OF MAN!

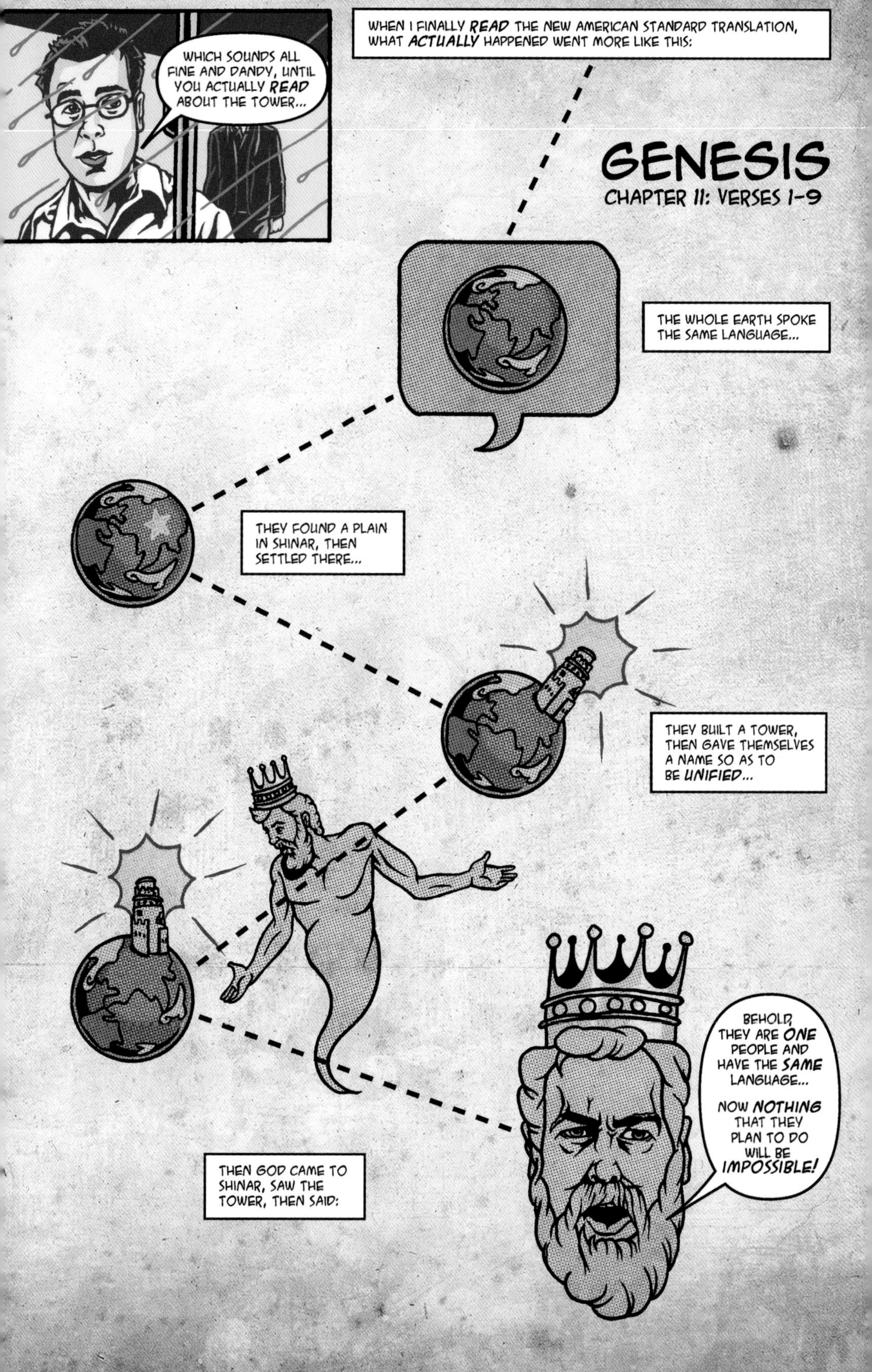

WHICH SOUNDS ALL FINE AND DANDY, UNTIL YOU ACTUALLY READ ABOUT THE TOWER...
WHEN I FINALLY READ THE NEW AMERICAN STANDARD TRANSLATION, WHAT ACTUALLY HAPPENED WENT MORE LIKE THIS:
GENESIS
CHAPTER 11: VERSES 1-9
THE WHOLE EARTH SPOKE THE SAME LANGUAGE...
THEY FOUND A PLAIN IN SHINAR, THEN SETTLED THERE...
THEY BUILT A TOWER, THEN GAVE THEMSELVES A NAME SO AS TO BE UNIFIED...
THEN GOD CAME TO SHINAR, SAW THE TOWER, THEN SAID:
BEHOLD, THEY ARE ONE PEOPLE AND HAVE THE SAME LANGUAGE...
NOW NOTHING THAT THEY PLAN TO DO WILL BE IMPOSSIBLE!

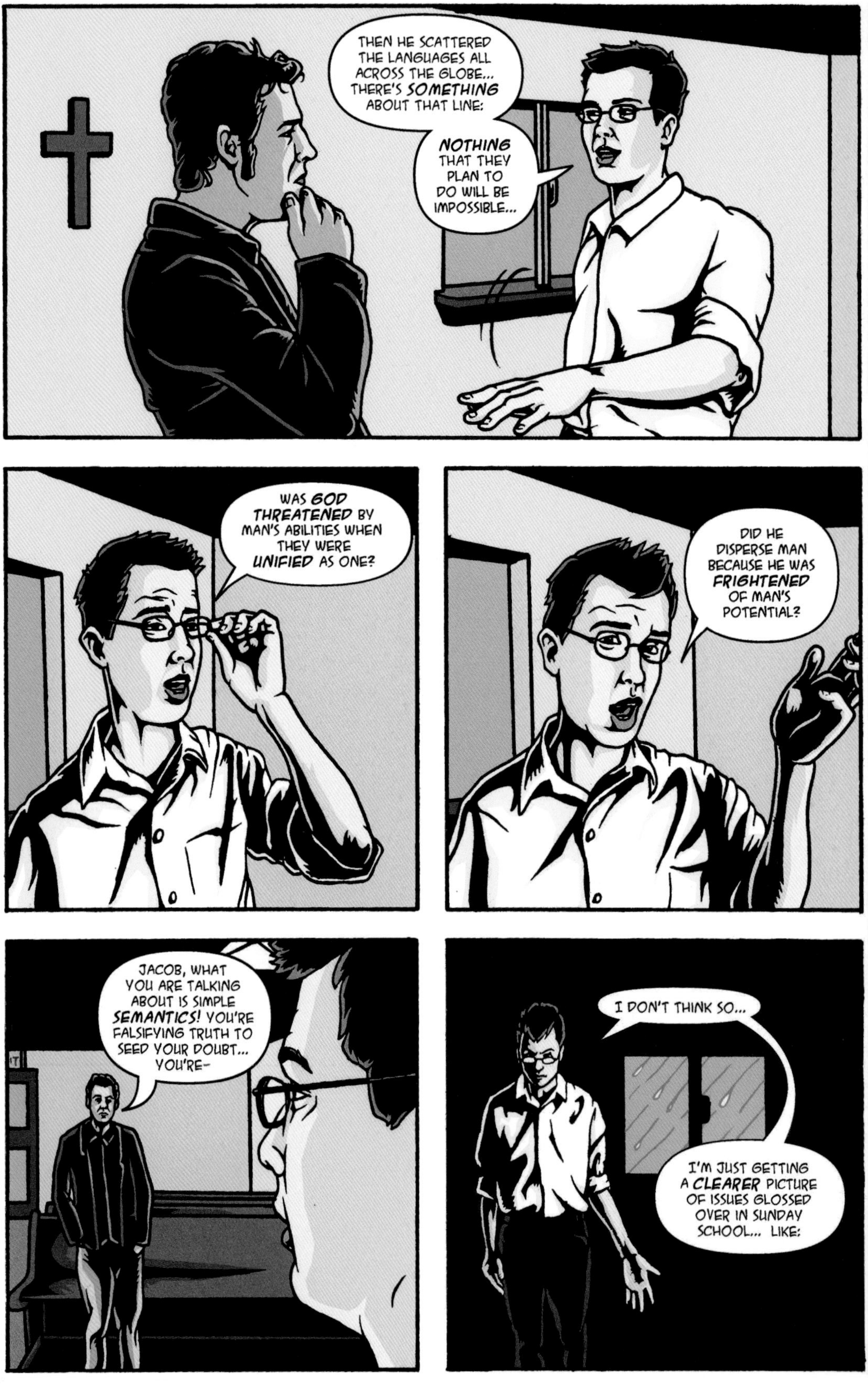
THEN HE SCATTERED THE LANGUAGES ALL ACROSS THE GLOBE... THERE'S SOMETHING ABOUT THAT LINE:
NOTHING THAT THEY PLAN TO DO WILL BE IMPOSSIBLE...
WAS GOD THREATENED BY MAN'S ABILITIES WHEN THEY WERE UNIFIED AS ONE?
DID HE DISPERSE MAN BECAUSE HE WAS FRIGHTENED OF MAN'S POTENTIAL?
JACOB, WHAT YOU ARE TALKING ABOUT IS SIMPLE SEMANTICS! YOU'RE FALSIFYING TRUTH TO SEED YOUR DOUBT... YOU'RE-
I DON'T THINK SO...
I'M JUST GETTING A CLEARER PICTURE OF ISSUES GLOSSED OVER IN SUNDAY SCHOOL... LIKE:

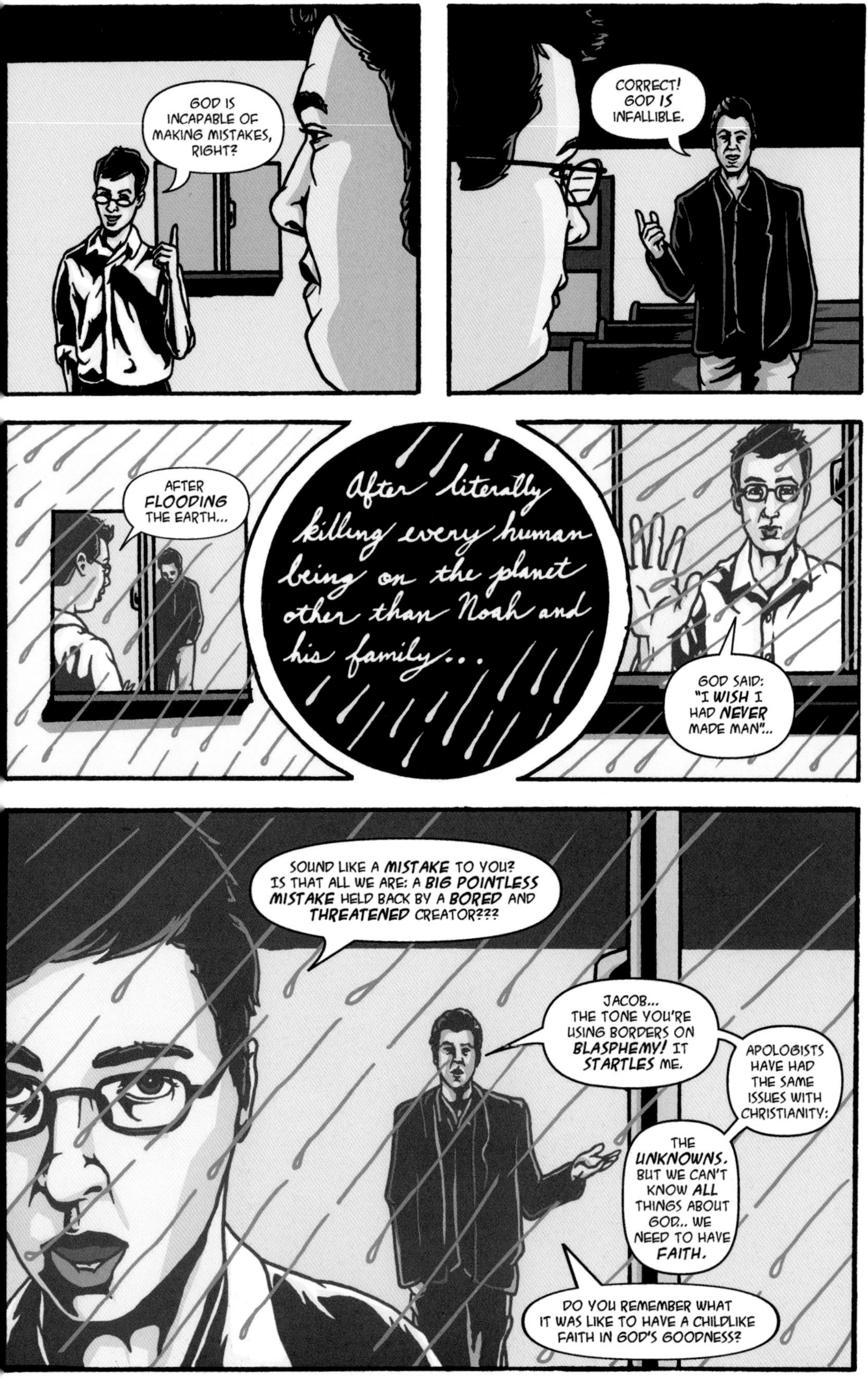
GOD IS INCAPABLE OF MAKING MISTAKES, RIGHT?
CORRECT! GOD IS INFALLIBLE.
AFTER FLOODING THE EARTH...
After literally killing every human being on the planet other than Noah and his family...
GOD SAID: "I WISH I HAD NEVER MADE MAN"...
SOUND LIKE A MISTAKE TO YOU? IS THAT ALL WE ARE: A BIG POINTLESS MISTAKE HELD BACK BY A BORED AND THREATENED CREATOR???
JACOB... THE TONE YOU'RE USING BORDERS ON BLASPHEMY! IT STARTLES ME.
APOLOGISTS HAVE HAD THE SAME ISSUES WITH CHRISTIANITY:
THE UNKNOWNS. BUT WE CAN'T KNOW ALL THINGS ABOUT GOD... WE NEED TO HAVE FAITH.
DO YOU REMEMBER WHAT IT WAS LIKE TO HAVE A CHILDLIKE FAITH IN GOD'S GOODNESS?

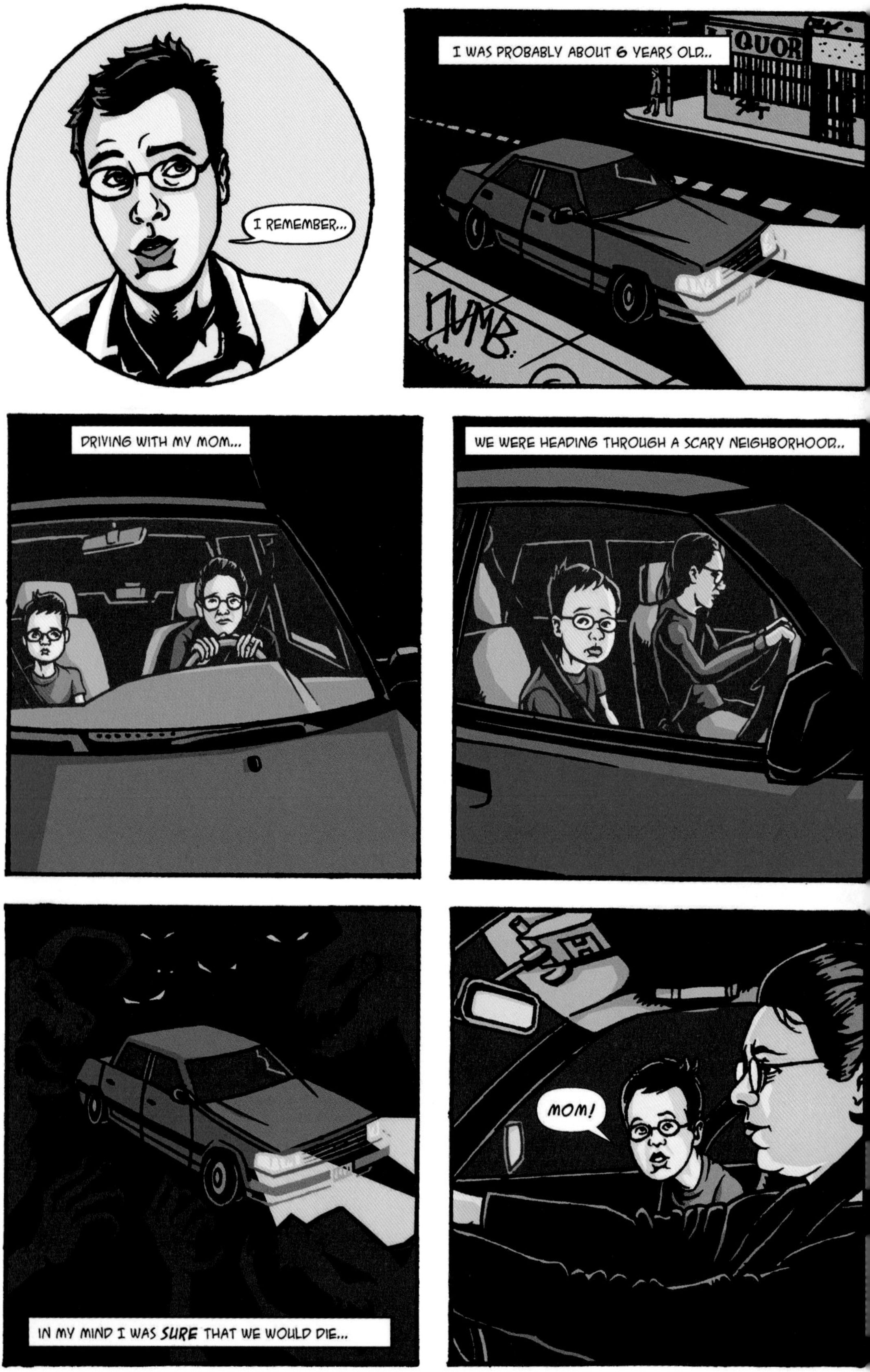
I REMEMBER...
I WAS PROBABLY ABOUT 6 YEARS OLD..
QUOR
NUMB
DRIVING WITH MY MOM...
WE WERE HEADING THROUGH A SCARY NEIGHBORHOOD..
IN MY MIND I WAS SURE THAT WE WOULD DIE...
MOM!

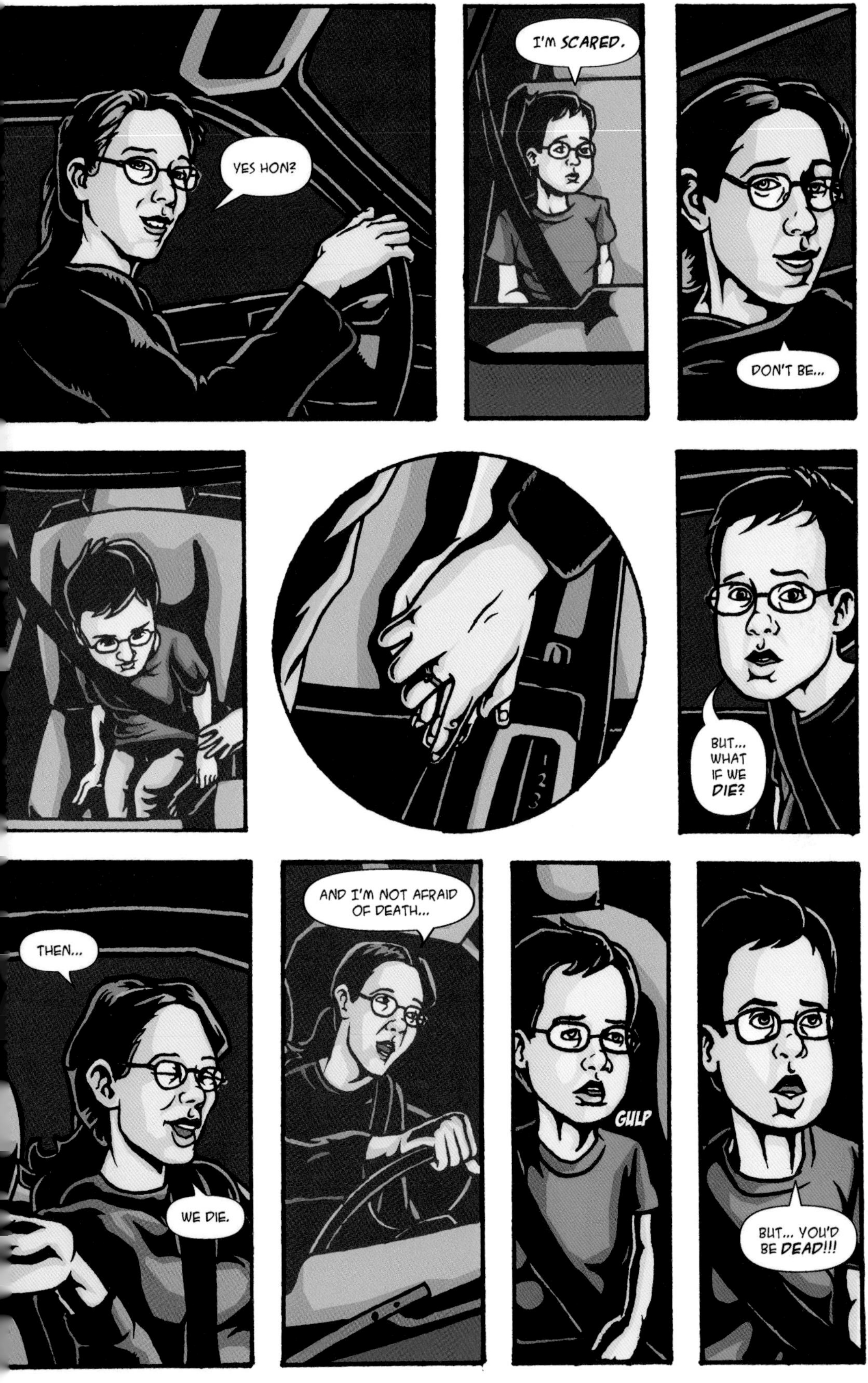

YES HON?
I'M SCARED.
DON'T BE...
BUT... WHAT IF WE DIE?
THEN...
WE DIE.
AND I'M NOT AFRAID OF DEATH...
GULP
BUT... YOU'D BE DEAD!!!

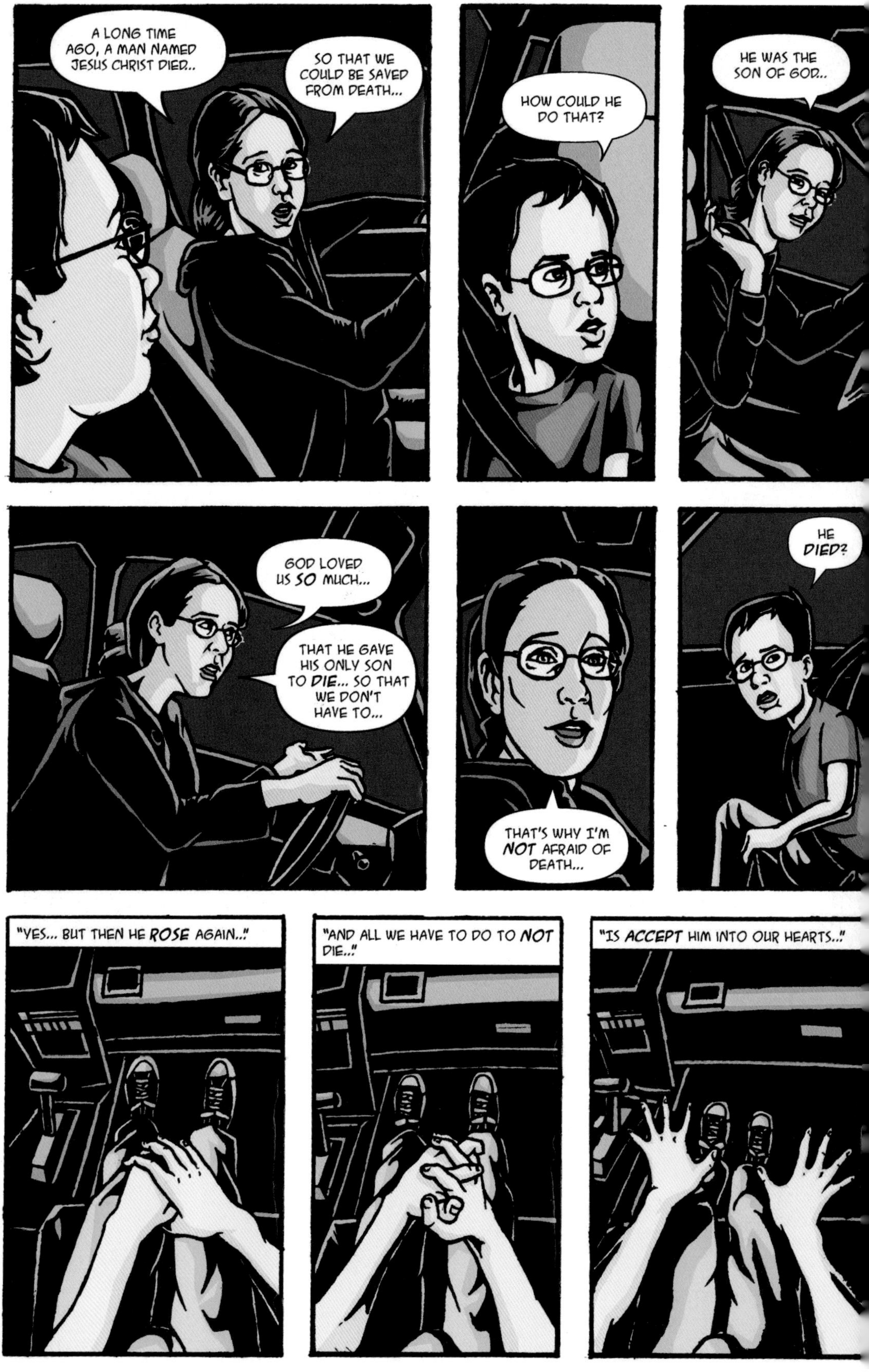
A LONG TIME AGO, A MAN NAMED JESUS CHRIST DIED..
SO THAT WE COULD BE SAVED FROM DEATH...
HOW COULD HE DO THAT?
HE WAS THE SON OF GOD..
GOD LOVED US **SO** MUCH...
THAT HE GAVE HIS ONLY SON TO **DIE**... SO THAT WE DON'T HAVE TO...
THAT'S WHY I'M **NOT** AFRAID OF DEATH...
HE **DIED**?
"YES... BUT THEN HE **ROSE** AGAIN..."
"AND ALL WE HAVE TO DO TO **NOT** DIE..."
"IS **ACCEPT** HIM INTO OUR HEARTS..."

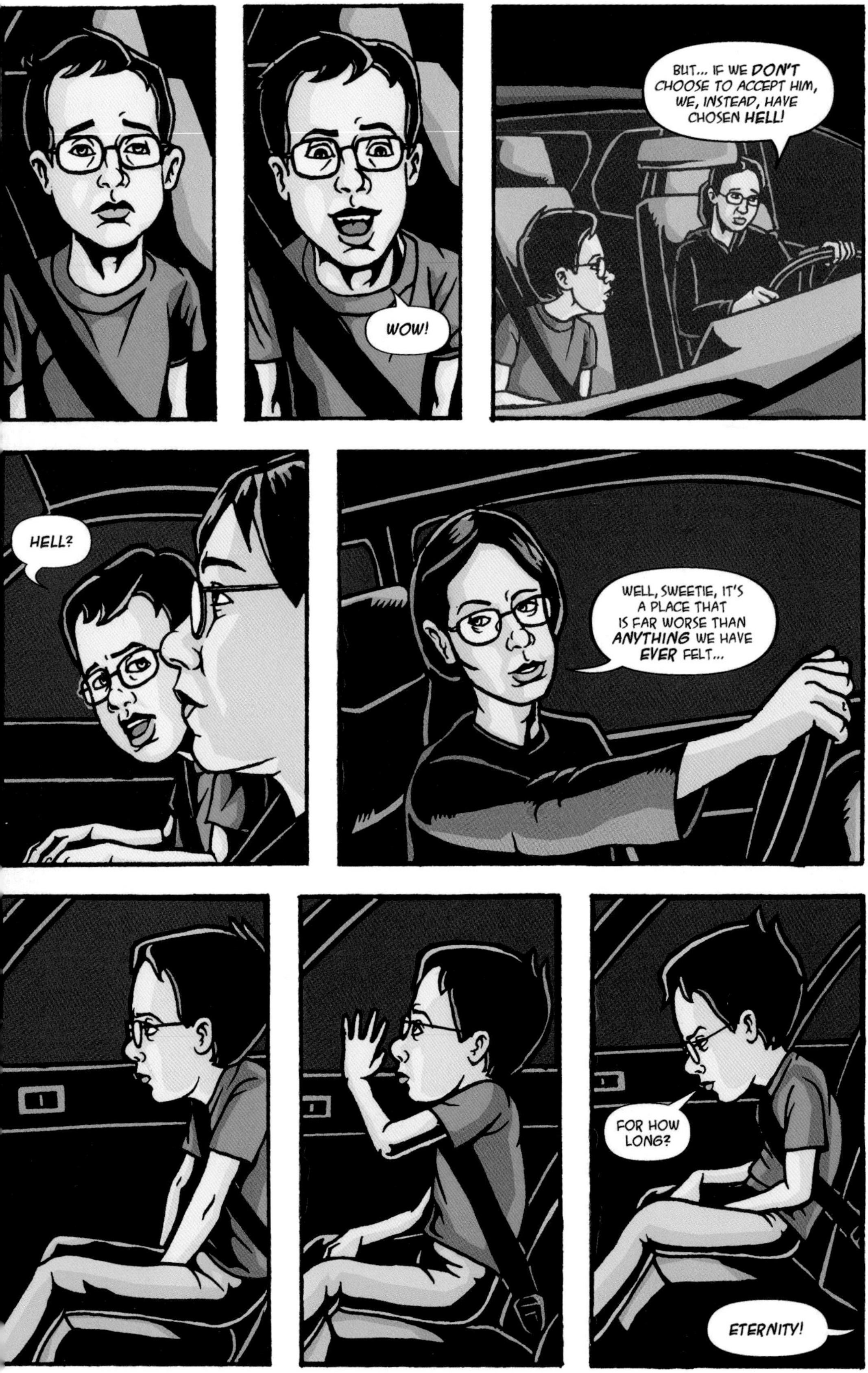
WOW!
BUT... IF WE DON'T CHOOSE TO ACCEPT HIM, WE, INSTEAD, HAVE CHOSEN HELL!
HELL?
WELL, SWEETIE, IT'S A PLACE THAT IS FAR WORSE THAN ANYTHING WE HAVE EVER FELT...
FOR HOW LONG?
ETERNITY!

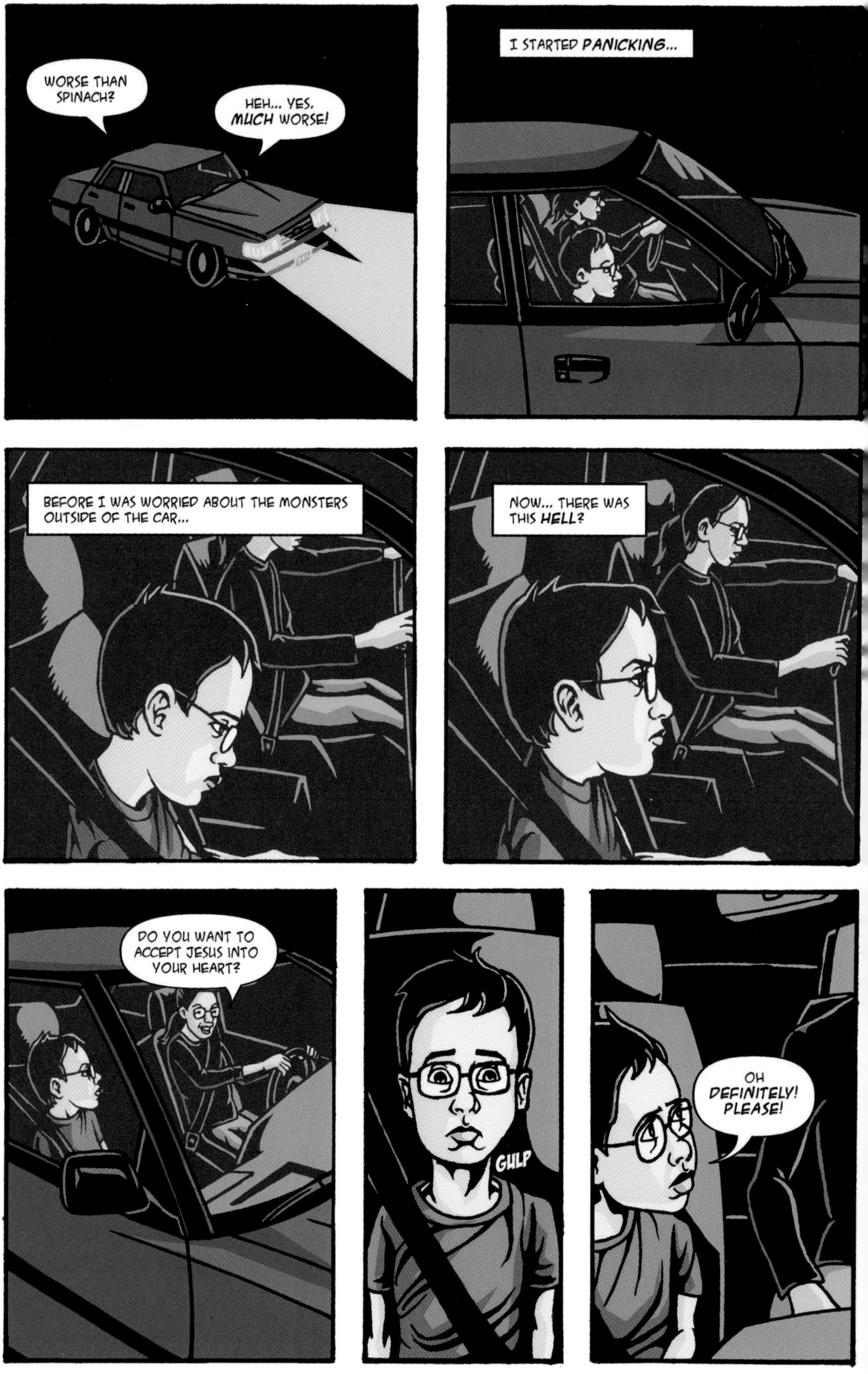
WORSE THAN SPINACH?
HEH... YES. MUCH WORSE!
I STARTED PANICKING...
BEFORE I WAS WORRIED ABOUT THE MONSTERS OUTSIDE OF THE CAR...
NOW... THERE WAS THIS HELL?
DO YOU WANT TO ACCEPT JESUS INTO YOUR HEART?
GULP
OH DEFINITELY! PLEASE!

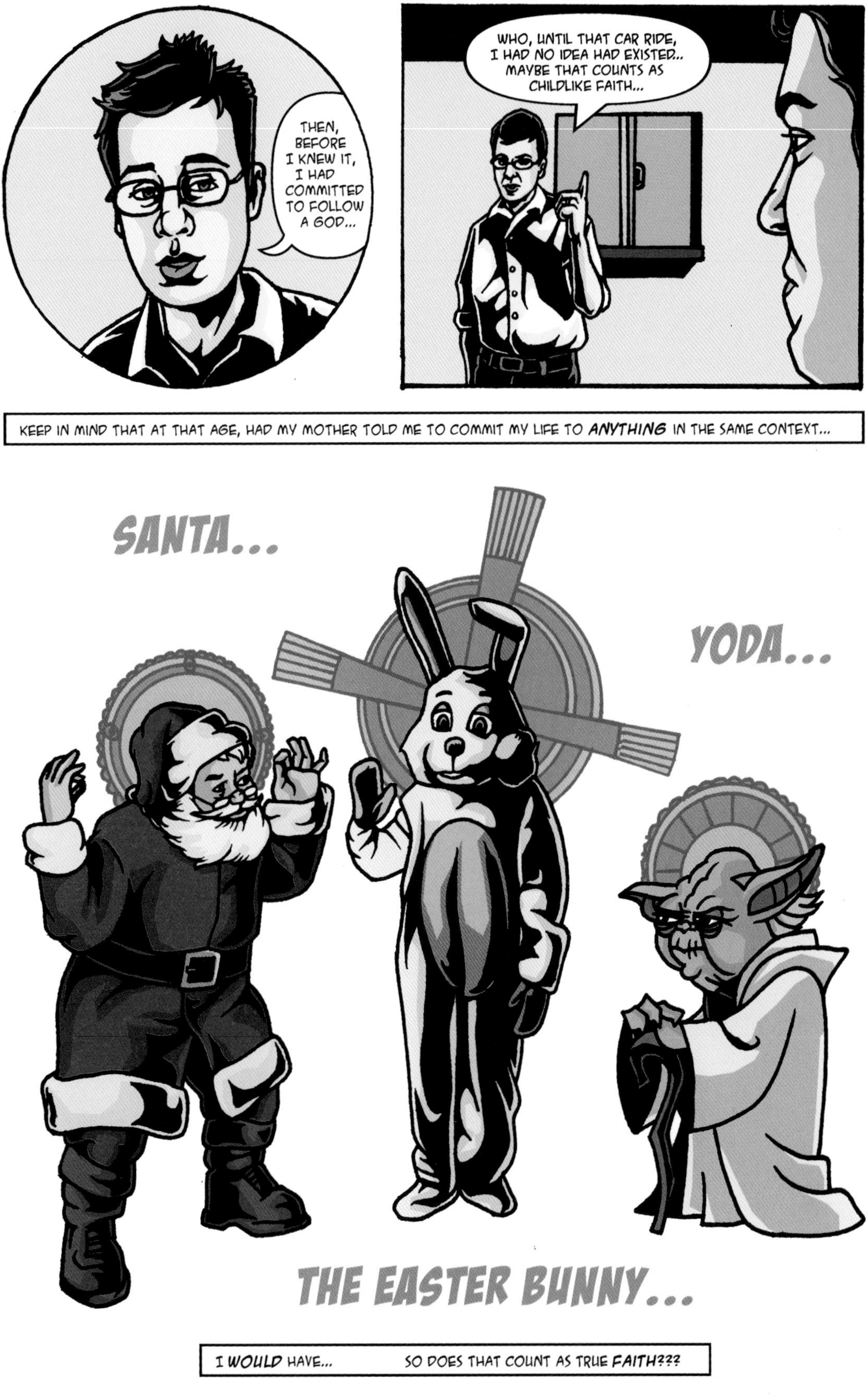
THEN, BEFORE I KNEW IT, I HAD COMMITTED TO FOLLOW A GOD...
WHO, UNTIL THAT CAR RIDE, I HAD NO IDEA HAD EXISTED.. MAYBE THAT COUNTS AS CHILDLIKE FAITH...
KEEP IN MIND THAT AT THAT AGE, HAD MY MOTHER TOLD ME TO COMMIT MY LIFE TO ANYTHING IN THE SAME CONTEXT...
SANTA...
YODA...
THE EASTER BUNNY...
I WOULD HAVE...
SO DOES THAT COUNT AS TRUE FAITH???

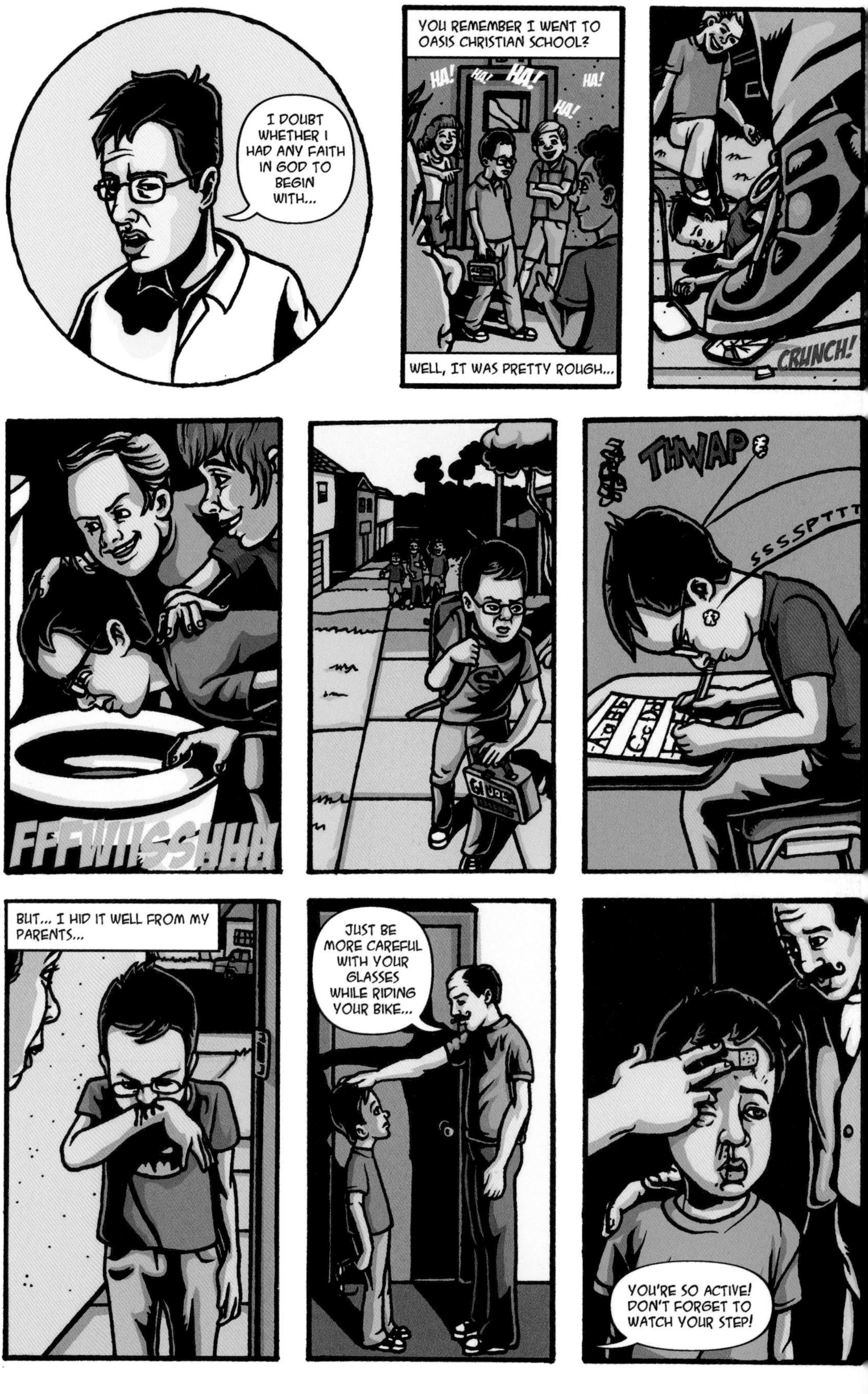
I DOUBT WHETHER I HAD ANY FAITH IN GOD TO BEGIN WITH...
YOU REMEMBER I WENT TO OASIS CHRISTIAN SCHOOL?
HA! HA! HA! HA! HA!
WELL, IT WAS PRETTY ROUGH...
CRUNCH!
FFFWIISSHHH
THWAP
SSSSPTTT
BUT... I HID IT WELL FROM MY PARENTS...
JUST BE MORE CAREFUL WITH YOUR GLASSES WHILE RIDING YOUR BIKE...
YOU'RE SO ACTIVE! DON'T FORGET TO WATCH YOUR STEP!

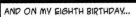

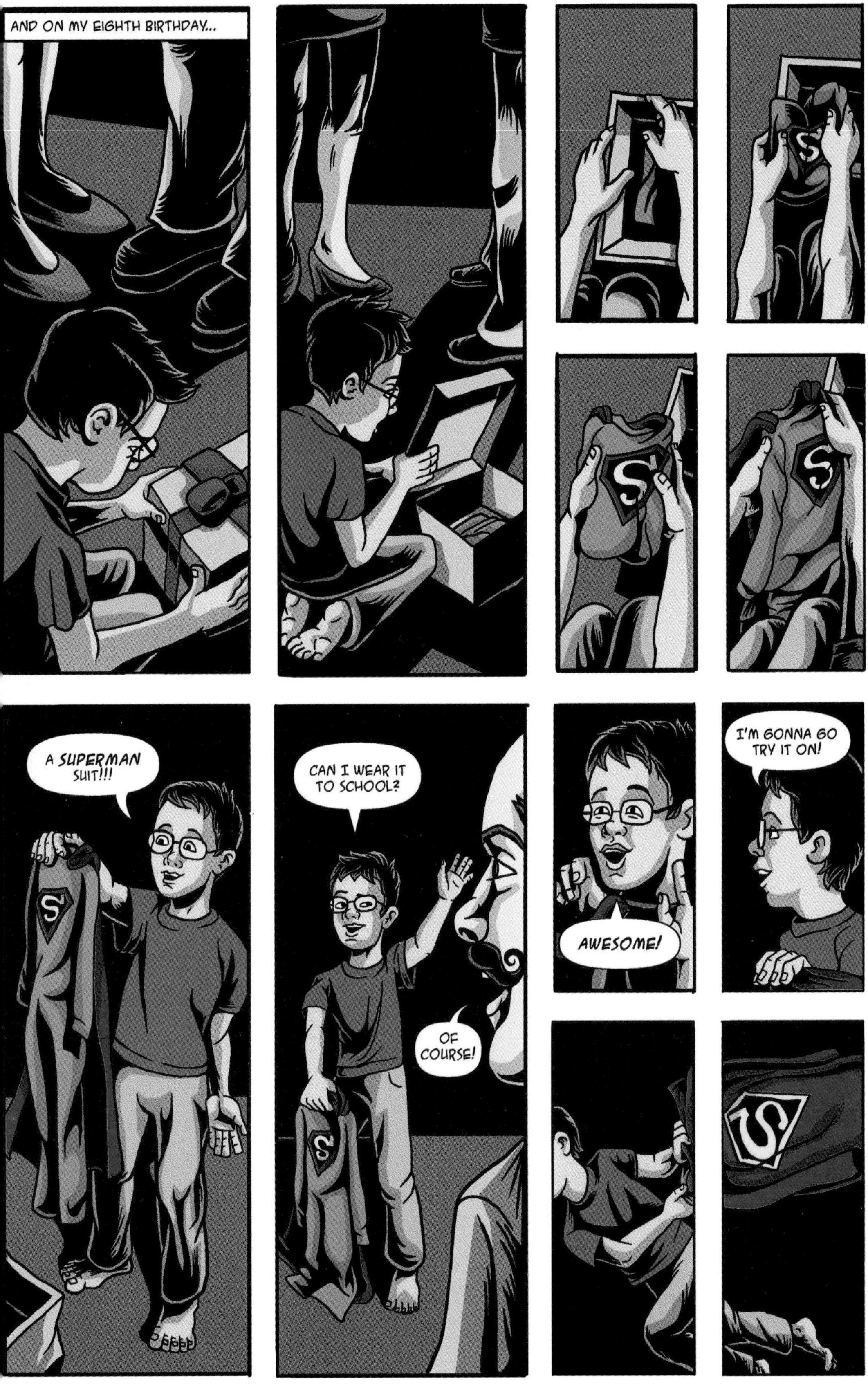
AND ON MY EIGHTH BIRTHDAY...
A SUPERMAN SUIT!!!
CAN I WEAR IT TO SCHOOL?
OF COURSE!
AWESOME!
I'M GONNA GO TRY IT ON!

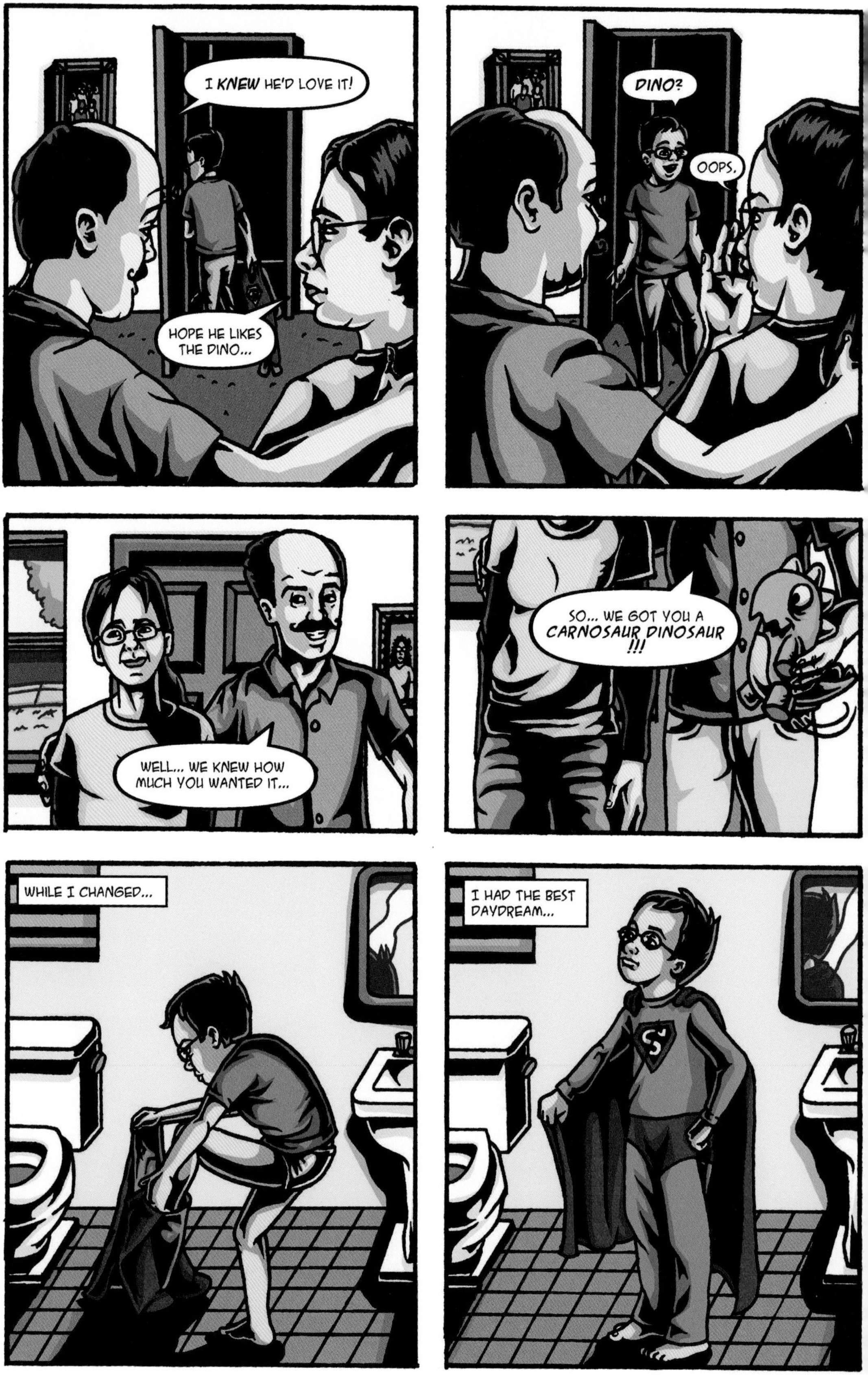
I KNEW HE'D LOVE IT!
HOPE HE LIKES THE DINO...
DINO?
OOPS.
WELL... WE KNEW HOW MUCH YOU WANTED IT...
SO... WE GOT YOU A CARNOSAUR DINOSAUR !!!
WHILE I CHANGED...
I HAD THE BEST DAYDREAM...

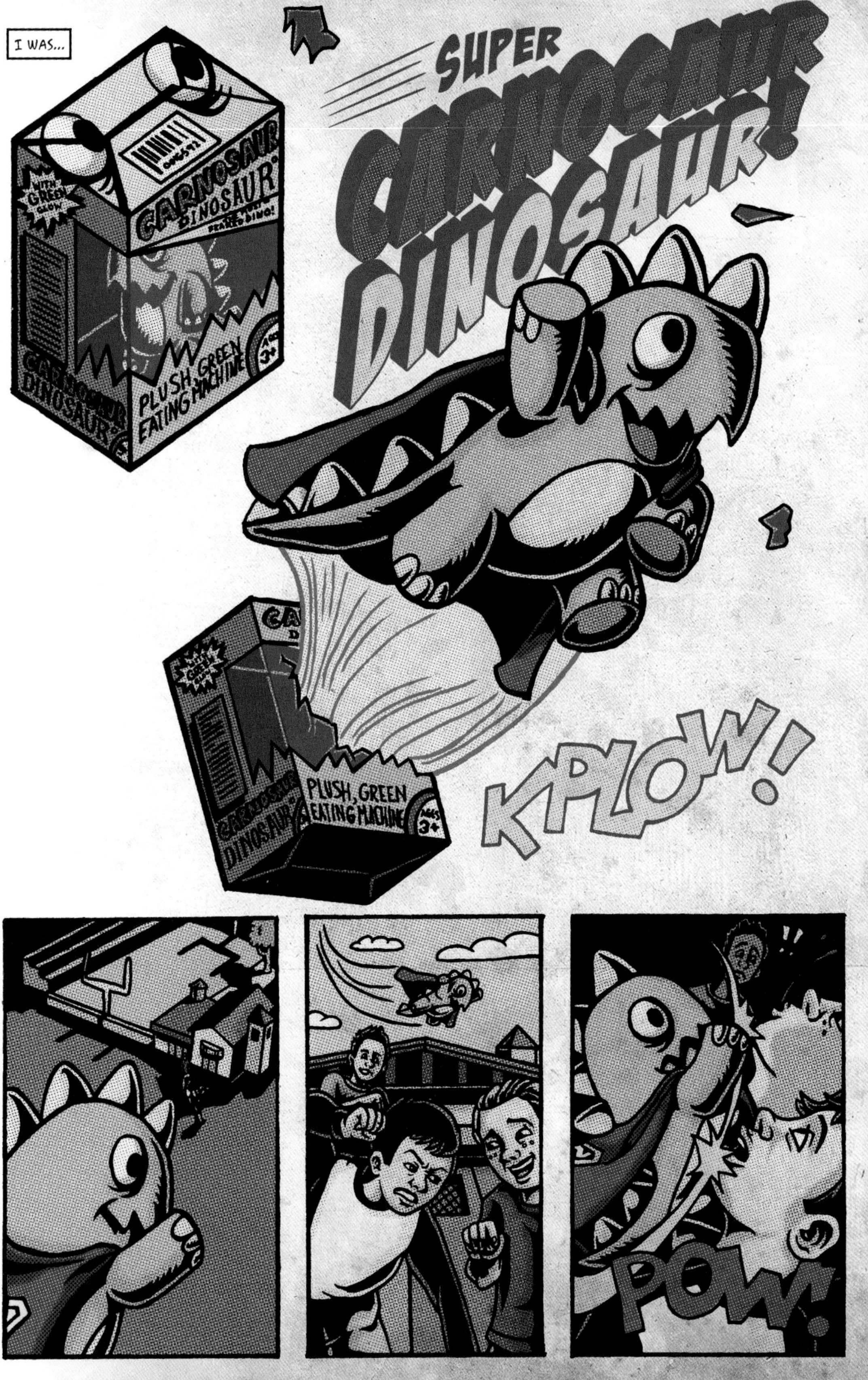
I WAS...
SUPER CARNOSAUR DINOSAUR!
WITH GREEN GLOW
CARNOSAUR DINOSAUR®
PLUSH GREEN EATING MACHINE
AGES 3+
CARNOSAUR DINOSAUR®
PLUSH, GREEN EATING MACHINE
AGES 3+
KAPLOW!
!!
POW!

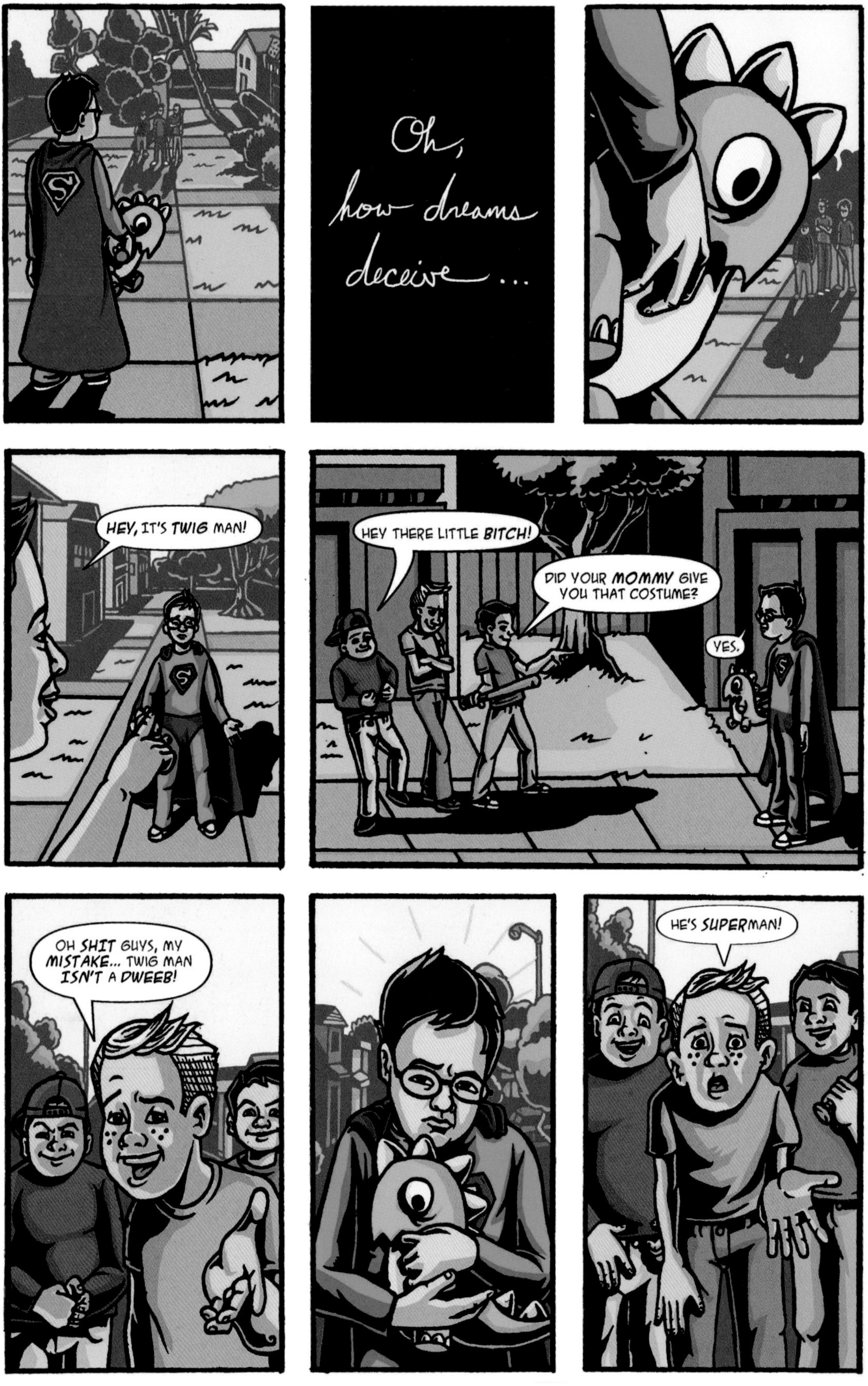
Oh,
how dreams
deceive...
HEY, IT'S TWIG MAN!
HEY THERE LITTLE BITCH!
DID YOUR MOMMY GIVE YOU THAT COSTUME?
YES.
OH SHIT GUYS, MY MISTAKE... TWIG MAN ISN'T A DWEEB!
HE'S SUPERMAN!

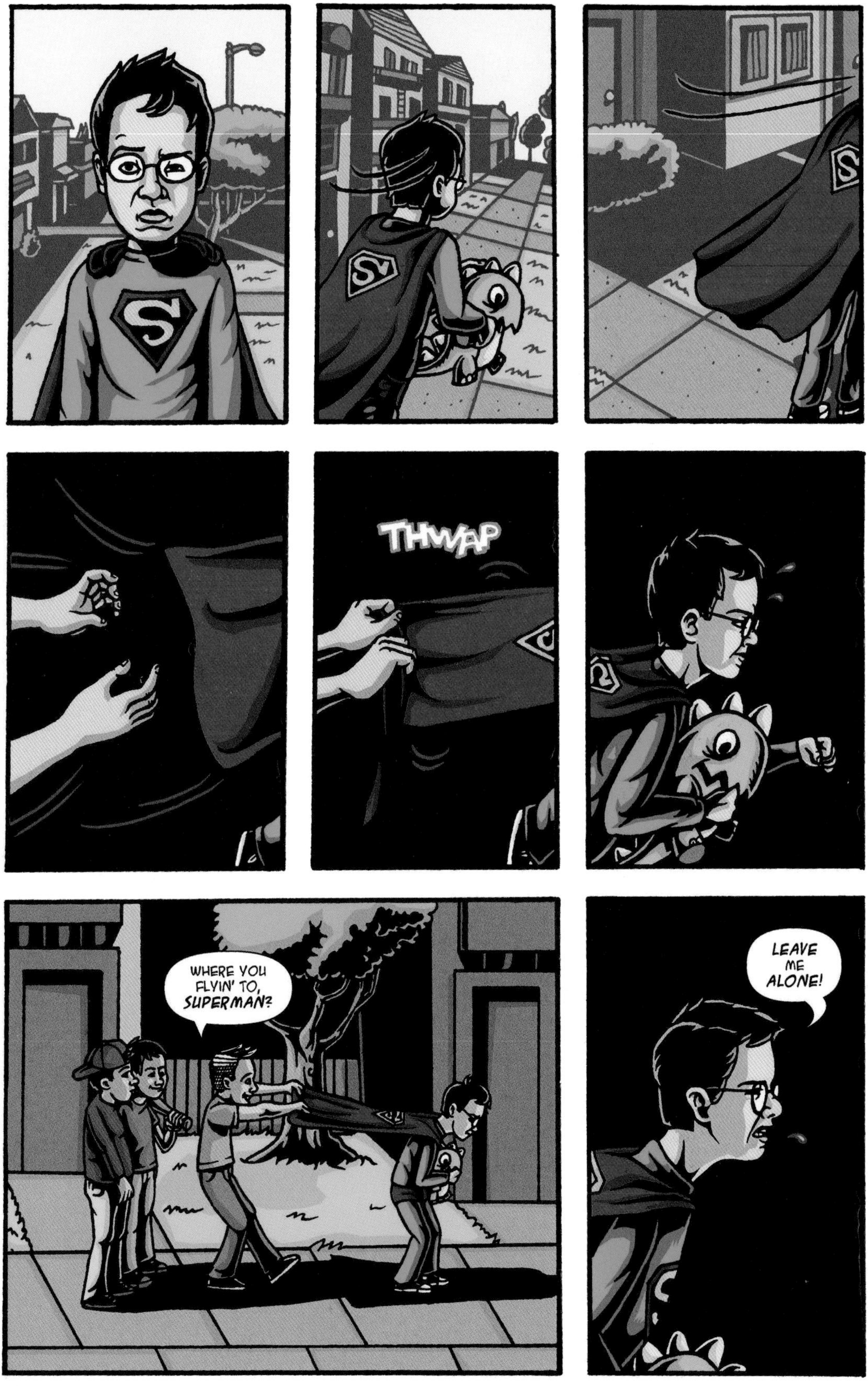
THWAP
WHERE YOU FLYIN' TO, SUPERMAN?
LEAVE ME ALONE!

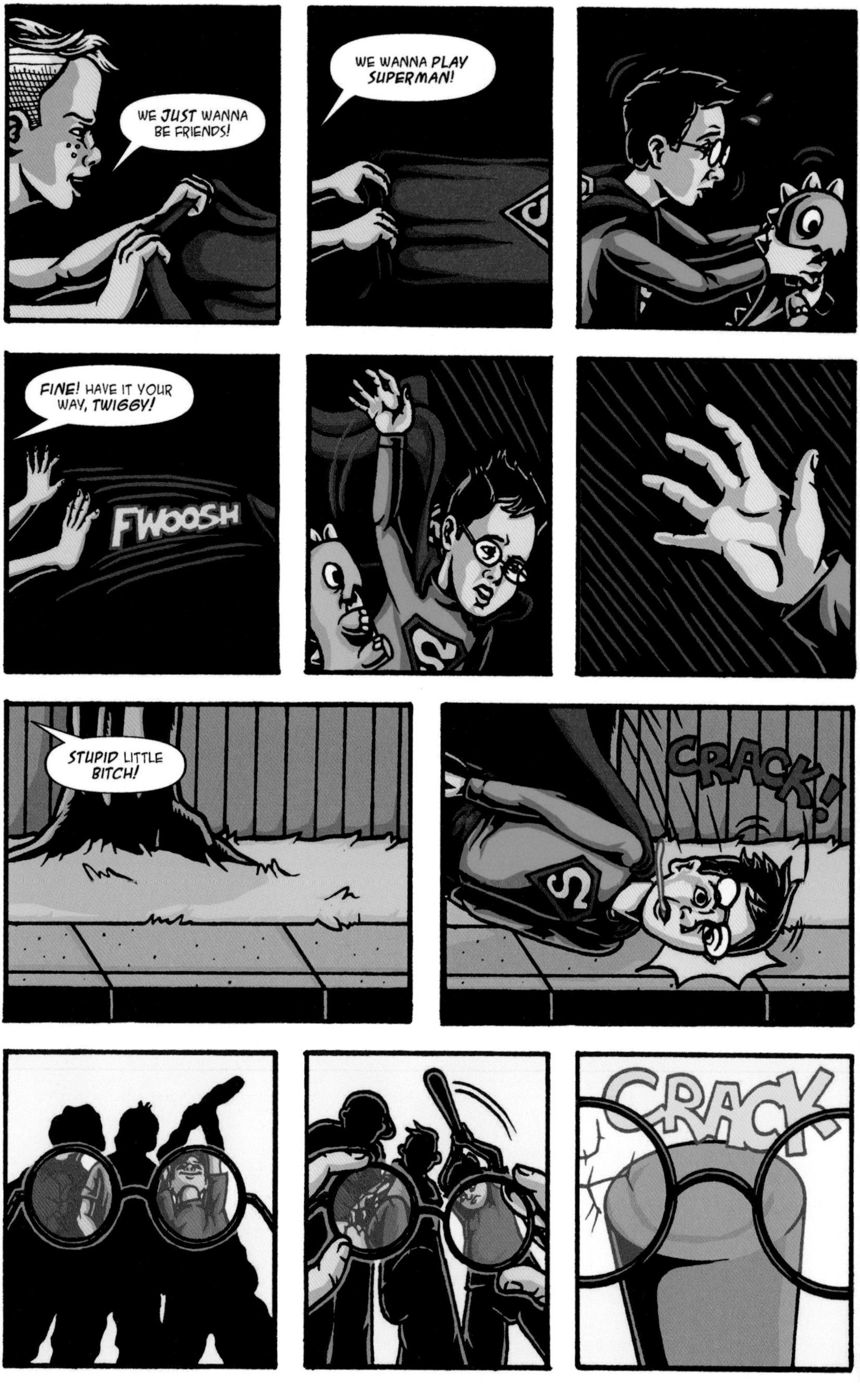
WE JUST WANNA BE FRIENDS!
WE WANNA PLAY SUPERMAN!
FINE! HAVE IT YOUR WAY, TWIGGY!
FWOOSH
STUPID LITTLE BITCH!
CRACK!
CRACK

HOPE THIS LITTLE *PUSSY* LIKES HIS *TOY.*

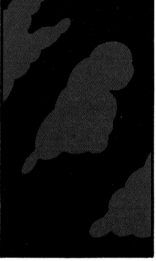

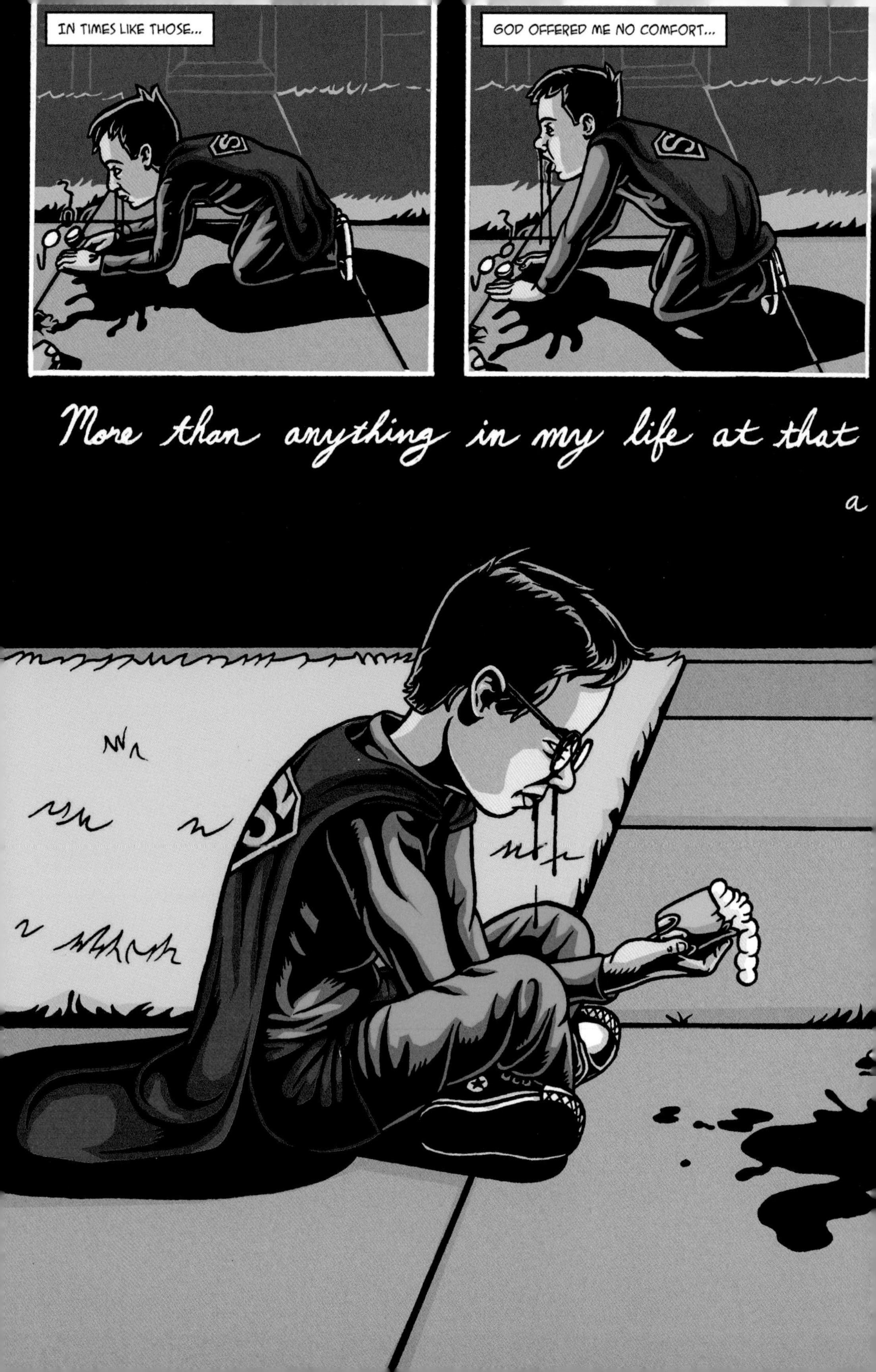
IN TIMES LIKE THOSE...
GOD OFFERED ME NO COMFORT...
More than anything in my life at that
a

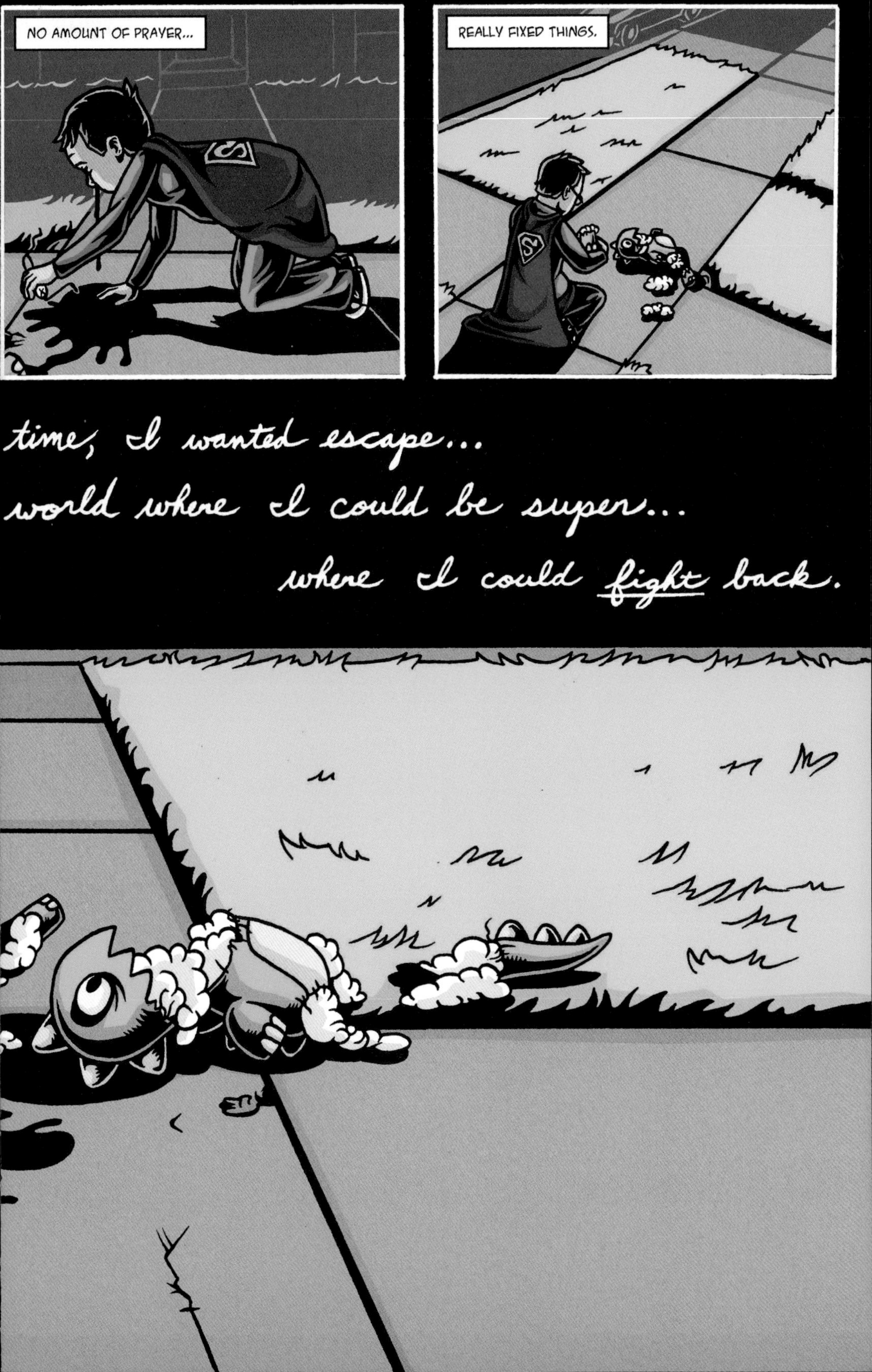
NO AMOUNT OF PRAYER...
REALLY FIXED THINGS.
time, I wanted escape...
world where I could be super...
where I could fight back.

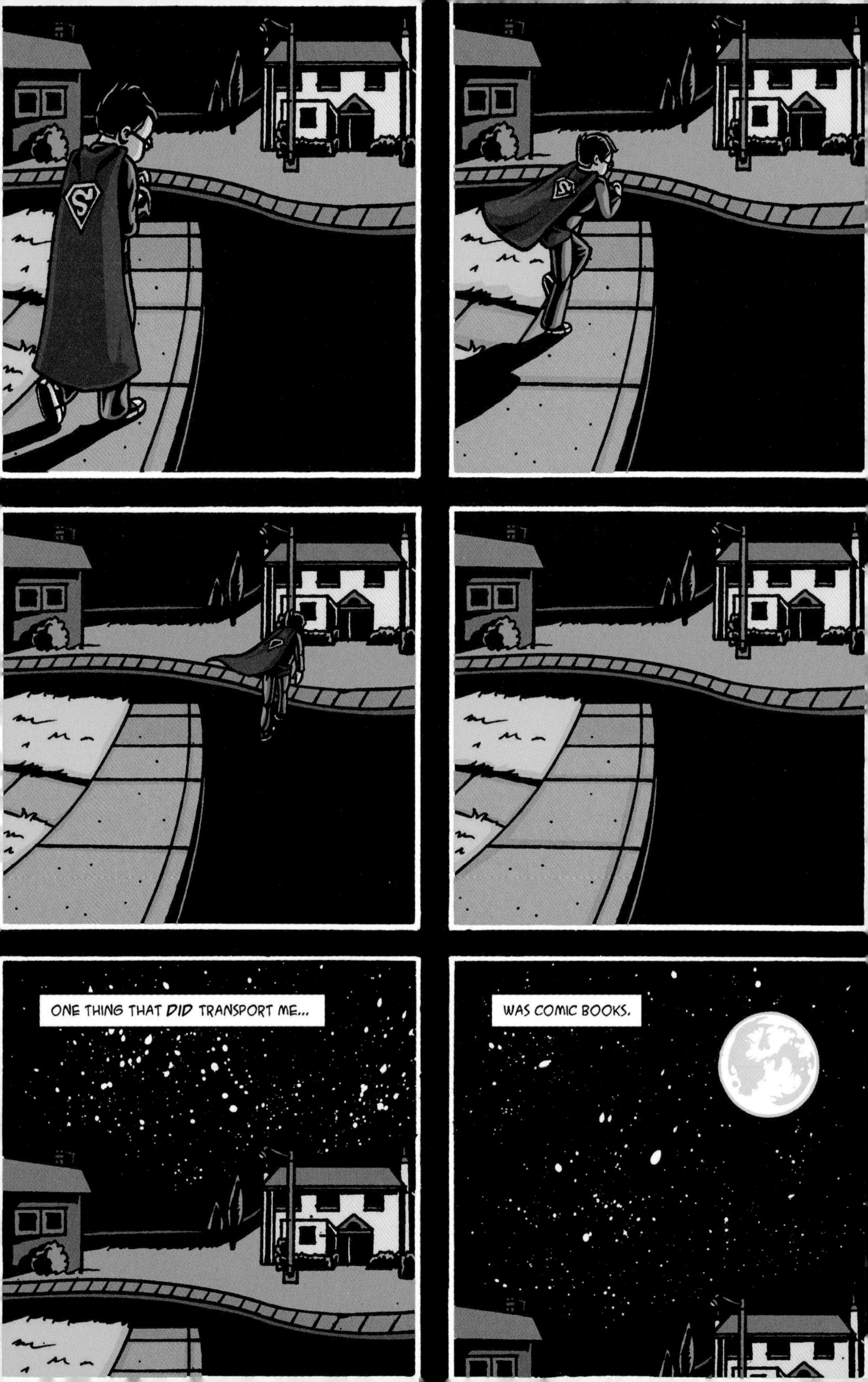
ONE THING THAT DID TRANSPORT ME...
WAS COMIC BOOKS.

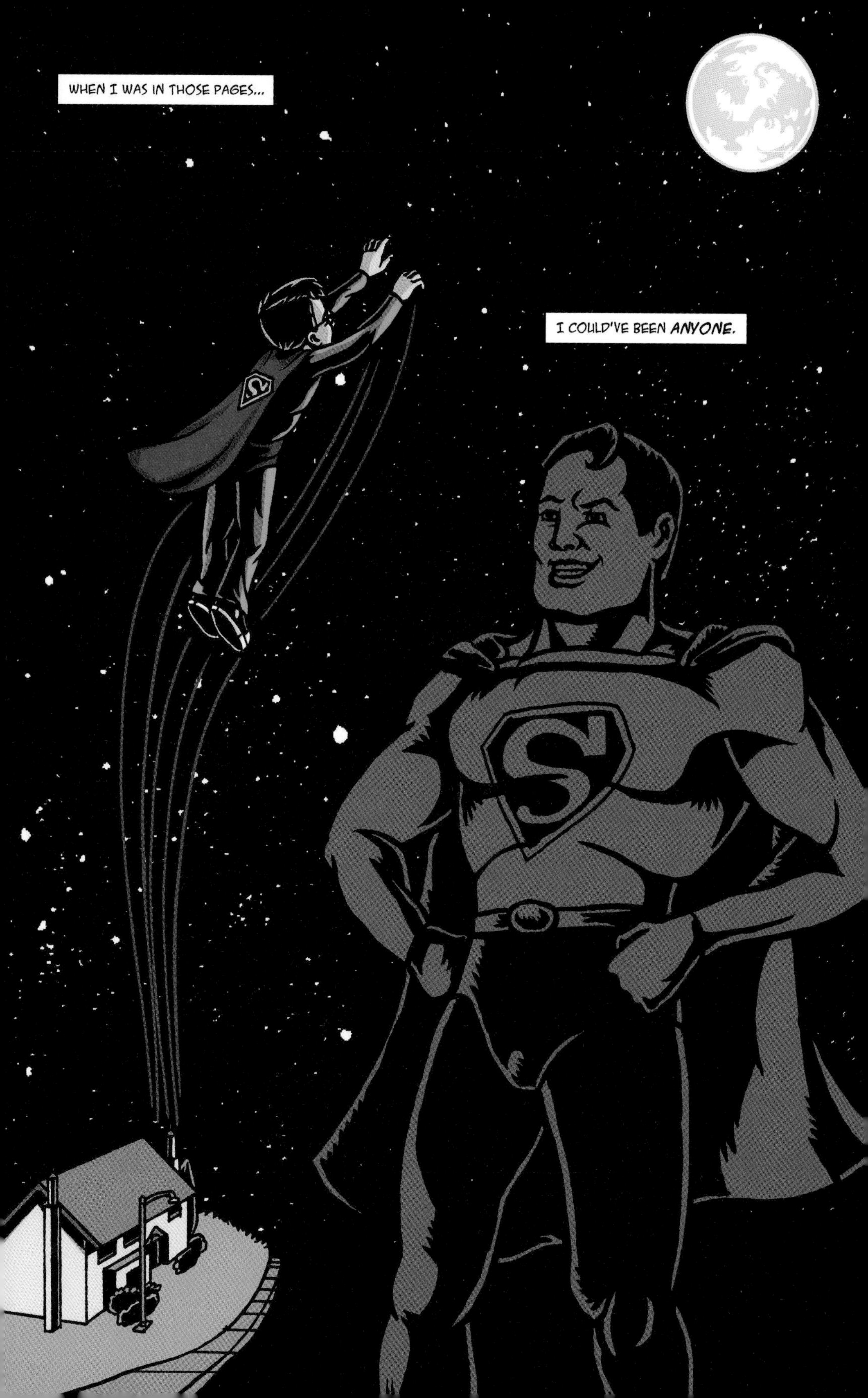
WHEN I WAS IN THOSE PAGES...
I COULD'VE BEEN ANYONE.

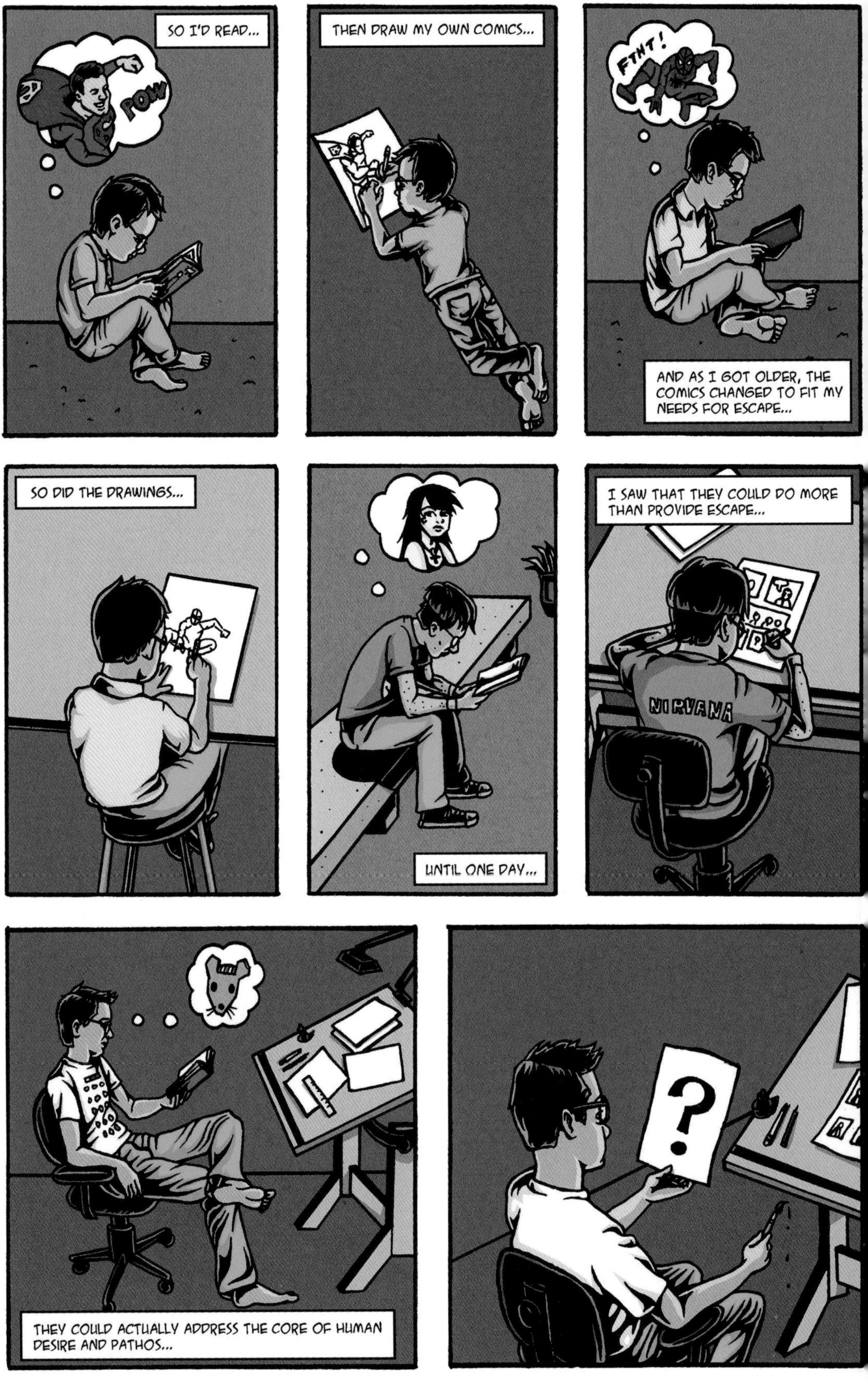
SO I'D READ...
POW
THEN DRAW MY OWN COMICS...
FTHT!
AND AS I GOT OLDER, THE COMICS CHANGED TO FIT MY NEEDS FOR ESCAPE...
SO DID THE DRAWINGS...
UNTIL ONE DAY...
I SAW THAT THEY COULD DO MORE THAN PROVIDE ESCAPE...
NIRVANA
THEY COULD ACTUALLY ADDRESS THE CORE OF HUMAN DESIRE AND PATHOS...
?

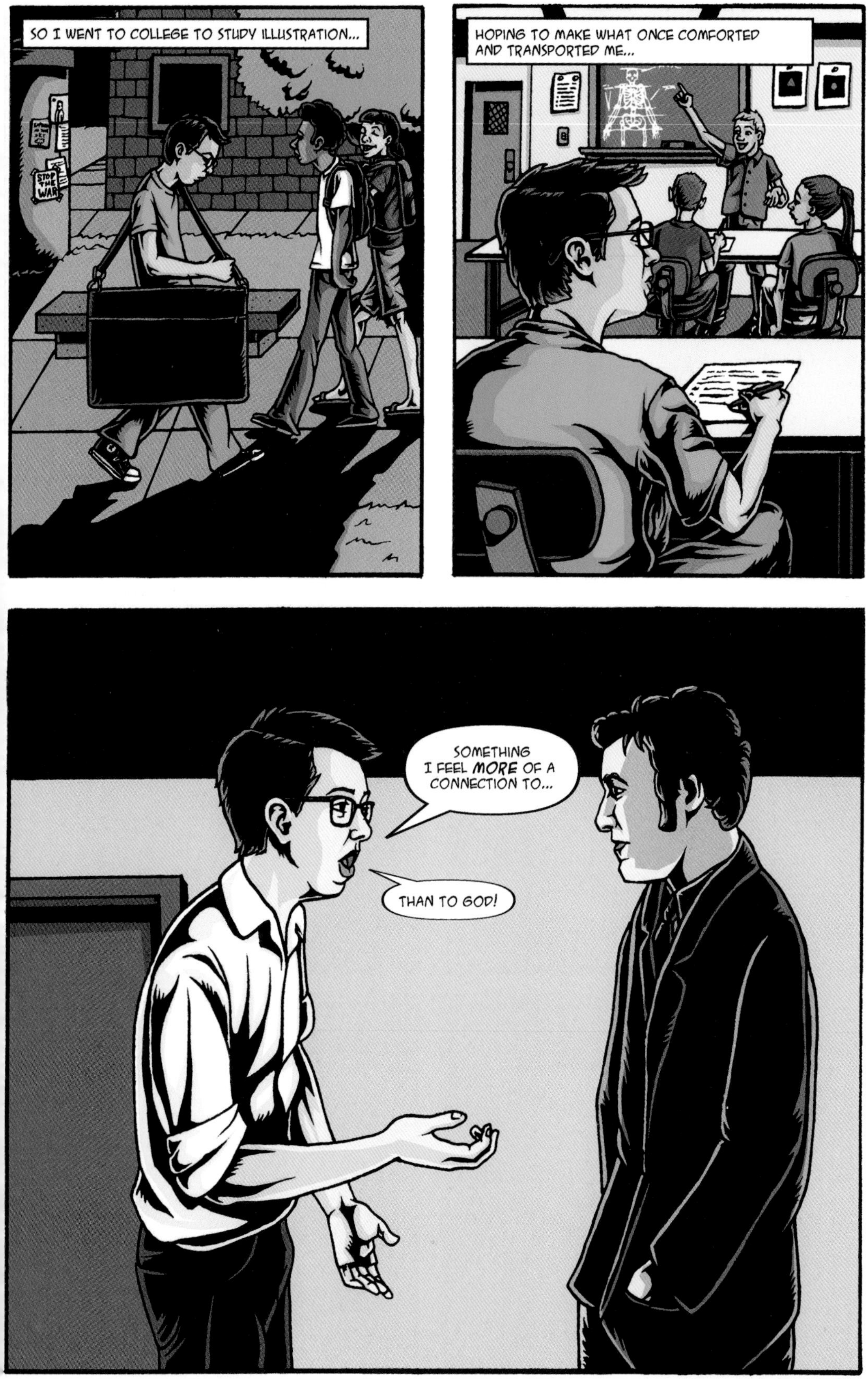

SO I WENT TO COLLEGE TO STUDY ILLUSTRATION...
STOP THE WAR
HOPING TO MAKE WHAT ONCE COMFORTED AND TRANSPORTED ME...
SOMETHING I FEEL *MORE* OF A CONNECTION TO...
THAN TO GOD!

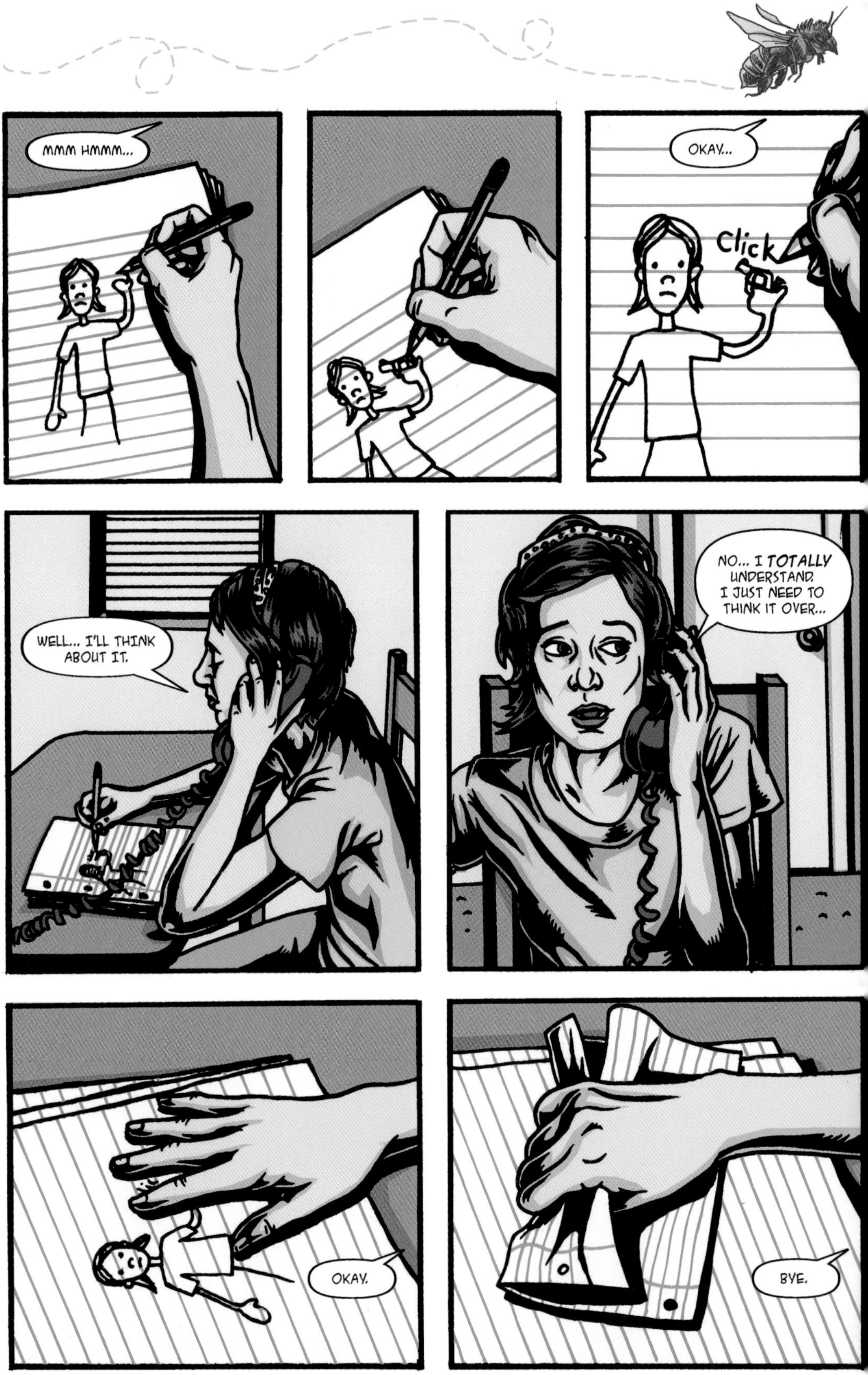
MMM HMMM...
OKAY...
Click
WELL... I'LL THINK ABOUT IT.
NO... I TOTALLY UNDERSTAND. I JUST NEED TO THINK IT OVER...
OKAY.
BYE.

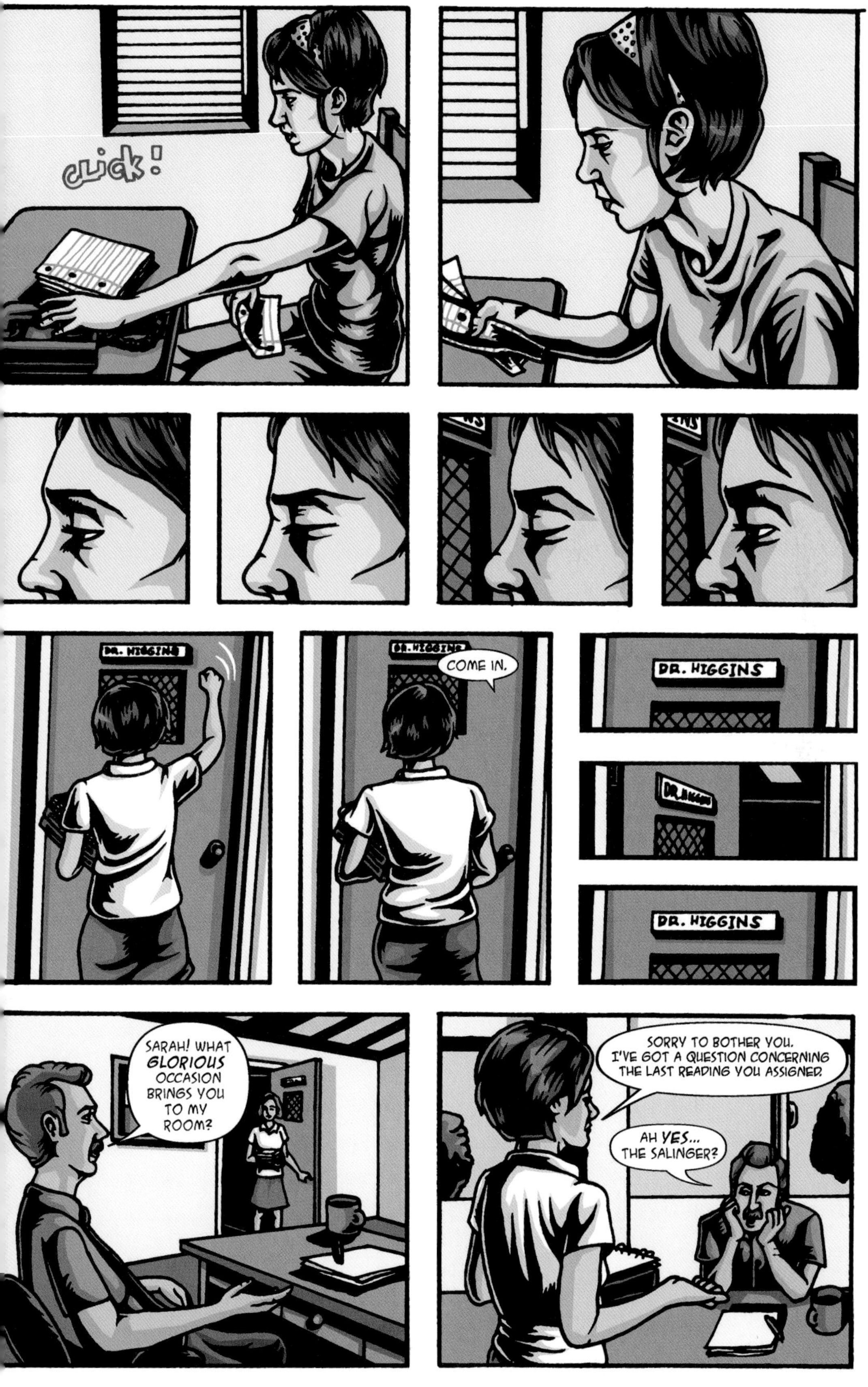
CLICK!
DR. HIGGINS
COME IN.
DR. HIGGINS
DR. HIGGINS
SARAH! WHAT GLORIOUS OCCASION BRINGS YOU TO MY ROOM?
SORRY TO BOTHER YOU. I'VE GOT A QUESTION CONCERNING THE LAST READING YOU ASSIGNED.
AH YES... THE SALINGER?

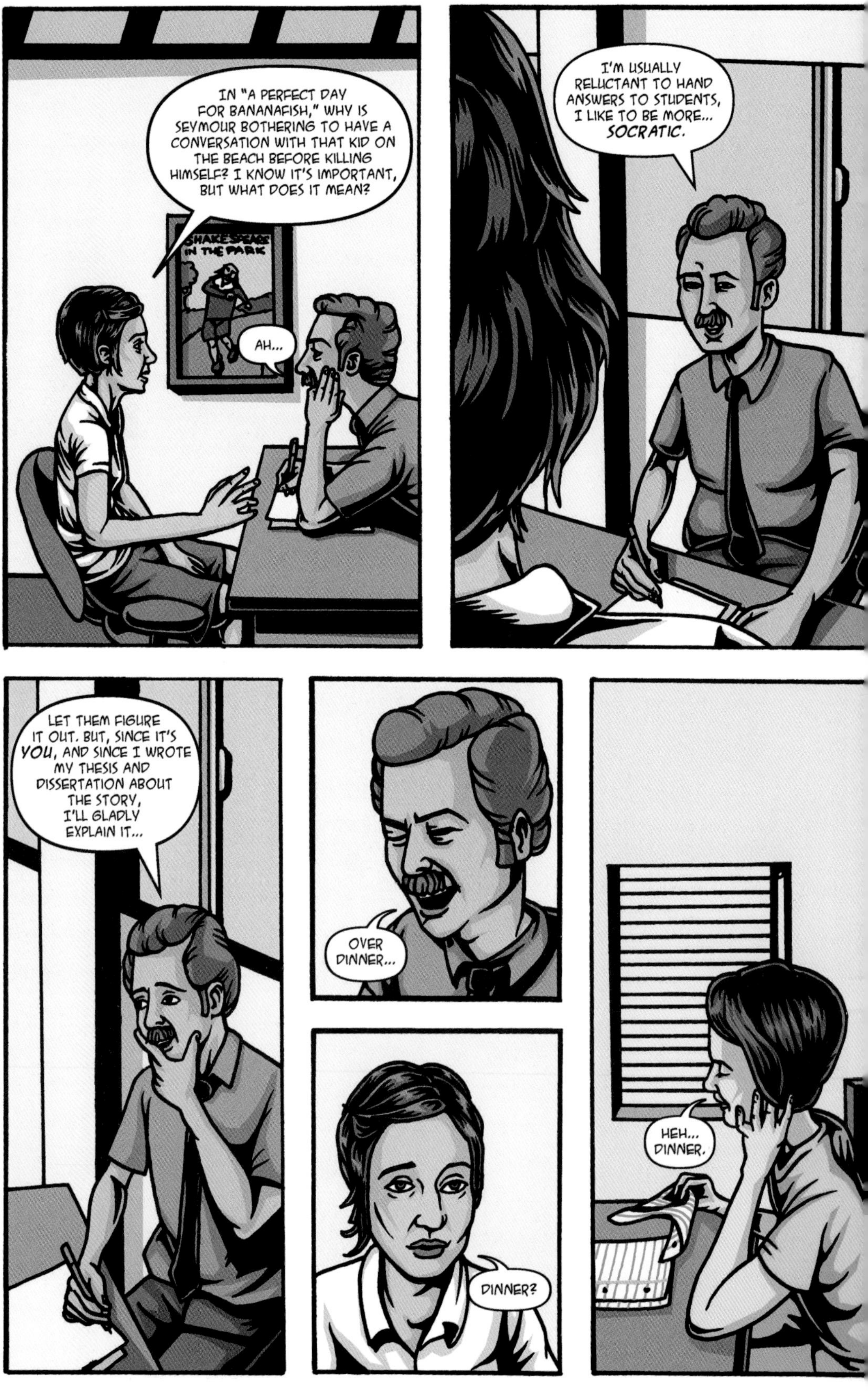
IN "A PERFECT DAY FOR BANANAFISH," WHY IS SEYMOUR BOTHERING TO HAVE A CONVERSATION WITH THAT KID ON THE BEACH BEFORE KILLING HIMSELF? I KNOW IT'S IMPORTANT, BUT WHAT DOES IT MEAN?
SHAKESPEARE IN THE PARK
AH...
I'M USUALLY RELUCTANT TO HAND ANSWERS TO STUDENTS, I LIKE TO BE MORE... SOCRATIC.
LET THEM FIGURE IT OUT. BUT, SINCE IT'S YOU, AND SINCE I WROTE MY THESIS AND DISSERTATION ABOUT THE STORY, I'LL GLADLY EXPLAIN IT...
OVER DINNER...
DINNER?
HEH... DINNER.

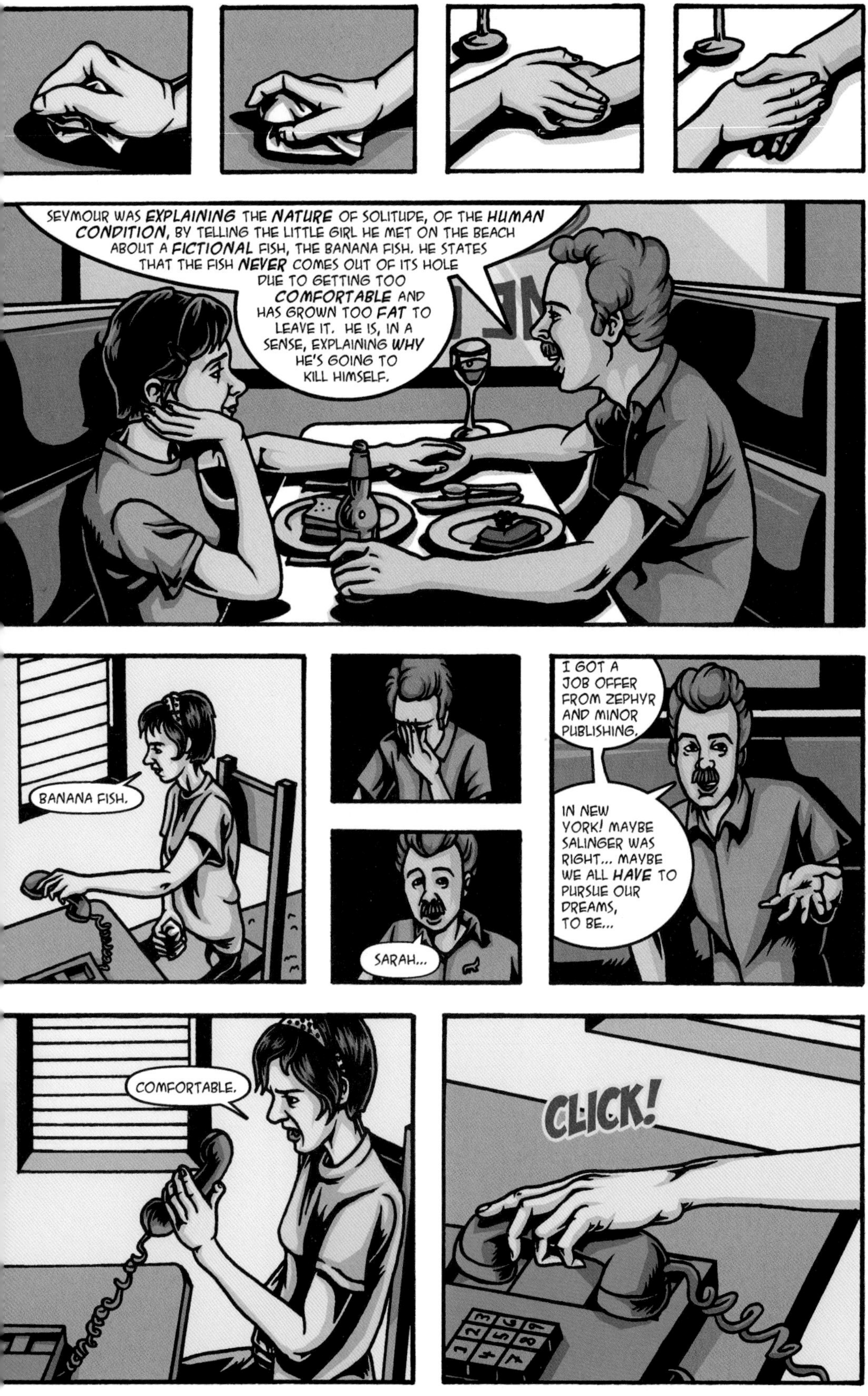
SEYMOUR WAS EXPLAINING THE NATURE OF SOLITUDE, OF THE HUMAN CONDITION, BY TELLING THE LITTLE GIRL HE MET ON THE BEACH ABOUT A FICTIONAL FISH, THE BANANA FISH. HE STATES THAT THE FISH NEVER COMES OUT OF ITS HOLE DUE TO GETTING TOO COMFORTABLE AND HAS GROWN TOO FAT TO LEAVE IT. HE IS, IN A SENSE, EXPLAINING WHY HE'S GOING TO KILL HIMSELF.
BANANA FISH.
SARAH...
I GOT A JOB OFFER FROM ZEPHYR AND MINOR PUBLISHING.
IN NEW YORK! MAYBE SALINGER WAS RIGHT... MAYBE WE ALL HAVE TO PURSUE OUR DREAMS, TO BE...
COMFORTABLE.
CLICK!

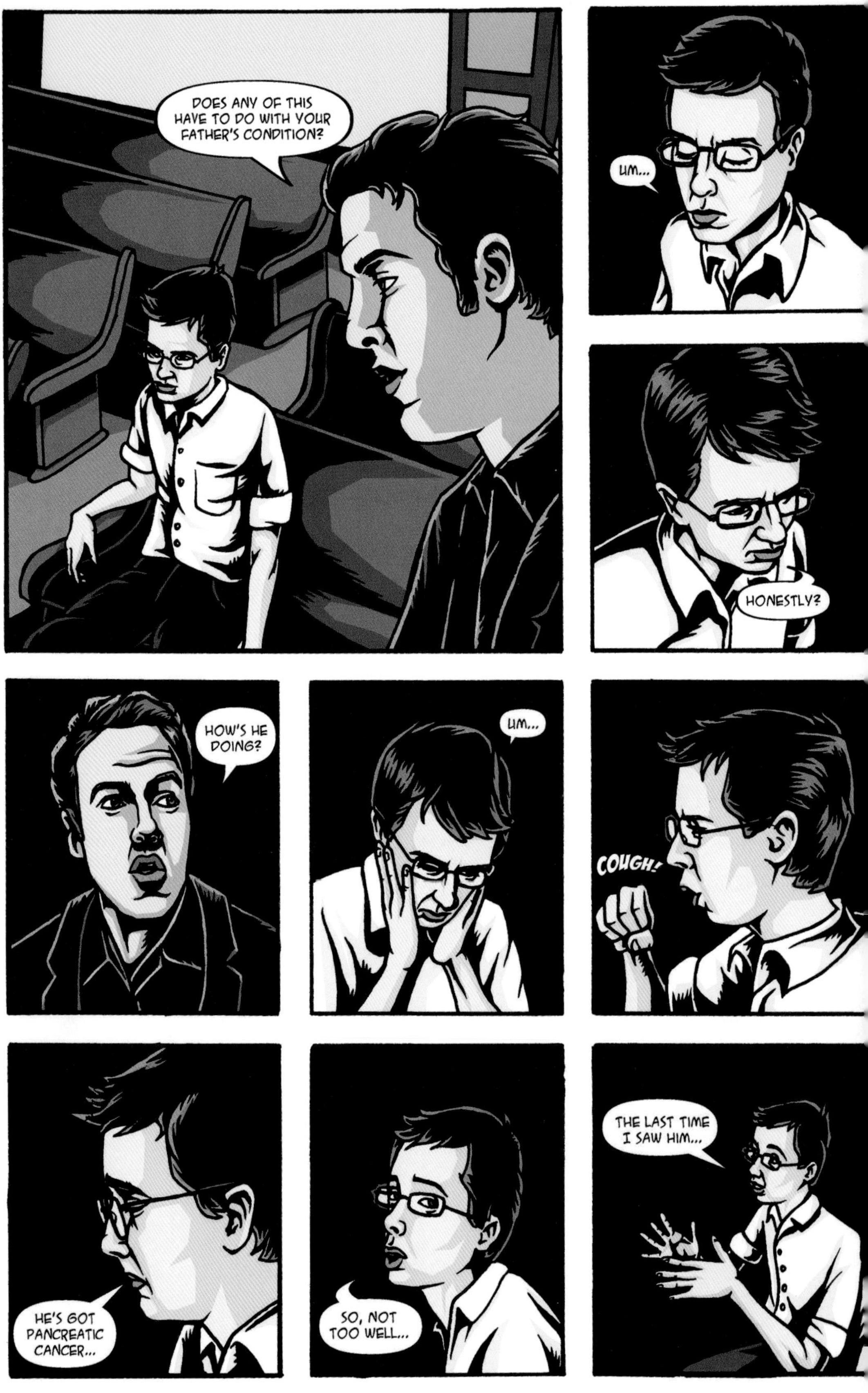
DOES ANY OF THIS HAVE TO DO WITH YOUR FATHER'S CONDITION?
UM...
HONESTLY?
HOW'S HE DOING?
UM...
COUGH!
HE'S GOT PANCREATIC CANCER...
SO, NOT TOO WELL...
THE LAST TIME I SAW HIM...

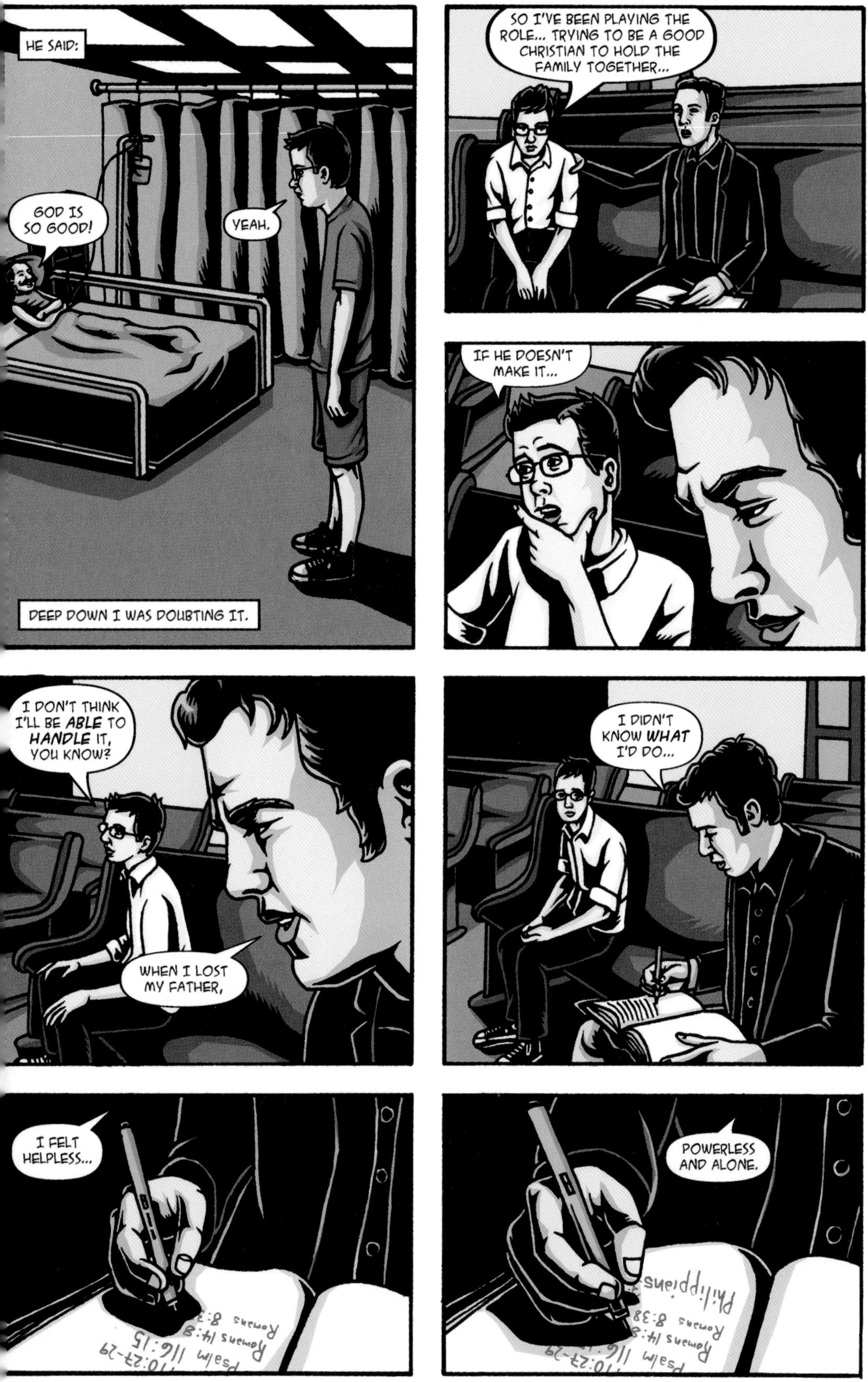
HE SAID:
GOD IS SO GOOD!
YEAH.
DEEP DOWN I WAS DOUBTING IT.
SO I'VE BEEN PLAYING THE ROLE... TRYING TO BE A GOOD CHRISTIAN TO HOLD THE FAMILY TOGETHER...
IF HE DOESN'T MAKE IT...
I DON'T THINK I'LL BE ***ABLE*** TO ***HANDLE*** IT, YOU KNOW?
WHEN I LOST MY FATHER,
I DIDN'T KNOW ***WHAT*** I'D DO...
I FELT HELPLESS...
POWERLESS AND ALONE.

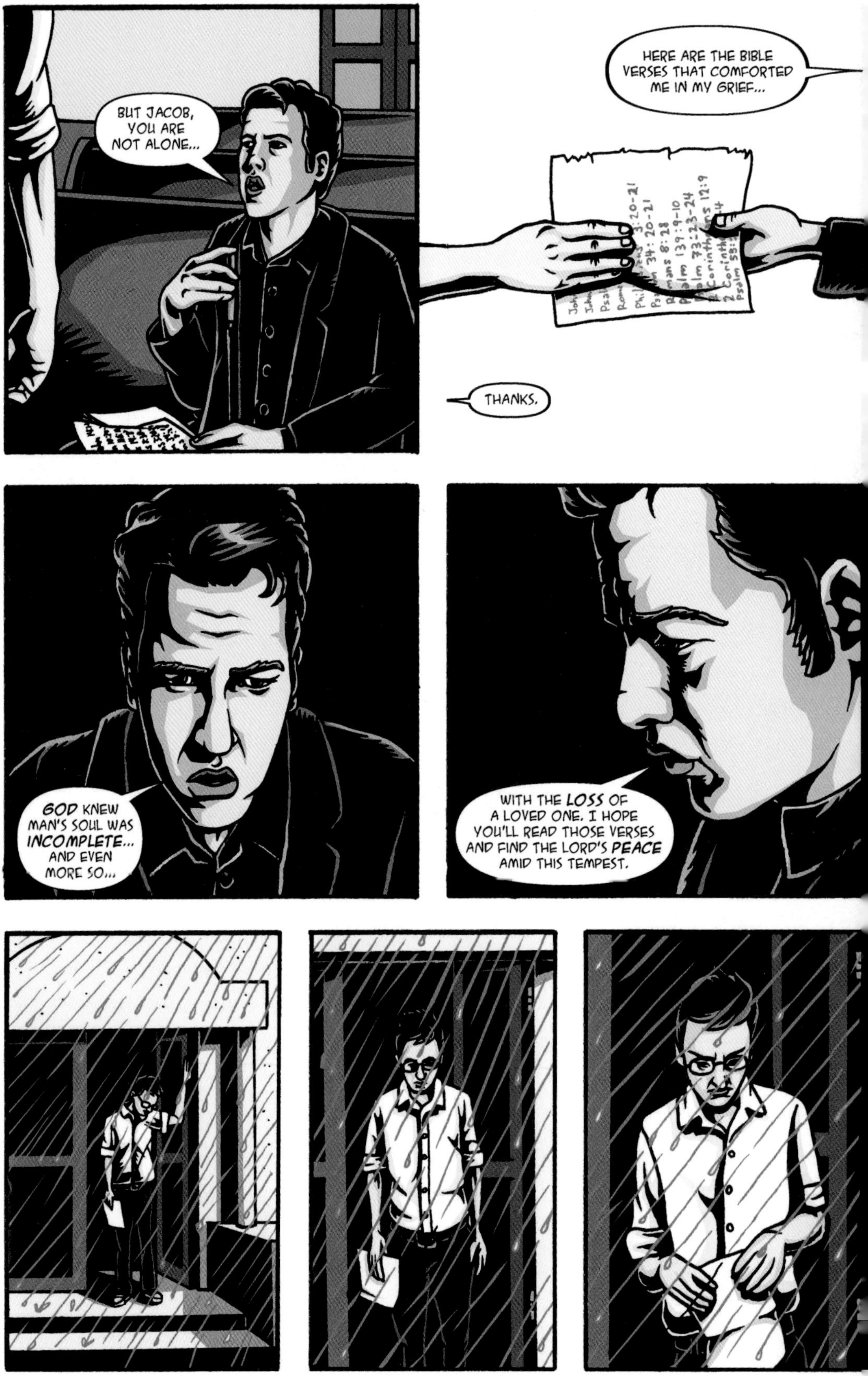
BUT JACOB, YOU ARE NOT ALONE...
HERE ARE THE BIBLE VERSES THAT COMFORTED ME IN MY GRIEF...
THANKS.
GOD KNEW MAN'S SOUL WAS INCOMPLETE... AND EVEN MORE SO...
WITH THE LOSS OF A LOVED ONE, I HOPE YOU'LL READ THOSE VERSES AND FIND THE LORD'S PEACE AMID THIS TEMPEST.

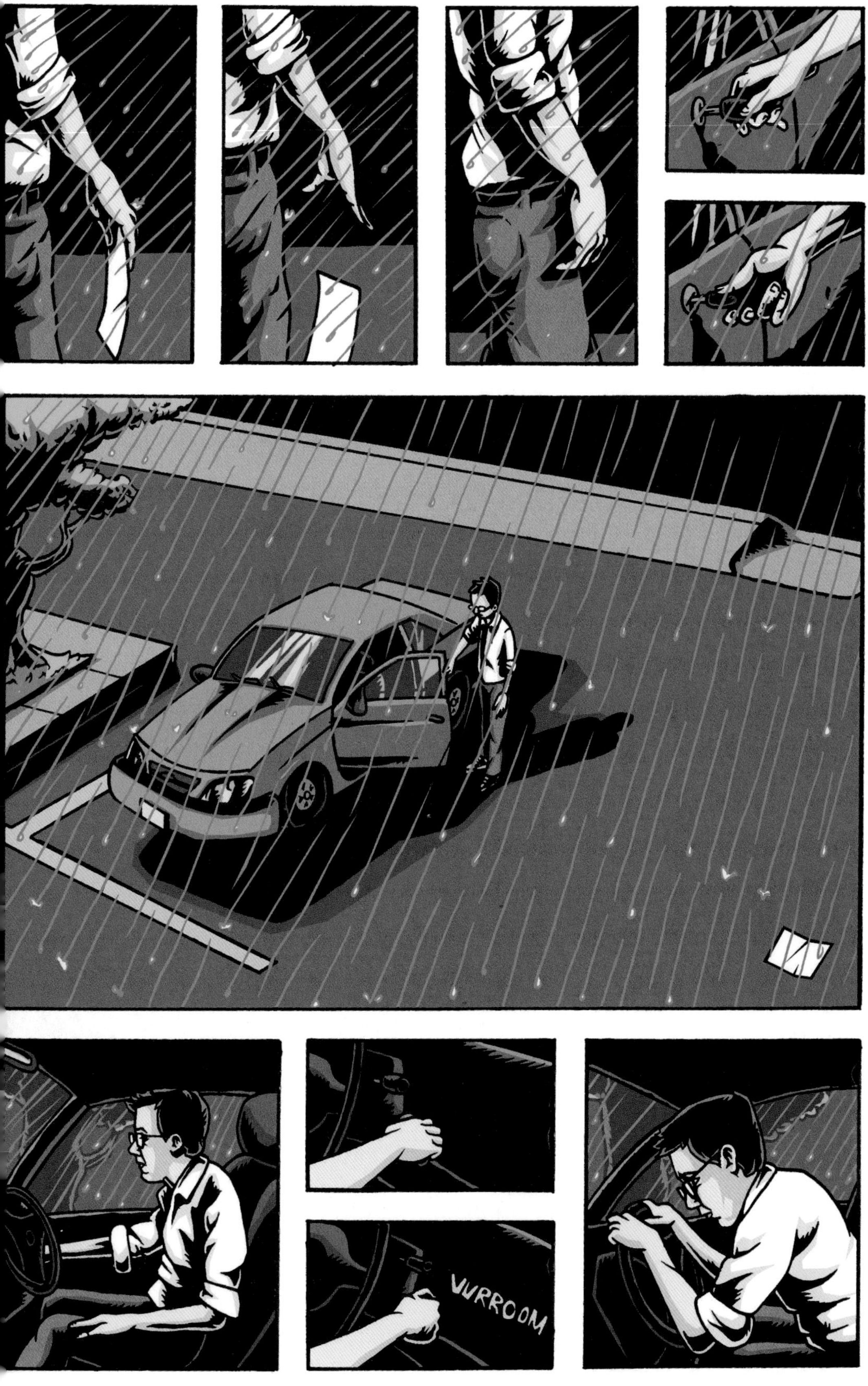
VVRROOM

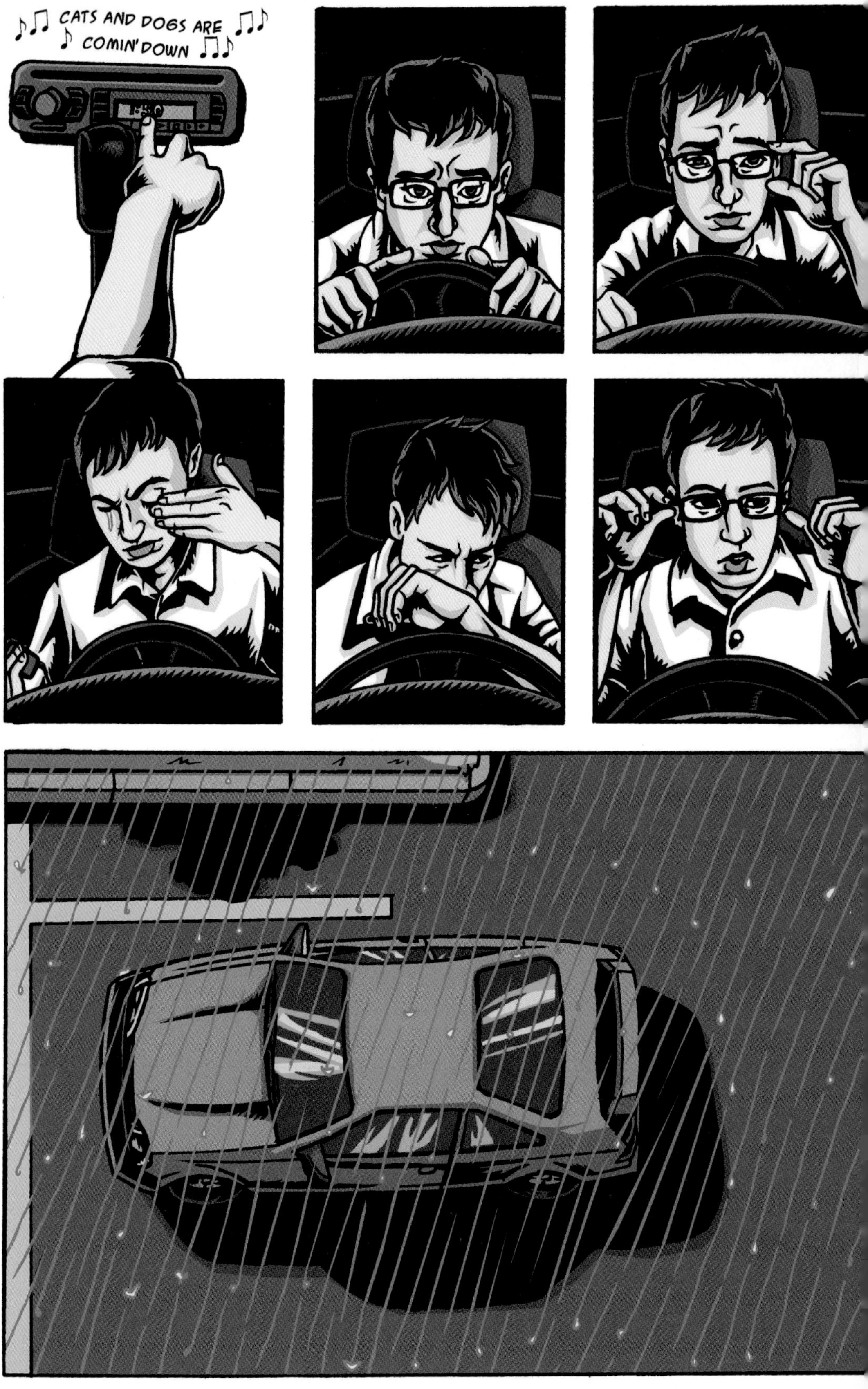
♪♫ CATS AND DOGS ARE ♫♪
♪ COMIN' DOWN ♫♪

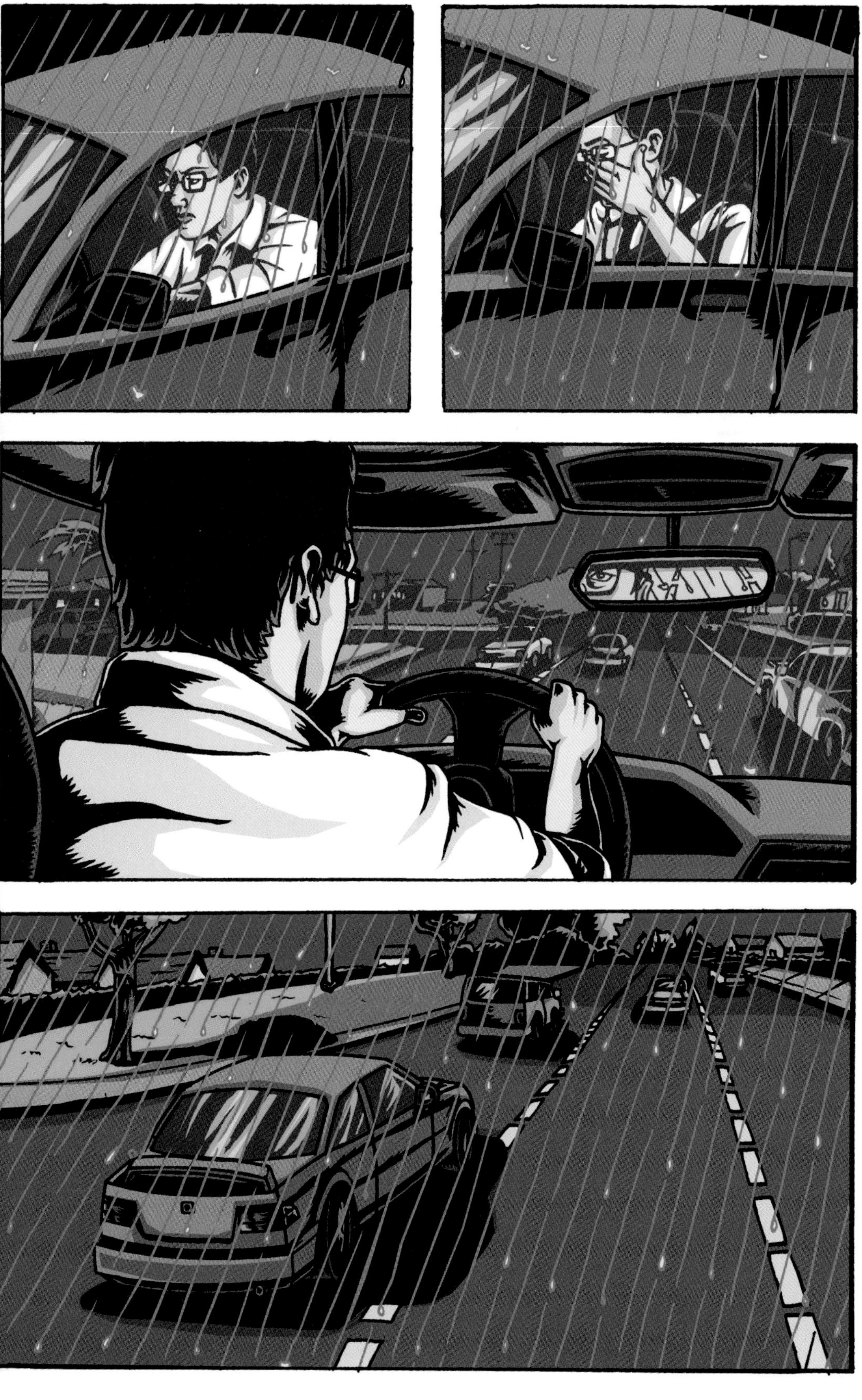

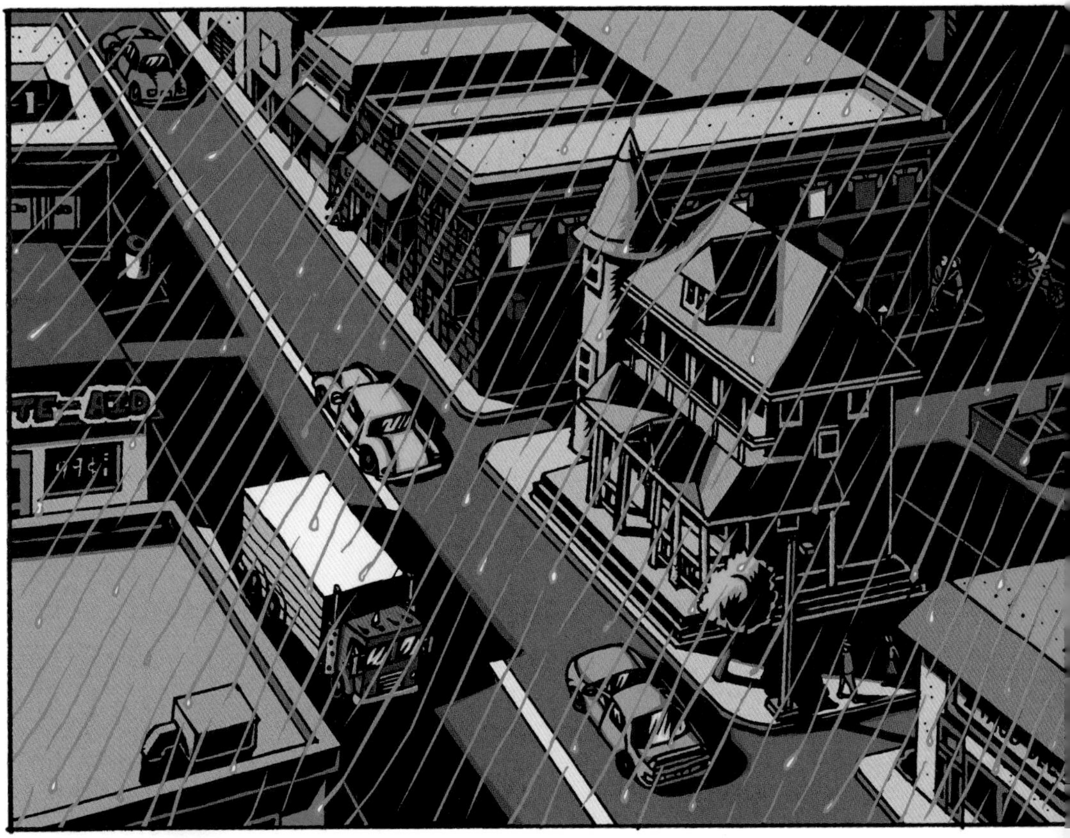

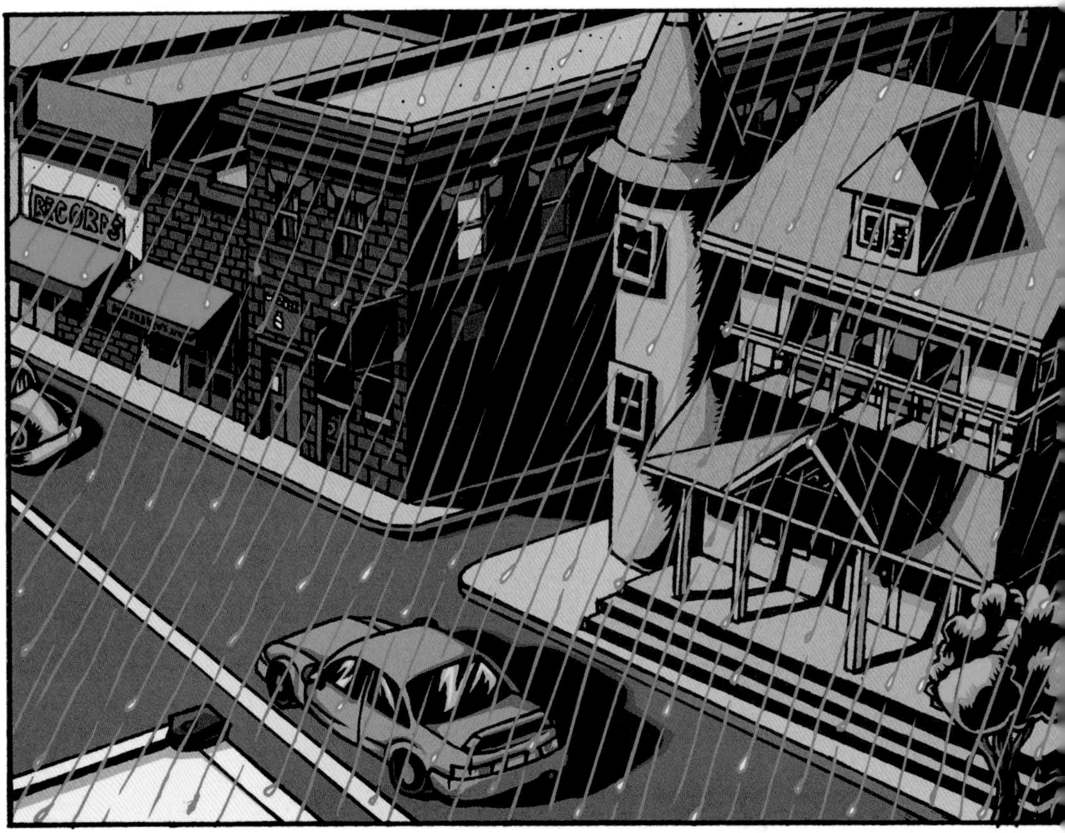
RECORDS

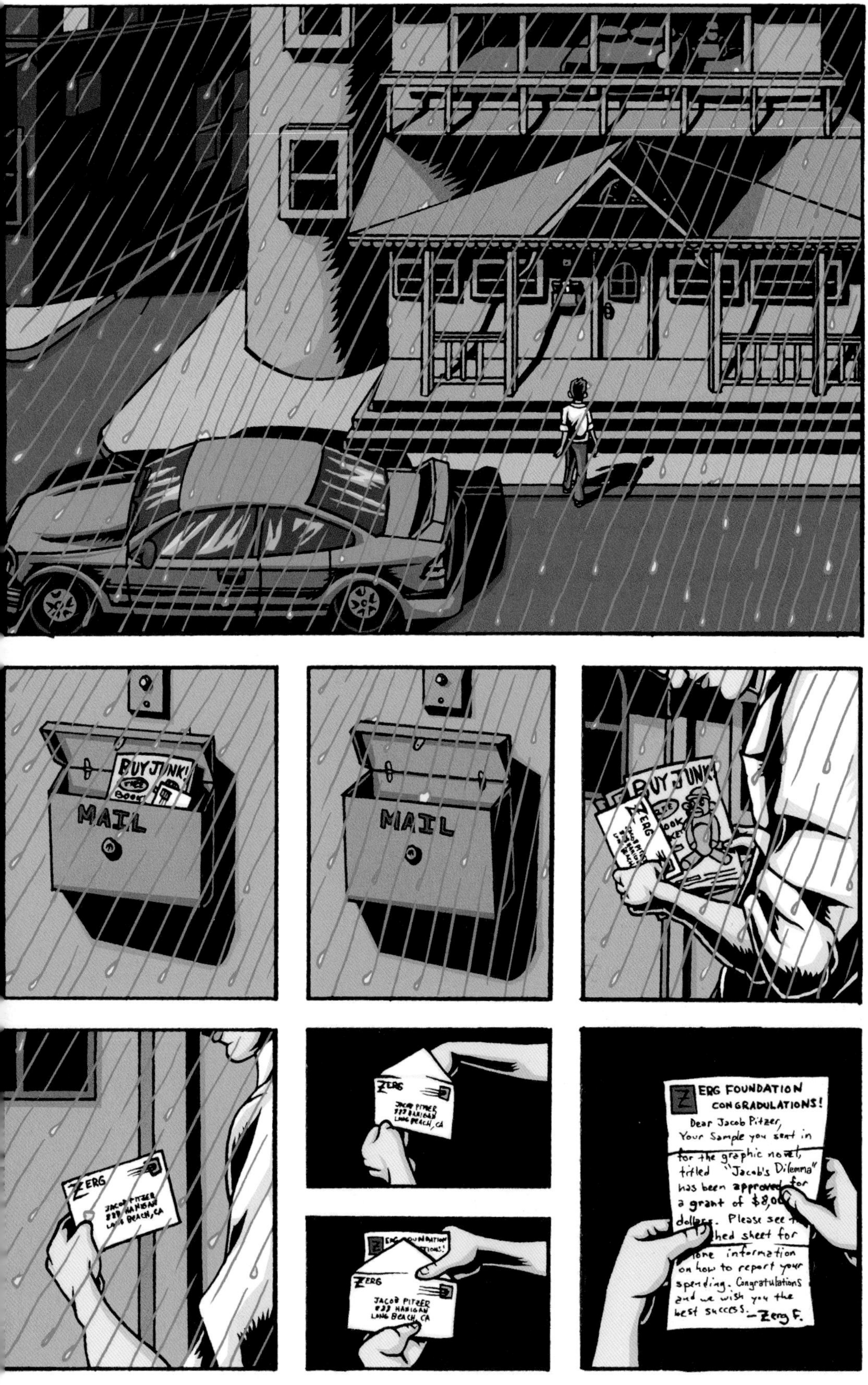
BUY JUNK!
MAIL
MAIL
ZERG
LONG BEACH, CA
ZERG
JACOB PITZER
LONG BEACH, CA
ZERG
JACOB PITZER
LONG BEACH, CA
ZERG FOUNDATION
CONGRADULATIONS!
Dear Jacob Pitzer,
Your Sample you sent in
for the graphic novel,
titled "Jacob's Dilemma"
has been approved for
a grant of $8,0
Please see
hed sheet for
information
on how to report your
spending. Congratulations
and we wish you the
best success. —Zerg F.

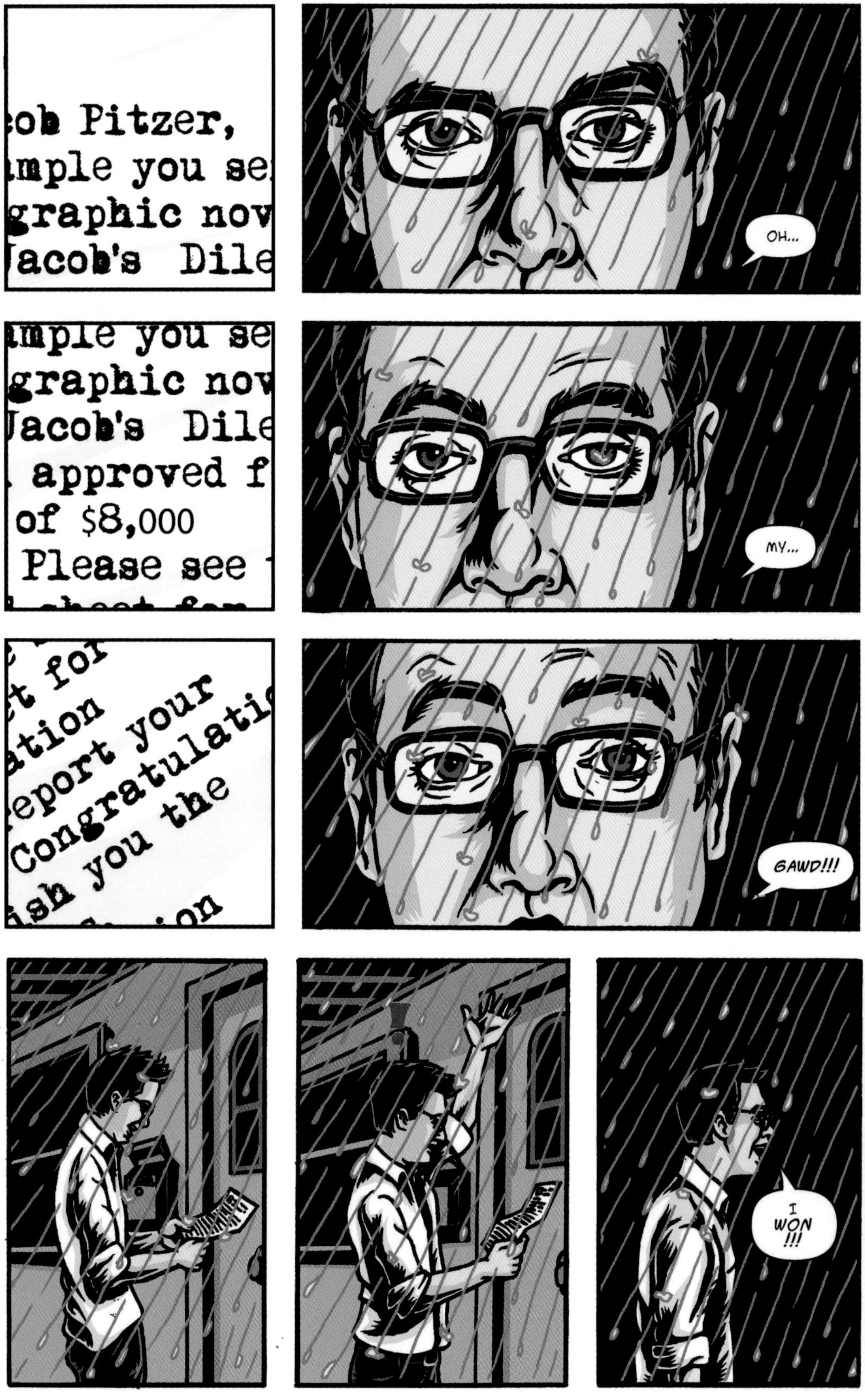

ob Pitzer,
mple you se
graphic nov
Jacob's Dile
OH...
mple you se
graphic nov
Jacob's Dile
approved f
of $8,000
Please see
MY...
t for
ation
eport your
Congratulati
you the
sh
on
GAWD!!!
I WON !!!

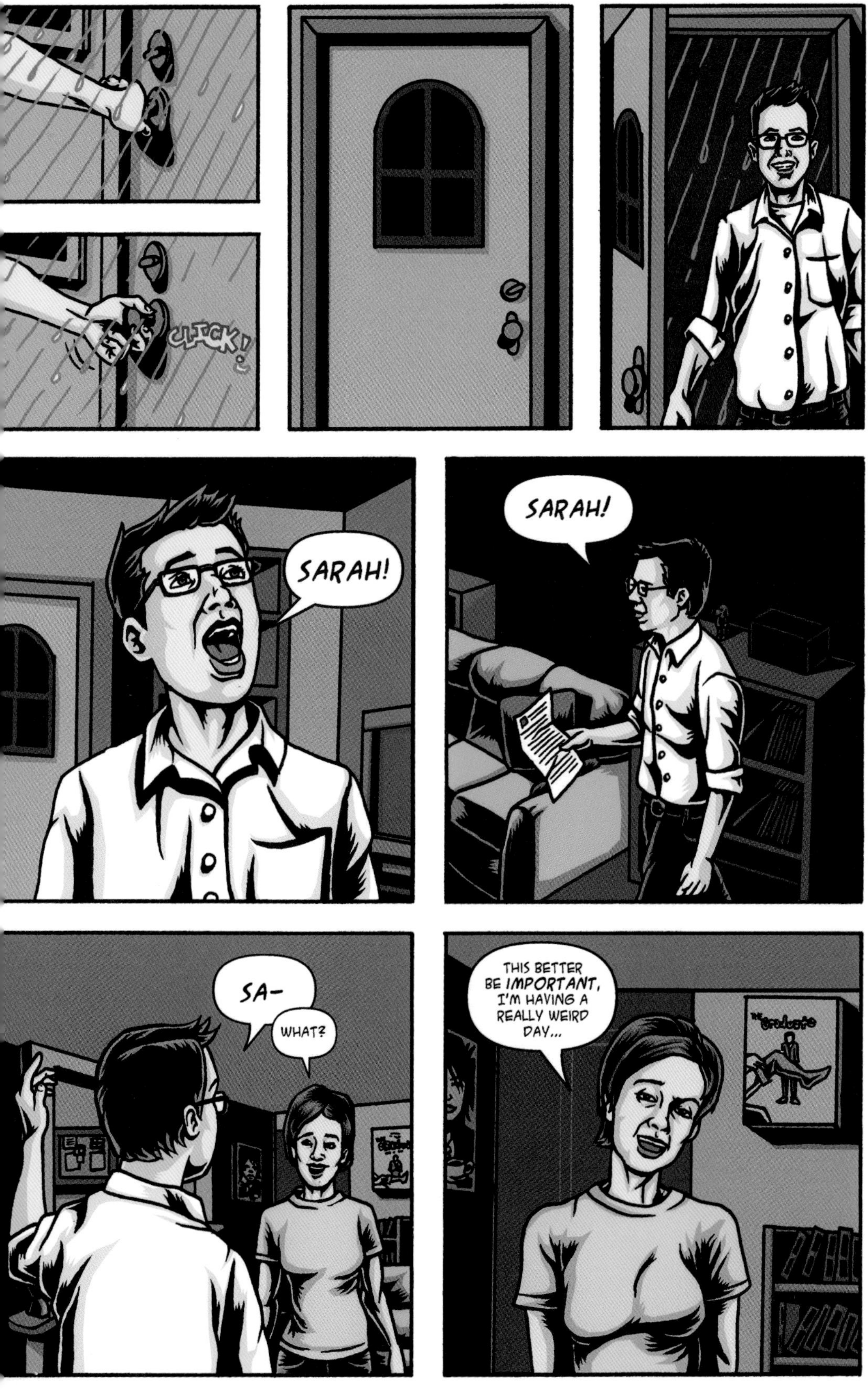
CLICK!
SARAH!
SARAH!
SA-
WHAT?
THIS BETTER BE IMPORTANT, I'M HAVING A REALLY WEIRD DAY...

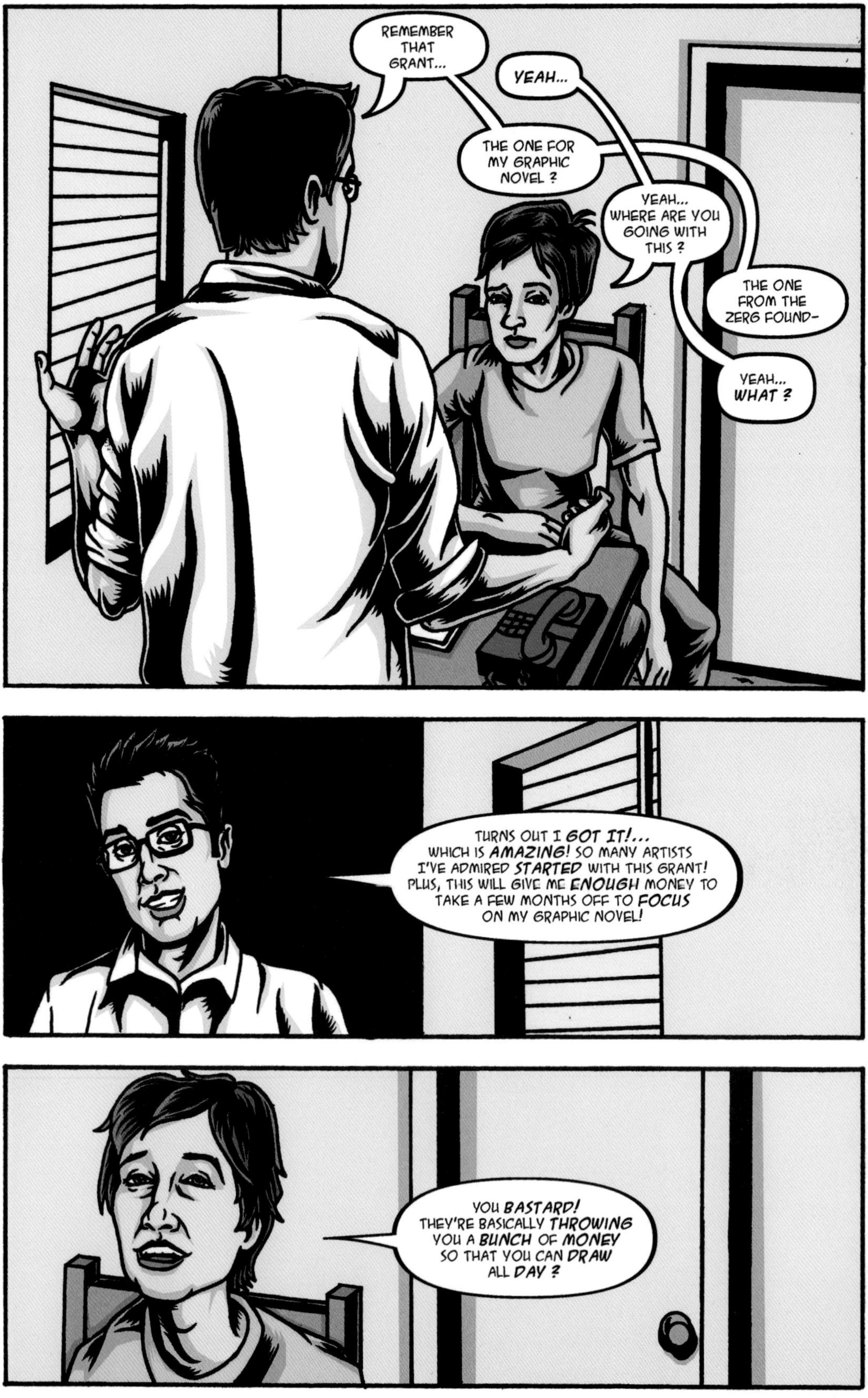
REMEMBER THAT GRANT...
YEAH...
THE ONE FOR MY GRAPHIC NOVEL ?
YEAH... WHERE ARE YOU GOING WITH THIS ?
THE ONE FROM THE ZERG FOUND-
YEAH... WHAT ?
TURNS OUT I GOT IT!... WHICH IS AMAZING! SO MANY ARTISTS I'VE ADMIRED STARTED WITH THIS GRANT! PLUS, THIS WILL GIVE ME ENOUGH MONEY TO TAKE A FEW MONTHS OFF TO FOCUS ON MY GRAPHIC NOVEL!
YOU BASTARD! THEY'RE BASICALLY THROWING YOU A BUNCH OF MONEY SO THAT YOU CAN DRAW ALL DAY ?

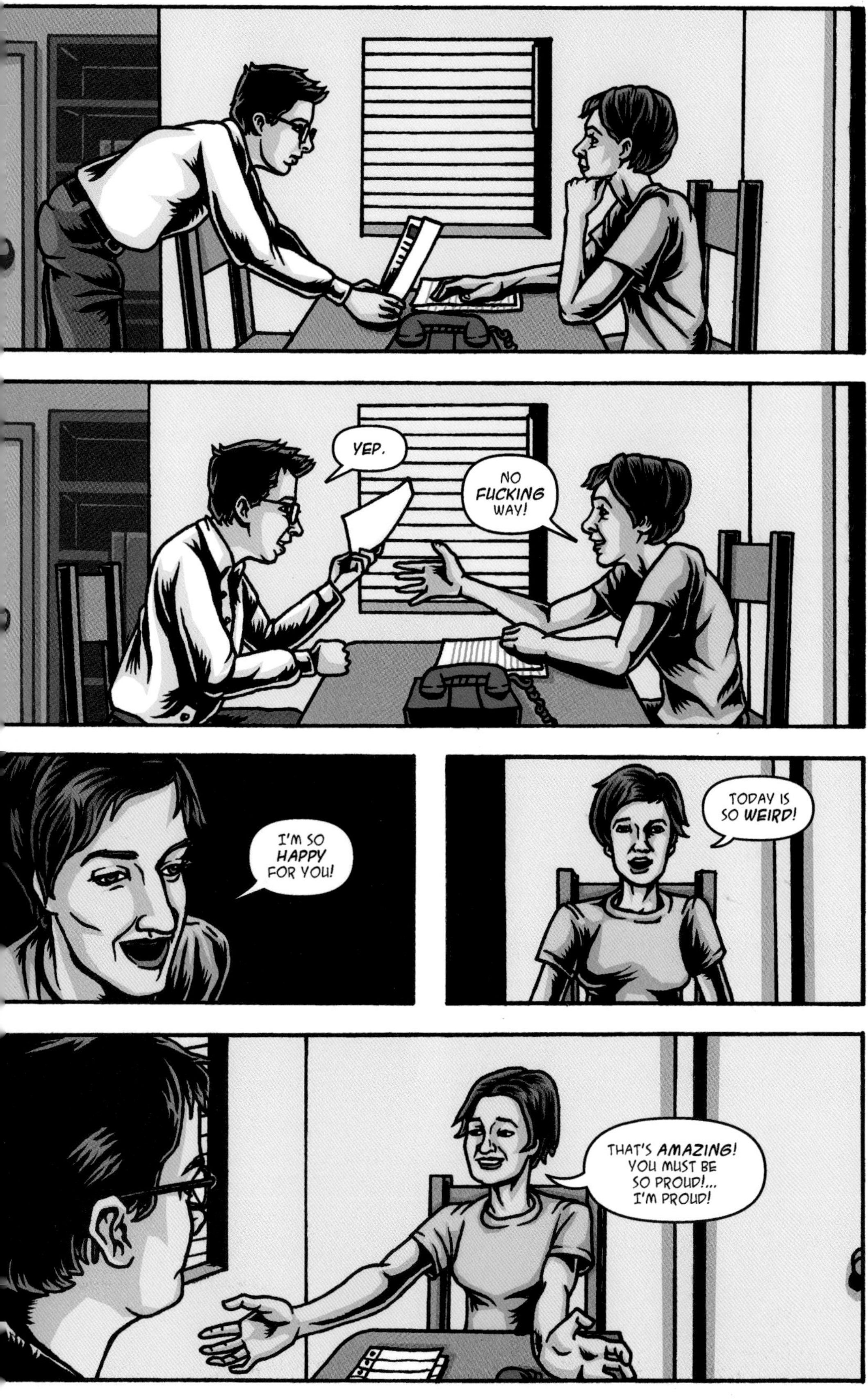
YEP.
NO FUCKING WAY!
I'M SO HAPPY FOR YOU!
TODAY IS SO WEIRD!
THAT'S AMAZING! YOU MUST BE SO PROUD!... I'M PROUD!

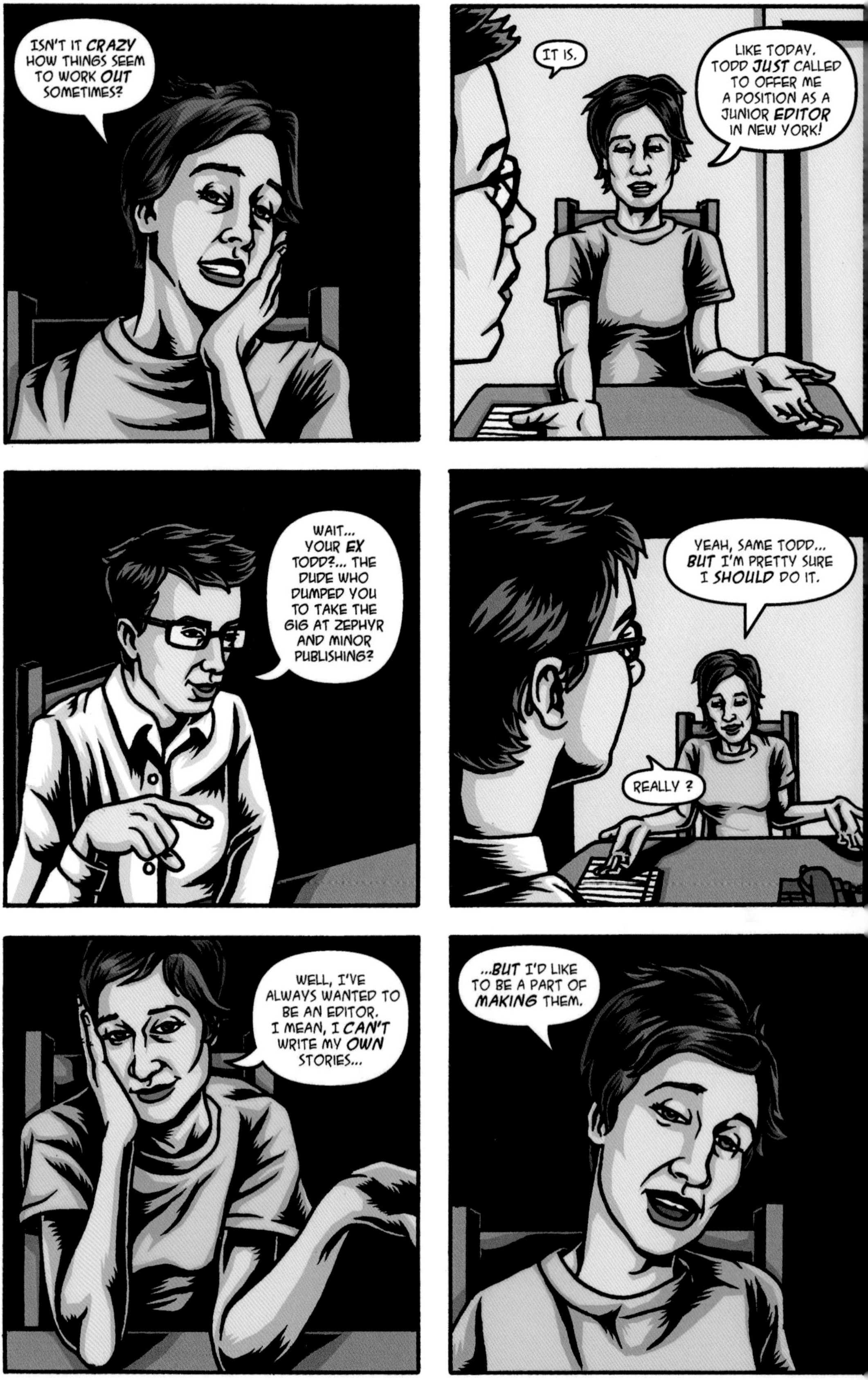
ISN'T IT CRAZY HOW THINGS SEEM TO WORK OUT SOMETIMES?
IT IS.
LIKE TODAY. TODD JUST CALLED TO OFFER ME A POSITION AS A JUNIOR EDITOR IN NEW YORK!
WAIT... YOUR EX TODD?... THE DUDE WHO DUMPED YOU TO TAKE THE GIG AT ZEPHYR AND MINOR PUBLISHING?
YEAH, SAME TODD... BUT I'M PRETTY SURE I SHOULD DO IT.
REALLY ?
WELL, I'VE ALWAYS WANTED TO BE AN EDITOR. I MEAN, I CAN'T WRITE MY OWN STORIES...
...BUT I'D LIKE TO BE A PART OF MAKING THEM.

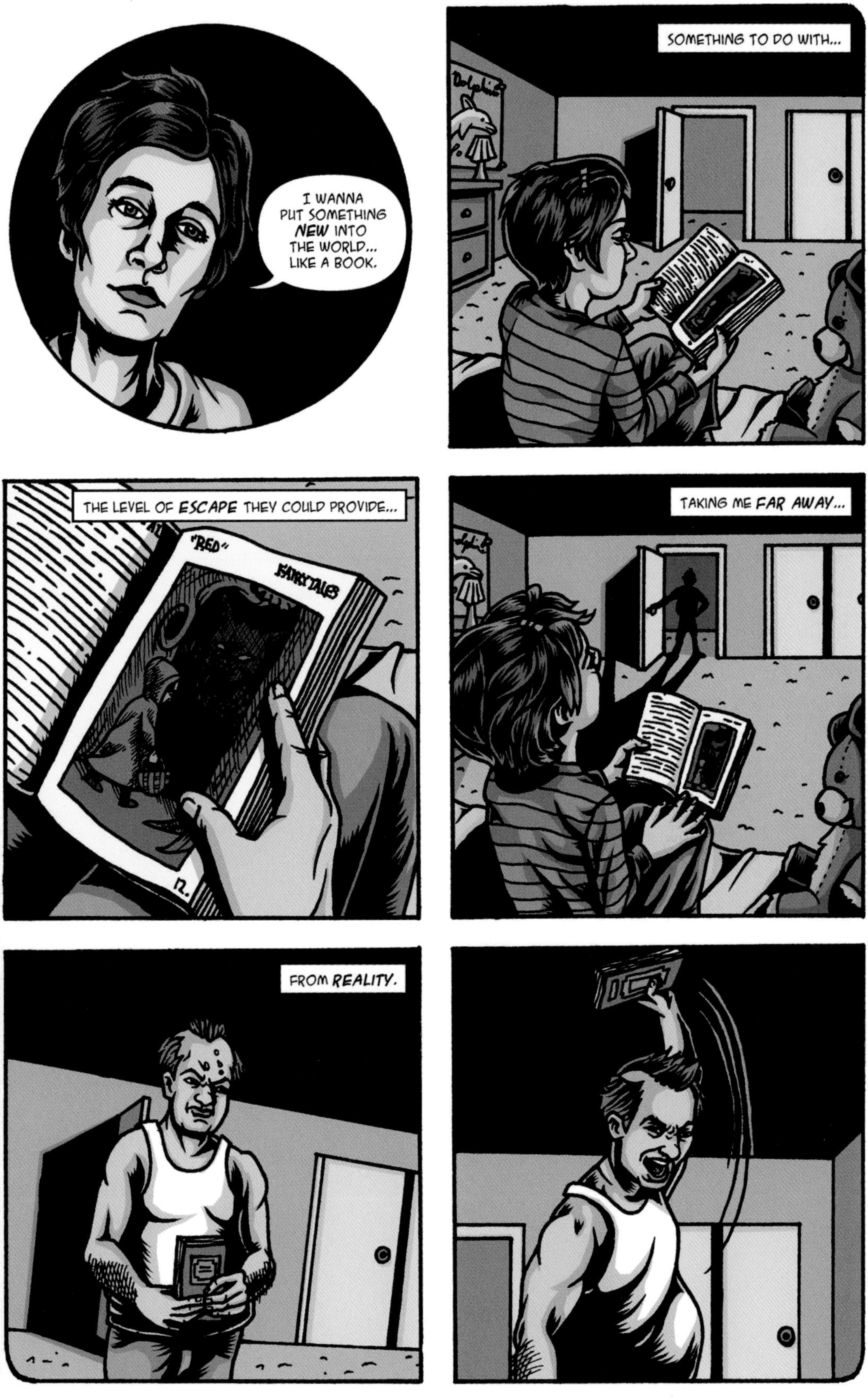
I WANNA PUT SOMETHING NEW INTO THE WORLD... LIKE A BOOK.
SOMETHING TO DO WITH...
THE LEVEL OF ESCAPE THEY COULD PROVIDE...
"RED"
FAIRY TALES
12.
TAKING ME FAR AWAY...
FROM REALITY.

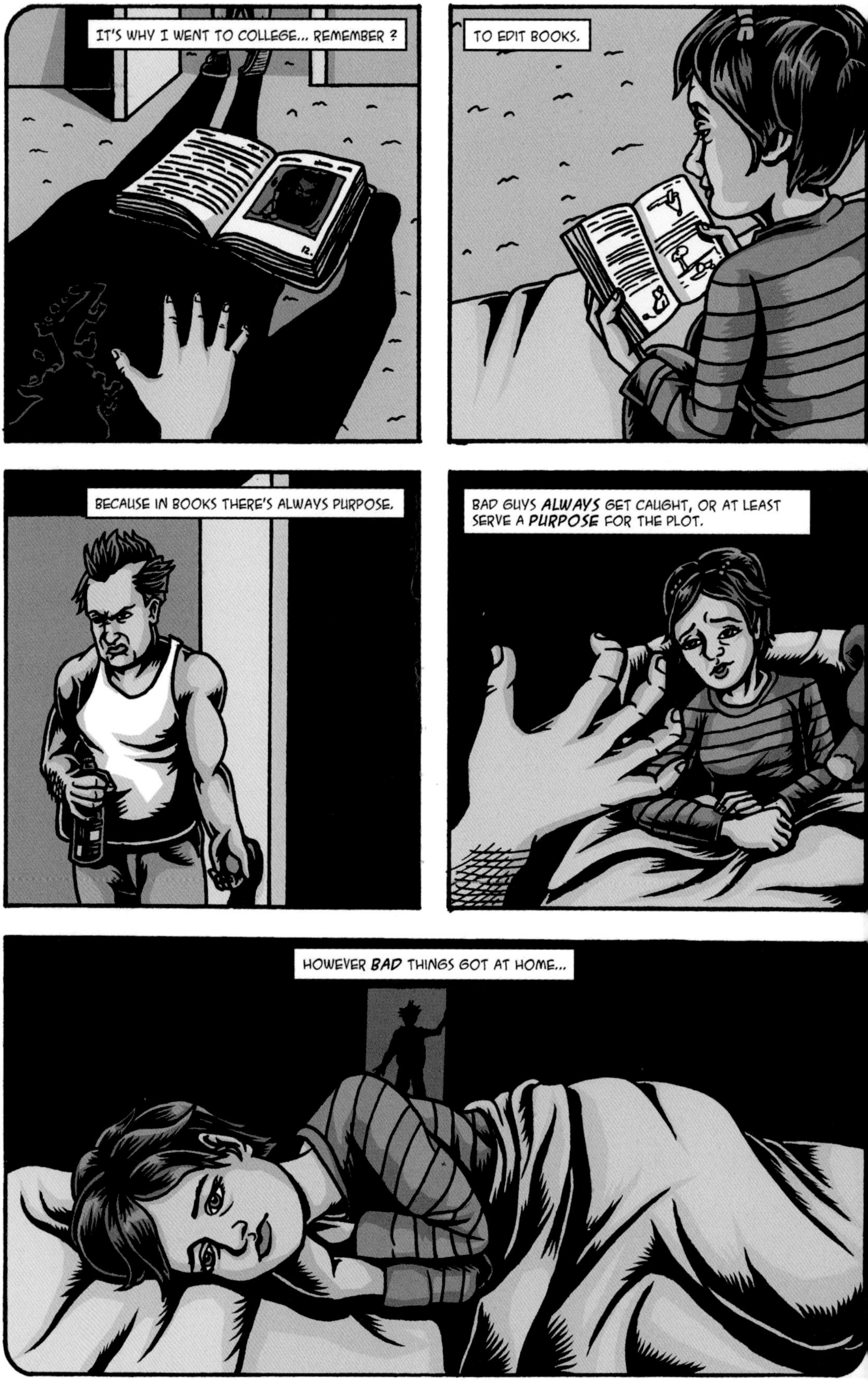
IT'S WHY I WENT TO COLLEGE... REMEMBER ?
TO EDIT BOOKS.
BECAUSE IN BOOKS THERE'S ALWAYS PURPOSE.
BAD GUYS ALWAYS GET CAUGHT, OR AT LEAST SERVE A PURPOSE FOR THE PLOT.
HOWEVER BAD THINGS GOT AT HOME...

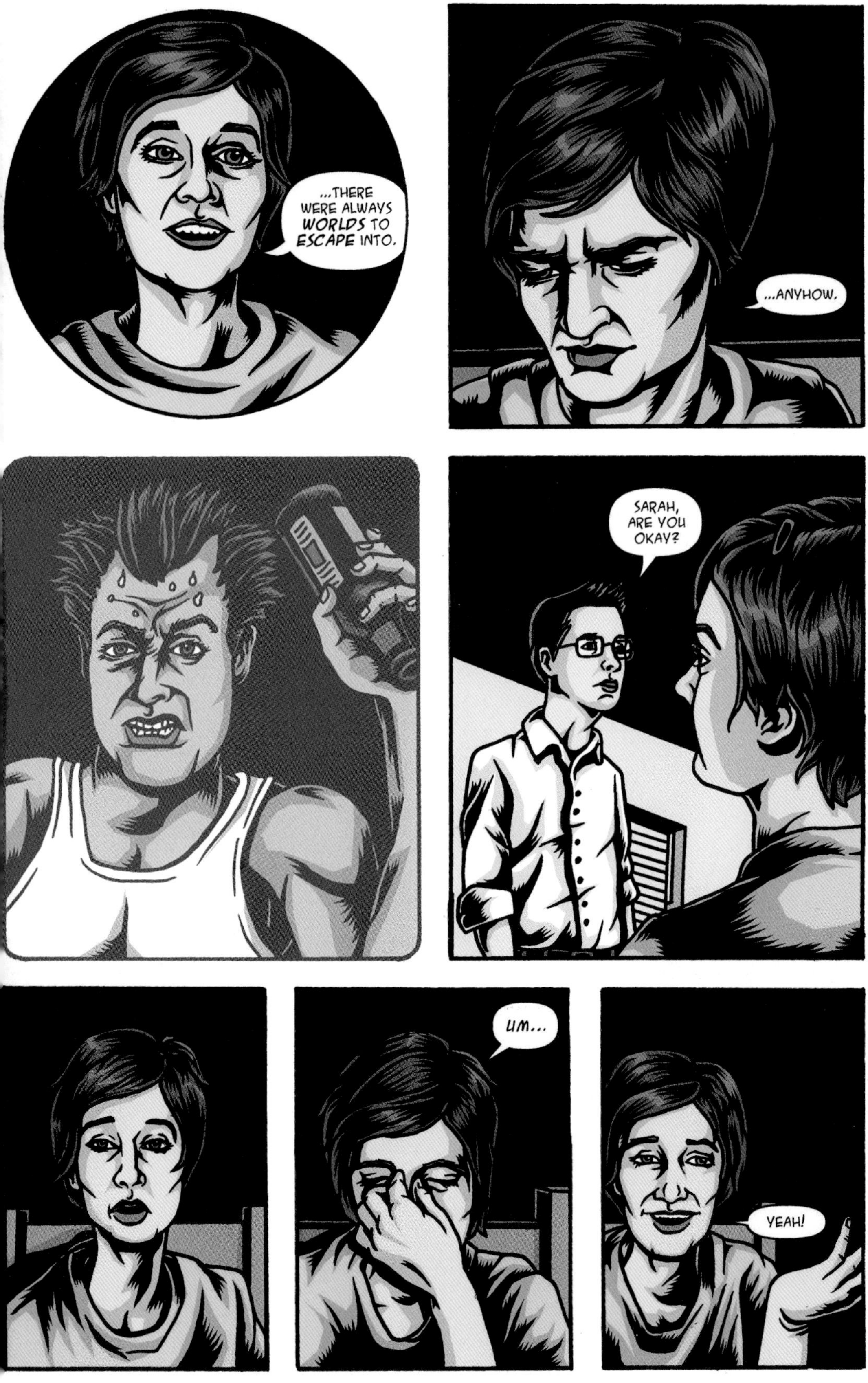
...THERE WERE ALWAYS WORLDS TO ESCAPE INTO.
...ANYHOW.
SARAH, ARE YOU OKAY?
UM...
YEAH!

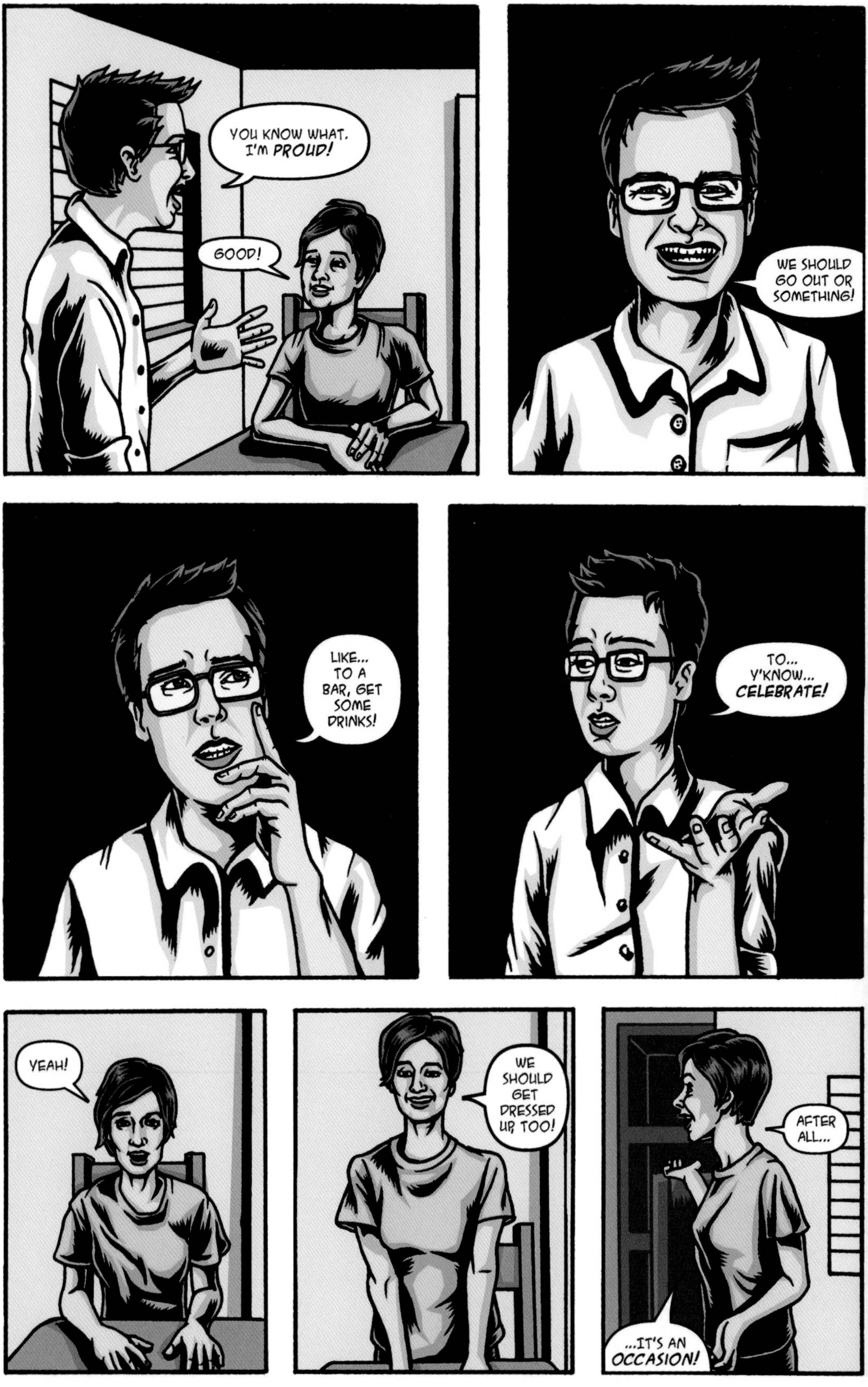
YOU KNOW WHAT. I'M PROUD!
GOOD!
WE SHOULD GO OUT OR SOMETHING!
LIKE... TO A BAR, GET SOME DRINKS!
TO... Y'KNOW... CELEBRATE!
YEAH!
WE SHOULD GET DRESSED UP, TOO!
AFTER ALL...
...IT'S AN OCCASION!

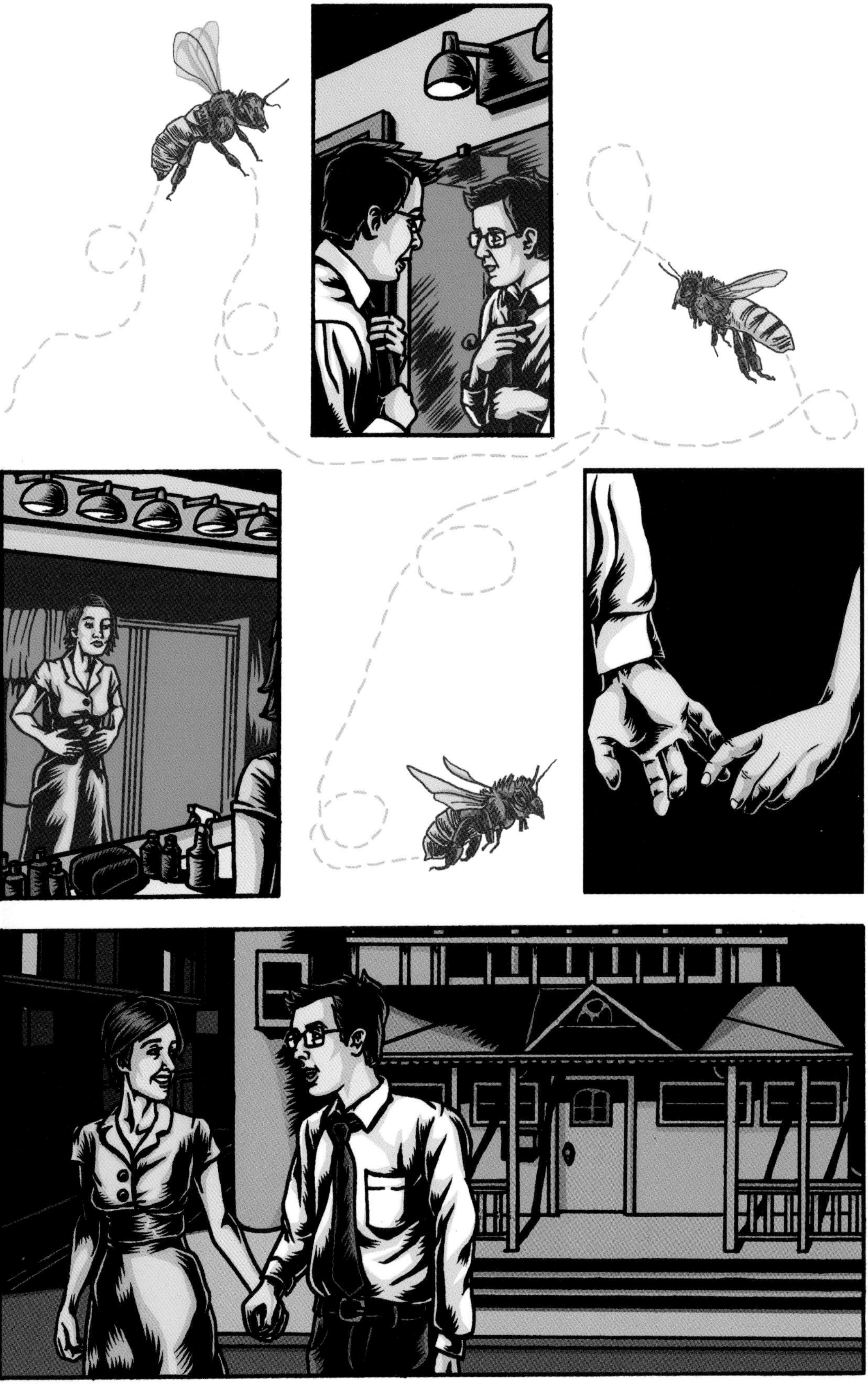

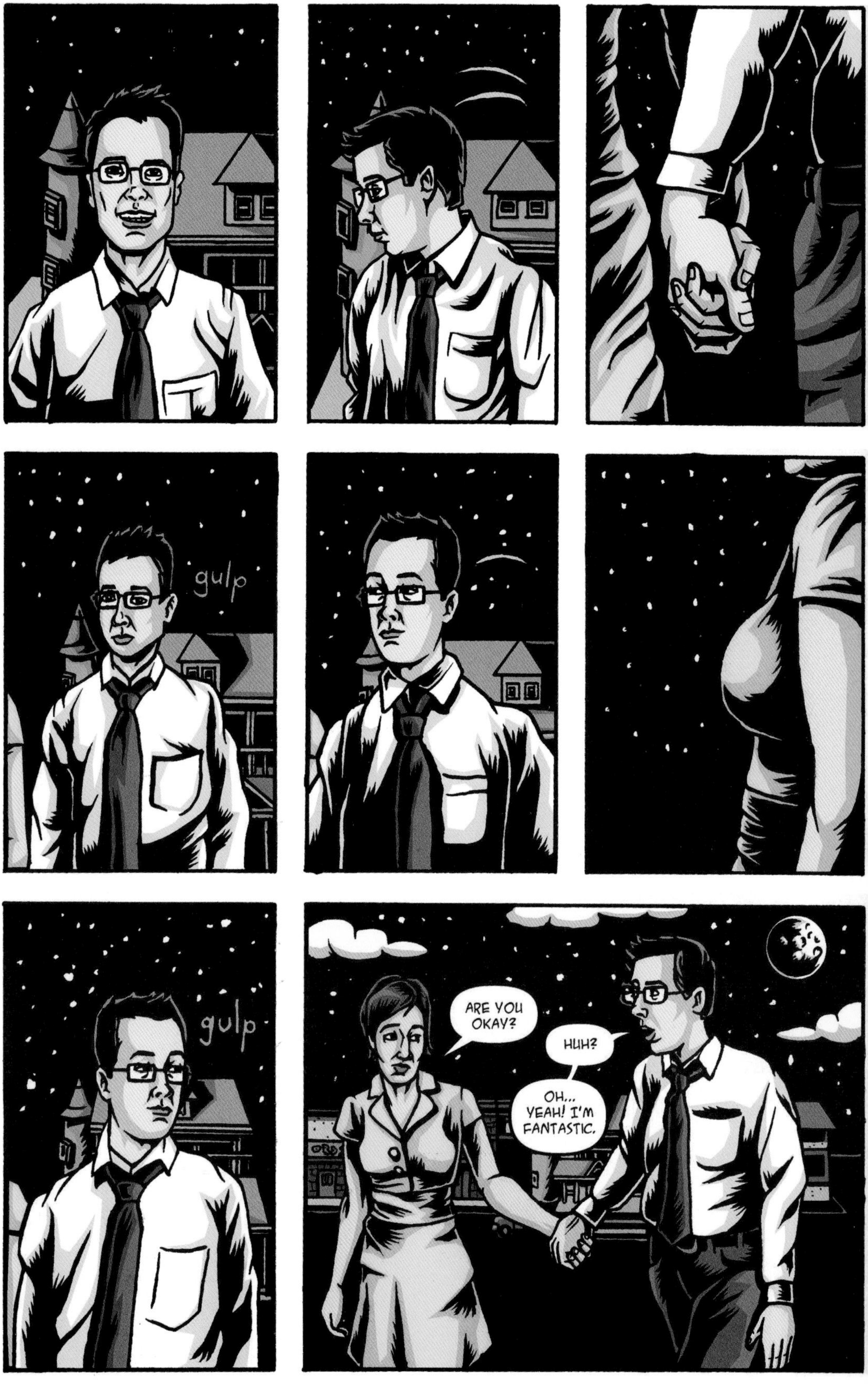
gulp
gulp
ARE YOU OKAY?
HUH?
OH... YEAH! I'M FANTASTIC.

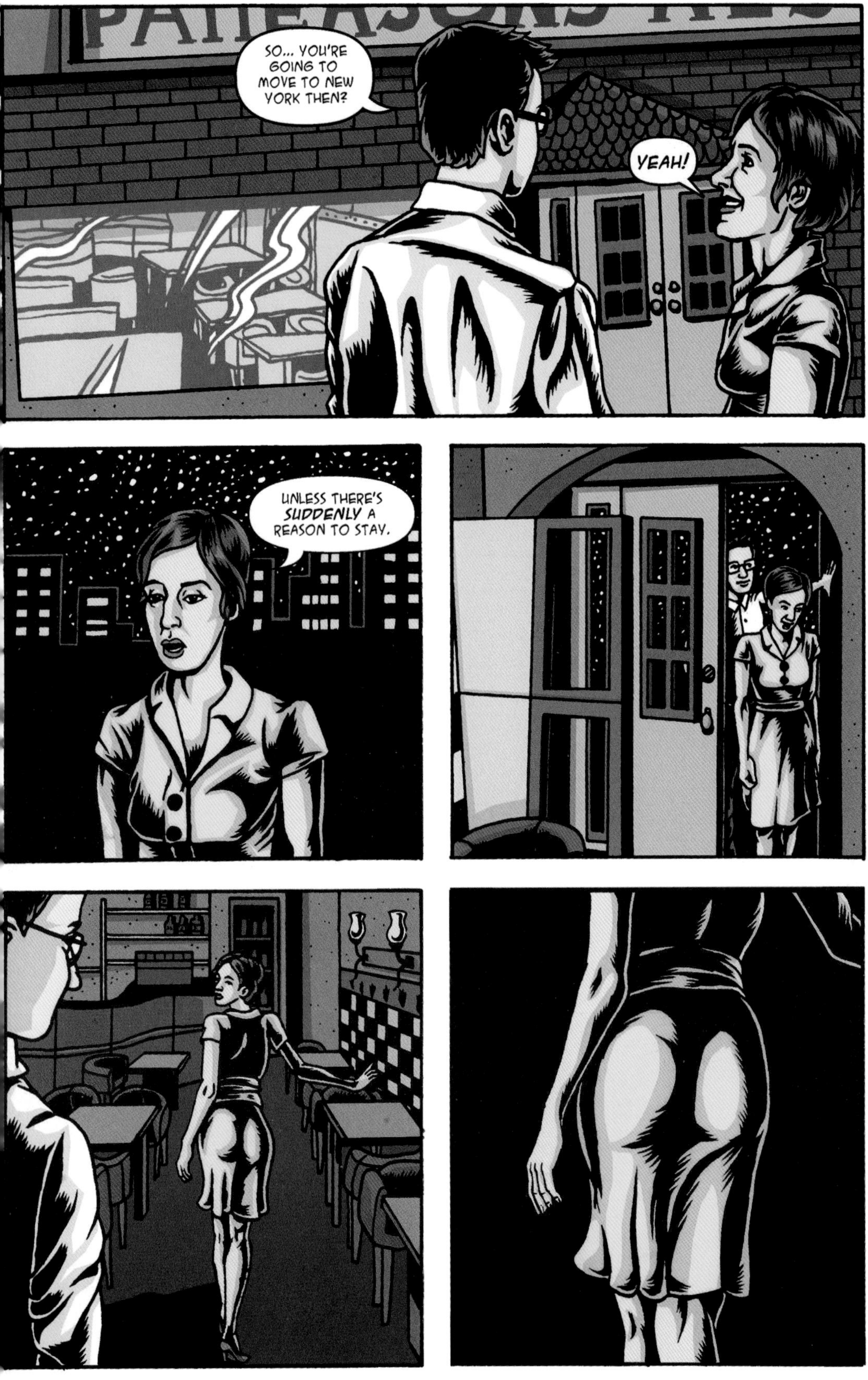
SO... YOU'RE GOING TO MOVE TO NEW YORK THEN?
YEAH!
UNLESS THERE'S SUDDENLY A REASON TO STAY.

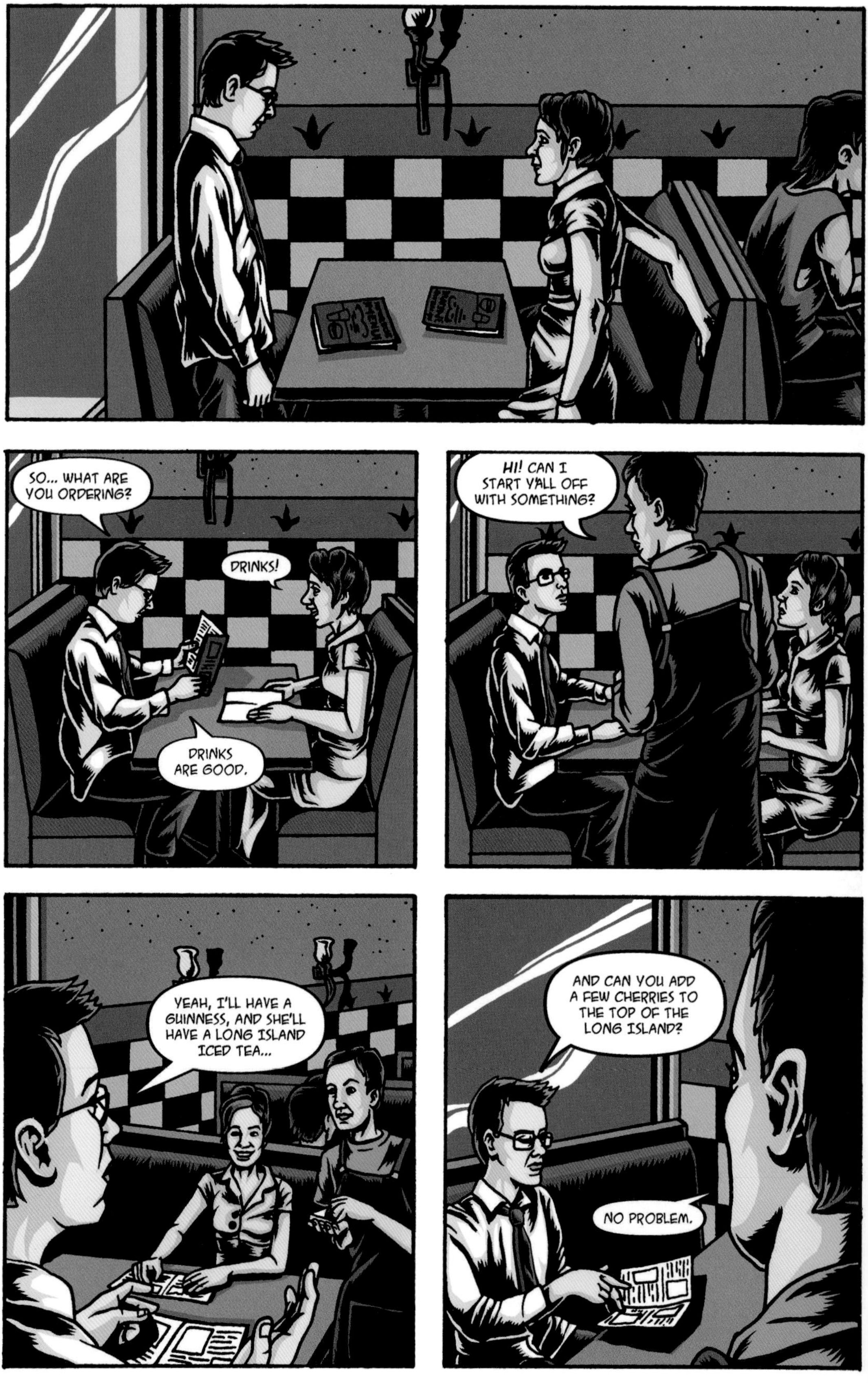
SO... WHAT ARE YOU ORDERING?
DRINKS!
DRINKS ARE GOOD.
HI! CAN I START Y'ALL OFF WITH SOMETHING?
YEAH, I'LL HAVE A GUINNESS, AND SHE'LL HAVE A LONG ISLAND ICED TEA...
AND CAN YOU ADD A FEW CHERRIES TO THE TOP OF THE LONG ISLAND?
NO PROBLEM.

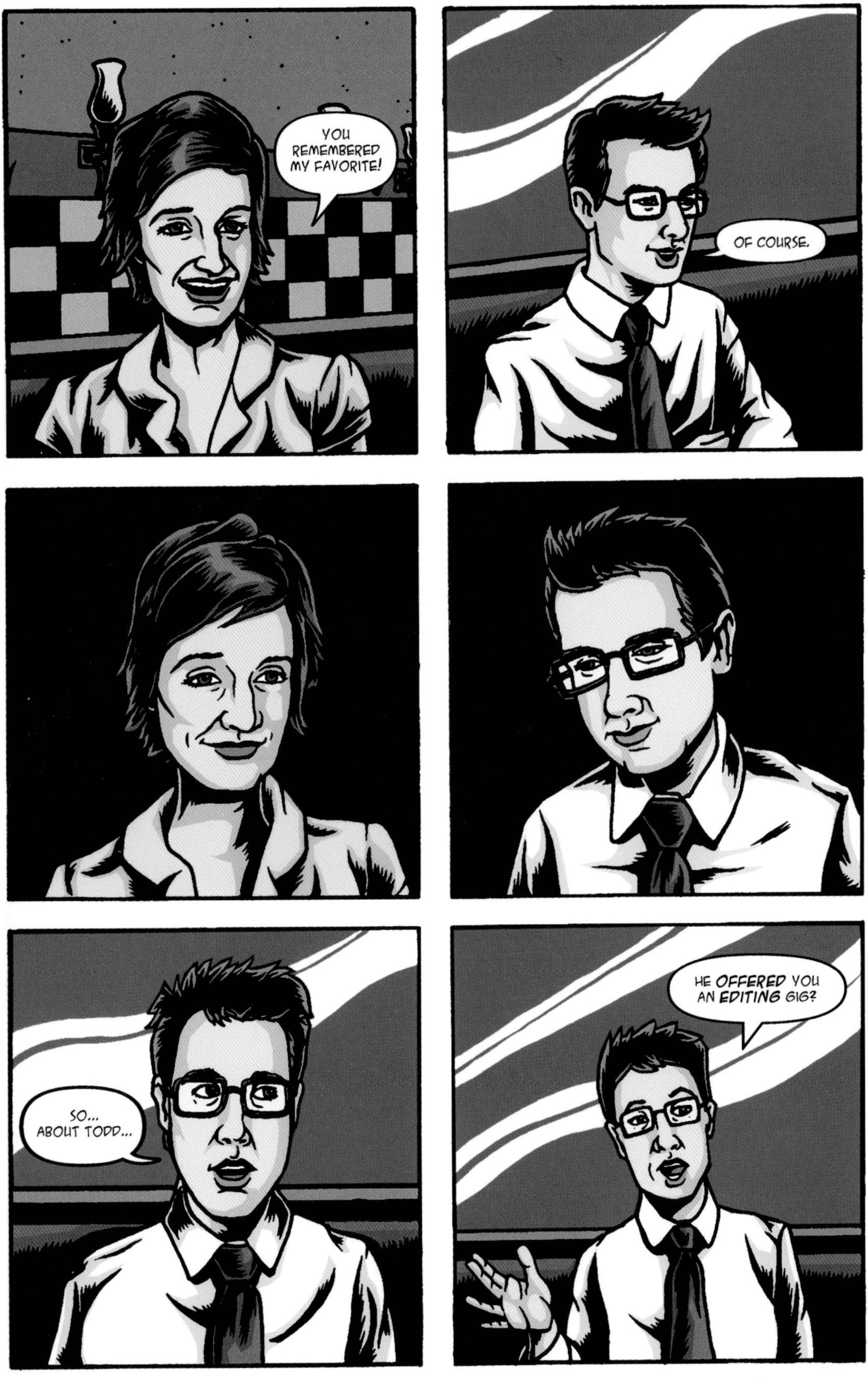
YOU REMEMBERED MY FAVORITE!
OF COURSE.
SO... ABOUT TODD...
HE OFFERED YOU AN EDITING GIG?

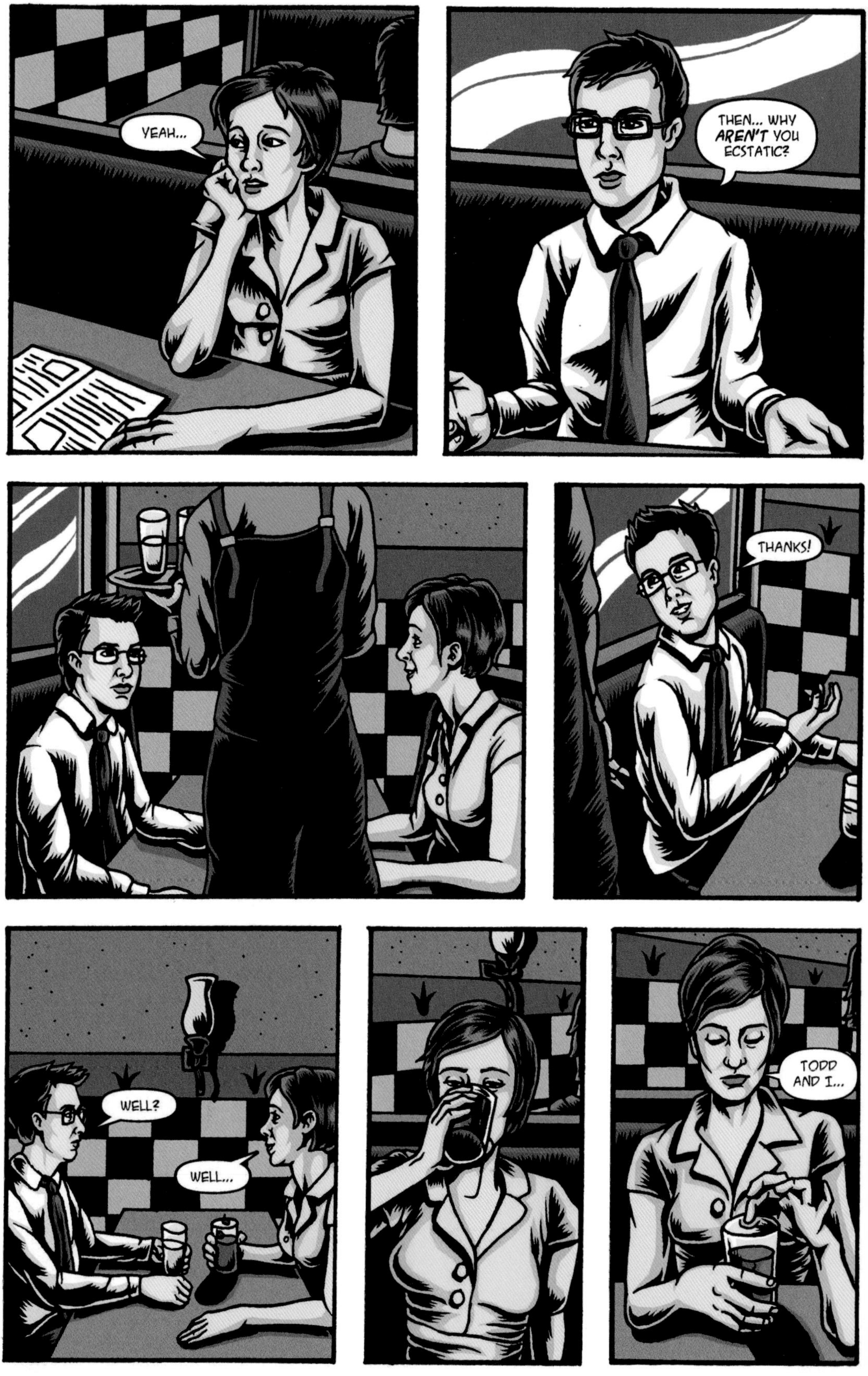
YEAH...
THEN... WHY *AREN'T* YOU ECSTATIC?
THANKS!
WELL?
WELL...
TODD AND I...

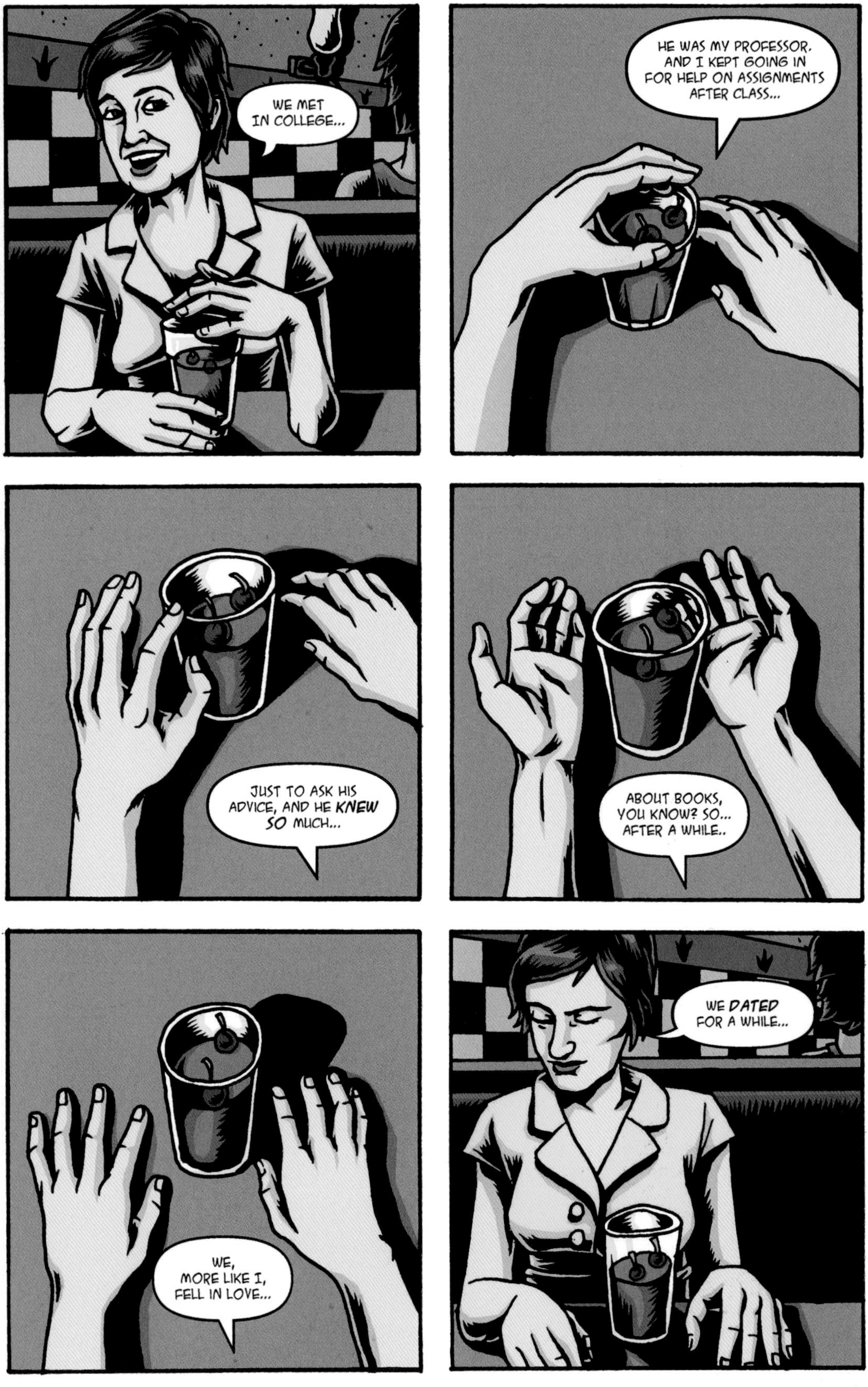
WE MET
IN COLLEGE...
HE WAS MY PROFESSOR.
AND I KEPT GOING IN
FOR HELP ON ASSIGNMENTS
AFTER CLASS...
JUST TO ASK HIS
ADVICE, AND HE KNEW
SO MUCH...
ABOUT BOOKS,
YOU KNOW? SO...
AFTER A WHILE..
WE,
MORE LIKE I,
FELL IN LOVE...
WE DATED
FOR A WHILE...

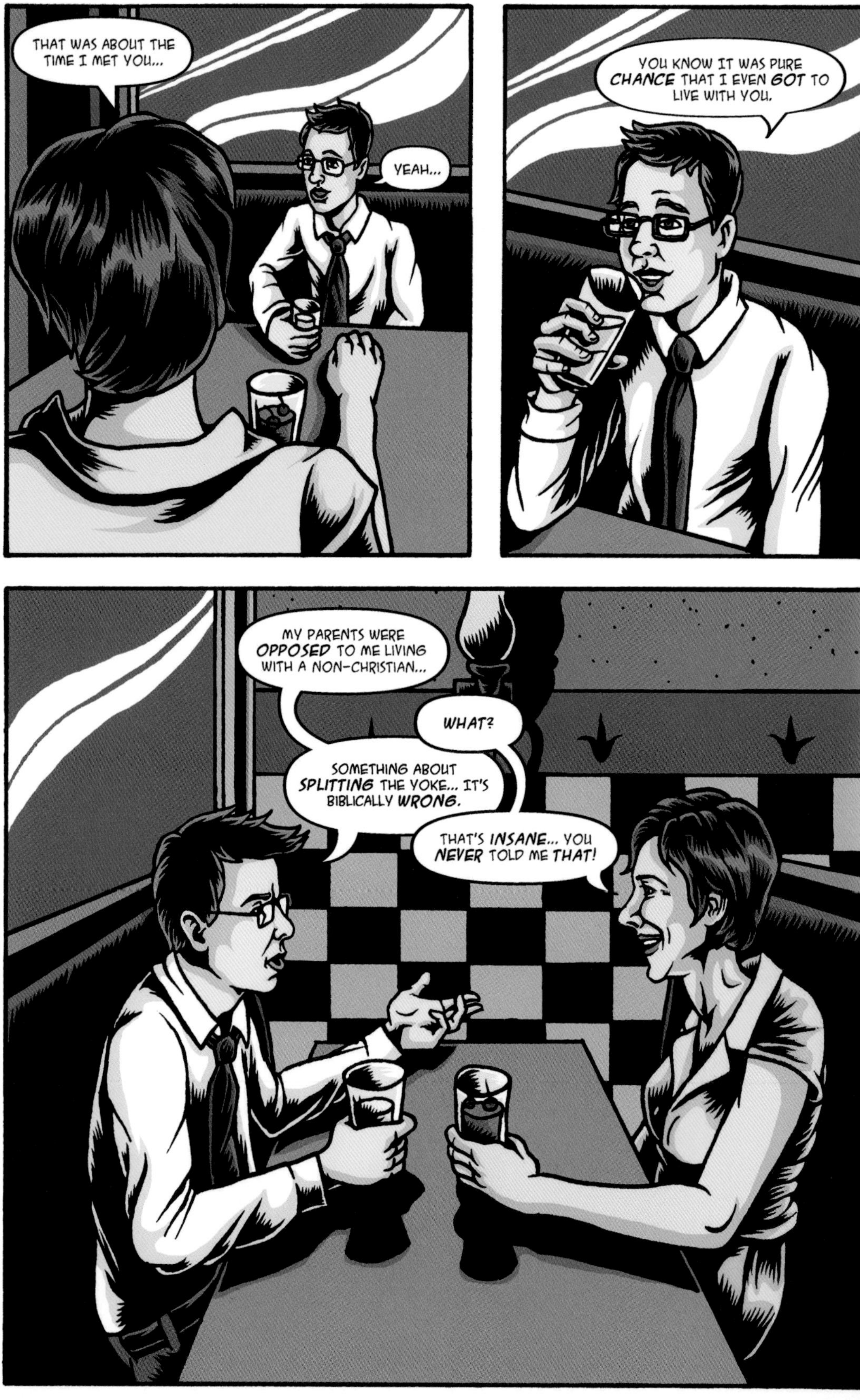
THAT WAS ABOUT THE TIME I MET YOU...
YEAH...
YOU KNOW IT WAS PURE CHANCE THAT I EVEN GOT TO LIVE WITH YOU.
MY PARENTS WERE OPPOSED TO ME LIVING WITH A NON-CHRISTIAN...
WHAT?
SOMETHING ABOUT SPLITTING THE YOKE... IT'S BIBLICALLY WRONG.
THAT'S INSANE... YOU NEVER TOLD ME THAT!

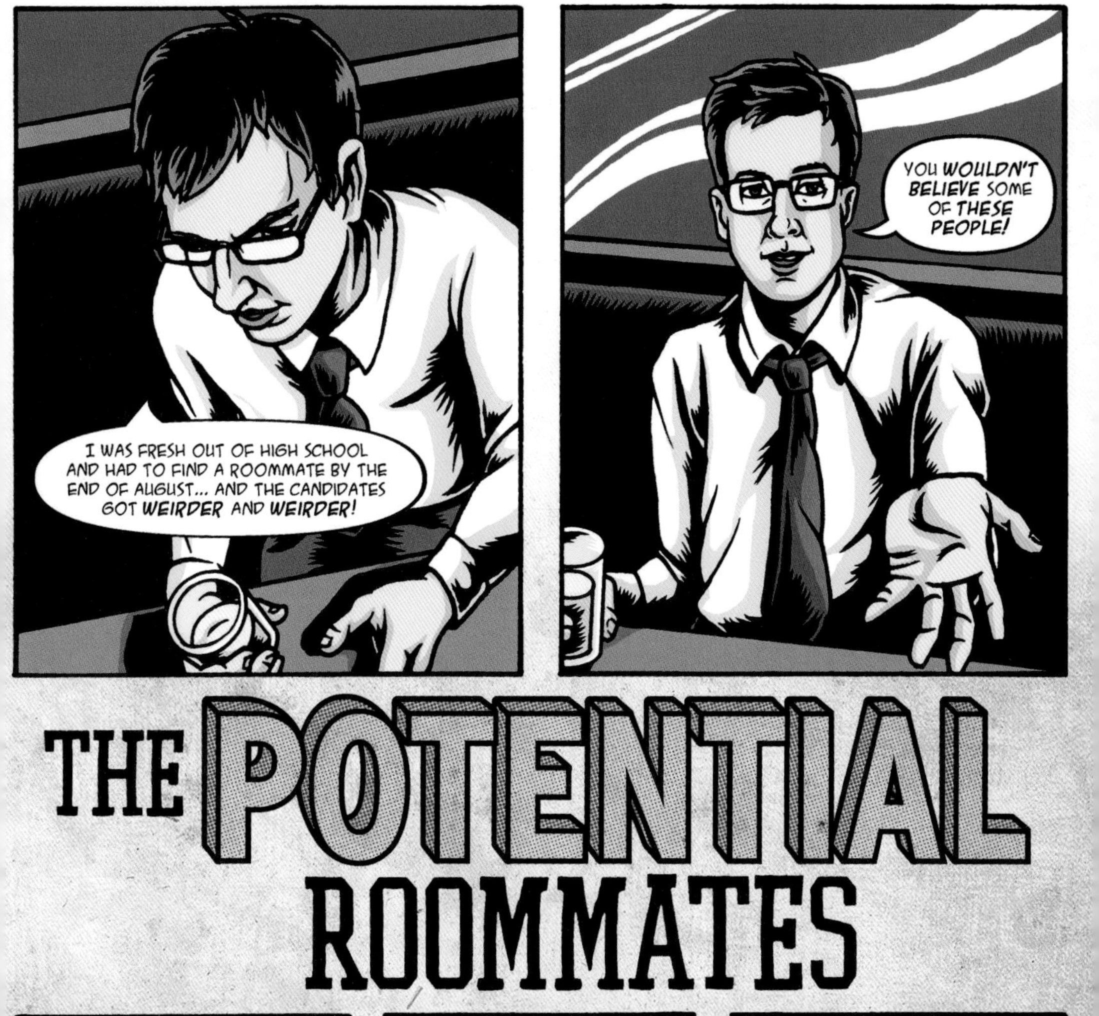
I WAS FRESH OUT OF HIGH SCHOOL AND HAD TO FIND A ROOMMATE BY THE END OF AUGUST... AND THE CANDIDATES GOT WEIRDER AND WEIRDER!
YOU WOULDN'T BELIEVE SOME OF THESE PEOPLE!

THE POTENTIAL ROOMMATES

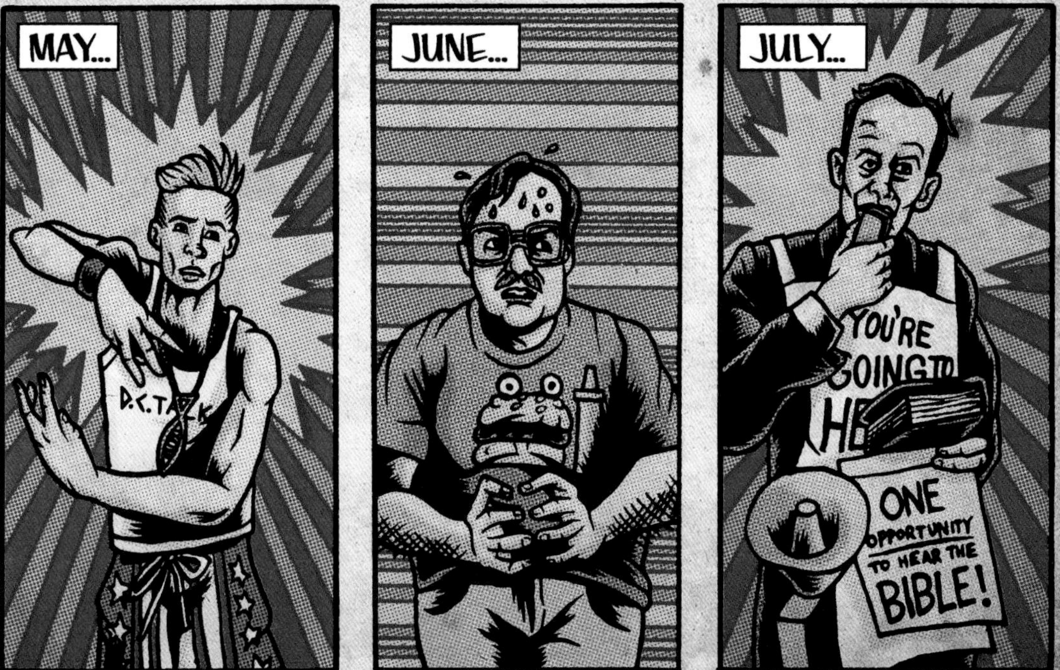
MAY...
JUNE...
JULY...
YOU'RE
ONE OPPORTUNITY TO HEAR THE BIBLE!

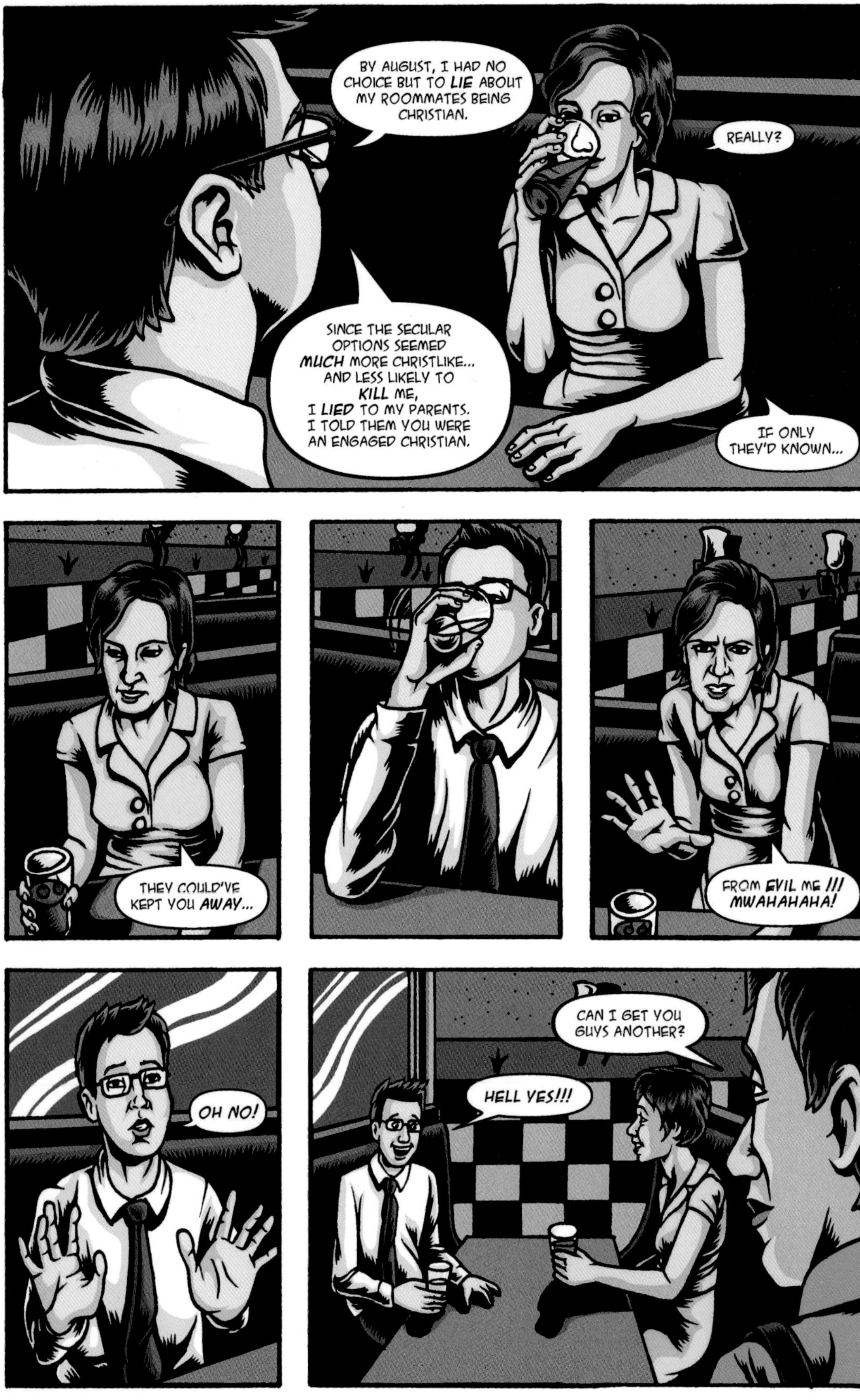
BY AUGUST, I HAD NO CHOICE BUT TO LIE ABOUT MY ROOMMATES BEING CHRISTIAN.
REALLY?
SINCE THE SECULAR OPTIONS SEEMED MUCH MORE CHRISTLIKE... AND LESS LIKELY TO KILL ME, I LIED TO MY PARENTS. I TOLD THEM YOU WERE AN ENGAGED CHRISTIAN.
IF ONLY THEY'D KNOWN...
THEY COULD'VE KEPT YOU AWAY...
FROM EVIL ME !!! MWAHAHAHA!
OH NO!
CAN I GET YOU GUYS ANOTHER?
HELL YES!!!

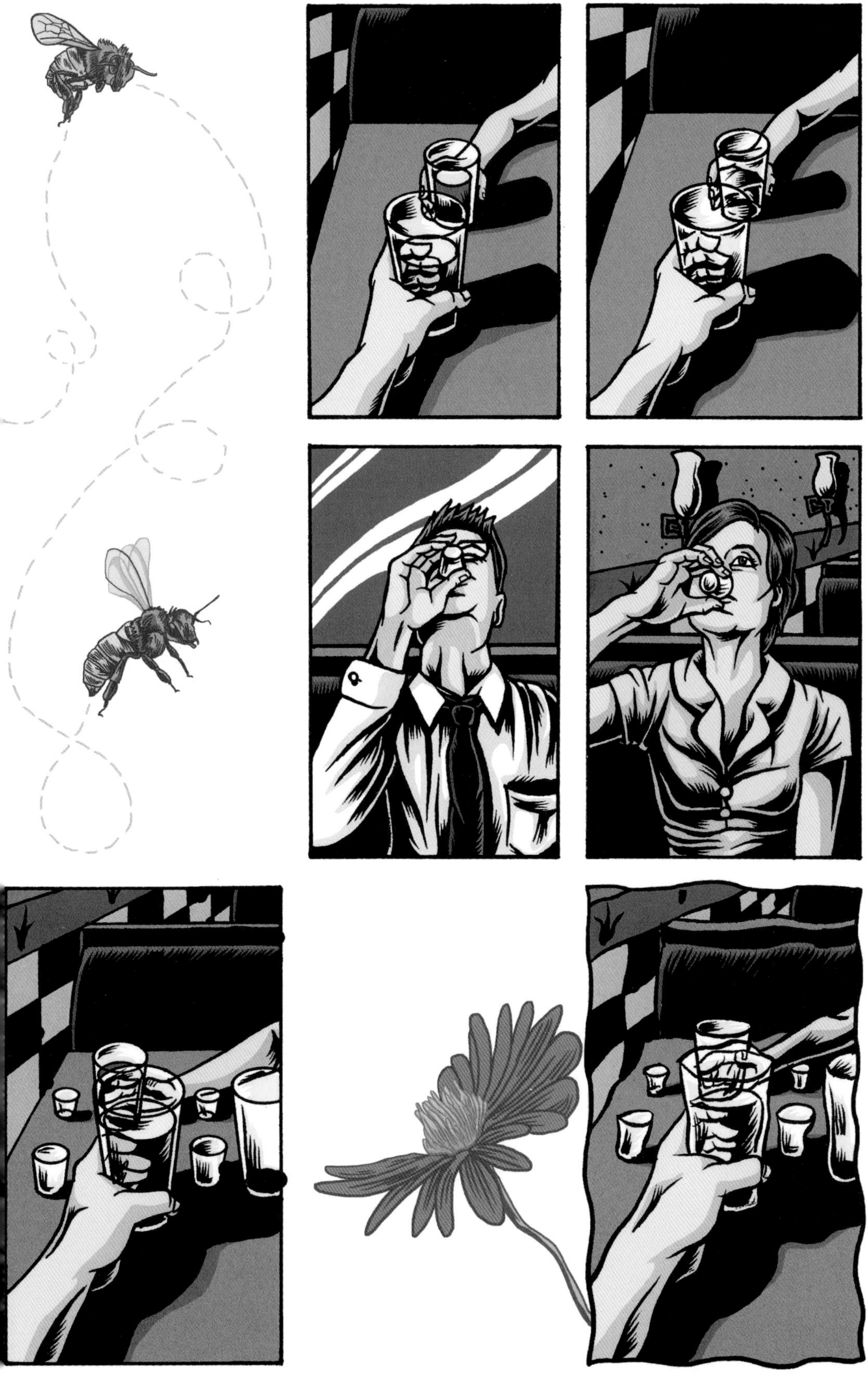

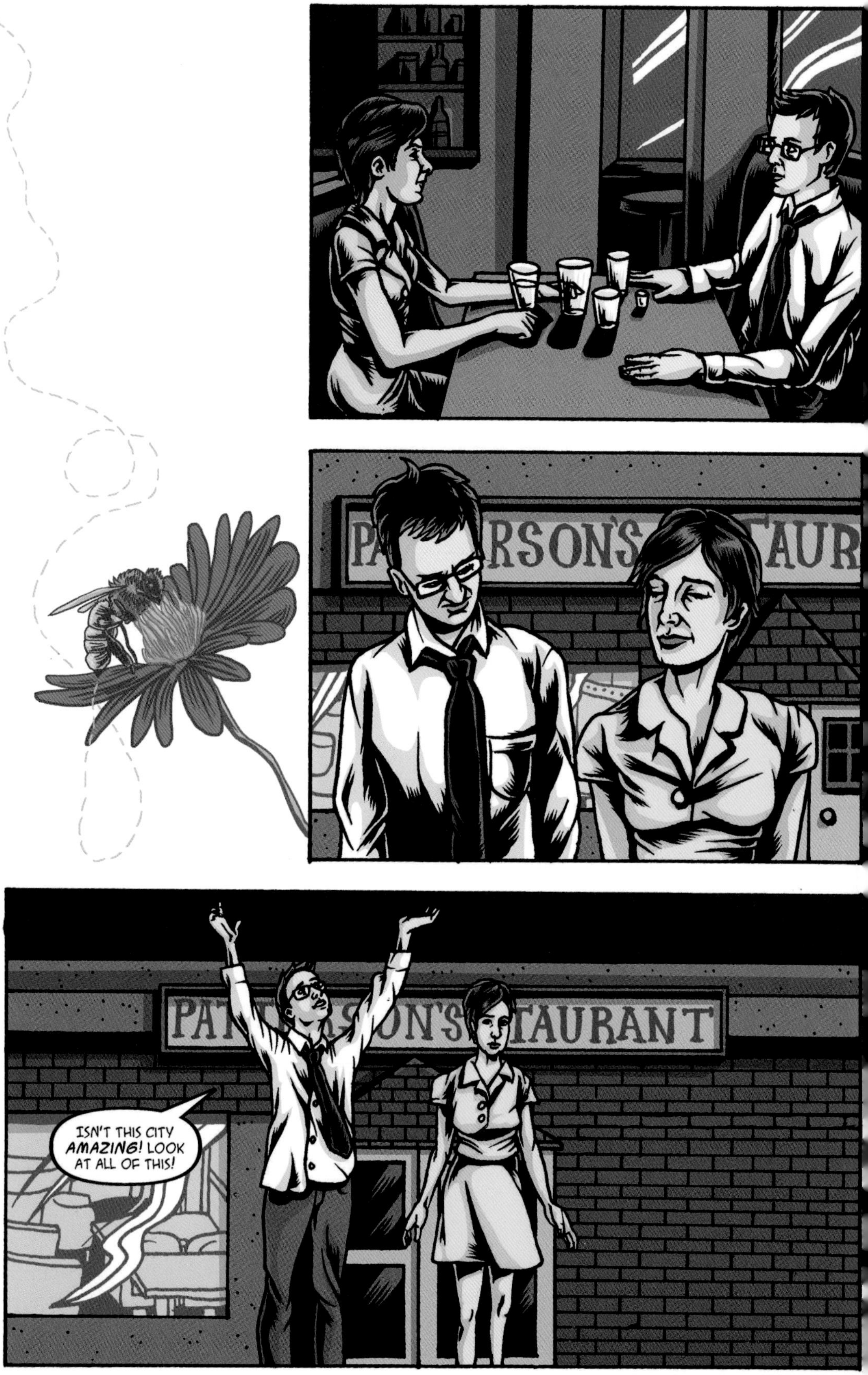
ISN'T THIS CITY AMAZING! LOOK AT ALL OF THIS!

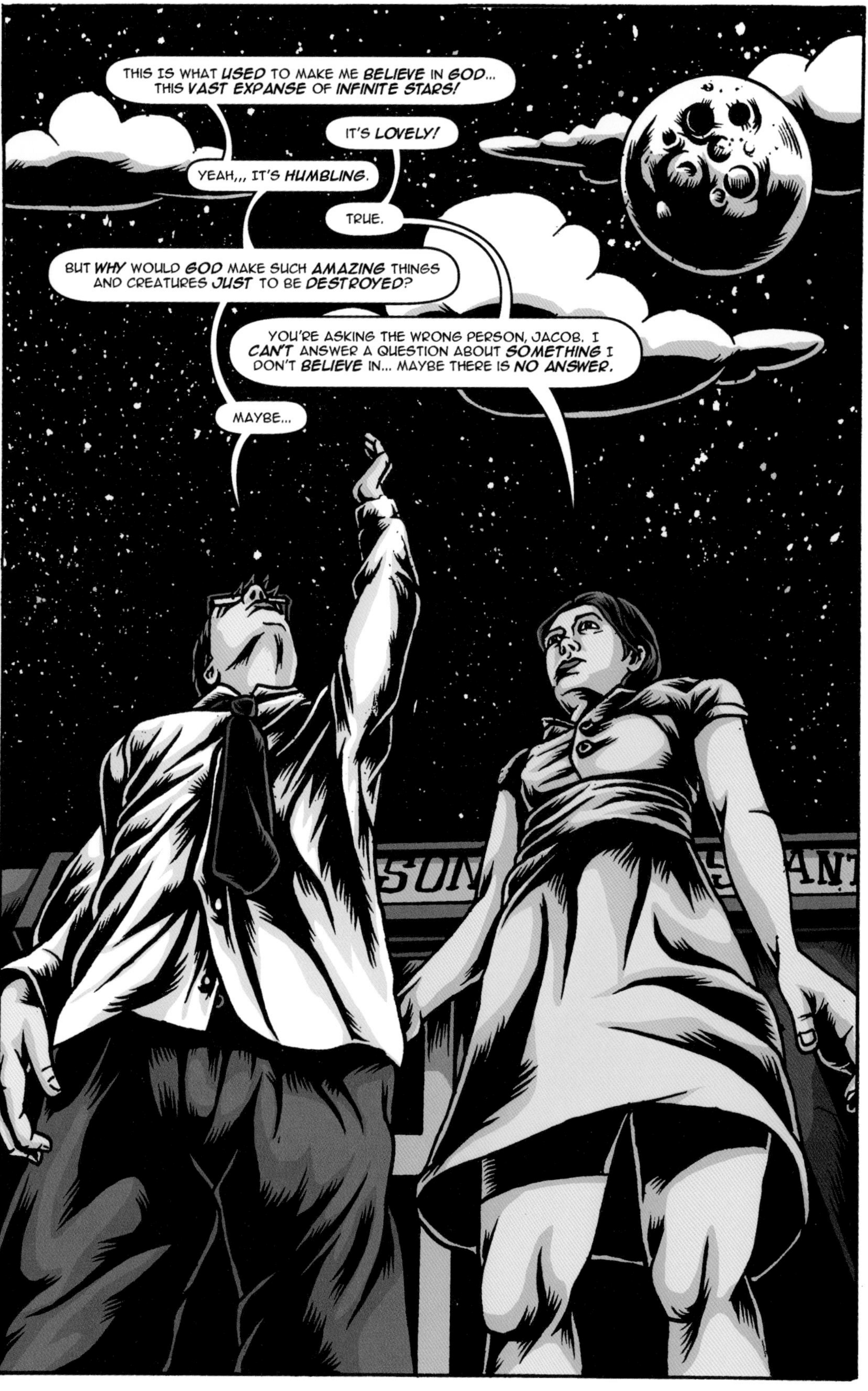
THIS IS WHAT USED TO MAKE ME BELIEVE IN GOD... THIS VAST EXPANSE OF INFINITE STARS!
IT'S LOVELY!
YEAH,,, IT'S HUMBLING.
TRUE.
BUT WHY WOULD GOD MAKE SUCH AMAZING THINGS AND CREATURES JUST TO BE DESTROYED?
YOU'RE ASKING THE WRONG PERSON, JACOB. I CAN'T ANSWER A QUESTION ABOUT SOMETHING I DON'T BELIEVE IN... MAYBE THERE IS NO ANSWER.
MAYBE...

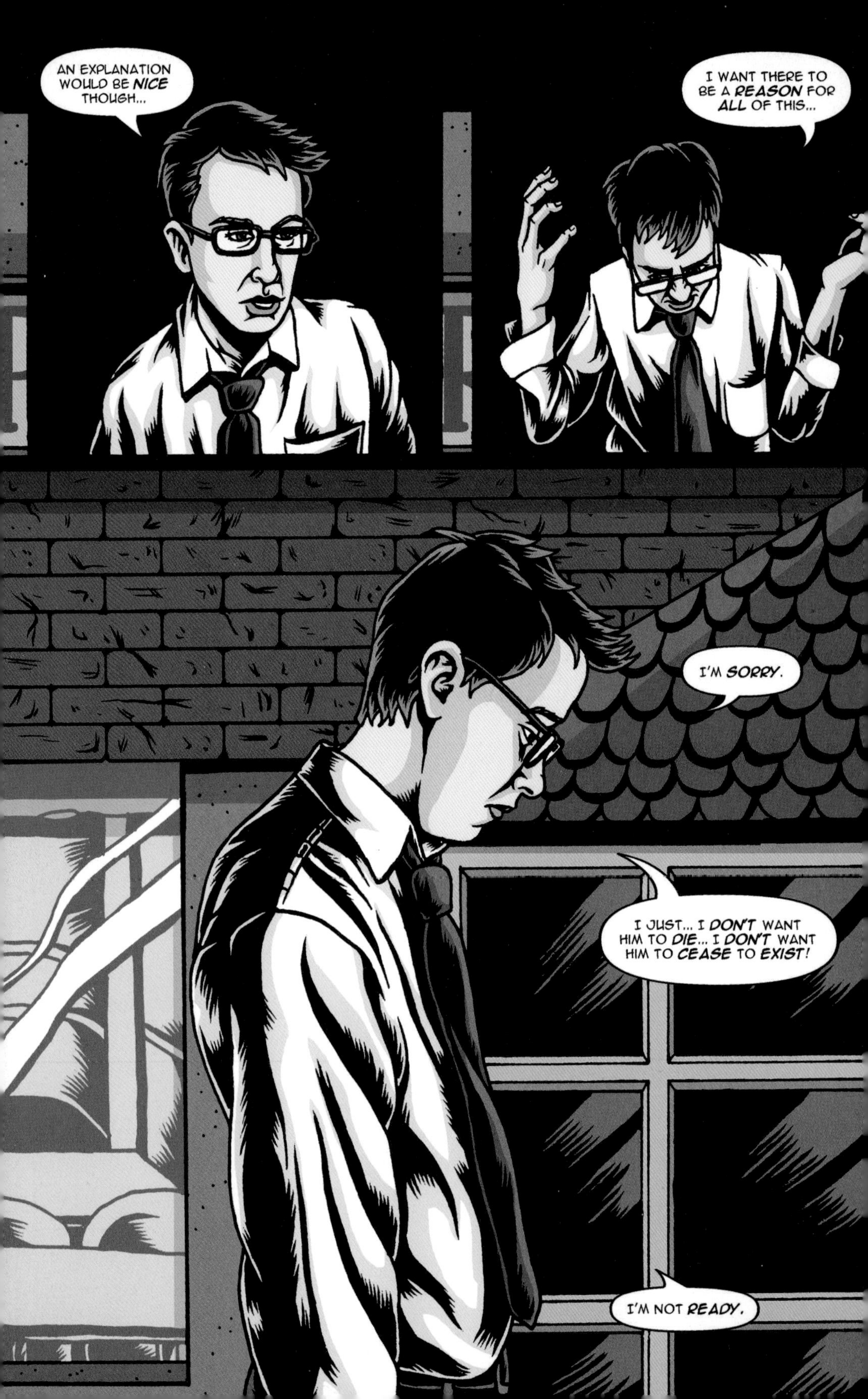
AN EXPLANATION WOULD BE NICE THOUGH...
I WANT THERE TO BE A REASON FOR ALL OF THIS...
I'M SORRY.
I JUST... I DON'T WANT HIM TO DIE... I DON'T WANT HIM TO CEASE TO EXIST!
I'M NOT READY.

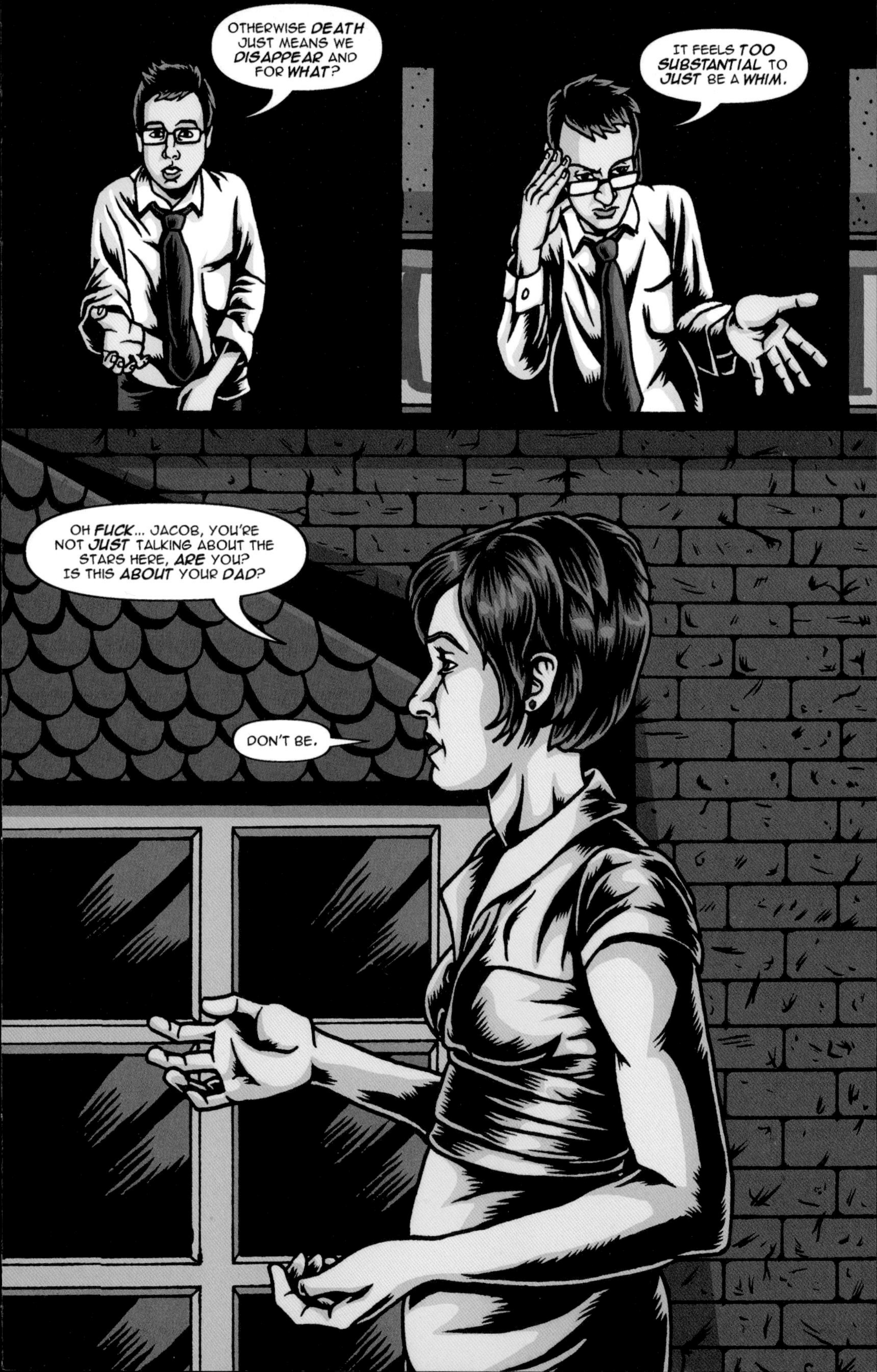

OTHERWISE DEATH JUST MEANS WE DISAPPEAR AND FOR WHAT?
IT FEELS TOO SUBSTANTIAL TO JUST BE A WHIM.
OH FUCK... JACOB, YOU'RE NOT JUST TALKING ABOUT THE STARS HERE, ARE YOU? IS THIS ABOUT YOUR DAD?
DON'T BE.

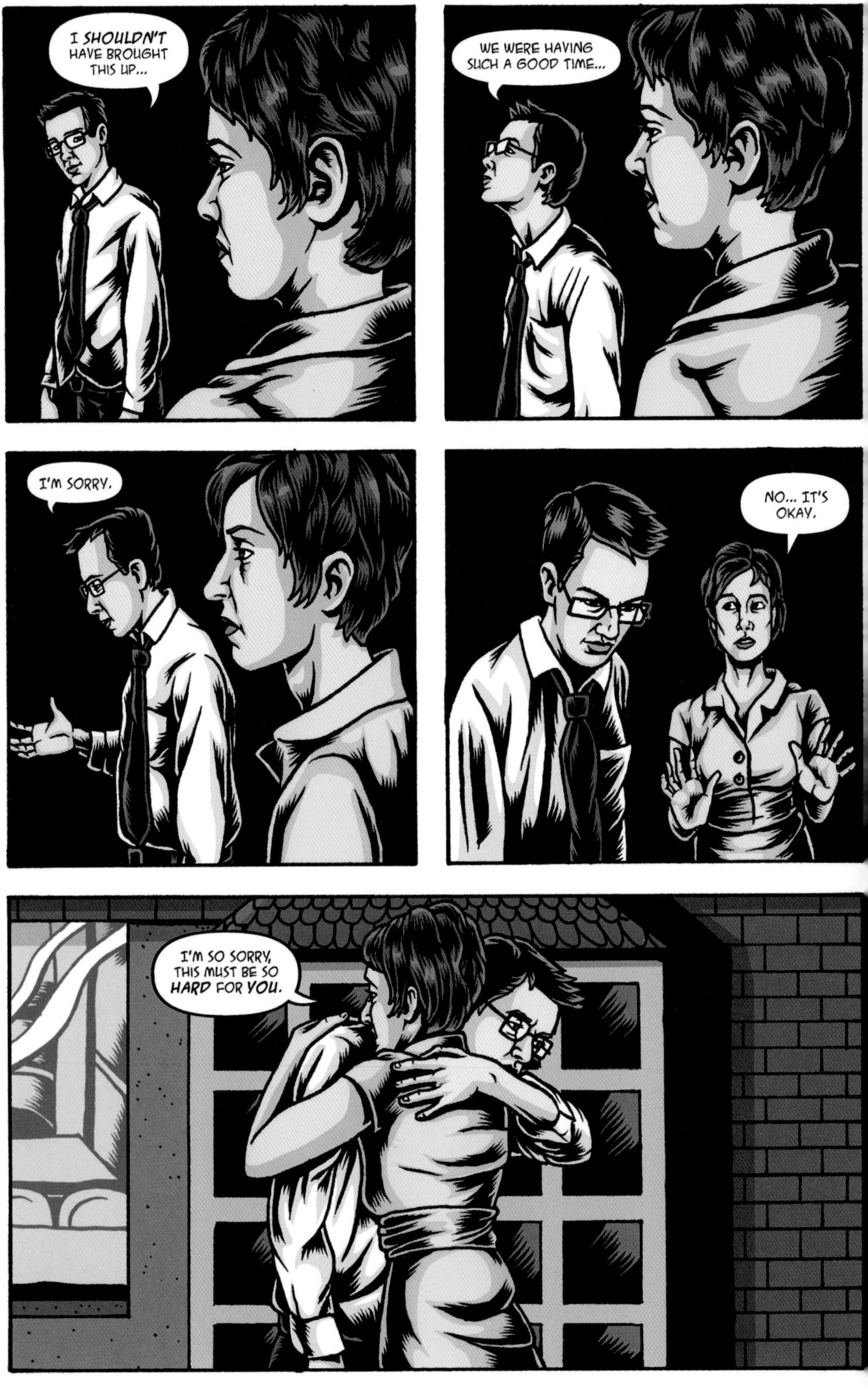
I SHOULDN'T HAVE BROUGHT THIS UP...
WE WERE HAVING SUCH A GOOD TIME...
I'M SORRY.
NO... IT'S OKAY.
I'M SO SORRY, THIS MUST BE SO HARD FOR YOU.

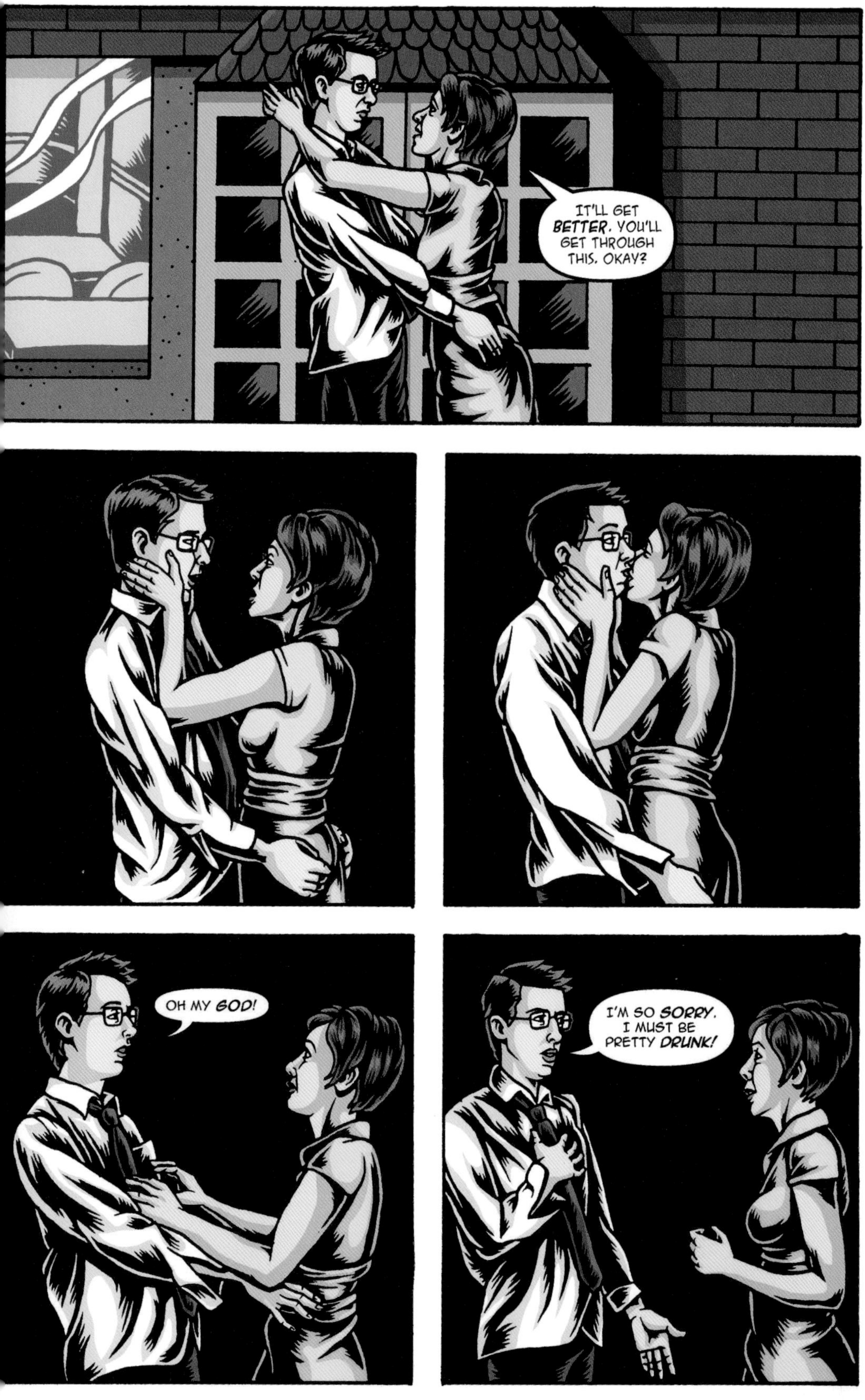
IT'LL GET BETTER. YOU'LL GET THROUGH THIS. OKAY?
OH MY GOD!
I'M SO SORRY. I MUST BE PRETTY DRUNK!

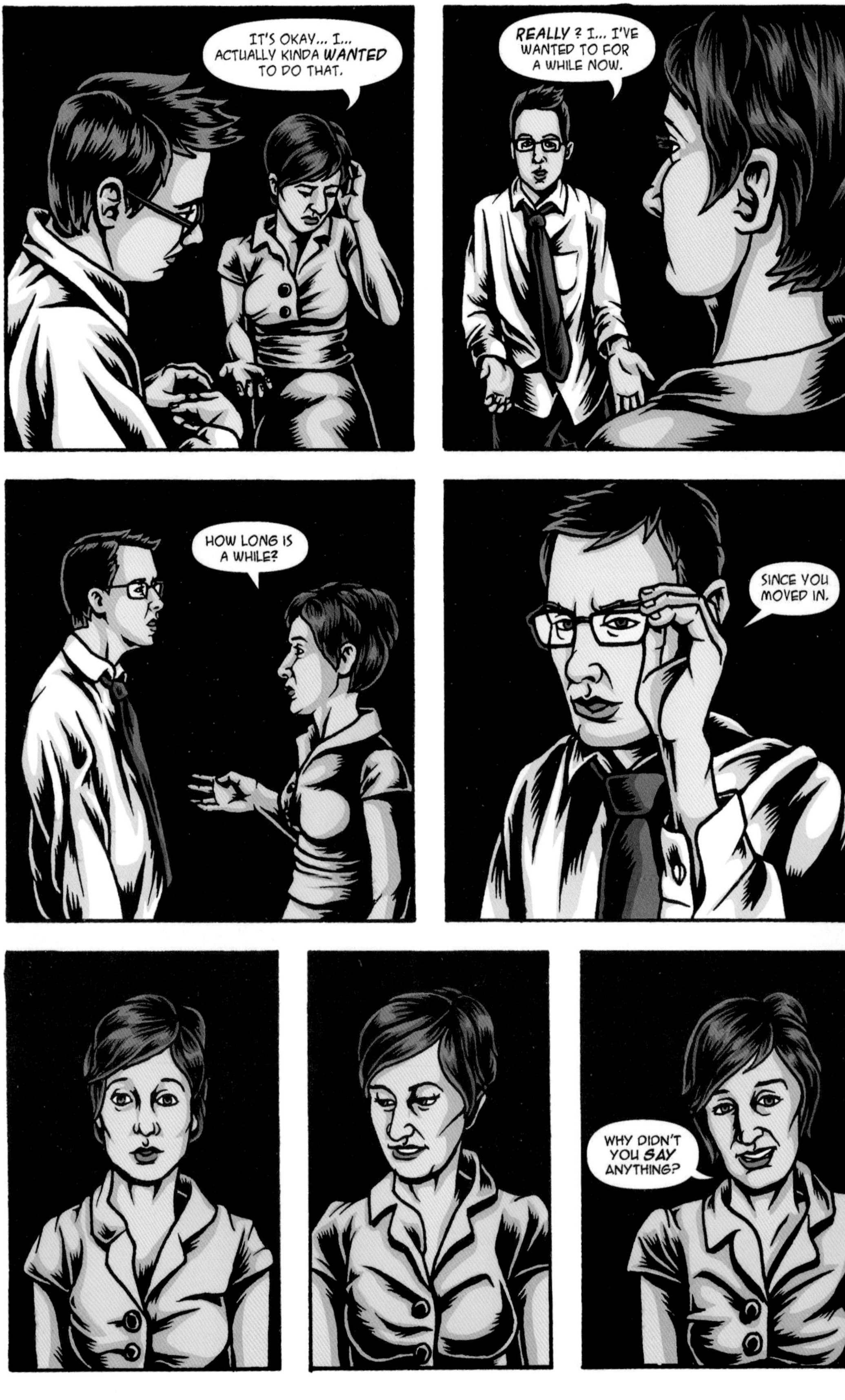
IT'S OKAY... I... ACTUALLY KINDA WANTED TO DO THAT.
REALLY? I... I'VE WANTED TO FOR A WHILE NOW.
HOW LONG IS A WHILE?
SINCE YOU MOVED IN.
WHY DIDN'T YOU SAY ANYTHING?

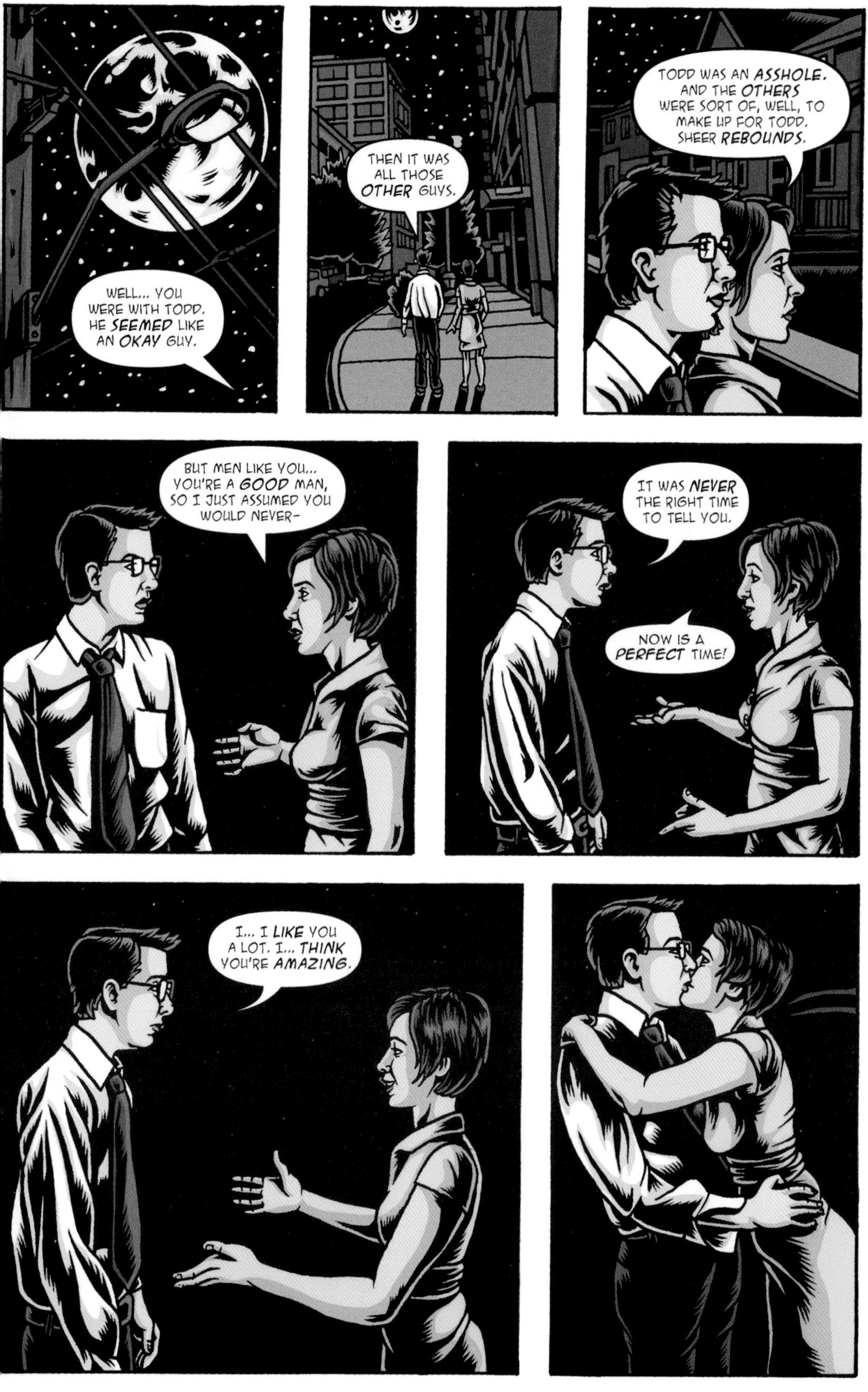
WELL... YOU WERE WITH TODD. HE SEEMED LIKE AN OKAY GUY.
THEN IT WAS ALL THOSE OTHER GUYS.
TODD WAS AN ASSHOLE. AND THE OTHERS WERE SORT OF, WELL, TO MAKE UP FOR TODD. SHEER REBOUNDS.
BUT MEN LIKE YOU... YOU'RE A GOOD MAN, SO I JUST ASSUMED YOU WOULD NEVER-
IT WAS NEVER THE RIGHT TIME TO TELL YOU.
NOW IS A PERFECT TIME!
I... I LIKE YOU A LOT. I... THINK YOU'RE AMAZING.

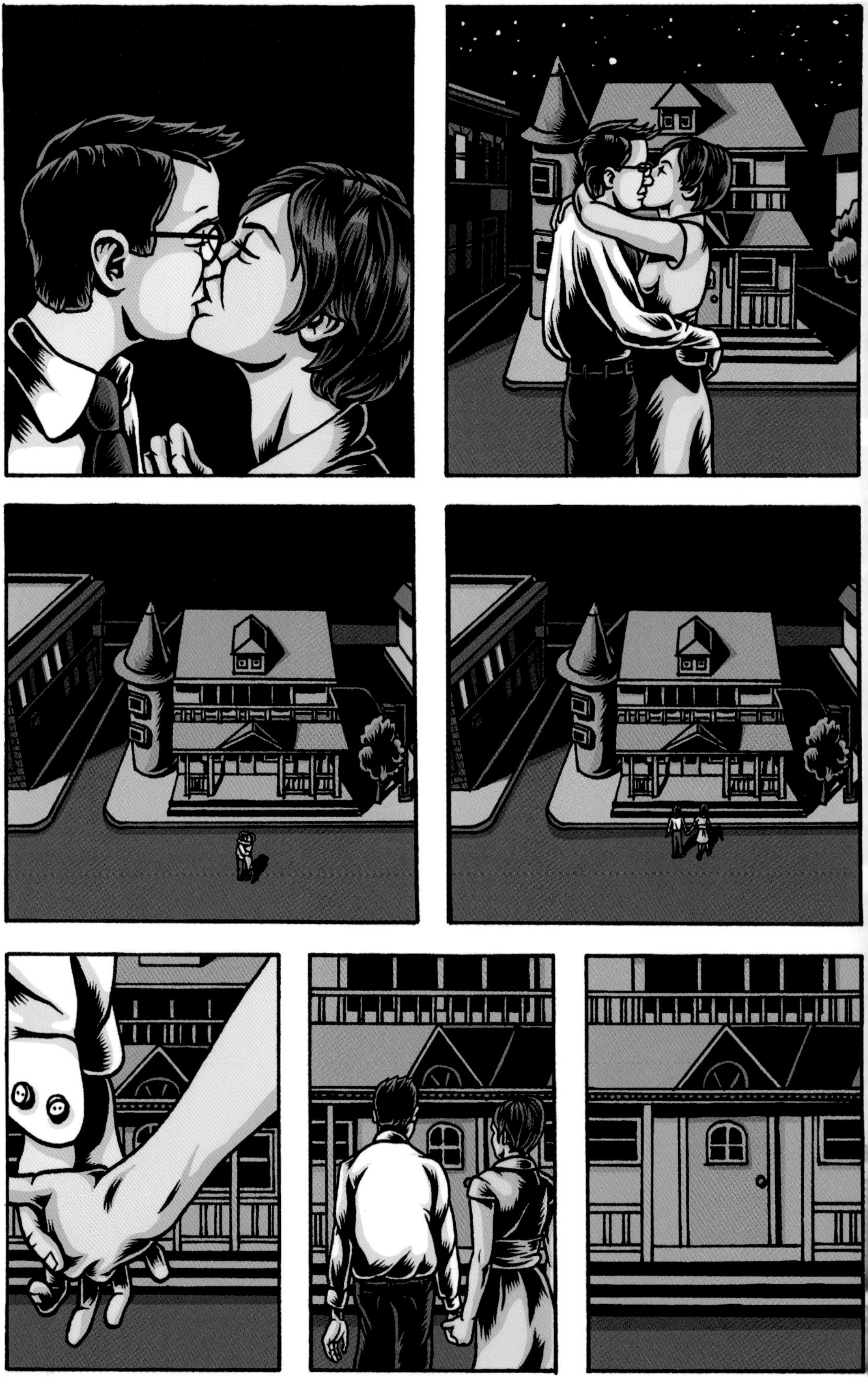

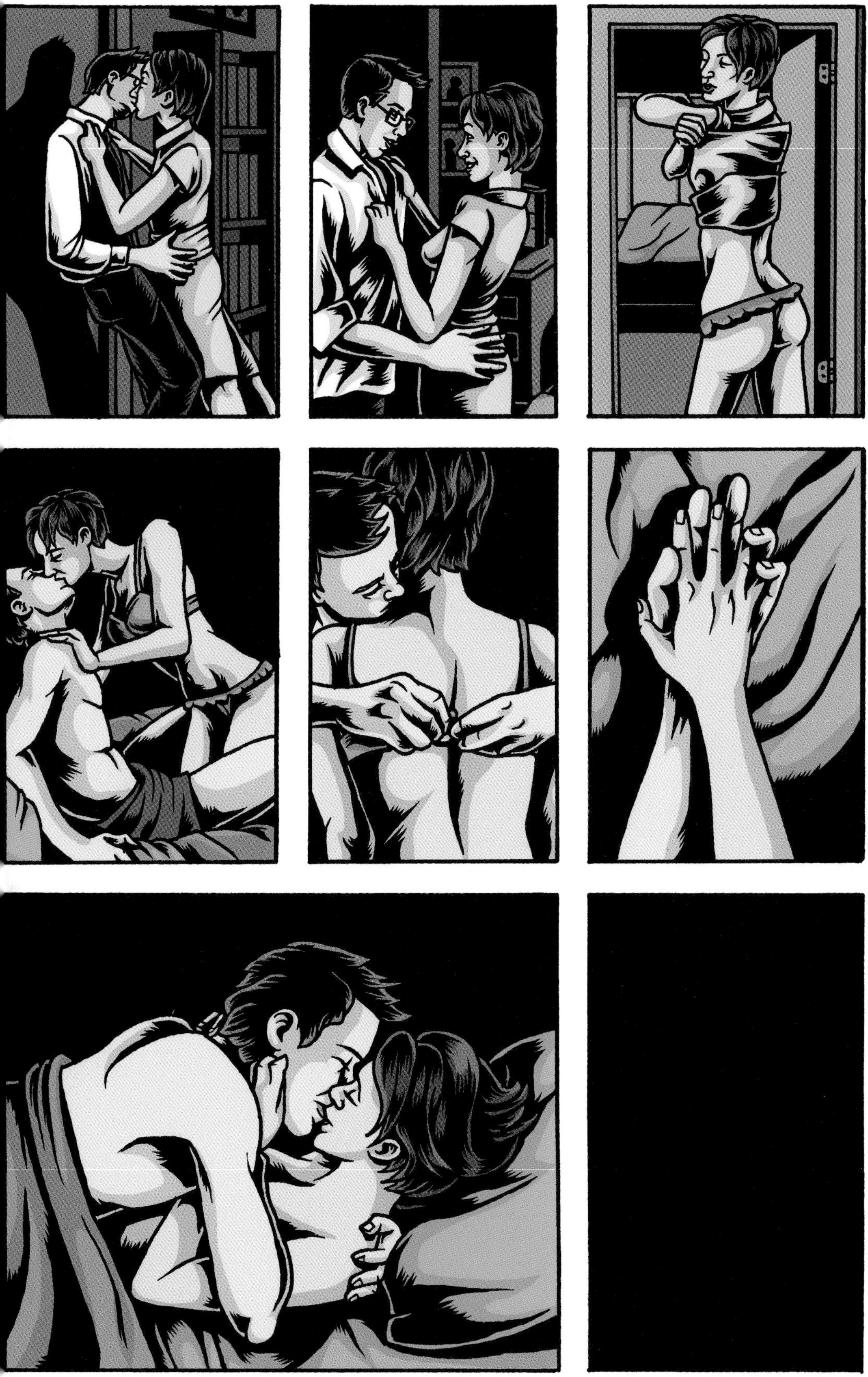

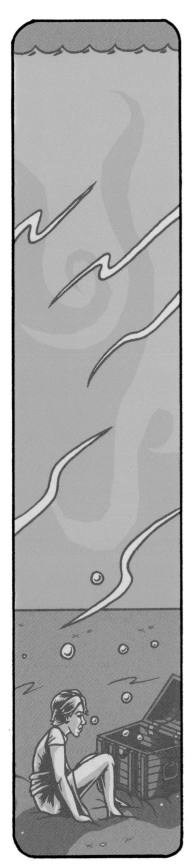

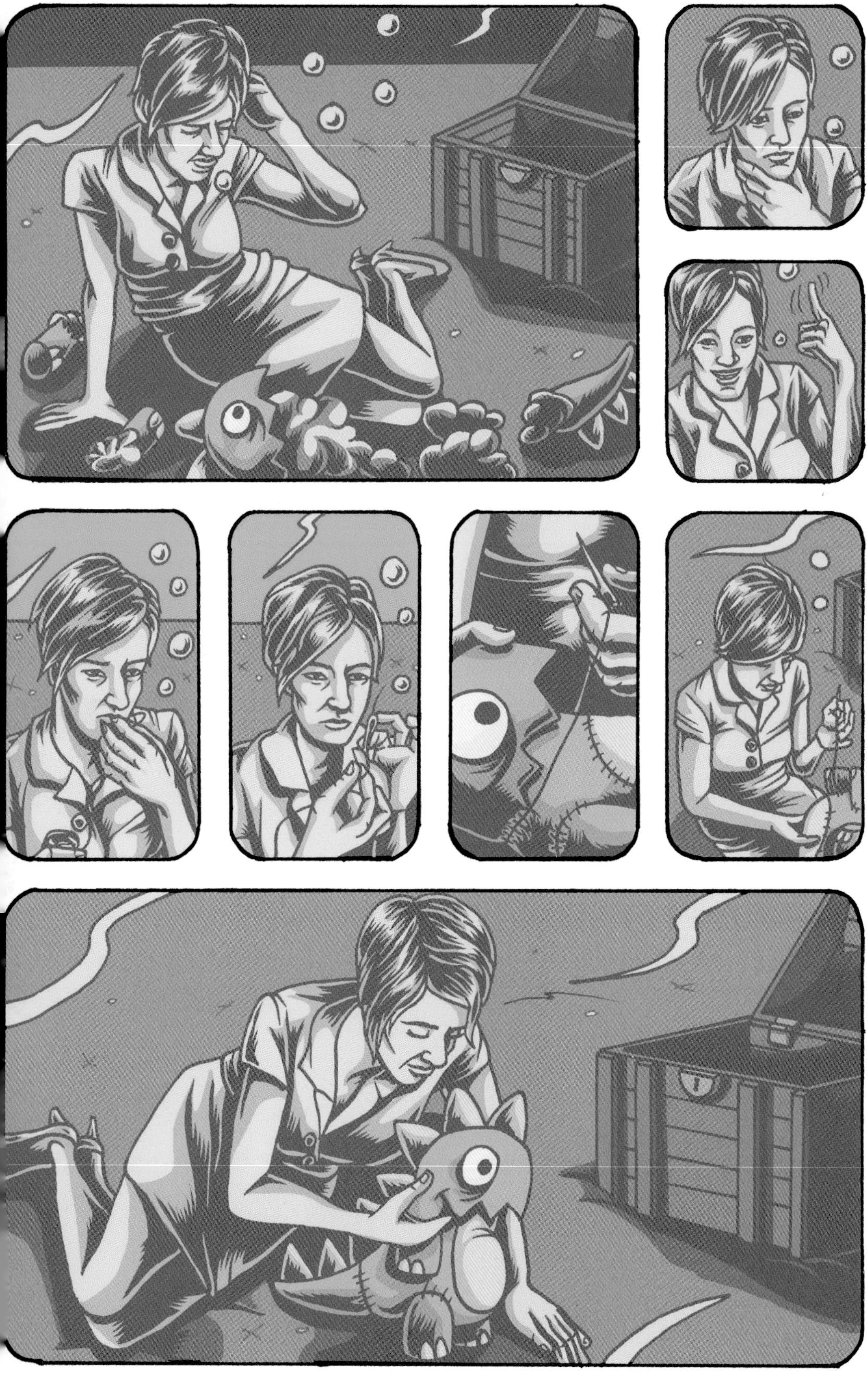

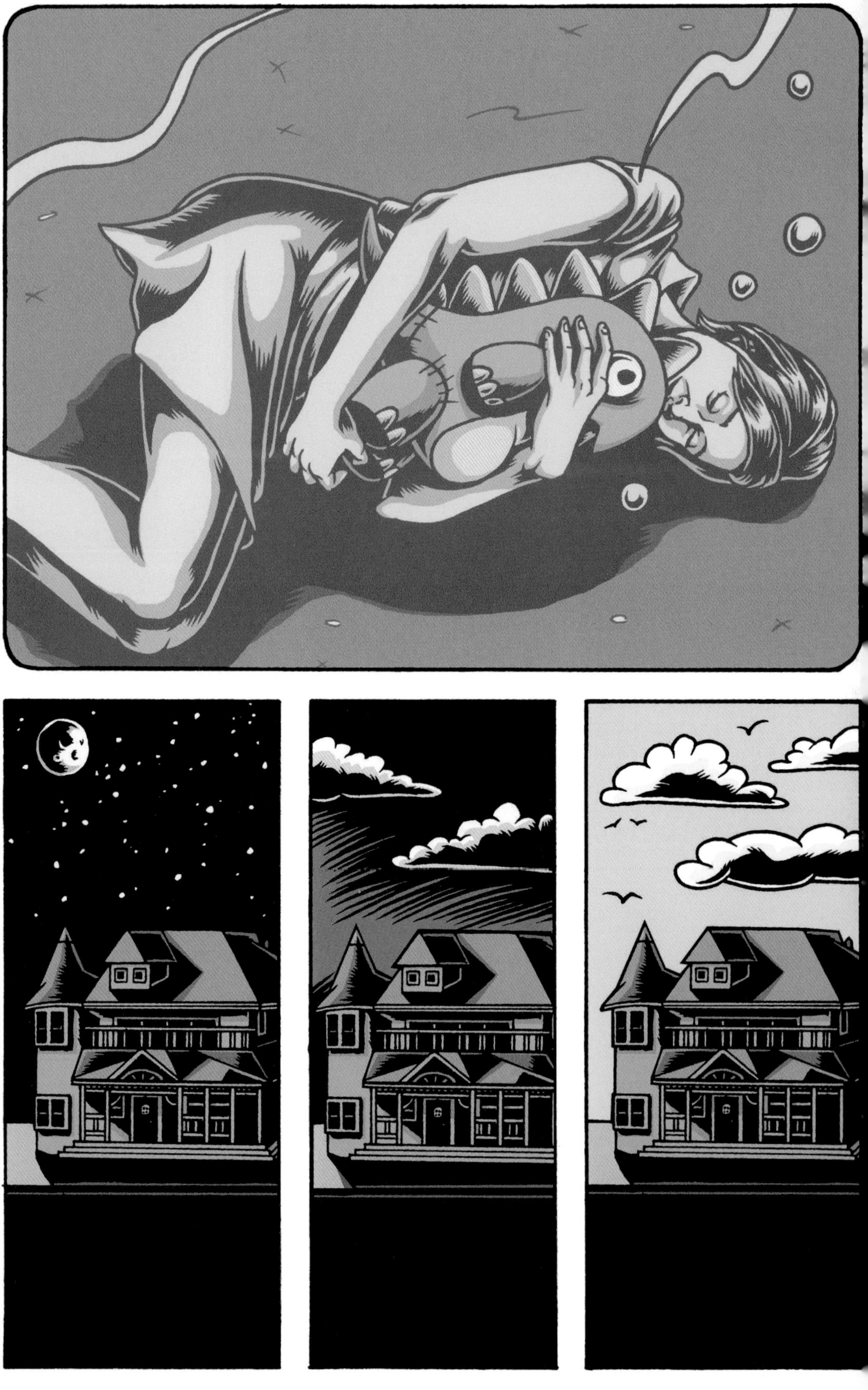

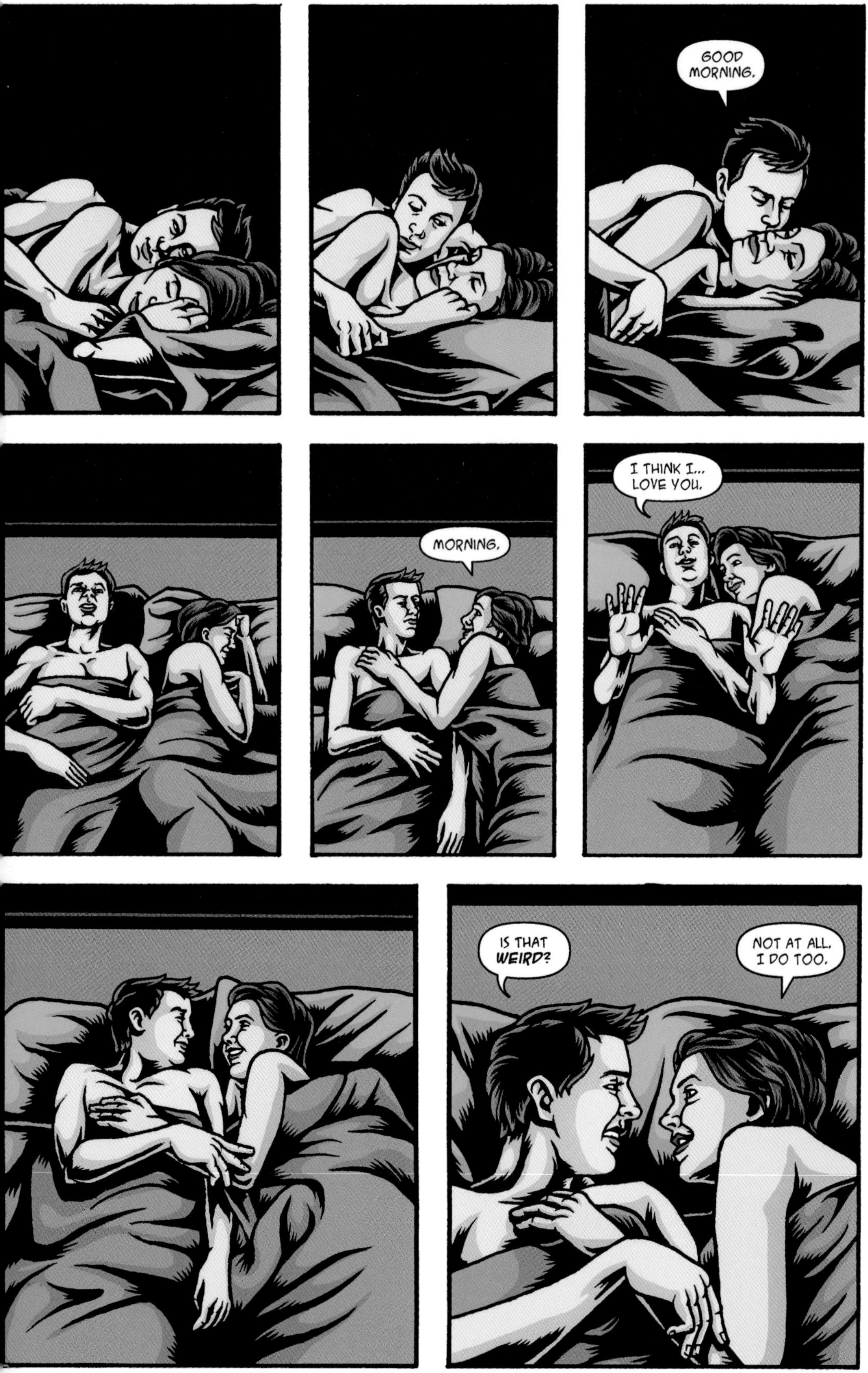
GOOD MORNING.
MORNING.
I THINK I... LOVE YOU.
IS THAT WEIRD?
NOT AT ALL. I DO TOO.

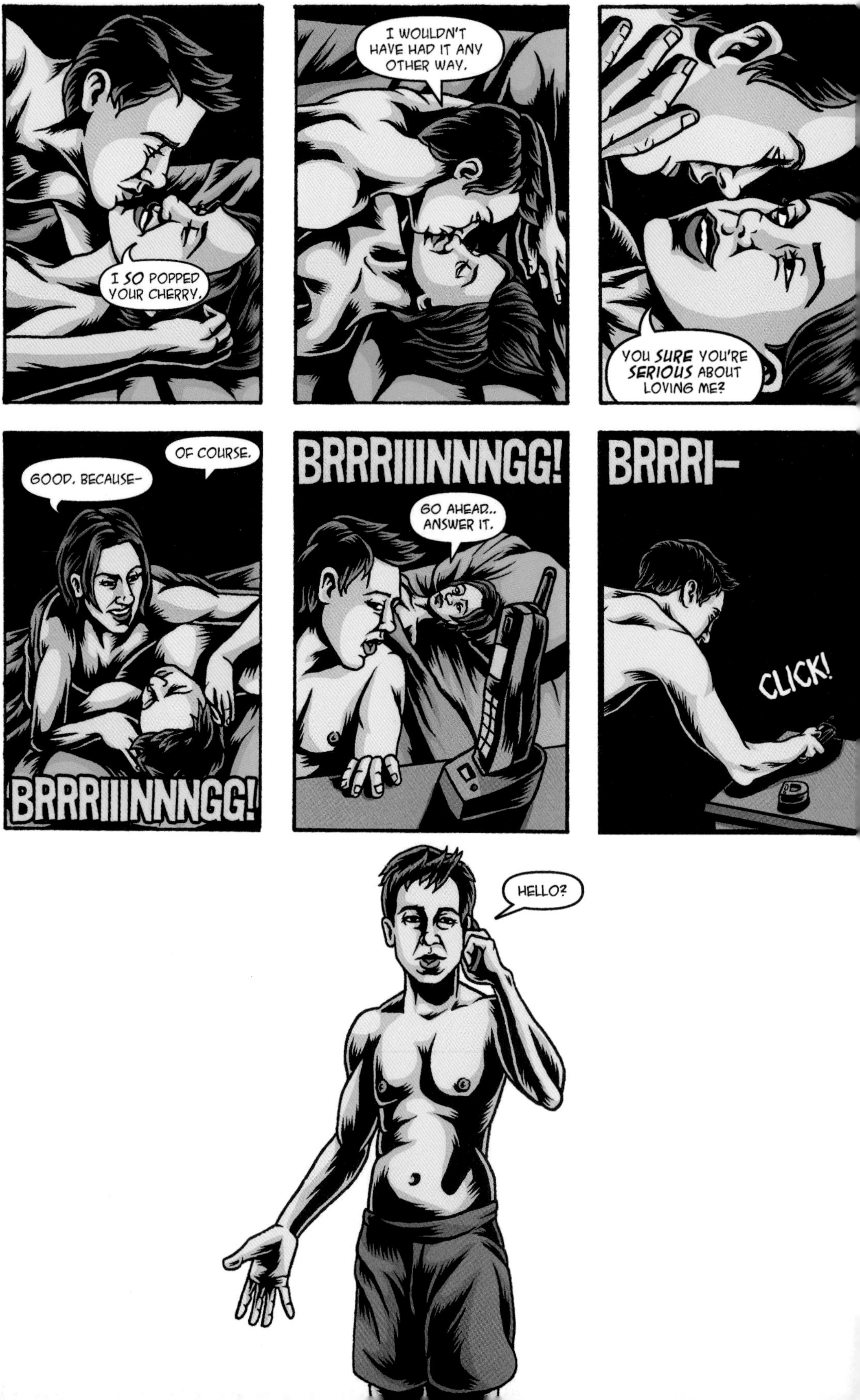
I SO POPPED YOUR CHERRY.
I WOULDN'T HAVE HAD IT ANY OTHER WAY.
YOU SURE YOU'RE SERIOUS ABOUT LOVING ME?
OF COURSE.
GOOD. BECAUSE-
BRRRIIIINNNGG!
BRRRIIIINNNGG!
GO AHEAD.. ANSWER IT.
BRRRI-
CLICK!
HELLO?

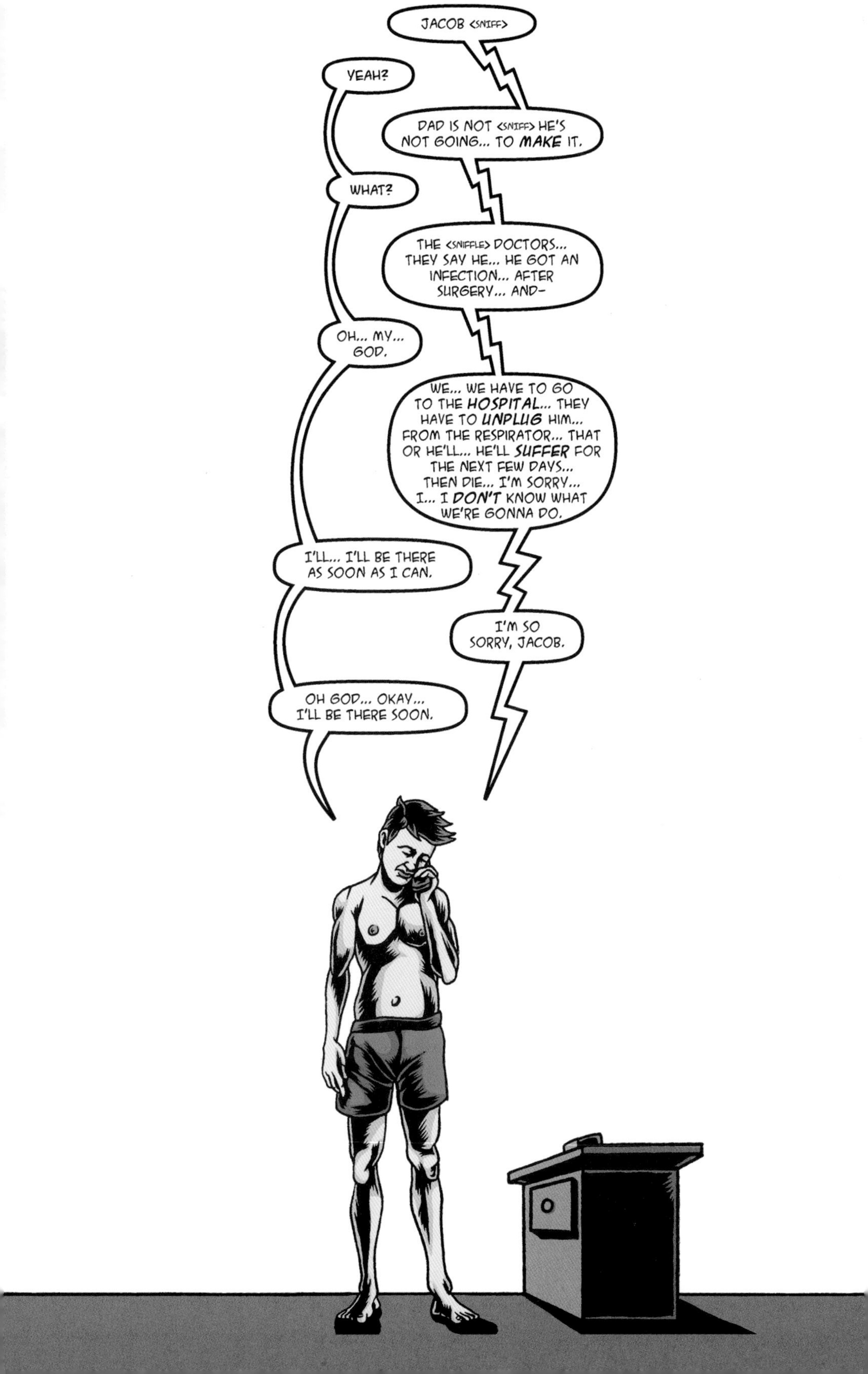
JACOB <SNIFF>
YEAH?
DAD IS NOT <SNIFF> HE'S NOT GOING... TO MAKE IT.
WHAT?
THE <SNIFFLE> DOCTORS... THEY SAY HE... HE GOT AN INFECTION... AFTER SURGERY... AND–
OH... MY... GOD.
WE... WE HAVE TO GO TO THE HOSPITAL... THEY HAVE TO UNPLUG HIM... FROM THE RESPIRATOR... THAT OR HE'LL... HE'LL SUFFER FOR THE NEXT FEW DAYS... THEN DIE... I'M SORRY... I... I DON'T KNOW WHAT WE'RE GONNA DO.
I'LL... I'LL BE THERE AS SOON AS I CAN.
I'M SO SORRY, JACOB.
OH GOD... OKAY... I'LL BE THERE SOON.

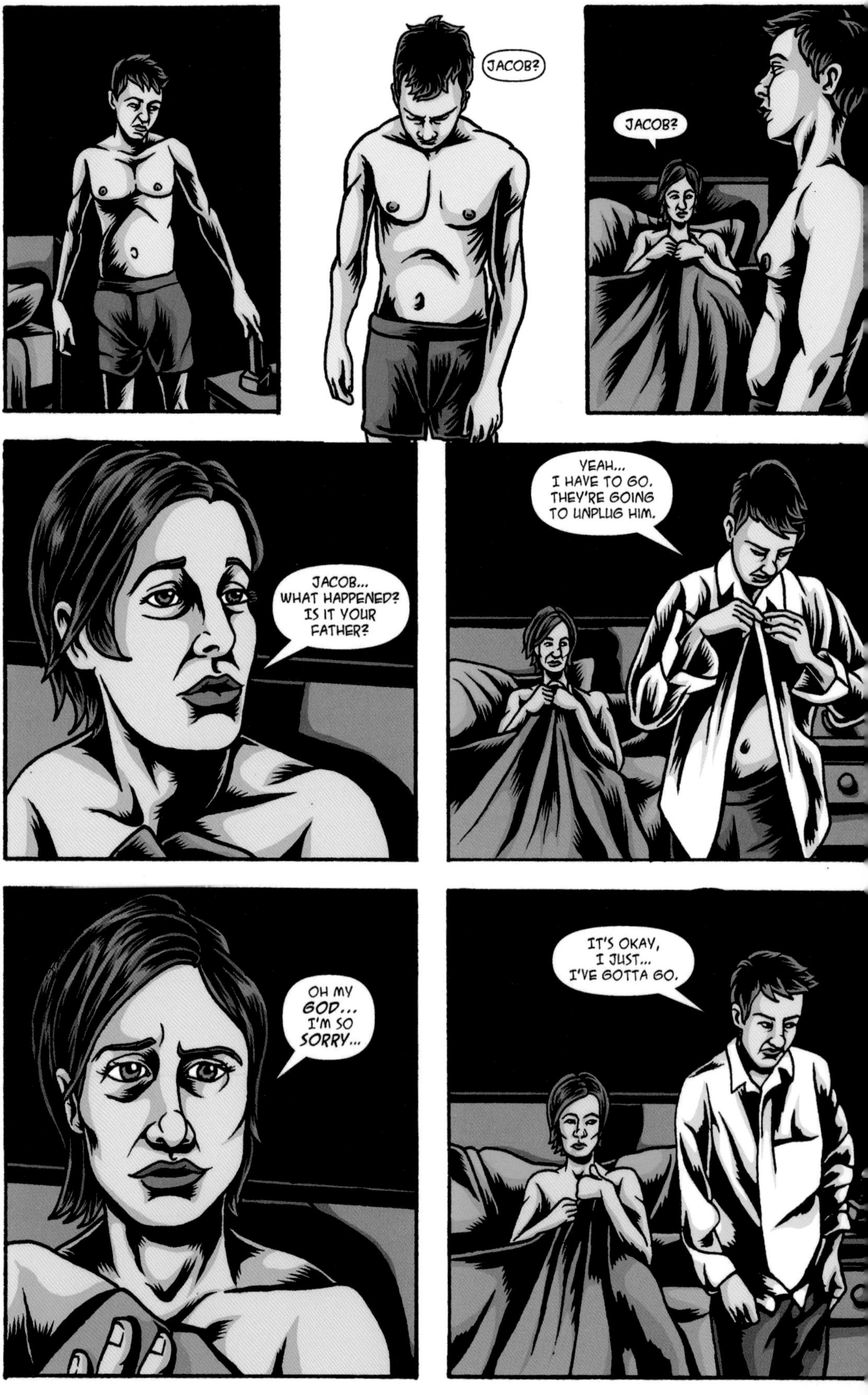
JACOB?
JACOB?
JACOB... WHAT HAPPENED? IS IT YOUR FATHER?
YEAH... I HAVE TO GO. THEY'RE GOING TO UNPLUG HIM.
OH MY GOD... I'M SO SORRY...
IT'S OKAY, I JUST... I'VE GOTTA GO.

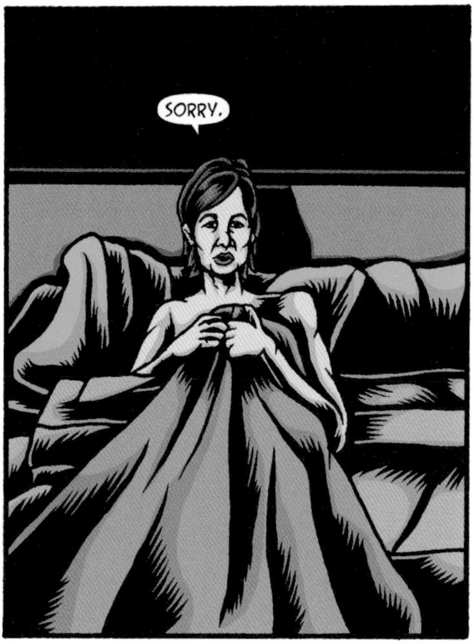
SORRY.

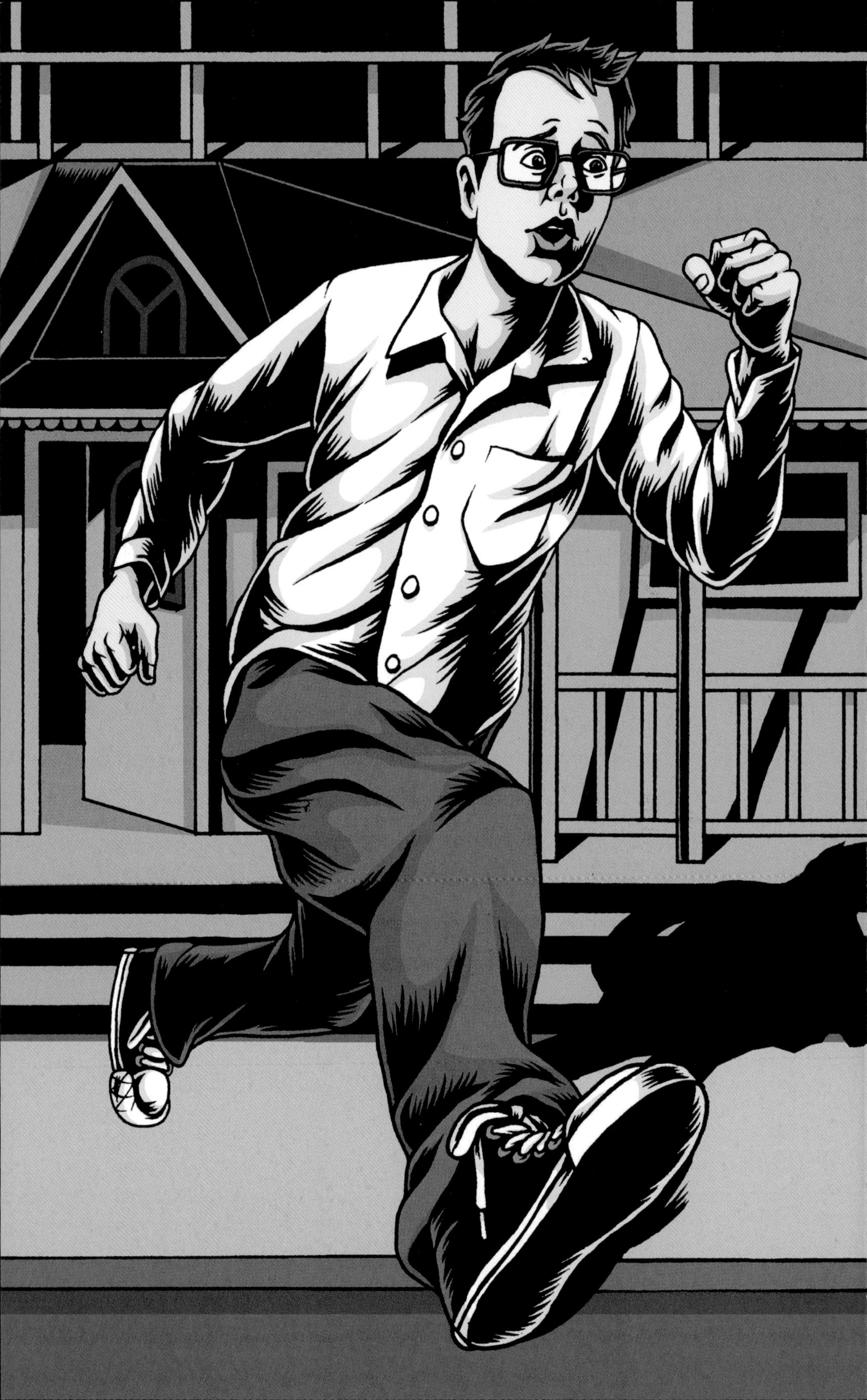

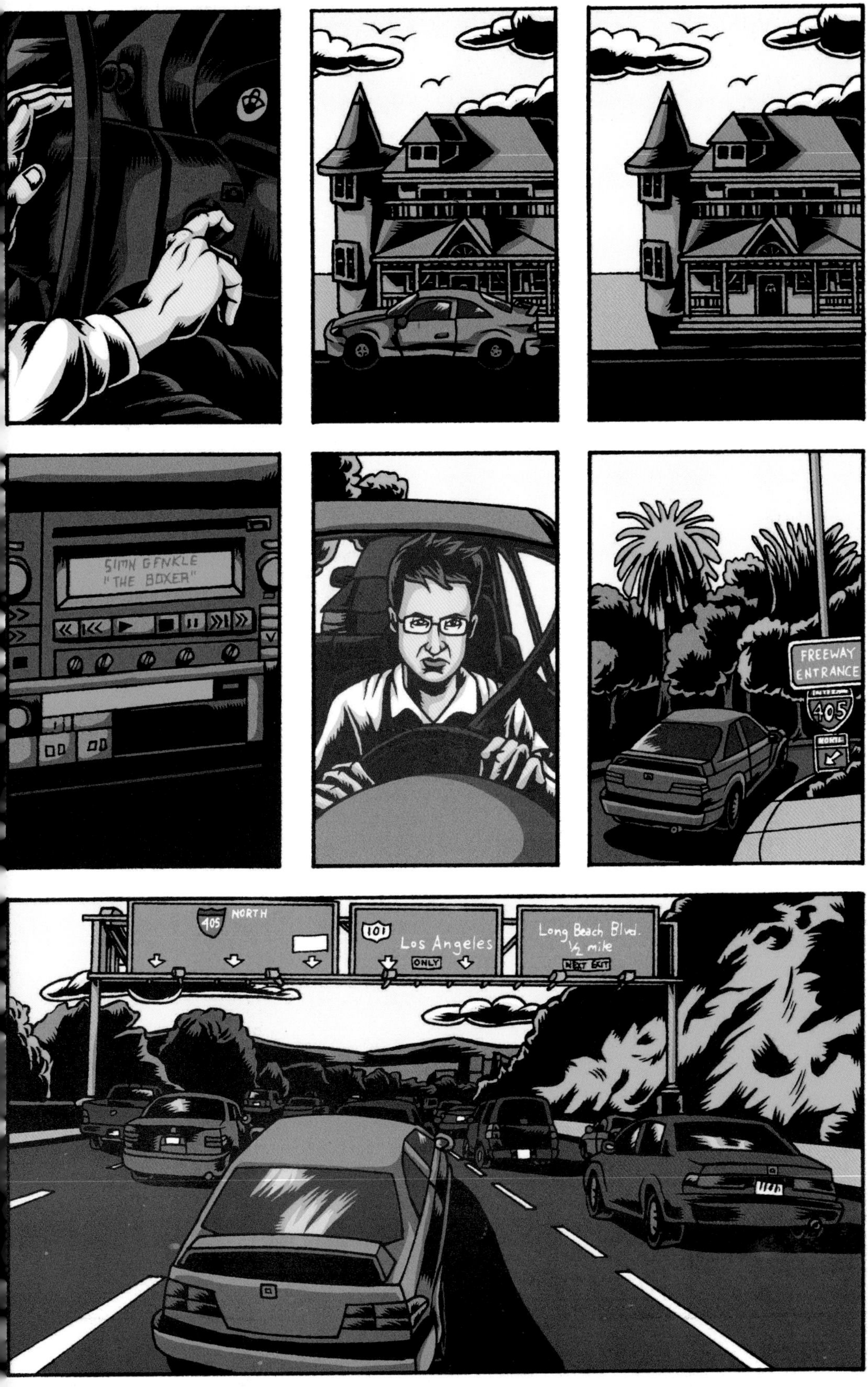
SIMN GFNKLE
"THE BOXER"
FREEWAY ENTRANCE
405
405 NORTH
101
Los Angeles
ONLY
Long Beach Blvd.
½ mile
NEXT EXIT

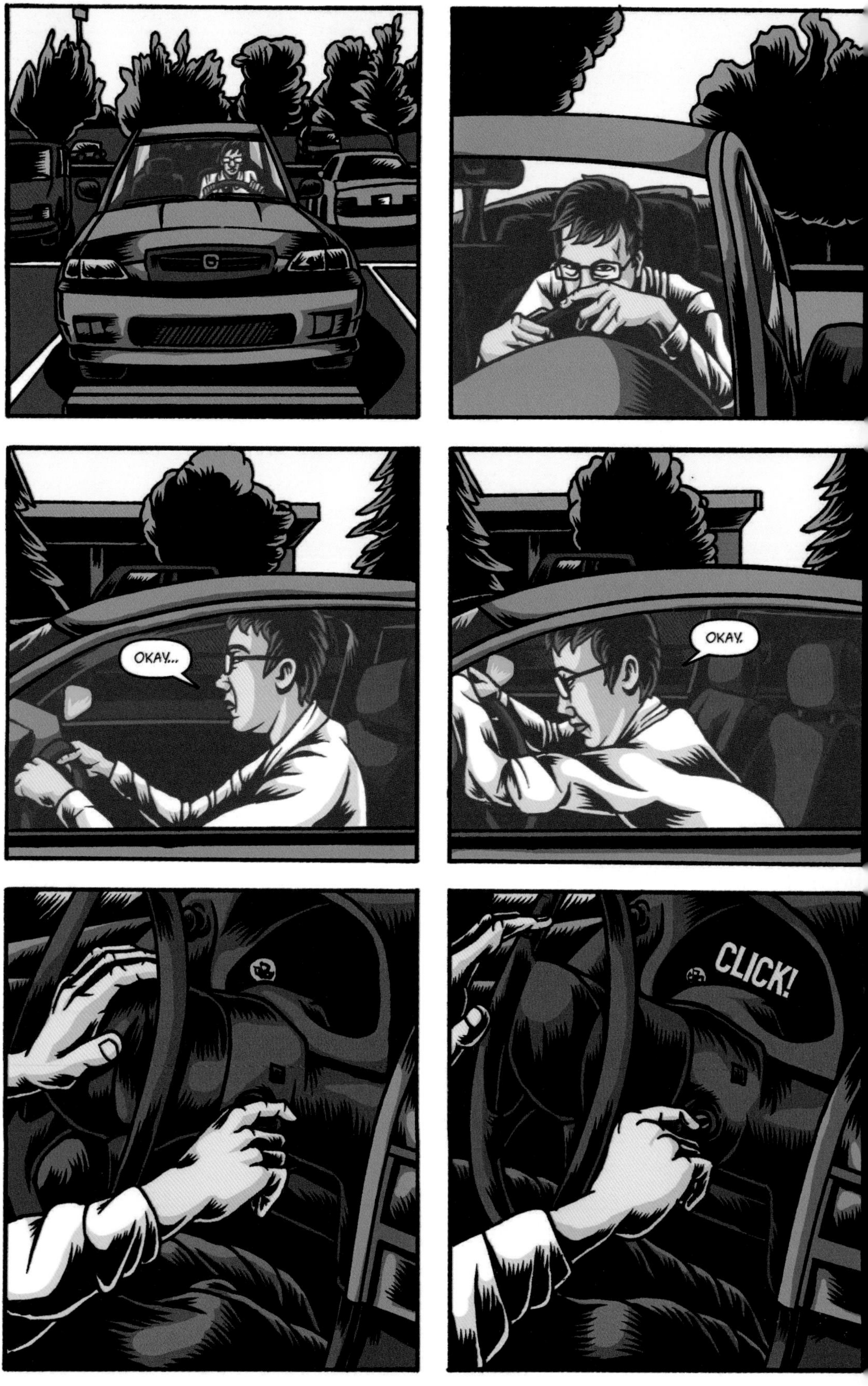
OKAY...
OKAY.
CLICK!

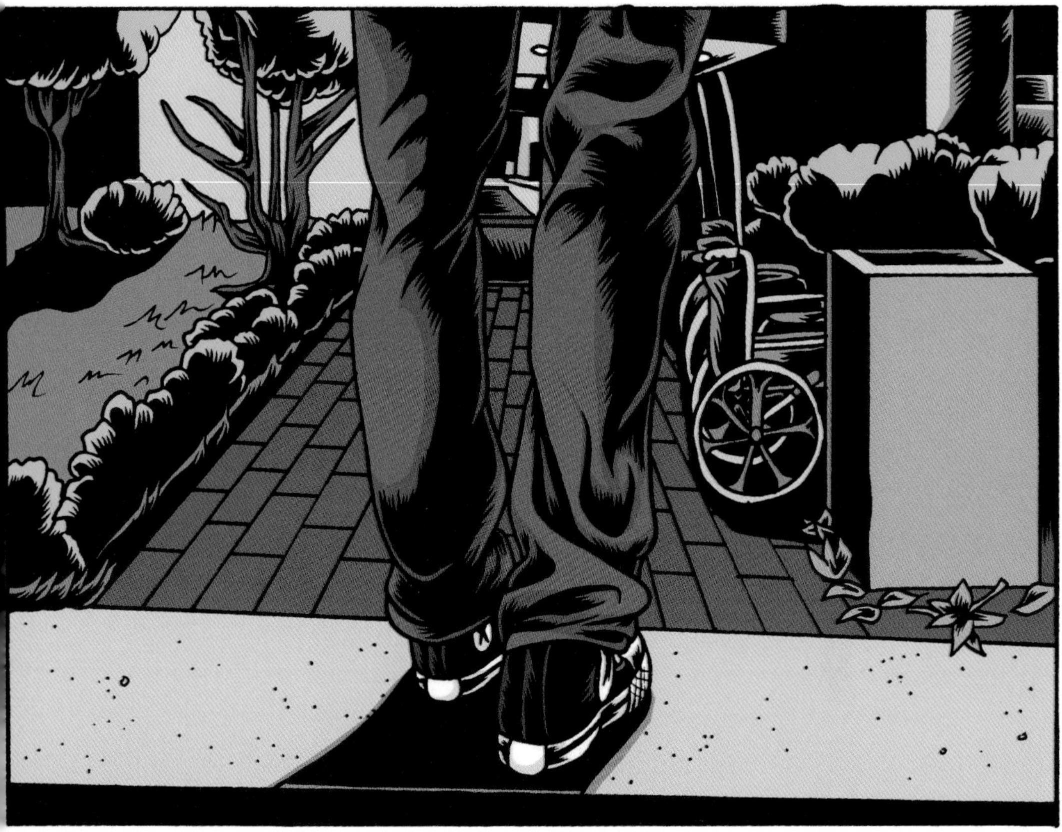
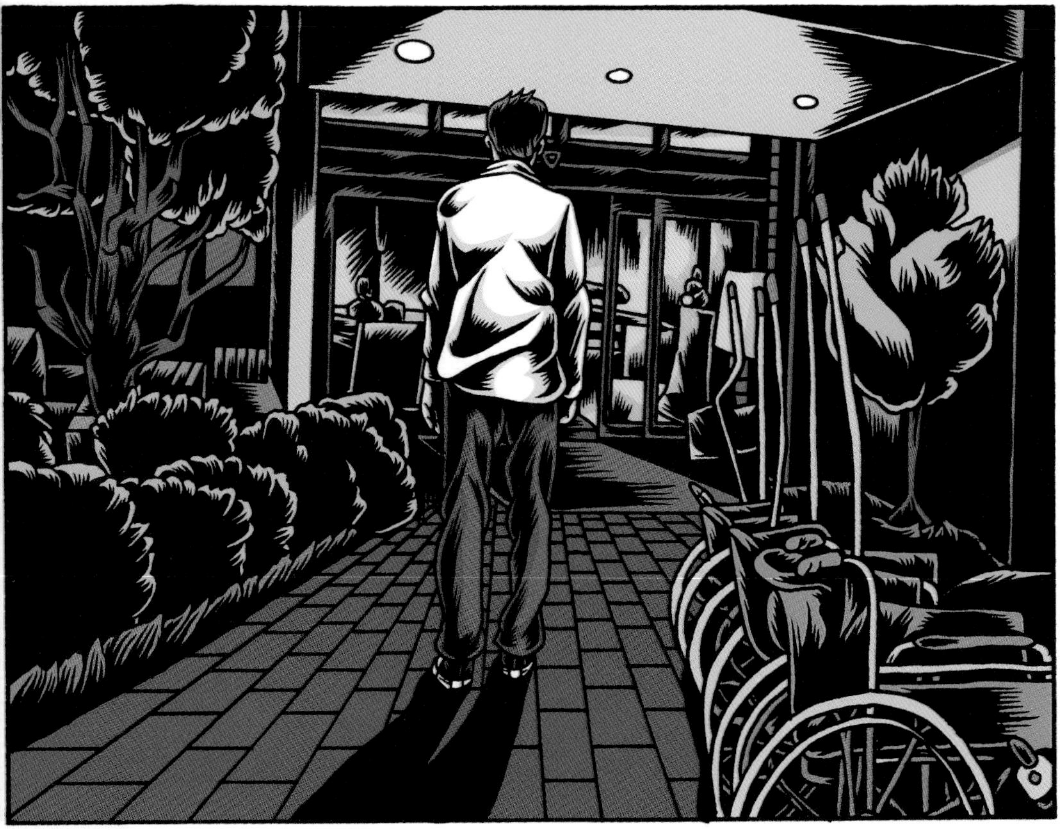

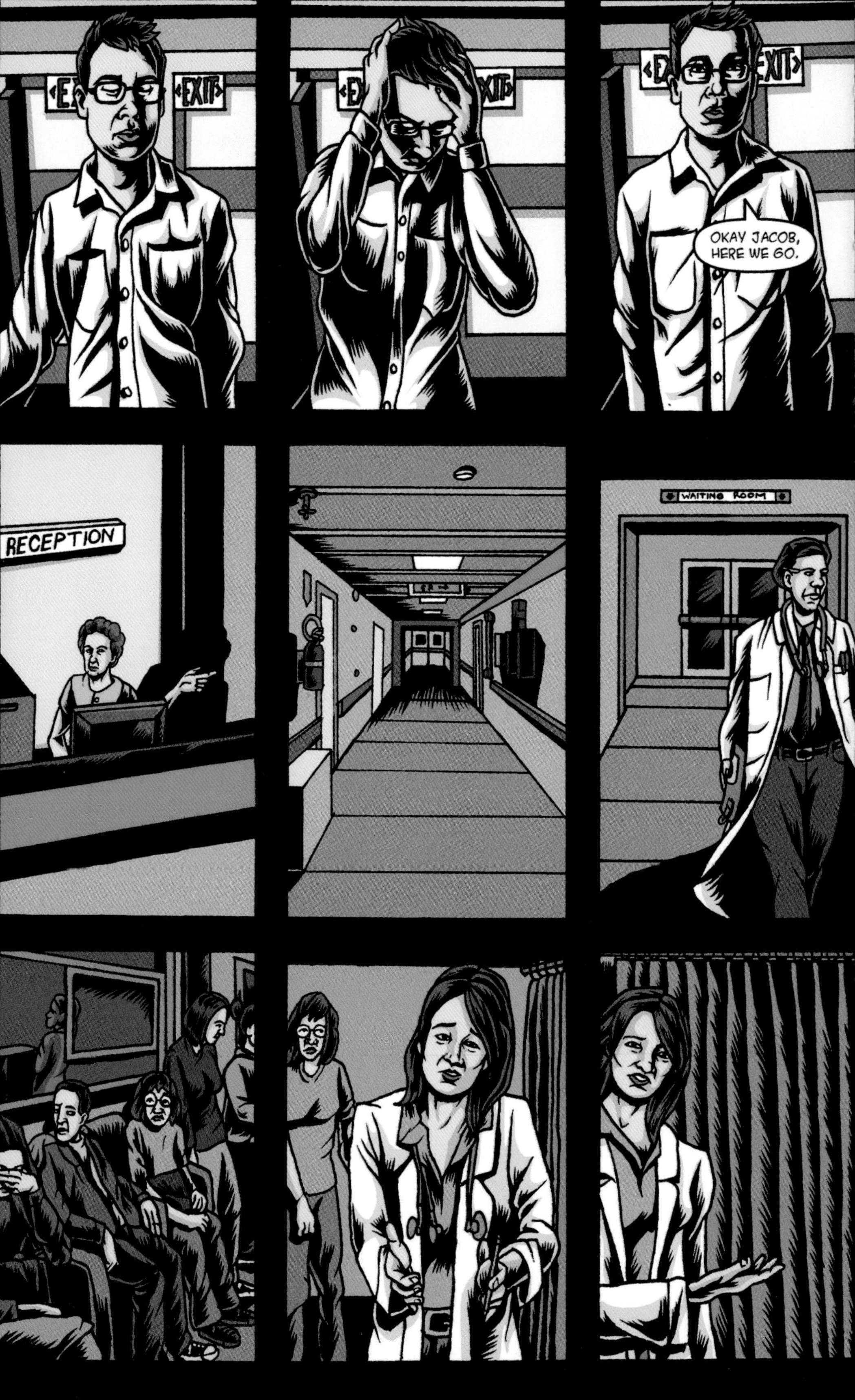
EXIT
EXIT
OKAY JACOB,
HERE WE GO.
RECEPTION
WAITING ROOM

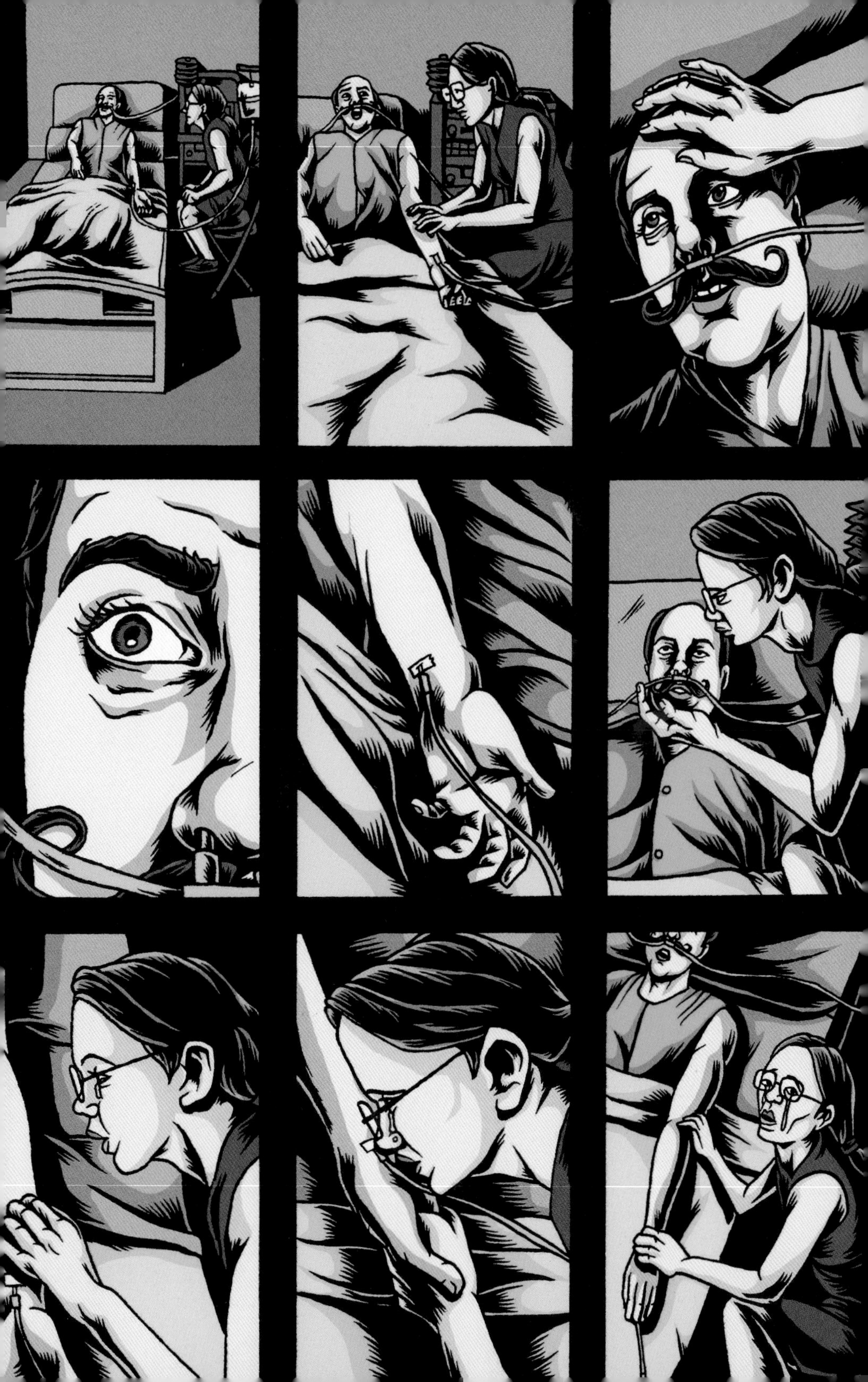

10
0 BPM

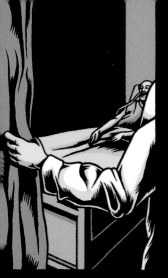

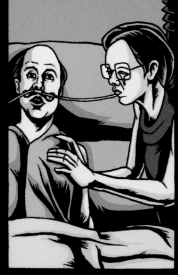

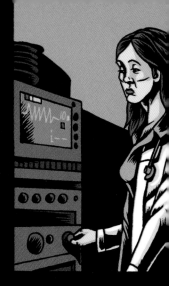

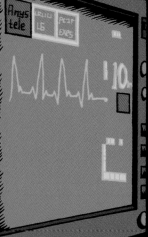

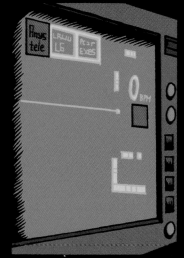

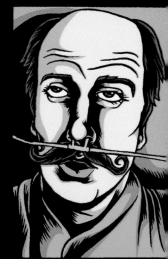

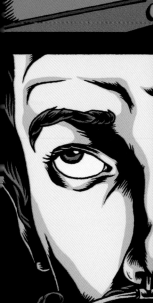

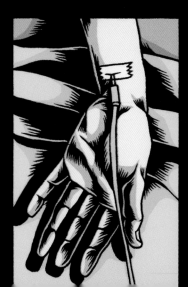

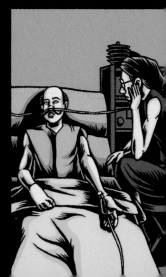

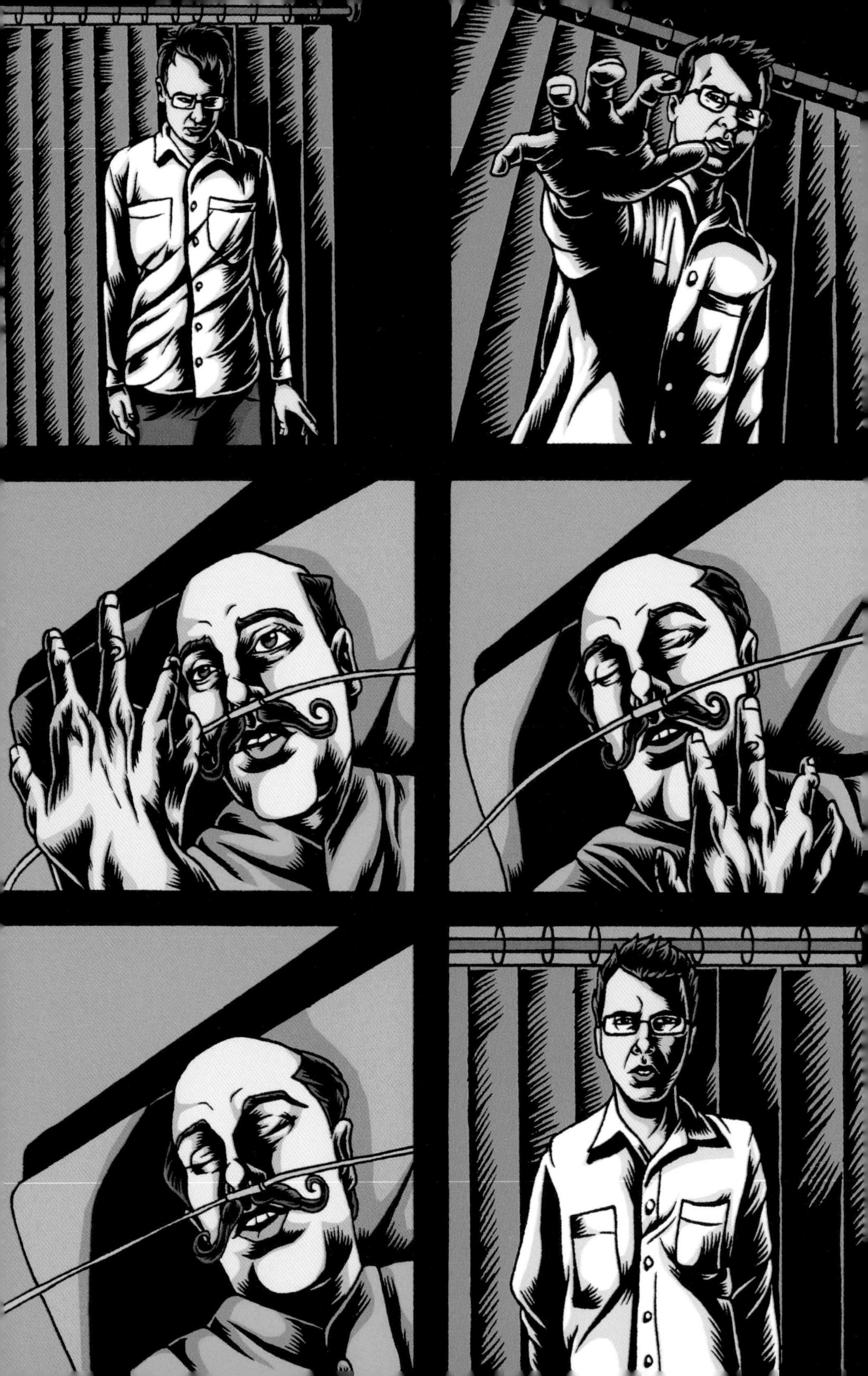

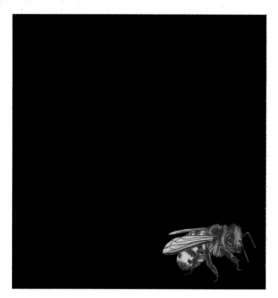

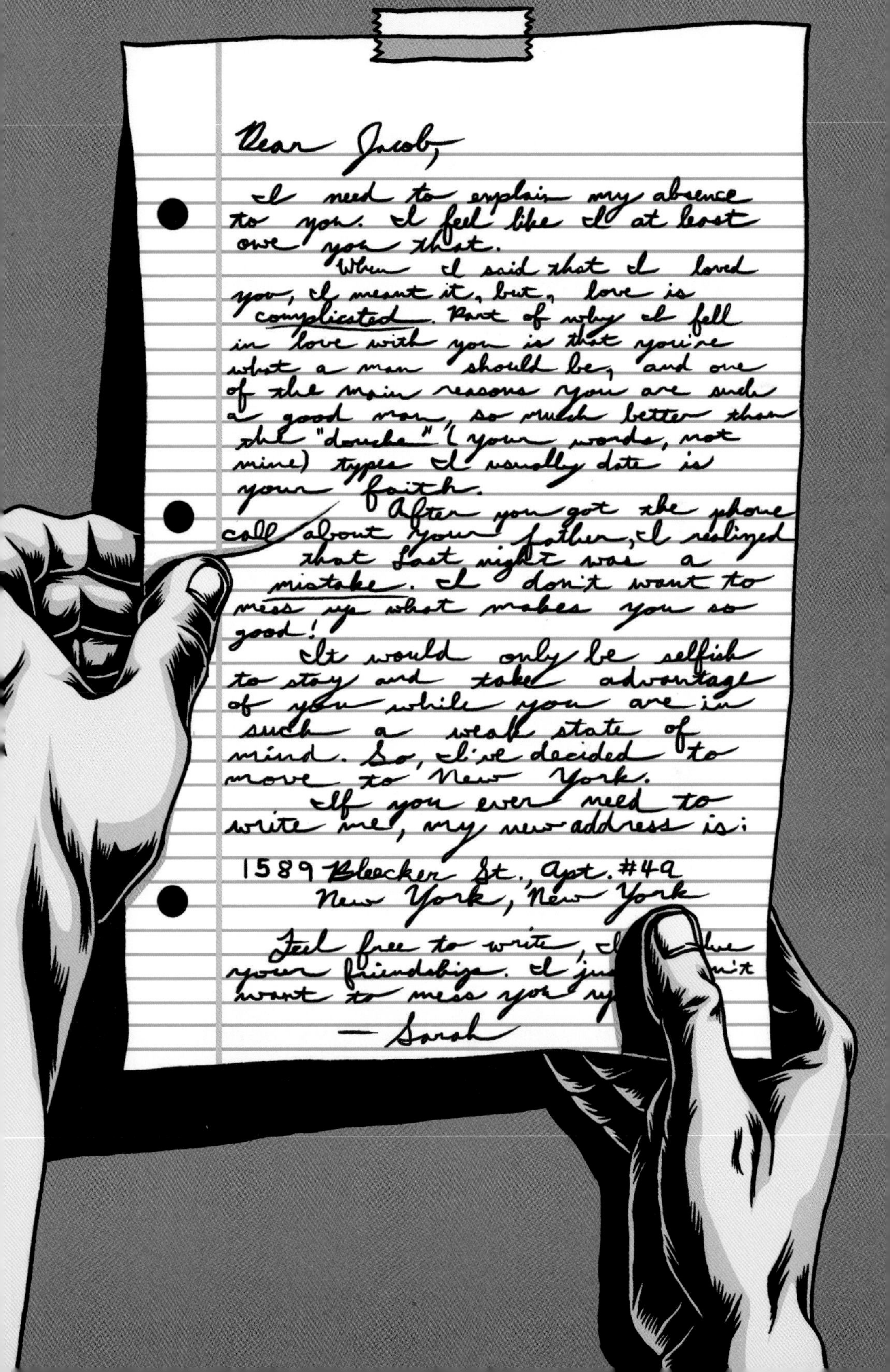

Dear Jacob,

I need to explain my absence to you. I feel like I at least owe you that.

When I said that I loved you, I meant it, but, love is complicated. Part of why I fell in love with you is that you're what a man should be, and one of the main reasons you are such a good man, so much better than the "douche" (your words, not mine) types I usually date is your faith.

After you got the phone call about your father, I realized that last night was a mistake. I don't want to mess up what makes you so good!

It would only be selfish to stay and take advantage of you while you are in such a weak state of mind. So, I've decided to move to New York.

If you ever need to write me, my new address is:

1589 Bleecker St., Apt. #49
New York, New York

Feel free to write, I ... lue your friendship. I ju... n't want to mess you u...

— Sarah

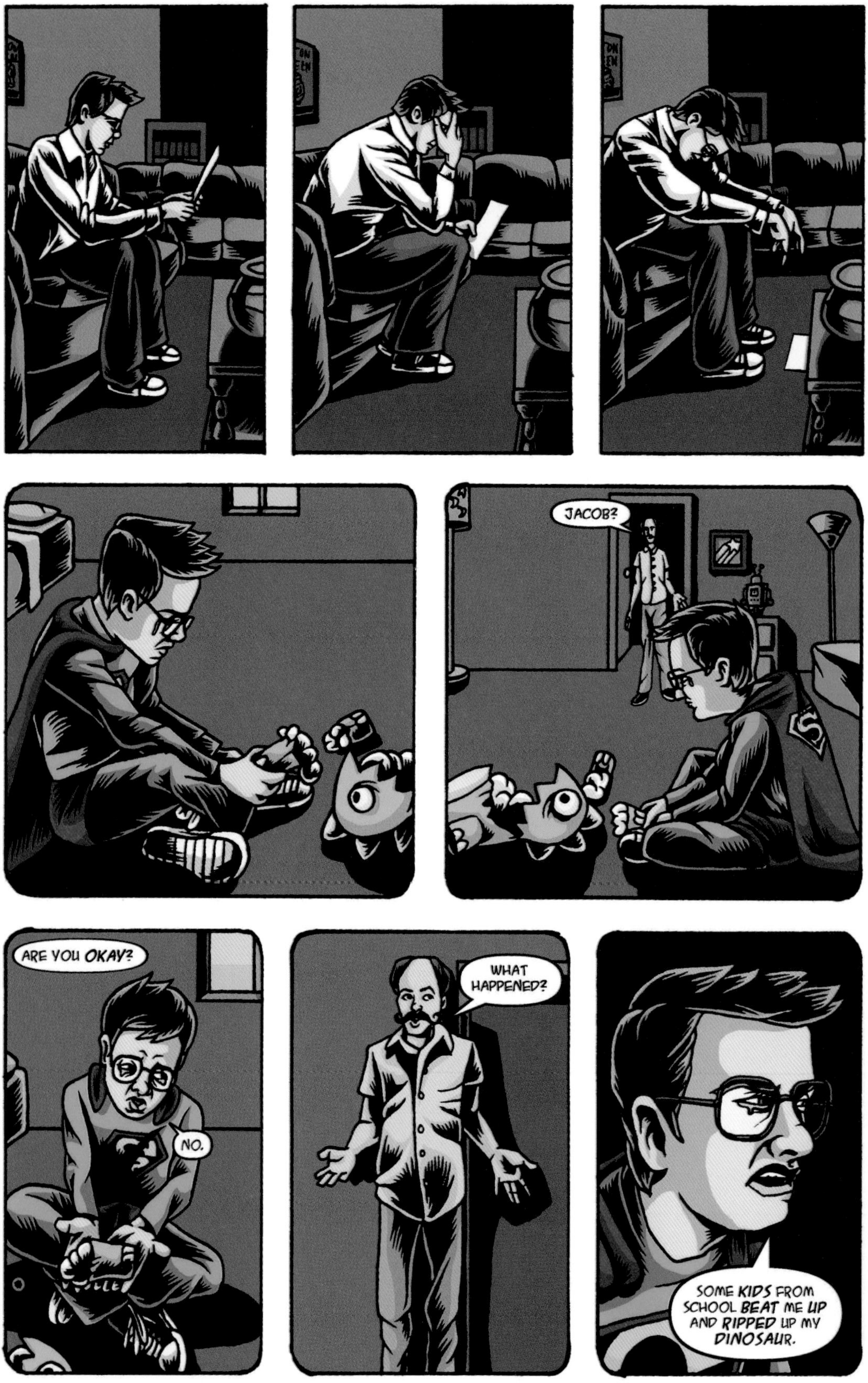
JACOB?
ARE YOU OKAY?
NO.
WHAT HAPPENED?
SOME KIDS FROM SCHOOL BEAT ME UP AND RIPPED UP MY DINOSAUR.

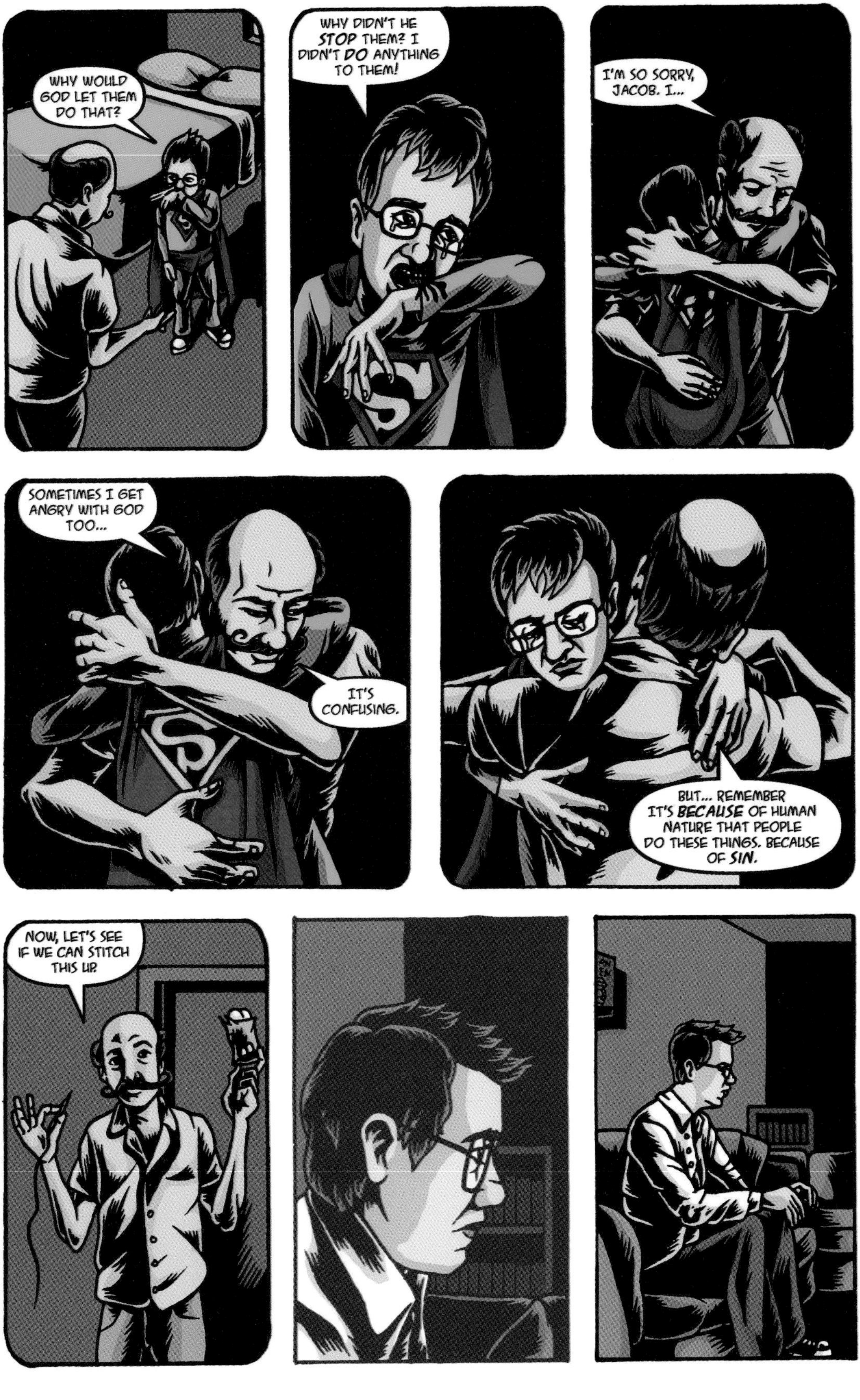
WHY WOULD GOD LET THEM DO THAT?
WHY DIDN'T HE STOP THEM? I DIDN'T DO ANYTHING TO THEM!
I'M SO SORRY, JACOB. I...
SOMETIMES I GET ANGRY WITH GOD TOO...
IT'S CONFUSING.
BUT... REMEMBER IT'S BECAUSE OF HUMAN NATURE THAT PEOPLE DO THESE THINGS. BECAUSE OF SIN.
NOW, LET'S SEE IF WE CAN STITCH THIS UP.

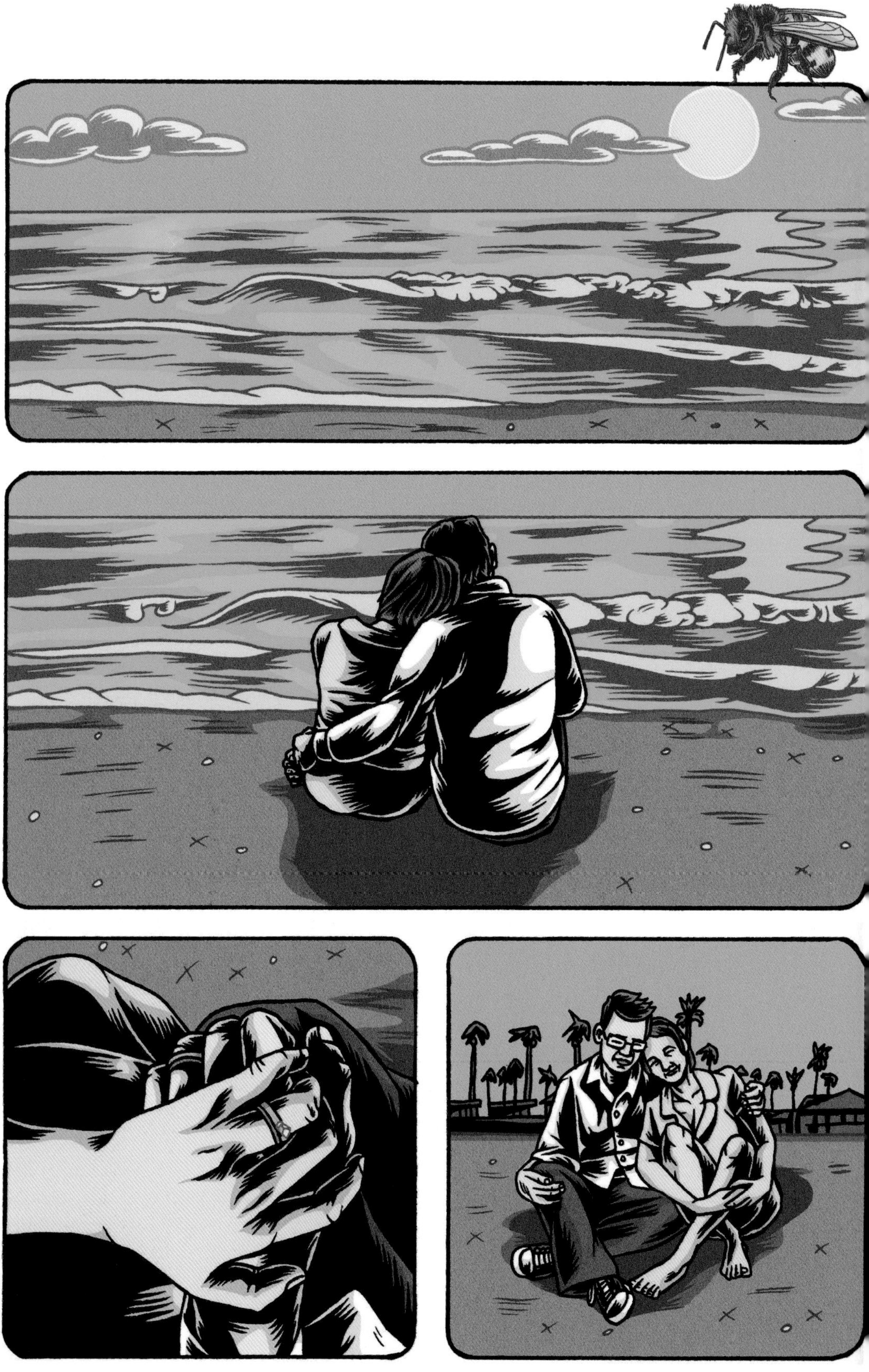

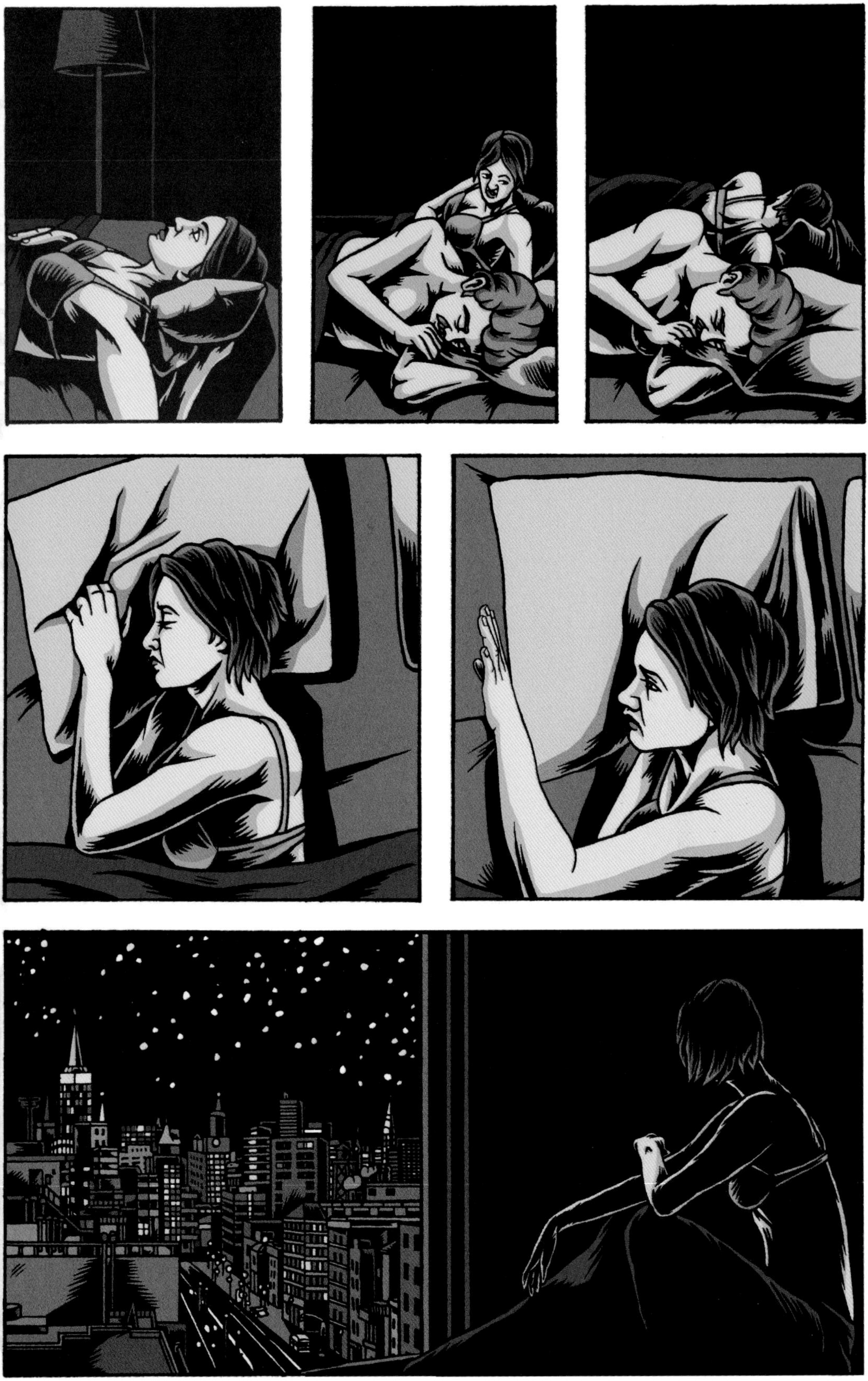

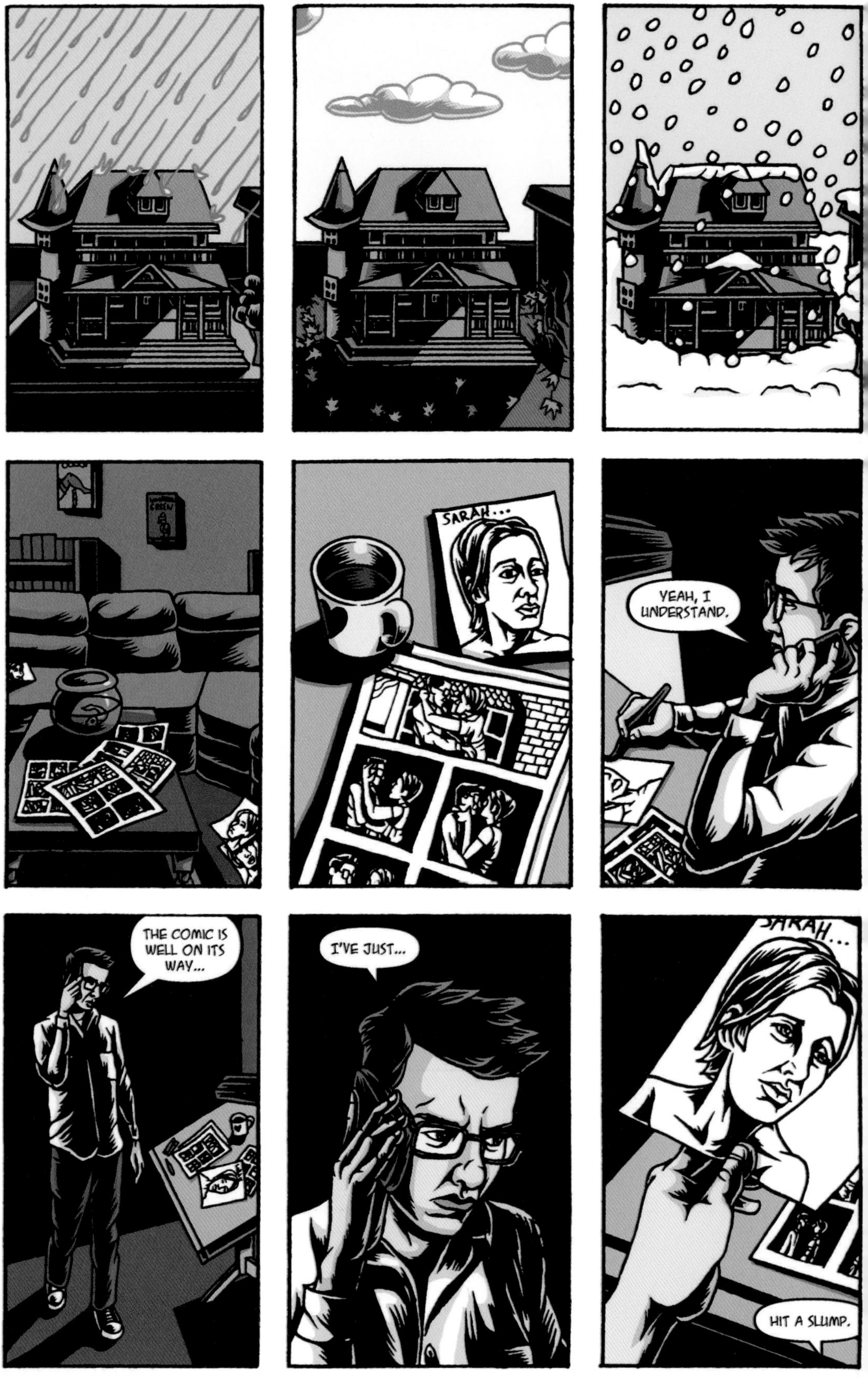
SARAH...
YEAH, I UNDERSTAND.
THE COMIC IS WELL ON ITS WAY...
I'VE JUST...
SARAH...
HIT A SLUMP.

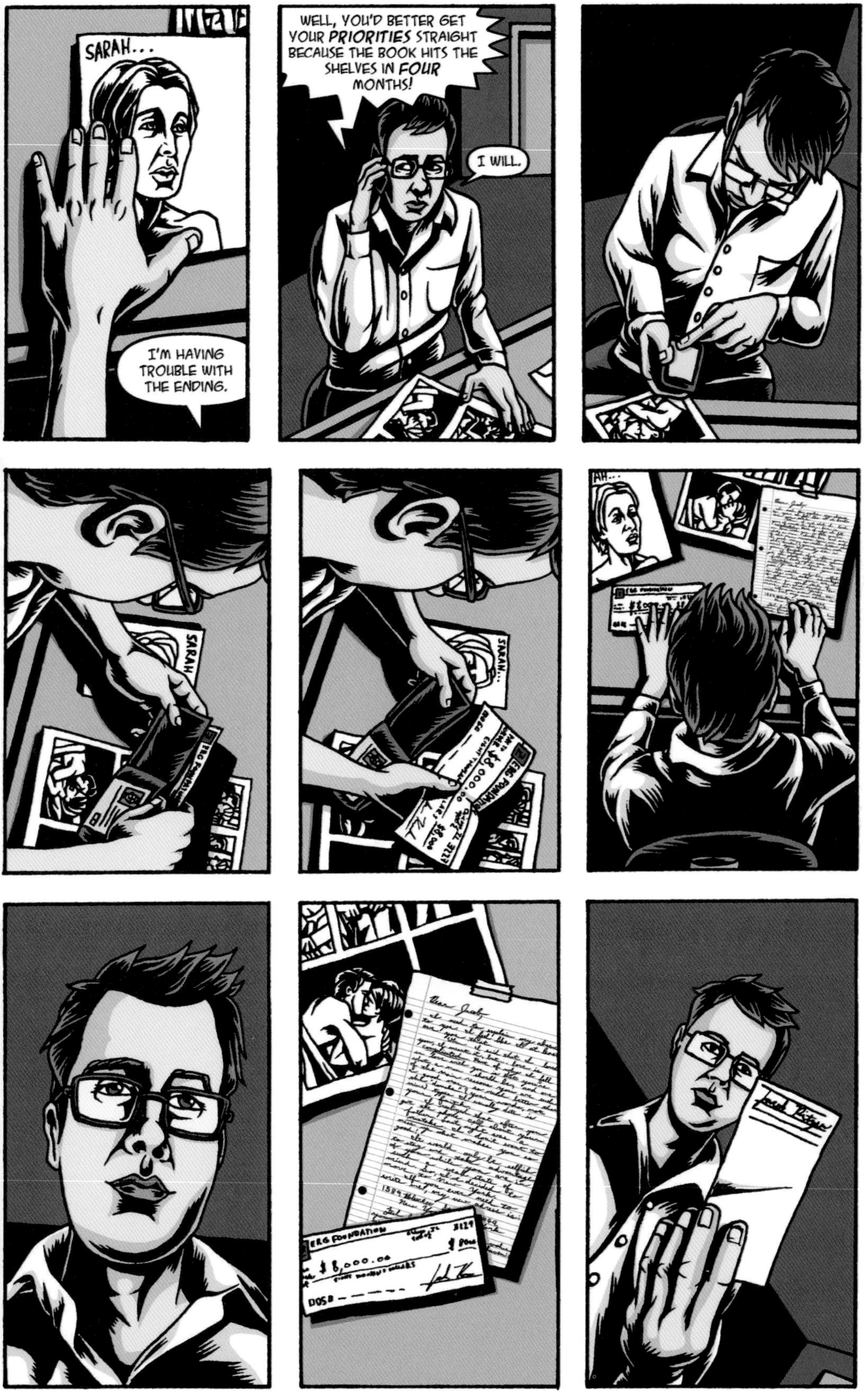
SARAH...
I'M HAVING TROUBLE WITH THE ENDING.
WELL, YOU'D BETTER GET YOUR PRIORITIES STRAIGHT BECAUSE THE BOOK HITS THE SHELVES IN FOUR MONTHS!
I WILL.
SARAH
SARAH...
ERG FOUNDATION
$8,000.00

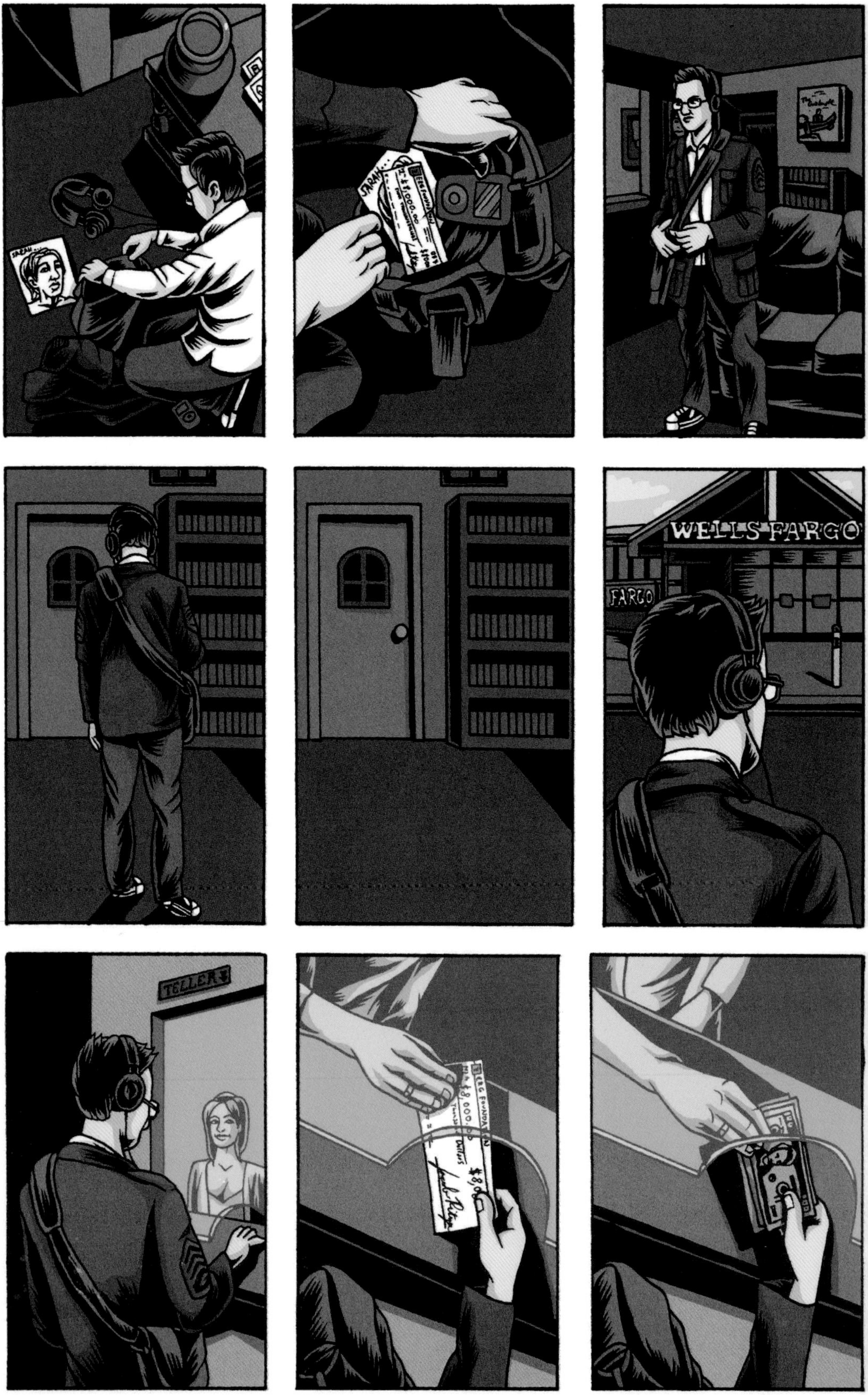
SARAH...
WELLS FARGO
FARGO
TELLER

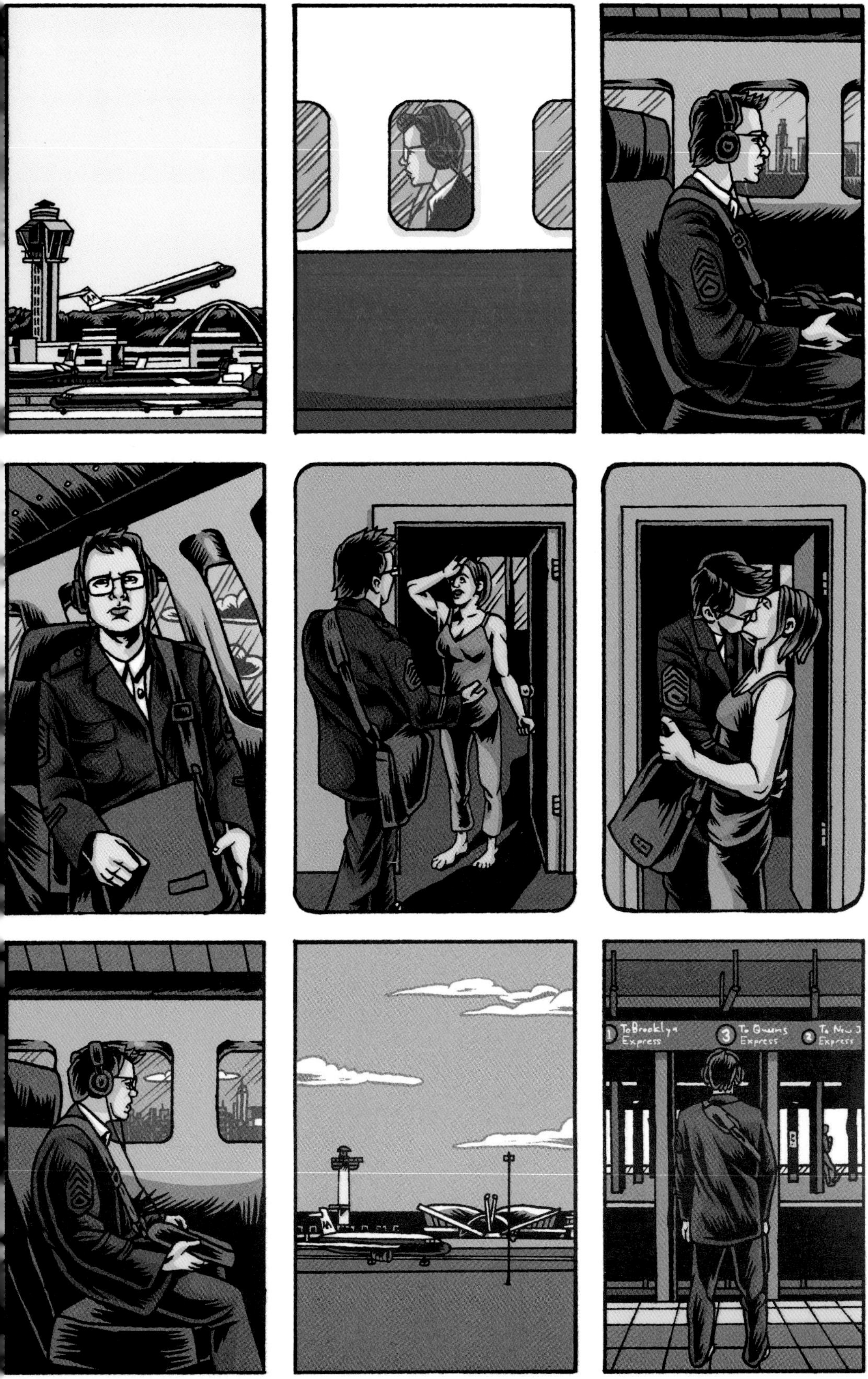
1 ToBrooklyn Express
3 To Queens Express
2 To New J Express

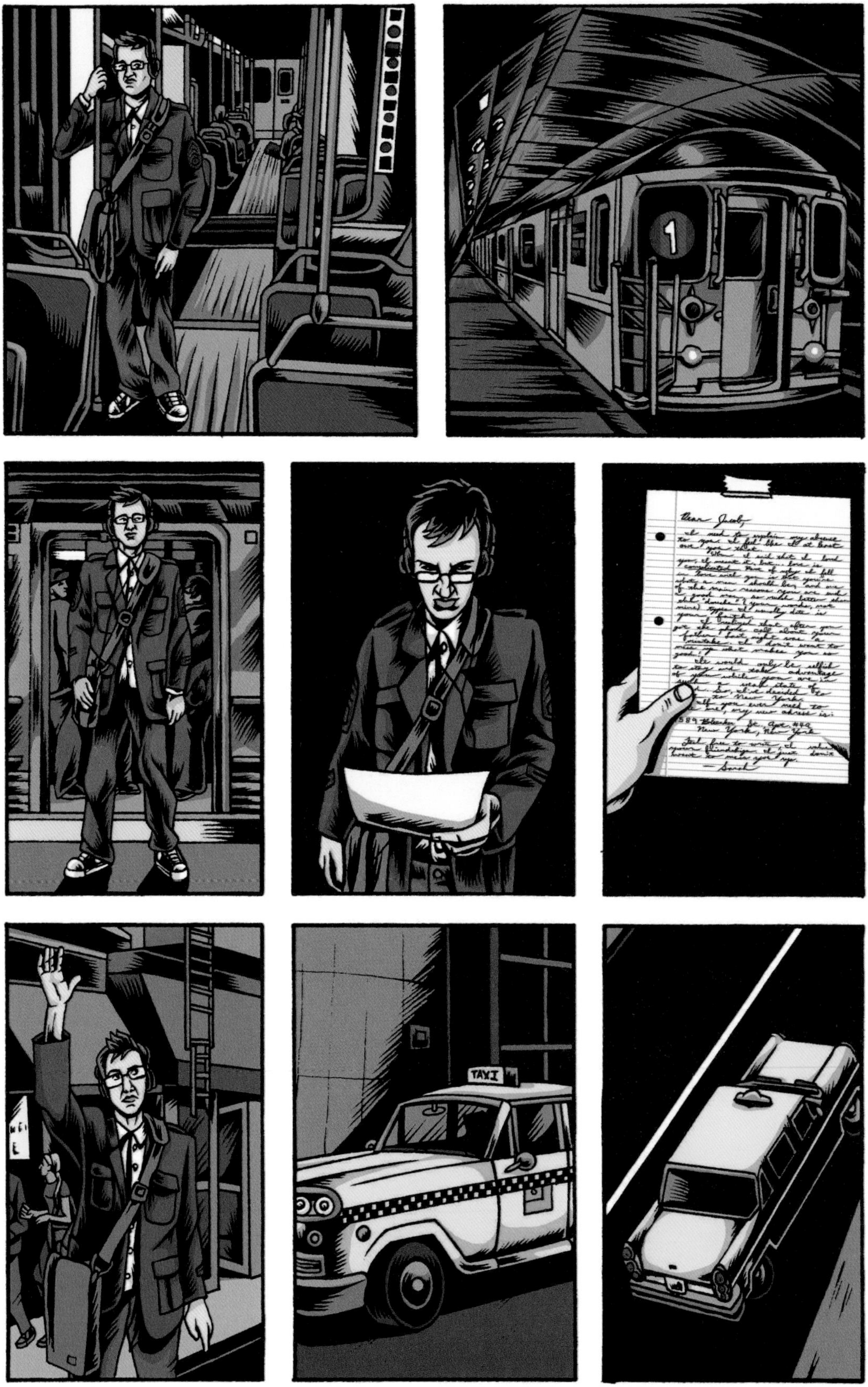
1
Dear Jacob,
I need to explain my absence to you. I feel like I at least owe you that.
When I said that I loved you, I meant it, but... love is complicated.
It would only be selfish to stay and take advantage of you while you are in such a weak state of
589 Bleecker St. Apt. #4Q
New York, New York
Feel free to write, I value your friendship. I just don't want to mess you up.
— Sarah
TAXI

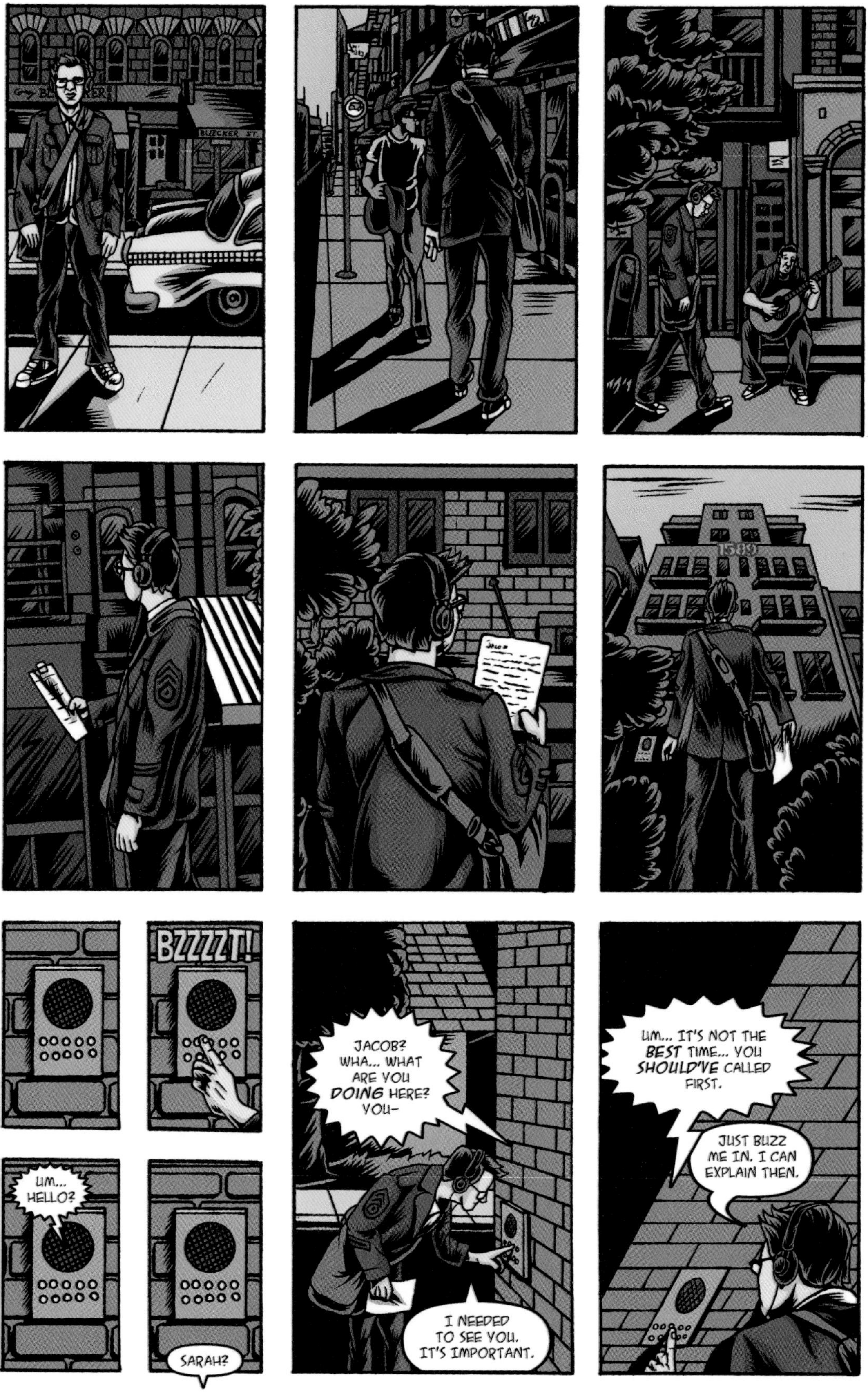
BLEECKER
BLEECKER ST.
1589
BZZZZT!
UM... HELLO?
SARAH?
JACOB? WHA... WHAT ARE YOU DOING HERE? YOU-
I NEEDED TO SEE YOU. IT'S IMPORTANT.
UM... IT'S NOT THE BEST TIME... YOU SHOULD'VE CALLED FIRST.
JUST BUZZ ME IN. I CAN EXPLAIN THEN.

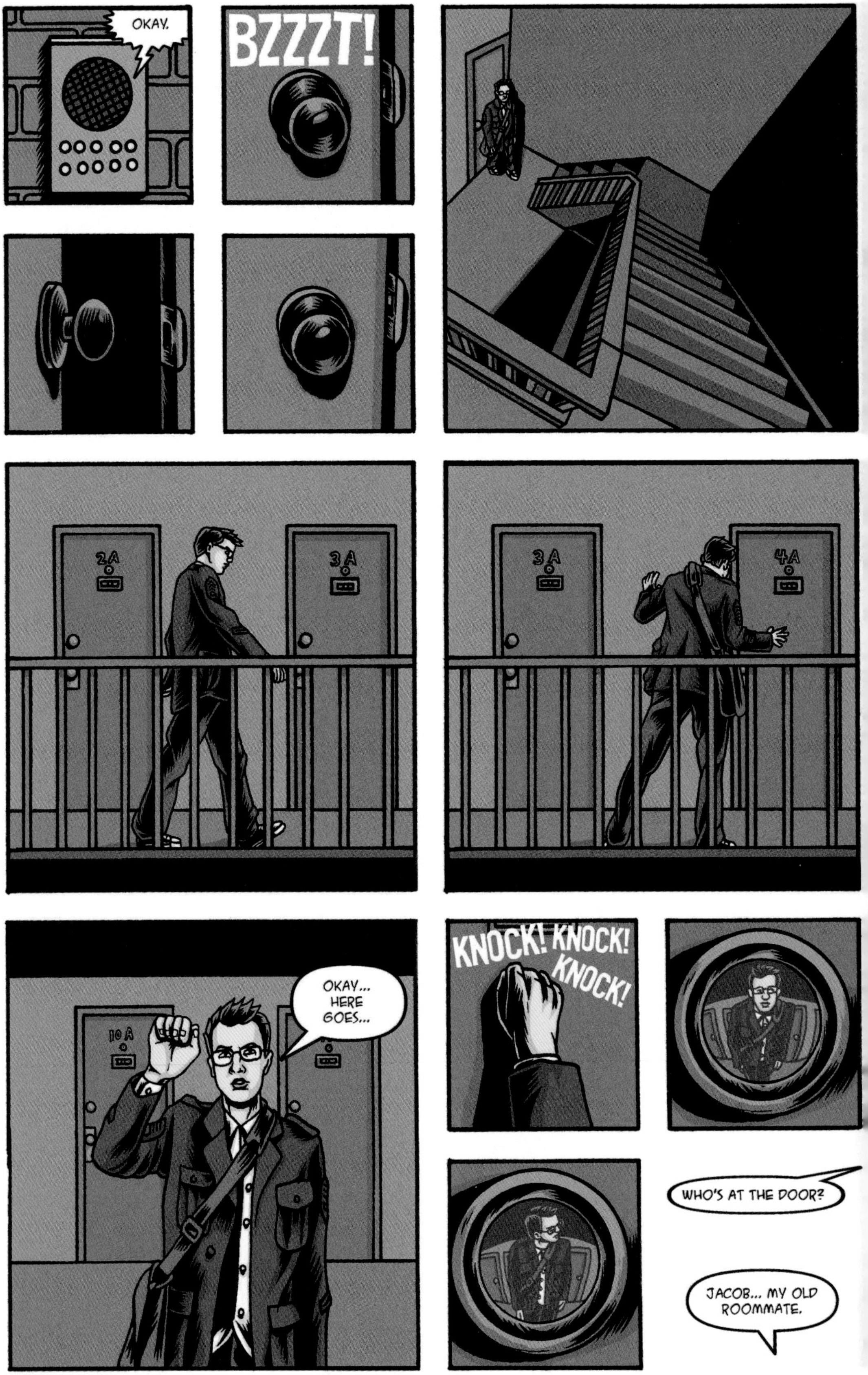
OKAY.
BZZZT!
OKAY... HERE GOES...
KNOCK! KNOCK! KNOCK!
WHO'S AT THE DOOR?
JACOB... MY OLD ROOMMATE.

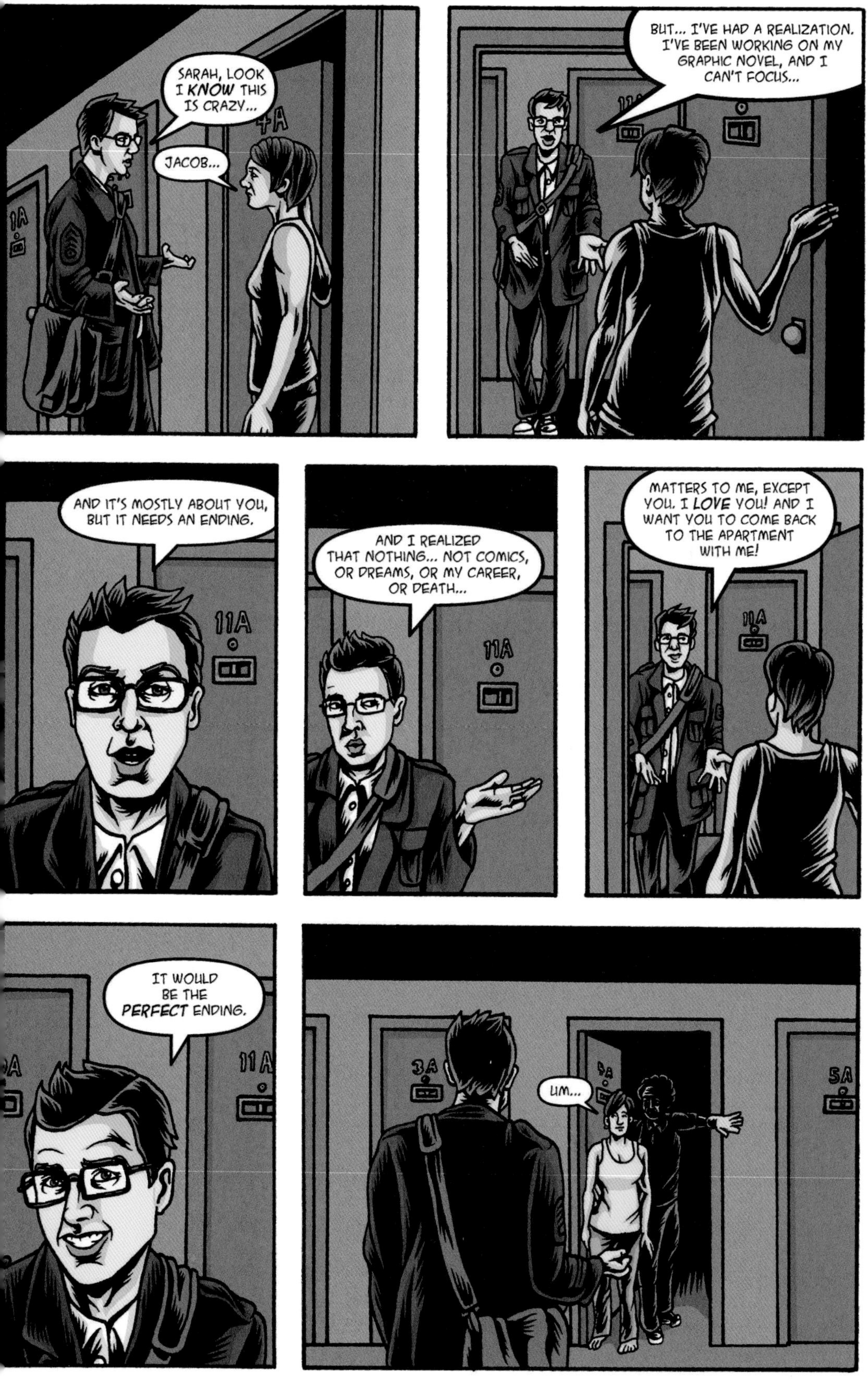
SARAH, LOOK I KNOW THIS IS CRAZY...
JACOB...
BUT... I'VE HAD A REALIZATION. I'VE BEEN WORKING ON MY GRAPHIC NOVEL, AND I CAN'T FOCUS...
AND IT'S MOSTLY ABOUT YOU, BUT IT NEEDS AN ENDING.
AND I REALIZED THAT NOTHING... NOT COMICS, OR DREAMS, OR MY CAREER, OR DEATH...
MATTERS TO ME, EXCEPT YOU. I LOVE YOU! AND I WANT YOU TO COME BACK TO THE APARTMENT WITH ME!
IT WOULD BE THE PERFECT ENDING.
UM...

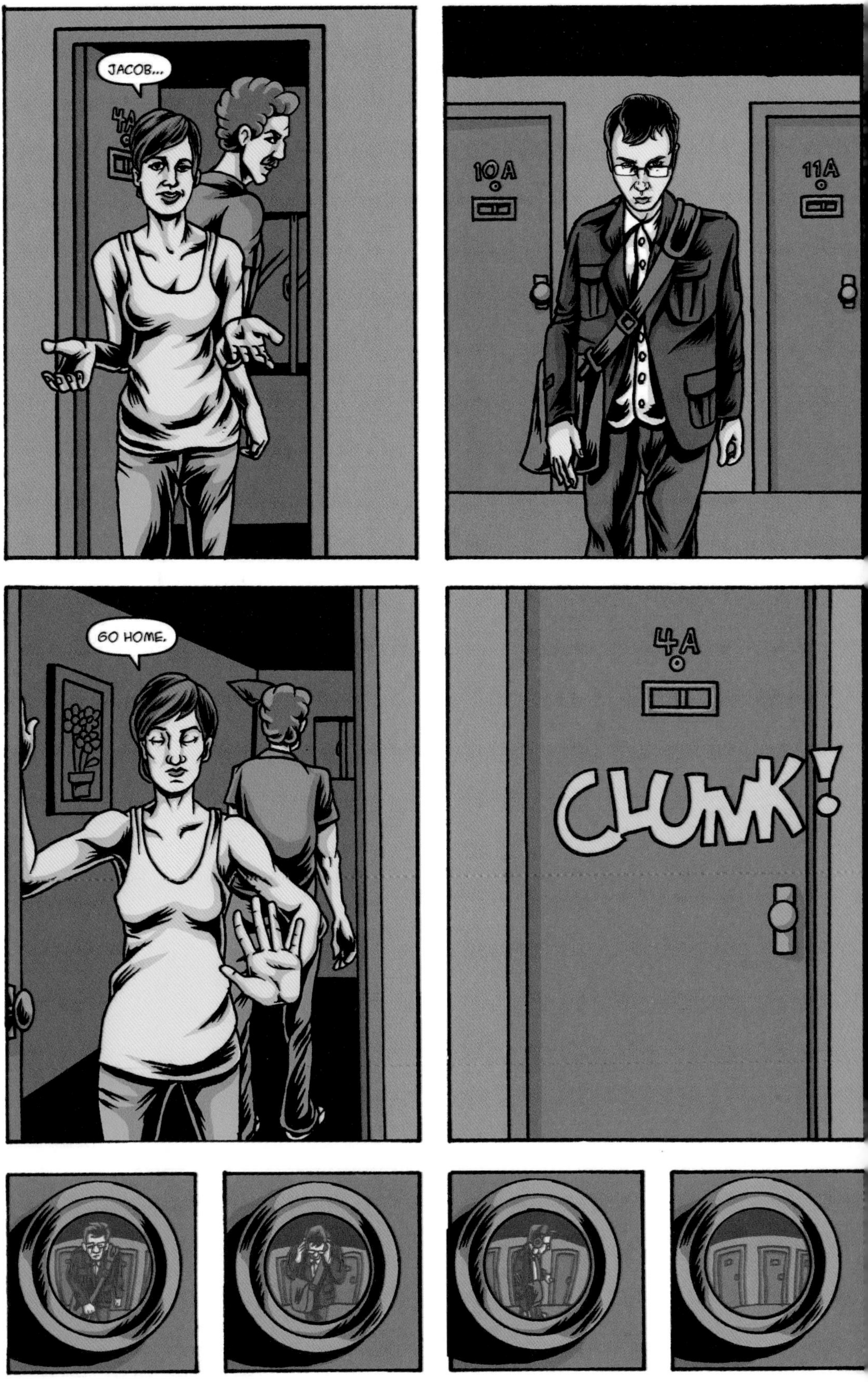
JACOB...
GO HOME.
4A
CLUNK!

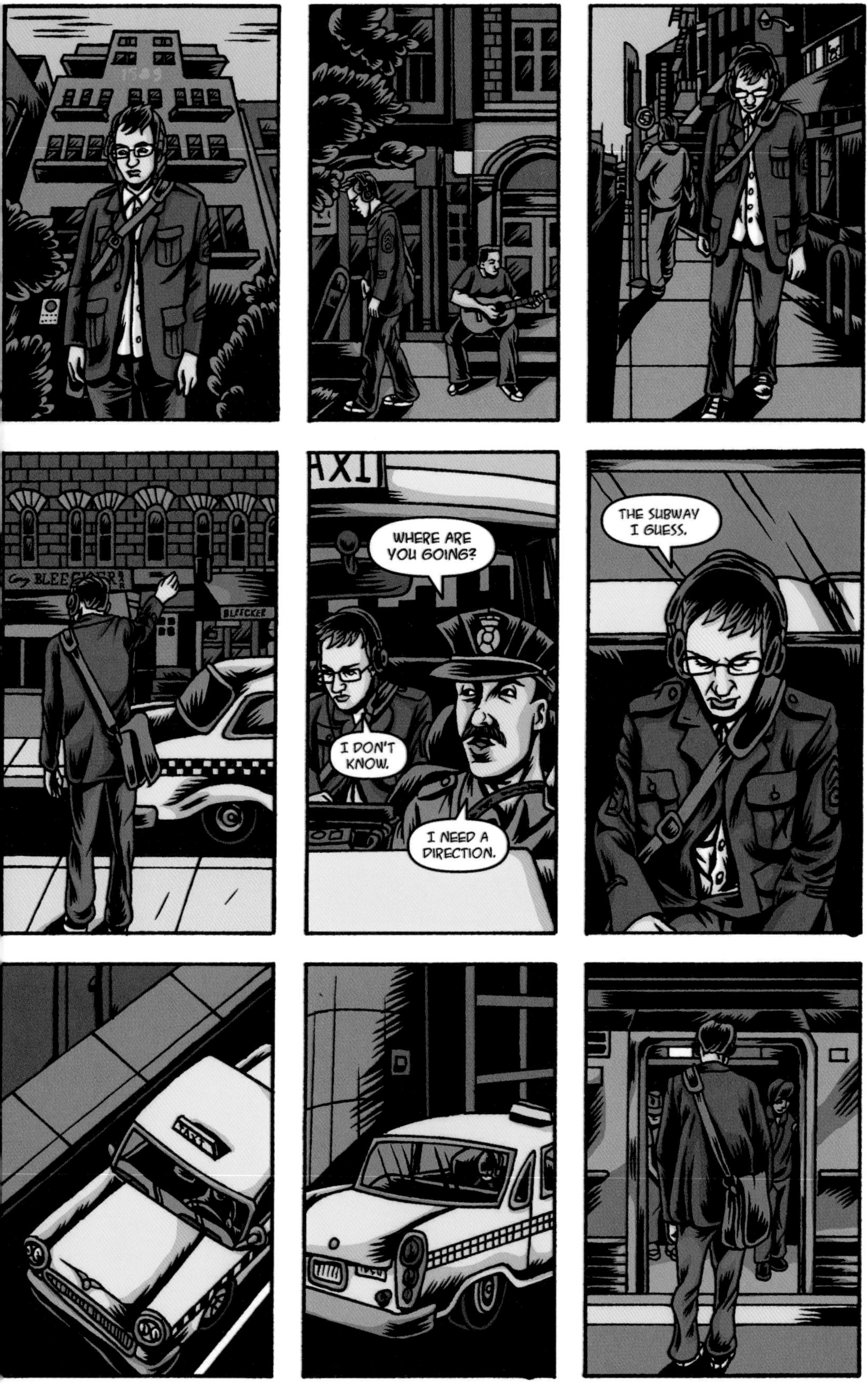
BLEECKER
WHERE ARE YOU GOING?
I DON'T KNOW.
I NEED A DIRECTION.
THE SUBWAY I GUESS.

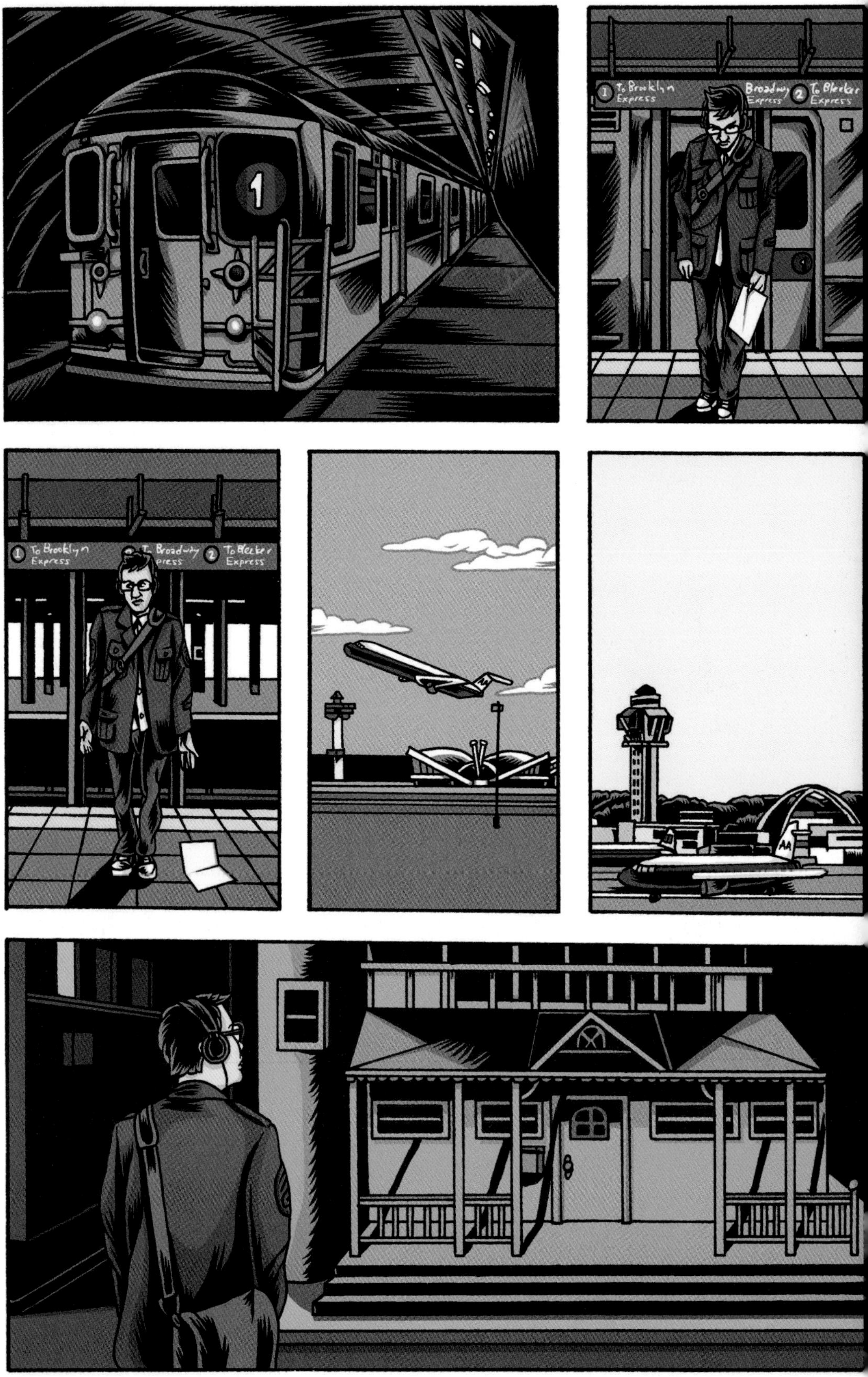
1
1 To Brooklyn Express
Broadway Express
2 To Bleeker Express
1 To Brooklyn Express
2 To Bleeker Express
AA
AA

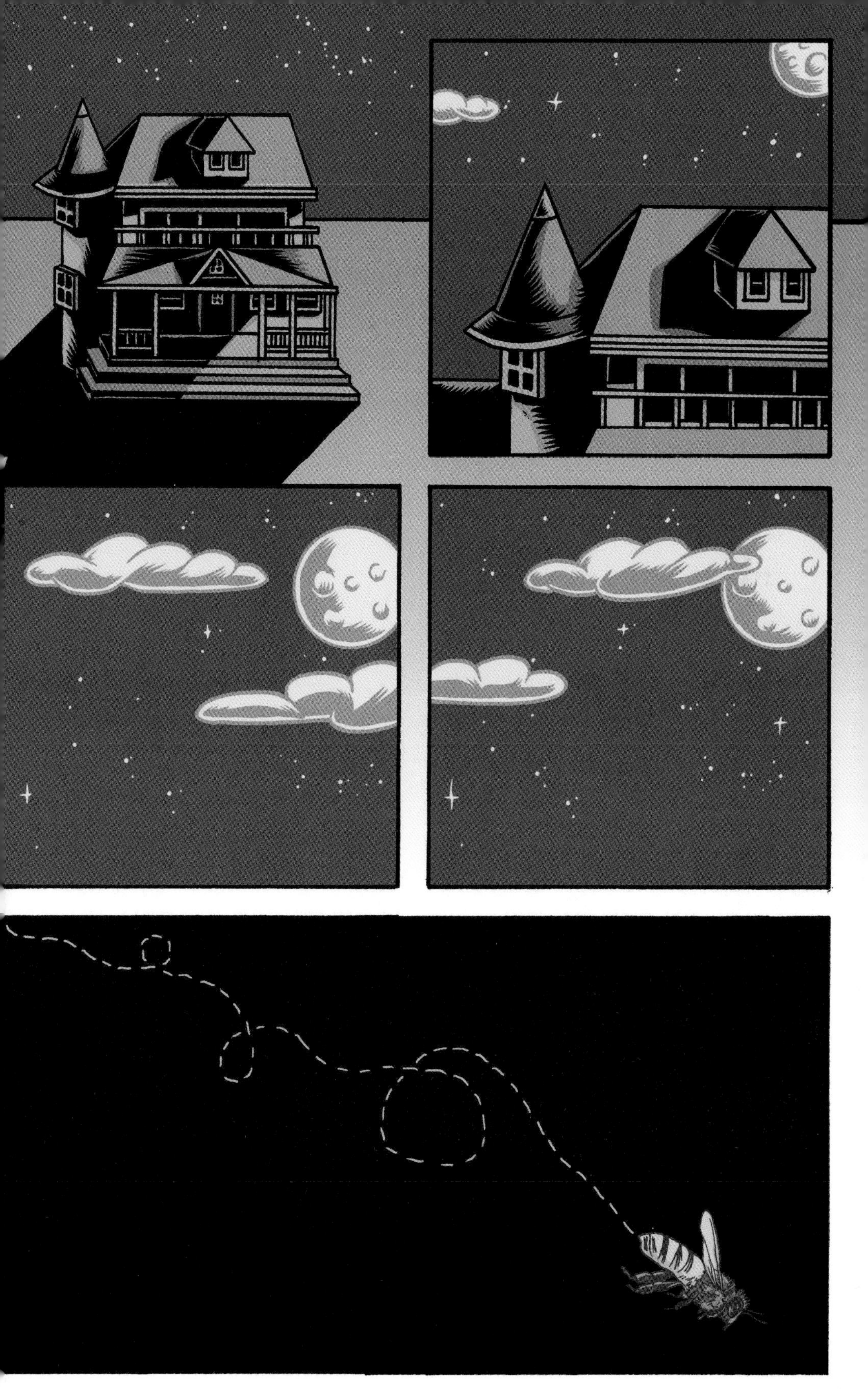

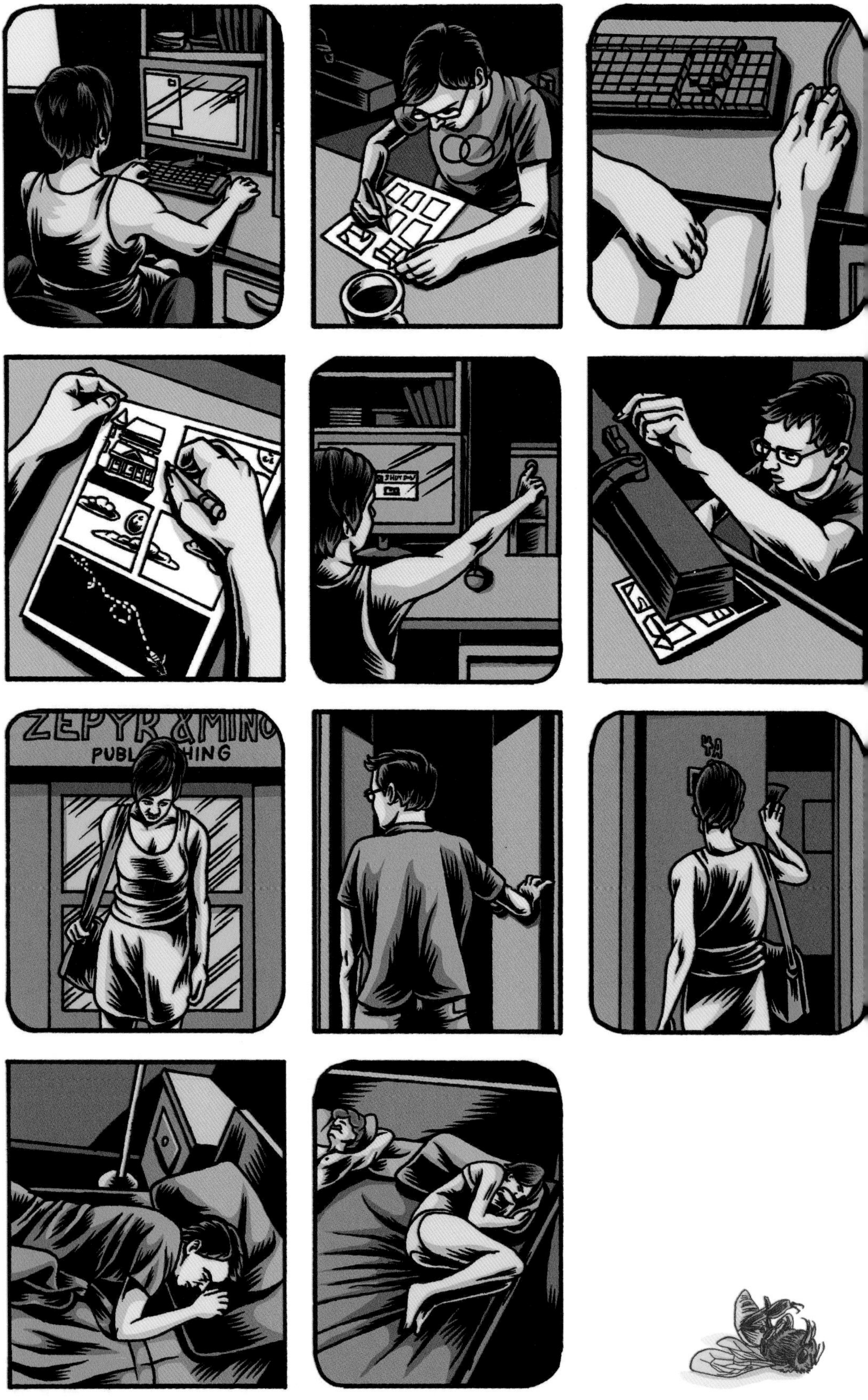
ZEPYR&MINO
PUBL HING
4A

DEDICATION

In memory of my father, Gordon Kemble.

ACKNOWLEDGMENTS

Making a graphic novel is no simple task. I appreciate everyone who assisted and supported me in the making of this work. I'm thankful for my amazing literary agent, Keely Boeving at WordServe Literary, who's been a godsend advocating for this publication. Thanks to Jeremy Clover for posing for endless reference photos for years while being patient and supportive of my artwork, as well as a good friend. To Robin Richesson, Rick Reese, David Hadlock, Mark Michelon, Margaret Black, and the other mentors/teachers at CSULB who first lit the spark and guided me through the process of getting into the graphic novel medium—some of these pages were made in your classrooms and in late nights at the FA4 graduate studio. To my cartoonist buddies Chris Kawagiwa, Brandon Clark, Kevin Cross, Mike Getsiv, David Chelsea, Scott Serkland, Cory Kerr, and the multiple others who supported and were beside me during the creation of this work. To Joshua Patterson for being the best friend and creative support a guy can have. To Diana Schutz, who took the time to first look at these pages, encouraging me by showing there was potential in the work. To my family, my Mom, Fawn, Lavender, Mei, Greg, and Dan, who've stuck by me and always been tolerant of my rather autobiographical work; it takes a village to make these things, and Fawn and Lavender are my secret sister editors who make my work twice as good as it is in the first draft. Finally, to my wife, Mai S. Kemble, for being a rock during the creative storm and being patient with endless nights at the drawing board, and to my son, Benjamin, for being the best kid a person can have.

ABOUT THE AUTHOR

Joshua Kemble is a full-time art director, a freelance illustrator, and a Xeric Award–winning cartoonist. He is currently writing and illustrating the graphic novel *Two Stories: Book Two*, the sequel to his debut graphic novel, *Two Stories: Book One*, while creating freelance illustrations for t-shirts, magazines, and other media. His various illustration clients have ranged from Scholastic to Random House, and his comic work has been published in a variety of anthologies and self-published minicomics.

An unabashed comic book geek, Kemble was born in 1980 in Tarzana, California, and grew up in the Antelope Valley. He received his BFA in illustration and MFA in studio art from California State University, Long Beach, and now resides in Lancaster, California, with his wife and fellow artist, Mai S. Kemble, and his son, Benjamin. He occasionally teaches college art courses in design and illustration, was the cohost of the illustration podcast Big Illustration Party Time, and currently cohosts the Artcasters and the Indie Review Show. He is a member of the Los Angeles chapter of the National Cartoonists Society. He also plays guitar and sings in the band No Saboteurs.

ALSO BY JOSHUA KEMBLE

Two Stories

Library of Congress Cataloging-in-Publication Data

Names: Kemble, Joshua, 1980– author, illustrator.
Title: Jacob's apartment / Joshua Kemble.
Description: University Park, Pennsylvania : Graphic Mundi, [2022]
Summary: "Follows the stories, in graphic novel format, of two twenty-something roommates, one Christian and one atheist, as they seek to find their place in the world. Explores the themes of faith deconstruction, identity, young love, and loss to create an engrossing world in which waking and sleeping dreams collide"—Provided by publisher.
Identifiers: LCCN 2021054184 | ISBN 9781637790229 (paperback)
Subjects: LCSH: Roommates—Comic books, strips, etc. | Cartoonists—Comic books, strips, etc. | Christianity and atheism—Comic books, strips, etc. | Faith and reason—Christianity—Comic books, strips, etc. | Loss (Psychology)—Comic books, strips, etc. | Man-woman relationships—Comic books, strips, etc.
Classification: LCC PN6727.K427 J33 2022
LC record available at https://lccn.loc.gov/2021054184

Printed in Lithuania by BALTO Print
Published by The Pennsylvania State University Press,
University Park, PA 16802–1003

The Author is represented by and this book is published in association with the literary agency of WordServe Literary Group, Ltd., www.wordserveliterary.com.

graphic mundi
drawing our worlds together

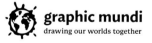

Graphic Mundi is an imprint of The Pennsylvania State University Press.

The Pennsylvania State University Press is a member of the Association of University Presses.

It is the policy of The Pennsylvania State University Press to use acid-free paper. Publications on uncoated stock satisfy the minimum requirements of American National Standard for Information Sciences—Permanence of Paper for Printed Library Material, ANSI Z39.48–1992.